TRAPPED

Center Point
Large Print

Also by Irene Hannon and available from
Center Point Large Print:

Fatal Judgment
Deadly Pursuit
Lethal Legacy
Vanished
That Certain Summer

**This Large Print Book carries the
Seal of Approval of N.A.V.H.**

Private Justice #2

TRAPPED

Irene Hannon

CENTER POINT LARGE PRINT
THORNDIKE, MAINE

This Center Point Large Print edition is published
in the year 2013 by arrangement with Revell,
a division of Baker Publishing Group.

The text of this Large Print edition is unabridged.
In other aspects, this book may vary
from the original edition.
Printed in the United States of America
on permanent paper.
Set in 16-point Times New Roman type.

ISBN: 978-1-61173-879-7

Library of Congress Cataloging-in-Publication Data

Hannon, Irene.
    Trapped : a Private Justice novel / Irene Hannon. — Center point
    Large Print edition.
        pages ; cm
    ISBN 978-1-61173-879-7 (library binding : alk. paper)
    1. Women journalists—Fiction. 2. Private investigators—Fiction.
    3. Large type books. I. Title.
PS3558.A4793T73 2013b
813′.54—dc23
                                                            2013020487

To Tom—
my real-life hero.
I give thanks every day
for the gift of your love.

Prologue

The house was quiet.

Too quiet.

Laura Griffith paused inside the back door and frowned.

Where was the thudding bass that usually shook the walls as it reverberated from behind Darcy's closed bedroom door?

Where was the soda can her half sister always left on the counter, despite repeated requests to rinse empties and put them in the recycle bin?

Where was the faint odor of burned bagel that had greeted her at the end of every workday since the teen's arrival in St. Louis four months ago?

She crossed the room and dropped her purse and tote bag on the kitchen table, the thump of the heavy satchel echoing in the uncharacteristic stillness. "Darcy?"

No response.

As a tingle of unease slithered along her nerve endings, Laura forced herself to take a deep breath.

Chill, okay? This could just be a new strategy. She hasn't tried the silent treatment yet. Stay calm.

As if.

Chagrin twisted her lips as she walked toward the living room. Her placid existence had

7

evaporated the day Darcy stepped inside the house, a hundred and two pounds of brashness, bravado, and attitude. It had taken mere hours for the girl to figure out her thirty-three-year-old half sibling had zero experience dealing with a sixteen-year-old—and Darcy had done her best to exploit that liability ever since.

Was it any wonder they clashed constantly?

Laura passed through the living room, giving it a quick scan. No gloves or hat thrown on the couch. No muffler trailing across the floor. No parka dumped in the wing chair.

Since it was doubtful Darcy had altered her typical behavior pattern and put her winter gear in the coat closet, the conclusion was obvious.

She'd broken the rule about coming straight home after school. Again.

With a sigh, Laura walked down the hall toward Darcy's room. Not much chance she'd find the teen poring over her homework on a Friday afternoon, but it couldn't hurt to check. Hope sprang eternal and all that—even if she was already psyching herself up for the battle of wills sure to come later in the evening.

As usual, Darcy's door was closed. Laura knocked and called her name. After waiting a few beats, she turned the knob.

Once again, apprehension skittered through her, along with a sudden chill that had nothing to do with the frigid early February weather outside or the icy wind whistling around the corner of the house. Darcy's bed was made, the desktop swept clean of clutter, the carpet pristine rather than littered with discarded pieces of clothing from the teen's ritual morning search for the perfect outfit.

But it was the folded sheet of paper on the pillow that caused her heart to stutter.

Rubbing her damp palms on her slacks, she forced herself to move toward the bed. Hesitated. Then, pulse pounding, she picked up the note and flipped it open.

It took her only a few seconds to read the brief message.

A few more to quiet her chaotic thoughts.

A full half minute to formulate a plan of action.

Then she strode back to the kitchen, reached for her phone . . . and started to pray.

1

Three Days Later

Stifling a yawn, James "Dev" Devlin pushed through the back door of Phoenix Inc., buffeted by a blast of Arctic-like air. Man, was he beat. His late date Saturday night had taken a toll, as had the Sunday double-shift surveillance gig for the insurance fraud case. At least those long hours of boredom in the cold van had paid off. He'd nailed the perp with that final batch of photos.

Dev detoured into the small kitchen, rubbing his hands together to restore circulation as he made a beeline for the coffeepot. Too bad he wouldn't be there to see the look on the claimant's face when he got a load of the incriminating shots. If you were alleging debilitating back damage from a slip on a wet floor at work, it wasn't too smart to play a lively game of Twister in front of a picture window where there was no reasonable expectation of privacy . . . and where any PI worth his salt could snap away in full compliance with the law.

The guy was not only a cheat, he was an idiot.

"About time you got here."

At the reproving comment behind him, Dev stifled a groan. So much for sneaking in an hour late.

He poured his coffee, took a long swallow, and braced himself as he turned.

With a pointed glance at her watch, Nikki folded her arms across her chest, raised an eyebrow, and waited.

"The streets are a sheet of ice." Why he felt the need to justify his behavior to the Phoenix receptionist/office manager escaped—and annoyed —him.

"I got here on time."

Touché.

He took another fortifying sip of java. "I had a busy weekend."

"I'll bet. Who was it this Saturday, the blonde rocket scientist you brought to the company picnic who forgot to refrigerate the potato salad she contributed and made us all sick, or the nuclear physicist from last year's Christmas party who thought computer forensics was a new video game?"

He did *not* need a razzing first thing on a Monday morning.

"For the record, I worked all day yesterday. And I mean all day. I put in a freezing double shift on the workman's comp case while you lazed around in your warm house and changed the color of the stripe in your hair." He squinted at the hot pink streak in her short platinum blonde spikes. "What happened to the purple?"

"I was in a pink mood. And don't try that best-defense-is-a-good-offense baloney on me. We have a new client in the waiting room, who fought her way here through the ice storm. She's been twiddling her thumbs for half an hour, which has not helped calm her down. Why haven't you been answering your phone?"

"It didn't ring."

"Is the battery dead?"

"No." He pulled it off his belt.

The battery was dead.

"I guess it needs to be charged."

11

"I guess it does. You want me to show her back?"

"In a minute." If this potential client was anything like the hysterical woman he'd dealt with last week, who suspected her husband was cheating on her and wanted Phoenix to gather incriminating evidence so she could sock him with a huge settlement, he needed a few slugs of caffeine before he explained that wasn't their kind of case and sent her on her way.

"It's not a marriage-on-the-rocks issue."

He narrowed his eyes at Nikki. What was she, psychic? Or was he that transparent? Had to be the latter—but how had he survived as an undercover ATF agent if he was that easy to read?

Then again, he almost hadn't.

Pushing that thought aside, he snagged a packet of sugar to cut the bitterness of the coffee.

If only he could cut the bitterness of his memories as easily.

Nikki gave him another disapproving look. "I bet you ate a bowl of sugarcoated cereal this morning too."

Without responding, he ripped the top off the packet and dumped the whole thing in—an act of defiance more than prudence.

"That's what I figured." She leaned a shoulder against the door frame, expression smug.

He grabbed a plastic stir stick, fighting down another surge of irritation. "Just because your new husband caved under your health-food crusade doesn't mean we all have to sign on to the cause."

"Hey." She lifted her hands, palms toward him, and shrugged. "It's your body—but I don't want to hear any complaints when it starts to fall apart. So can I show this woman to your office? With Cal on his honeymoon and Connor tied up with that protection gig, you're it."

Lucky him.

"How come Connor gets all the glamorous assignments? I wouldn't mind protecting a Hollywood star for a week while she films a movie in town."

"If you were a former Secret Service agent, you might get a few of those plum jobs too. As it is, you get a distraught woman by the name of Laura Griffith. It's a runaway case, by the way. I'll stall her for three more minutes. Drink up."

She swiveled in her high-heeled leather boots and exited into the hall with a swish of her short skirt.

Dev took a sip of his coffee as he watched her disappear. Grimacing, he dumped the rest down the drain. It was far too sweet—unlike their saucy office manager. But she knew her stuff. They'd be hard-pressed to find someone else who was not only a skilled administrator but also happened to have a gift for bookkeeping and computer forensics . . . not to mention a heart of gold—though he'd never admit that to anyone.

Especially her.

After refilling his cup and leaving it black, he followed in her wake. When she said three minutes, she meant it—ready or not . . . unless she took pity on him and decided to give him more breathing space to get his act together.

But he wasn't going to count on her generosity.

"He'll be with you in a couple of minutes."

Laura turned as the receptionist reentered the waiting area through the door behind her desk. "Thanks."

Clasping her hands in her lap, she switched her focus to one of the larger-than-life nature-themed photos that decorated the walls. The office was nicer than she'd expected. Based on what she'd read about real-life private investigators, most PIs bore little resemblance to the glorified Hollywood version of the profession. A lot of them sounded like sleazy, work-out-of-the-car-and-at-the-fringes-of-the-law types.

This setting, however, didn't fit that image. The nubby Berber carpet, the neutral, patterned fabric of the three chairs, the glass-topped coffee table— classy. And the prominent rectangular wooden plaque with the Justice First brass lettering was comforting.

The receptionist, on the other hand, was more than a bit off-putting.

Laura stole a look at the woman. Her streak of

hot-pink hair, miniskirt, boots, clunky metal jewelry, and heavy-handed makeup were a disconnect with the low-key, discreet setting. But Darcy would no doubt approve of her splashy look.

Just one more example of the 180-degree difference in their viewpoints.

On the other hand, if she hadn't called the receptionist's teenaged brother last night after stumbling across his name and number scribbled on a slip of paper in Darcy's room, she'd have been on her own with the daunting task of finding a reputable PI firm. Instead, the boy had passed the phone to this woman, who'd sounded businesslike and capable. The Phoenix website had also been impressive, as had the law-enforcement backgrounds of the three PIs. So here she was.

For better or worse.

She hoped it was the former. Because so far, she hadn't been impressed by official law-enforcement reaction to her sister's disappearance. She needed expert help—and she needed it fast.

"I can show you back now."

As the receptionist spoke again, she rose and joined her at the door behind the desk. The woman pushed through, then led the way down a carpeted hall to the first office on the right, where she paused and gave a discreet knock on the half-closed door.

"Your client is here." She stepped aside and gestured for Laura to enter.

"Thanks." As Laura murmured the word, she slipped past the receptionist, crossed the threshold . . . and did a double take.

While glitzy Hollywood-type PIs might be more fabrication than reality, the athletic-looking man who rose to greet her did fit the stereotype. As he circled the desk to shake her hand, she did a quick assessment. He was tall, topping her five-and-a-half-foot frame by a good six inches, and definitely handsome, his herringbone jacket emphasizing his broad shoulders. But he missed the mark on the dark attribute. Instead, he had striking, deep auburn hair and eyes the color of polished jade.

"Ms. Griffith, I'm James Devlin." He took her hand, his firm grip warm and somehow reassuring.

As their gazes locked, Laura's throat tightened. All weekend, she'd borne her worry and stress alone. Yet as his fingers squeezed hers, some of that burden lifted. The PI seemed strong, confident, and capable—the kind of man who could take on any challenge and succeed.

Her relief was palpable . . . and she hoped not premature.

"Thanks for seeing me on short notice." If he noticed the slight quiver beneath her words, he didn't let on.

A dimple dented one cheek as he smiled and released her hand. "Short notice is par for the course in the PI world. Please, have a seat." He indicated a small round table off to one side of his office.

As she walked over and slid onto a chair, he picked up a pad of lined paper and a pen from his desk. "Did Nikki offer you a beverage?"

"Yes. I turned her down, but I'm rethinking coffee. It's been a long, sleepless weekend."

"Not a problem. Cream or sugar?"

"Just cream, please."

"I'll be back in a minute. Make yourself comfortable."

Once he disappeared out the door, Laura tried to follow his advice. She took a deep breath. Let it out slowly. Repeated the process as she scanned his office. Better. The vibrating hum in her nerves quieted, and the knot in her stomach loosened—thanks perhaps in part to the impressive ATF-related awards and honors on the walls that confirmed her favorable impression of James Devlin. Distinguished Service medal. Medal of Valor. Framed letters of commendation, including one to her left that included the words *tenacious, professional, diligent,* and *courageous.*

That was just the kind of person it would take to track down Darcy, who'd left few clues.

And her half sister needed tracking down.

Because no matter how mature she thought she

was, Darcy wasn't anywhere close to being old enough to survive on her own. And Laura was counting on James Devlin and his Phoenix colleagues to help her find the runaway teen before she wound up in far deeper trouble than she'd ever encountered during her past forays into independence.

Maybe he hadn't drawn the short straw after all.

As Dev poured a cup of coffee for Phoenix's newest client, he grinned. While he hadn't been psyched up to launch his week with a demanding case, when the client was as pretty as Laura Griffith . . . not so bad.

He dumped a container of cream into the steaming brew and stirred, watching the dark color lighten to mocha. Interesting that he would find their new client appealing. Brunettes didn't usually attract him. Not that her hair was a plain mousy brown or anything. Not with those gold highlights that glinted every time she moved. Too bad she wore it in that single French braid, becoming as the style was. He'd much prefer to see it loose and full. Still, the more severe style did draw attention to her long-lashed blue eyes, soft lips, and model-like high cheekbones.

Still grinning, he straightened his tie, tossed the stir stick in the trash, and started toward the door. Even though Phoenix had an unwritten hands-off rule for active clients, there was no law against looking . . . and enjoying. Discreetly, of course.

Discretion top of mind, he used the short return trip to his office to shift back into professional mode.

After setting the coffee in front of Laura, he took his own seat. "So how can I help you, Ms. Griffith? Our office manager mentioned a runaway situation?"

She knitted her fingers into a tight knot on top of the table. "Yes. My sixteen-year-old half sister, Darcy Weber. She left Friday. I verified she was in class all day, so it was sometime after three. I'm assuming she came home first, because she was only carrying her usual stuff when she caught the bus in the morning. I've called everyone I can think of, but I haven't been able to find a trace of her."

"Did you notify the police?"

"Yes, not that they appeared to be overly concerned. An officer came by, read the note she left, and took some basic information. He said all the precinct officers would be made aware of the situation and they'd put her in the National Crime Information Center database. They did follow up yesterday to see if I'd learned anything else or heard from her, but that's about it." She leaned forward, her knuckles whitening. "Shouldn't they be doing more?"

He hesitated, tempted to sugarcoat the truth and ease her anxiety with some vague reassurances.

But he never lied to clients.

"Police resources are always stretched thin, Ms. Griffith. A runaway won't be their highest priority unless there's a suspicion of foul play. However, since running away is a juvenile offense in Missouri if you're under seventeen, they'll do what they can. But their efforts will be constrained by staffing levels and more urgent cases. That's why private investigation is a reasonable option in a situation like this. You mentioned a note?"

"Yes." Laura shifted sideways in her chair and dug through the purse she'd slung over the back. She withdrew a single sheet of paper and held it out, the vibration in the paper betraying the tremor in her fingers.

He took it, flipped open the folded sheet, and read the brief note.

Laura: This isn't working out for either of us. I'll be seventeen in four months, old enough to be on my own. So I'm heading out to meet up with a friend. Once I get settled and find a job, I'll repay the money I took from the stash you keep in the shoe in your closet. Please keep my stuff and I'll send for it down the road. Don't worry about me. I'll be fine. This is better for both of us. No more rules for me, no more trouble for you. Thanks for trying.

It was signed "Darcy" in a scrawling hand.

Dev set the sheet of paper on the table and picked up his pen. "Based on that note, I'm assuming there were some problems on the home front."

"Yes." Laura rubbed at the twin vertical lines etched above her nose. "Darcy and I had the same mother, who died three years ago. They lived in New York. Mom and I rarely visited in person because of distance and my limited vacation time, so Darcy and I were practically strangers. But when her father died four months ago, there was no one else to take her in. If I hadn't offered, she'd have ended up in foster care."

"Admirable."

She dismissed his praise with a rueful shake of her head. "My intentions were good, but I had no idea what I was getting into. Darcy's had a few minor problems since Mom died—truancy, a possible pot-smoking incident, a couple of drinking parties that got busted, another runaway attempt last summer that lasted all of twelve hours—but I thought I could handle her, maybe help her get her act together." She sighed and stared into the dark depths of her coffee. "Talk about wishful thinking. We clashed from day one. Her dad was a lot older than our mom and not in the best of health his last year, and I've gathered she got away with a lot. I assume she expected to do the same here."

"And you didn't let her."

21

"I *tried* not to let her, but she's smart, and she'd already become adept at evasion tactics. If I told her to tone down her makeup for school, she stashed it in her locker and put it on there. I found that out one day when she forgot to take it off before she came home. If I told her to be back at seven, she'd push it to eight. That kind of thing."

"Was there a precipitating incident for this?" Dev gestured toward the note.

"No. Nothing out of the ordinary happened. We argue almost every day about something. Thursday night we got into it about the length of her skirt and a paper she needed to finish that was due Friday."

Laura took a sip of coffee, wrapping her fingers around the mug as if trying to warm them. "Part of the problem is the New York City to St. Louis transition. That's been tough for her. As far as I can tell, she hasn't made any real friends here— nor tried very hard to connect. She thinks this is a cow town and everyone is 404." Laura sighed. "I had to look that term up in the urban teen slang dictionary, by the way. It means a worthless person, place, or thing and comes from the web code for 'web page not found.' I've been spending a lot of time with that dictionary in the past four months."

Taking a sip of his own brew, Dev considered the information Laura had offered about her half sister. Fights with her guardian. Adjustment problems. The typical I'm-grown-up-and-can-take-care-of-myself attitude of many teenagers.

It was the recipe for a runaway.

"So this probably wasn't a spur-of-the-moment decision." Dev set his mug down. It was always more difficult when teens planned their exits versus leaving in a huff, as most did. "What did she take, other than the money she mentioned?"

"Not much. Some clothing, her laptop, and a couple of photos from her dresser. Based on a quick kitchen inventory, I think she also made some sandwiches and took some granola bars. She left her cell phone, but she removed the SIM card."

Smart kid. She'd eliminated the possibility of GPS tracking and left them with very little retrievable electronic data.

"Okay. Tell me what you've already done to try and track her down."

Once more, Laura reached into her purse, removed a sheet of paper, and laid it on the table. "I went online and pulled up the log for her cell, which is billed to me. I've called all the numbers that appeared more than once in the past two months."

He gave the printout a quick skim. Most of the area codes were from New York—and one number dominated.

"Who's this?" He indicated the recurring number.

"Darcy's best friend, Brianna. She was the first one I called. If anyone would know Darcy's plans, it would be her, but if she's in on this, she's not talking and I haven't a clue how to reach her parents. I don't even know her last name. Everyone at the other numbers I called seemed clueless."

"We can get the billing name for Brianna's cell. I assume it's her parents. I'll call them, but they may want you to verify it's okay to talk with me. Any problem if I give them your number?"

"No."

"What about any contacts Darcy might have had here?"

"The only name I found in her room was your office manager's brother, which is why I'm here. When I called him last night, he passed the phone to her and she suggested I come by this morning if Darcy still hadn't turned up."

Nikki had recommended Phoenix to Laura?

Nice of her to tell him.

Positioning the tablet in front of him, he picked up his pen. "Why don't I get some basic information from you about Darcy and then we'll talk next steps."

He ran through the usual checklist of questions —date of birth, social security number, height, weight, hair color and style, eye color, scars/tattoos, identifying mannerisms, glasses/contacts, preferred type of dress, past boyfriends, what she

24

might have been wearing when she left. The butterfly tattoo on her left wrist was helpful. He put an asterisk beside that.

"Did she have an ATM or credit card?"

"No."

"Do you have a recent photo?"

Once more, Laura dug into her purse. She pulled out two snapshots and handed them over.

"I took that one at Christmas." Laura leaned closer to view the first photo too, bringing with her a subtle sweet scent. "She was in an upbeat mood that day. I hoped it would last, that we'd mend our fences and start the new year on better terms. It would be nice to have some family ties again. I didn't have any brothers or sisters, and my only relations are distant cousins I never see. Same with Darcy."

"No dice?" Dev studied the image. The blonde, blue-eyed teen, attired in jeans and a sweatshirt, was sitting on the floor with a Christmas tree behind her and smiling for the camera.

"No. That happy little interlude lasted all of one day. The other photo is one I found in her dresser, taken in New York, I assume."

He shuffled the other photo to the top. It was a professional image, the sophistication of Darcy's upswept hair, glitzy makeup, and somewhat suggestive attire more appropriate for a woman-of-the-world twenty-six than sweet sixteen.

"Quite a transformation."

"I know. In that getup, she'd have no problem passing for midtwenties. And that could get her into a lot of trouble on the street."

So could looking sixteen. Maybe more so. But Dev let that pass. The woman beside him was already worried enough.

"How would you describe her mental state?"

Laura tipped her head, her expression pensive as another whiff of that faint, appealing scent wafted his way. He tried to ignore it. "Deep down, I think she's still angry about Mom dying—and still grieving, even after three years. They had similar go-with-the-flow personalities and were very close. I also sense some guilt over her father's death."

That piqued his interest. "Why would she feel guilty about that?"

"He died of a heart attack a month after she ran away. He had heart issues anyway, but I have a feeling she suspects her escapades might have contributed to his demise."

So the situation was more complex than a simple defiance of house rules or an inappropriate show of independence. And anger, grief, and guilt could lead to compromised judgment and vulnerability.

Bad combination.

"Could she have been depressed too?"

"It's possible, though she hid it under a veneer of bravado if she was. I did try to get her to talk to a counselor at school when she first came, but she refused so I didn't push. It wasn't as if there were any serious problems here. No more truancy or pot smoking or alcohol-related incidents, just clashes on normal, everyday-life kinds of issues."

He caught a subtle glimmer in her eyes as she dipped her chin to pull a nonexistent piece of fuzz from the sleeve of her sweater. "Maybe I was too hard on her. Maybe my rules *were* old-fashioned, as she claimed. I can hardly remember being sixteen. Besides, it's a different world now."

The whisper of tears in her voice tugged at his heart, and he blinked in surprise. That was weird. His standard procedure was to offer clients a sympathetic ear but limit personal involvement. For whatever reason, that tactic wasn't working today. "I wouldn't be too hard on myself if I were you. Kids like to push the limits. Sometimes parents—or guardians—have to be the bad guys. That whole tough love thing."

She flicked a glance at his left hand. "Do you have children?"

"No. I'm not married, and *I'm* old-fashioned about that. No wife equals no kids." He paused, frowning. Now where had *that* come from? Sharing personal information wasn't part of his usual client spiel, either.

Time to lighten the serious tone with a little humor.

Leaning back in his chair, he adopted a more

casual pose. "But I do remember being sixteen, and with this hair, trust me—I got into my share of scrapes. Kids like me need a firm hand, and I'm forever grateful to my mother for reining me in."

More personal revelations. His lips flattened. Okay, this had to stop. But at least some of the tension and uncertainty in Laura's features had eased.

"Thanks for saying that. Is there any other information I can give you that might help?"

"How much money did Darcy take?"

"Whatever small amount of cash she might have had on hand, plus my three hundred dollars."

"Your shoe money?"

Pink spots appeared on her cheeks. "It's a strange place to keep extra cash, isn't it?"

"I've heard stranger. A litter box, for one."

She wrinkled her nose. "Seriously?"

"Yep. One of our clients told me he liked to put fifty-dollar bills there. He claimed he wrapped them in plastic, but I always washed my hands after any exchange of cash with him."

Her sudden smile blindsided him. The twinkle in her eyes lit up her face, chasing away the worry. Her lips softened and parted, revealing rows of even white teeth. Her features relaxed, giving him a glimpse of a different, carefree version of this woman.

A woman who, under other circumstances, he might be interested in getting to know better.

Not going to happen, buddy. She's a client.

Right.

He forced himself to look back down at his notes. "With three hundred dollars and change, she won't get far. Flying would eat up too much of her money, and she'd run into issues trying to buy a ticket at her age—unless she used a credit card and did it online?"

Laura shook her head. "No charges have shown up on my card for any sort of transportation."

"Could someone have sent her a ticket or money?"

"Maybe. But I don't think she's close enough to anyone here, and Brianna's younger than Darcy. I don't know how she'd manage to pull that off without alerting her parents. I do think New York is where Darcy is headed, though. She loves it there, and she knows the city well. I called Greyhound, but I didn't get anywhere."

"We can probably do better. And a bus would be my guess too. She could pay cash for a ticket with no questions asked. The only other possibility would be hitchhiking." Laura's complexion went a few shades paler, and Dev tacked on a caveat. "But in this weather, I'd say that's unlikely. Not much is moving on the roads."

"I hope that's true." She tapped a finger against the handle of her mug, her expression thoughtful. "Besides, I can't imagine Darcy hitching rides. She's savvy about some of the seedier sides of life, as most New Yorkers are." The words seemed meant to reassure her as much as him—but her next comment told him a lot of doubts remained. "I've been trying to think positive, to believe she'll be okay even if it takes me awhile to find her. But tell me the truth—am I kidding myself?"

Dev played with his pen. The simple answer was yes. Runaways faced threats on numerous fronts—drugs, gangs, alcohol, assault, to name a few. And the danger intensified the longer they stayed away, especially if they were wandering the streets. Theft—and worse crimes—could fast become a way of life as money ran low and desperation set in. Seventy-five percent of runaways who remained on the street for more than two weeks found themselves in big trouble.

But as he looked into Laura's anxious face, he couldn't bring himself to share that disheartening statistic. There would be plenty of time to bring it up later, if his initial steps to find Darcy proved fruitless.

"Not necessarily. Given the weather, she may have holed up somewhere with a friend you don't know about, waiting for a break in the storm."

"I hope that's true."

He did too—but he wouldn't lay odds on it after all the stuff he'd seen.

Before she could press him for further reassurance, he stood and moved to his desk. After retrieving a client contact form from a drawer, he passed it to her. "I'd appreciate it if you'd fill this out for our records. We always do a brief background check on new clients to help ensure our services aren't being used for some illegal end."

She skimmed the form, sufficiently distracted by his request to drop her previous line of questioning. "I guess that makes sense. We haven't talked about fees yet, either."

"We work on an hourly basis for most cases." He quoted her the hefty amount; she didn't blink.

"Whatever it takes." She reached for the pen he'd left on the table. "When Darcy's dad died, he left us equal shares in his and Mom's estate. I can't think of a better use for some of that money than finding Darcy."

She bent to her task, and Dev returned to his desk. The window rattled as a gust of wind shook the glass, and he looked out. The winter storm the weather gurus had said would bypass St. Louis had instead launched a frontal attack, beginning Friday night with sleet. Steady freezing rain the past two days had coated the streets and the tree branches, weighing down the limbs of the pine outside his office window. The needled boughs were bending, trying to hold up under the strain, but if the assault continued, they'd eventually reach a breaking point—as most things did under pressure.

For the second time in an hour, the bad

31

memories edged into his consciousness, trying to scale the wall he'd erected. Shoving them back, he focused on the slim woman at his office table instead. She'd slipped on a pair of glasses and was bent over the form, faint furrows of concentration marring her brow. Her studious air, simple makeup, and understated attire were in marked contrast to the double-pierced ears and world-here-I-come attitude that had come through loud and clear in the second photo of Darcy.

No wonder they'd clashed.

But despite their differences, it was obvious Laura cared deeply about the younger girl's welfare. The faint smudges below her lashes, the creases at the corners of her eyes, and her taut posture spelled worry in capital letters.

And it wasn't misplaced.

Girls like Darcy were easy prey for the wrong kind of people, New York street savvy notwithstanding.

A flicker of movement at the door caught his attention, and he looked over as Nikki gestured to him. Leaving Laura to her task, he slipped into the hall and closed the door behind him.

"You could have told me she came here at your recommendation."

"You're complaining because I brought in business?" Nikki arched an eyebrow, then shrugged. "I didn't know if she'd follow through —and what difference does it make, anyway?"

"I might need to talk to Danny, since he obviously knows the missing girl."

"Not well. He's smitten, but near as I can tell, your client's sister has been ignoring him. It was all one way."

"Still, he could have some piece of information that might be helpful."

"Fine. I'll tell him you might be in touch—which will make his day. He's had a strong case of hero worship since he stayed with you while Steve and I were on our honeymoon. Go figure." She rolled her eyes, then gestured to the window behind him. "It's starting to snow, and the weatherpeople are predicting ten inches by tonight. Despite their bad call on the ice, I'm apt to believe them on this, given the accumulating evidence. If you don't need me, I'd like to head home. I can do the monthly billing from there."

"What about the files in the corner of my office? I thought you were going to get to those today. The pile's about to topple."

She gave him a disgruntled look. "The pile's always about to topple. The faster I file them, the faster the stack grows. The world won't end if they have to wait a day or two."

"Fine. I'll hold down the fort alone today."

"Not quite." She nodded toward the closed door. "My client will be leaving shortly."

"Maybe you can stall her."

"Why would I want to do that?"

33

Nikki grinned but remained silent.

He blew out an exasperated breath. "She's my client, Nikki."

"So? Moira was Cal's client, and they ended up getting married."

"That's different."

"Yeah? How?"

"Look, just because you walked down the aisle a few months ago and are still the glowing bride doesn't mean everyone has the same goal." He shot her his most intimidating ATF-agent glare.

It didn't work.

So what else was new?

"Suit yourself. However, your eyes did light up when she walked through the door." Nikki sashayed back down the hall, throwing one final comment over her shoulder. "But she may not be the one. I can't imagine you getting with a librarian."

Librarian?

He gaped at Nikki's retreating back. Based on his usual choice of dates, she was right. That would be a stretch.

Still processing that latest bit of news, he pushed back through the door.

Laura stood as he reentered, handing him the form as he joined her. A quick glance at the place-of-employment question confirmed her profession. She worked at one of the St. Louis County Library branches.

"So what are the next steps?"

He looked at her. She removed her reading glasses, and those big blue eyes fixed on him. The faint sprinkling of freckles across the bridge of her nose was cute too. Not that he'd darkened the door of many libraries, but she didn't fit his stereotype of a . . .

"Mr. Devlin?"

Her uncertain tone registered, and he shifted gears. Next steps. Right.

He cleared his throat. "Just make it Dev, okay? We're not into formalities around here. My next step is to get the contact information for Brianna's parents and give them a call, see if they can exert a little pressure on their daughter for information. I'll also look into the Greyhound bus possibility. Any idea how she might have gotten downtown to the station?"

"No, but being a New Yorker, she's adept at public transportation."

"Then we'll assume she took a bus or cab or found her way to a Metrolink station. With the city shut down since late Friday, she might not have made it out of town yet. That works to our advantage."

"Is there anything more I can do to help?"

"Let me do some preliminary digging and I'll get back to you on that. But please call if you come across anything that might offer us some other clues." He plucked a card out of the holder on his desk and handed it over. "Use my cell number. I always have my BlackBerry with me."

She took the card, and as her cold fingers brushed his, he had to fight a sudden urge to warm her hands in his.

Get a grip, Devlin. She's a client—and not your type, anyway.

"Thanks." She slipped the card in the pocket of her black slacks.

"I'll show you out." He followed down the hall to the reception area, retrieved her calf-length wool coat from the rack, and held it as she slipped her arms inside. "Let me walk you to your car."

She eyed his dress shoes as she tugged a knit hat over her hair and wrapped a muffler around her neck. "Thanks, but I'm right in front . . . and better dressed for the weather."

No argument there. Her footwear was designed for practicality, as were the insulated gloves she pulled out of a pocket. Both would serve her well in the swirling snow that was already obliterating the landscape. As it was, he'd be lucky to make it to his own car without slipping on the ice and breaking an arm.

Today's attire wasn't the finest example of his planning skills.

"Good point. I'll walk you to the door instead."

She accepted that offer with a nod. Circling

behind Nikki's desk, he pressed the release button on the floor with his foot before joining her at the entrance.

"You have quite a security setup here."

"It pays to be cautious. The bad guys aren't always happy with the results of our work." He grasped the handle on the door. "Be careful driving home."

"I will." She tucked her muffler closer as she prepared to plunge into the swirling snow. "Wherever Darcy is, I hope she's warm and safe."

"Hold that thought."

She sent him a quick smile in response.

But as he watched her carefully navigate the icy sidewalk, clinging to her late-model red Civic for support as she rounded the hood, his own lips flattened. More often than not, teen runaways got into trouble—especially ones who thought they had street smarts. Minor delinquency and a brush with pot and alcohol wouldn't prepare a girl like Darcy for the gritty rawness of the life she'd escaped to, where one out of three runaways were lured into prostitution within forty-eight hours.

And while the blizzard might delay her departure and keep her close to home for a couple of extra days, that scenario had a downside he hadn't shared with his client. Darcy had limited funds and few friends in St. Louis. With her plans thwarted by the crippling storm, she'd need to

seek temporary shelter somewhere until traffic
started flowing again.

He just hoped she didn't take refuge in the
wrong place.

2

Nothing had gone according to plan.

Blanket draped over her shoulders, Darcy
huddled on the cot, back propped against the
wall in the church basement where she'd tossed
and turned for the past two nights.

She was supposed to be in Chicago by now,
settled in with Brianna's friend at the apartment
the aspiring actress shared with three other girls,
and looking for a job.

Instead, she was spending her days seeking
warmth in fast-food joints and her nights in a
homeless shelter.

This wasn't at all what she'd envisioned when
she'd walked out the door of Laura's house three
days ago.

A shudder rippled through her as she surveyed
the rows of cots. Most of the makeshift beds were
empty now that daylight was peeking through the
small windows at the top of the walls, but a slight
stench hovered in the air from the dozens of
unwashed bodies that had occupied them. The
long table at one end of the room, where she'd

grabbed a stale doughnut for breakfast, had also been cleared. Volunteers were straightening up the facility in preparation for another onslaught of homeless later tonight, since the storm showed no signs of abating.

Too bad she hadn't picked a more opportune time to leave.

But who'd have guessed the meteorologists would miss the mark by such a wide margin? And how could she have known Greyhound would shut down operations after two of their buses got stranded in the blizzard west of town? The behind-schedule local buses hadn't helped, either. After her second transfer dumped her out near the Civic Center, she'd slipped and slid her way to Gateway Station—only to discover she'd missed the last Chicago-bound Greyhound by fifteen minutes.

Darcy heaved a sigh.

Total bummer.

But going back to Laura's with her tail between her legs wasn't an option. Even after spending Friday night scrunched in a hard chair in the station while she waited for word on schedules— and having her hat and gloves stolen when she dozed off for a few minutes. Even after the last two nights in this place.

Groping beneath the cot, she verified her backpack was still there. And she'd slept with her purse, so that was safe too—not that there was much of value inside. She wasn't dumb enough to put her cash there. Every dollar, along with her bus ticket, had gone into the money belt hidden under her clothes. Although she'd almost accepted the discount hotel vouchers Greyhound had offered to stranded travelers, she was glad she hadn't succumbed to temptation. She needed to preserve her cash until she made it to Chicago and found a job.

"You ready to go?"

At the question, Darcy looked over at the lanky young woman on the adjacent cot. Lucky thing she'd run into the almost-eighteen-year-old at the bus terminal. After being on her own close to two years, Star knew her way around the system. If it hadn't been for her, Darcy would have been afraid to go with the two older ladies who'd shown up at the station claiming they were part of a winter outreach team and offering to give them food and a bed for the night in an emergency shelter. They'd seemed respectable, but you never knew.

Star, however, had told her she'd run into do-gooders like them in other cities and had convinced her they were legit. She'd been right. Everything had worked out okay.

"Yeah. I guess." Darcy pulled the blanket from around her shoulders, tugged her backpack from beneath the cot, and stood.

"I asked around." Star shifted the strap of her guitar case into a different position on her shoulder. "I thought someone might know of a squat where we could hang out today, but no luck. I guess we'll crash at the Burger King down the street until they toss us out. There aren't any malls nearby."

"Okay. But what's a squat?" Darcy had learned a lot of new words over the past two days while hanging out with Star. Spanging was begging. Busking was playing an instrument for money. Star did a lot of the latter, and she was talented, based on the sample Darcy had heard at the station after they hooked up. Talented enough to make it in Nashville, where she was headed now, since neither Chicago or New York had panned out. But squat was a new one.

Star shook her head, her long, dark hair swinging around her face. "You really are green, aren't you? But you'll learn. A squat is an abandoned building. They're okay in nice weather, but a heated place is better when it's cold."

"You think the buses might be running today?" Darcy hefted her backpack into position.

"Nah. It's still snowing like crazy. My guess is we're stuck here for another day or two. But hey . . . the food's free, the place is warm, and the bedding is clean. Can't ask for more than that, can you?"

Yeah, you could—but not in her present situation.

The other girl started to turn toward the exit, then paused. "Looks like your friend wants to say good-bye. I'll fade into the background and meet you at the door."

As Star stepped aside, Darcy caught a glimpse of Mark Hamilton walking their direction. He was hardly a friend, but they'd spent a lot of time talking the past two nights during his volunteer shift. Well, truth be told, she'd done most of the talking. He'd just listened. Nice guy too, even if he was closer to Laura's age—and her type. The sandy-haired, clean-cut, all-American-boy look was much too boring for her taste. Give her a little dark and dangerous any day.

Still, Mark had earned a lot of brownie points by not only lending her a willing ear but letting her in that first night at the intake desk despite the fact she was underage—and putting a fake name in the registration book.

"Heading out?" He stopped beside her and smiled.

"Yeah. How come you're still here? Won't you be late for work?" Hadn't he mentioned a day job at one point? Something to do with kids?

"The shelter's shorthanded because of the weather, and the daycare center where I work is closed today. So I've got some spare time. Where are you off to?"

"Star suggested Burger King."

"Not a bad idea. It's not far from here."

"Do you think they'll have a pay phone?"

"Hard to say in this cellular age." He studied her. "Are you thinking of calling your sister?"

"No. And it's half sister, remember?" She was grateful he hadn't pushed her to go home during their long talks—and she didn't want him to start now. "Like I told you . . . we don't get along. I completely disrupted her life when I showed up. Trust me, she's glad I disappeared."

Conscience prickling, she shifted from one foot to the other. That was a stretch. Laura did care about her. She knew that. But she was way too strict. More strict than her dad had been—and much stricter than their mom. Even if Laura's intentions were good, rules were for kids. If she stayed, they'd keep clashing, just as she and her dad had. And look how that had ended.

Swallowing past the sudden lump in her throat, she tightened her grip on the strap of her backpack and tried to ignore the question that continually strobed across her brain: Would he still be around if she hadn't given him so much grief?

Maybe.

Her shoulders drooped as the usual answer echoed back at her.

"Hey." Mark touched her arm. "You okay?"

"Yeah." She sniffed and swiped at her eyes. "It's just been a tough couple of days."

His features softened in sympathy. "I hear you. So who did you need to call?"

"The girl I was supposed to stay with in Chicago. I don't know her, and she doesn't care when I show up, but I did tell her I'd be there over the weekend. I should give her an update."

After a brief hesitation, Mark pulled out his cell, pressed a few keys, and handed it over. "You can use my phone."

"Are you sure?" She reached for it even as she asked the question.

"No problem."

"I'll keep it short." She angled away and dug the girl's contact information out of her money belt, then tapped in the number. After three rings, it rolled to voice mail. She was probably working an early shift at IHOP, the job that paid the bills while she waited for her acting break. "Hi, Rachel. It's Darcy Weber. I'm stranded in St. Louis because of the blizzard, but I'll be coming up as soon as the roads are clear. I'll give you a call when I'm on the way. See you soon." She handed the phone back. "Thanks."

Mark slipped the cell back in his pocket, looked around, and lowered his voice. "Listen . . . this isn't normal procedure, so please keep it to yourself . . . but I feel bad for you, having to stay in a place like this. It's obvious you don't belong in a homeless shelter. I have plenty of room at my house if you'd like to hang out there until the buses start running again. And I live in Soulard, which isn't far."

Darcy stared at him, alarm bells clanging. Go with a man she didn't know to his house? No way, no how. That would be just plain dumb.

As if he'd read her mind, Mark grinned. "I'm not an ax murderer, if that's what you're thinking, but I don't blame you for being suspicious. We live in a crazy world. If it makes you feel more comfortable, you can invite her too." He gestured toward Star, who was lingering by the door. "You can share the guest room. It has twin beds and its own bath. I can't promise you luxurious accommodations, but they beat this. And I'm not a bad cook."

Star was invited too? That put a better spin on things. Safety in numbers and all that. And it would be so much better than this place.

Torn, Darcy chewed on her lower lip. Maybe Mark was simply being a good Samaritan. He volunteered in a homeless shelter, after all. You had to be a kind, decent person to do that, didn't you? Plus, he was offering a home-cooked meal and a private room with a shower.

Her resolve to say no wavered.

Apparently sensing her indecision, Mark pulled out a card, jotted a phone number on the back, and handed it to her. "I'll tell you what. Take this and give me a call later if you decide to accept. I'm sure someone will loan you a cell phone. I have a four-wheel drive, and I don't mind picking you both up. That's my work card, so you can see

I'm gainfully employed. And FYI, I had to have a background check to work both here"—he gestured around the shelter—"and here." He tapped the card.

Darcy read the rectangular piece of cardboard. Mark was the supervisor at the daycare facility where he worked, and there were initials after his name. She had no idea what CCP or NAC stood for, but acronyms like that meant he had some smarts. Her dad had been proud of the CPA on his business card. He'd always said those kinds of credentials added a certain prestige and legitimacy.

Tempted but wary, she tucked the card in her coat. "I'll think about it, okay?"

"Sure."

"Mark! Can you give me a hand with this table?"

With a wave, he acknowledged the older man who'd summoned him. "I'll be there in a sec." Then he turned back to her. "I'm not working here tonight, so if you decide to pass on my offer, I wish you luck." He stuck his hand out.

Darcy took it, searching his eyes. She saw nothing but sincerity in their depths. "Thanks. And thanks for talking to me these past two nights."

"I'm glad I was here for you. It's tough to be on your own." He gave her fingers one more squeeze and released them. "See you around." With a mock salute, he zigzagged through the cots in the direction of the waiting volunteer.

On the far side of the room, Star raised a hand and motioned her over. Darcy moved toward the exit, scanning the shelter. She didn't want to spend another night—or two—here. Mark was right. She didn't belong in a place like this, and he'd offered her an out. Better yet, he'd offered both of them an out.

She could imagine what her father would say if he knew she was thinking about accepting the man's invitation, and Laura would blow a gasket. Her mom, on the other hand, would get it. Not that she'd approve, but with her treat-life-like-an-adventure attitude, she'd understand Darcy's point of view. Still . . . even she might think this was foolish.

But Star had been around. She'd talked a bit to Mark too, and so far, all her advice and suggestions had been sound. As Darcy joined her at the door, she fingered the card—and made a decision.

Once they found a warm place to hunker down for a few hours, she'd get her new friend's take on his invitation.

And she'd trust her judgment.

Marcia and Daniel Chapman.

The corners of Dev's mouth lifted. What would he do without phone validator and the crisscross directory?

Contact information in hand for Brianna's parents, he picked up his desk phone and tapped in their home number.

As it rang, he swiveled in his chair. For once the weatherpeople appeared to have been right. In the half hour since Laura Griffith had left, the snow had intensified. Large flakes swirled outside the window, reducing visibility to a few yards. If this kept up, he'd have to hail a dogsled to get home—or camp out at the office. Given that the refrigerator in the break room held only six cans of soda and two pieces of curled-up pizza that had been in there for more than a week, however, the latter was not an appealing prospect.

When a woman's voice greeted him on the other end of the line, he swung back to face his desk. "Mrs. Chapman?"

"Yes."

He introduced himself, gave her a brief recap of the situation, and concluded with his request. "Since the two girls are best friends, it's likely Darcy confided in Brianna. Your daughter didn't offer my client any information, but perhaps you'll have better luck. While you're at it, you might want to remind her that contributing to the delinquency of a minor is against the law."

"Of course, my husband and I will help in any way we can. I'll talk to Brianna as soon as she gets home from school. You said you were with a company called Phoenix?"

"Yes. You can check out our website." He gave her the URL. "And if you'd like to verify our involvement, let me give you my client's number as well as the one for my cell phone." He slid Laura's contact sheet in front of him and recited her information. "We're in the midst of a blizzard here in St. Louis, which means Darcy may still be in town. If so, time is critical."

"I understand. I'll call you as soon as I speak with Brianna."

After ending the conversation with a thank-you, Dev dropped the phone back in its cradle and picked up the slip of paper with the names and work schedules of the two Greyhound ticket agents who'd been on duty Friday night. The manager of the facility had been helpful a few weeks ago with another missing person case, and with the relationship legwork already done, the man had been happy to pass on the information . . . though he hadn't been willing to divulge home phone numbers.

But that's what telephone directories were for.

Dev pulled up the white pages on his computer and began his search. There was only one listing for the first agent's unusual last name, and within thirty seconds he had the phone number. The second name turned up three possibilities. Not ideal, but better than if the guy's name had been John Smith.

He started with the first agent. She was pleasant

enough, and sympathetic, but had no recollection of anyone fitting Darcy's description on Friday night, and no memory of a girl with a butterfly tattoo.

One down, one to go.

The first two numbers for the second agent were dead ends, but he hit pay dirt with the third.

"Yes, you've got the right guy. And I do remember that little lady." Dev pegged the speaker at once as a friendly, older gent who was eager to help. Excellent. "I noticed the tattoo when she hoisted her backpack. Sixteen, you say? Could have fooled me. I thought she was twenty-one, twenty-two. She seemed nervous, and I wondered if she might be running away from a boyfriend."

"No. From a sister who's very worried about her. It's the typical teen stuff, plus house rules were too strict."

"I hear you. I've got a grandson who thinks that way too. Up till now, though, he's stuck it out at home, praise the Lord. It's a tough world out there, and we see our share of down-and-outers at the station. A lot of them look ripe for trouble— either starting it or falling into it."

"We're hoping to find this girl before either happens." Dev picked up his pen. "Do you happen to remember her destination?"

"Sure do. Chicago. It stuck in my mind, because

my cousin lives there and this girl reminded me of his daughter."

So it wasn't New York, as Laura had suspected. Who did Darcy know in the Windy City? He jotted that question on his tablet.

"Did you notice what she did after the trip was canceled?"

"Yeah. She hung around for a long time. I kind of kept an eye on her, because she seemed out of place. For a while, she curled up on a seat, like she was trying to catch a few winks. As I was leaving after my shift, I saw her talking to a girl with a guitar. They were both still there when I came back the next day, but a couple of hours later I did a walk-through to pass out some coffee to the folks who were stranded, and both of them were gone."

"This would have been what time?"

"Around seven o'clock Saturday night."

"And the buses haven't started running again, according to your manager."

"Nope. Talk is they might be able to get a few through by tomorrow night, but I'm not holding my breath. This storm is a doozy."

Dev doodled a spiral on the pad of paper. The good news was that Darcy most likely hadn't left town yet.

The bad news was they had no idea where she'd gone to wait out the storm.

"Can you describe the girl with the guitar?" He

doubted that was going to help him much, but it was always better to have too much information than too little.

"I didn't pay a whole lot of attention to her. Tall, thin, long black hair. Her kind comes through all the time. The drifters, I call them. They have this rootless look. I can't describe it, but I've seen it often enough to recognize it."

So had Dev.

"Do you have any guesses where the two of them might have gone?" The question was a long shot, and he was preparing to thank the man and hang up even as he asked it.

But the agent surprised him.

"I can't say for sure, because I didn't see them leave. The little gal you're after didn't take the discount coupon for the hotel we offered, but there are numbers for a homeless shelter or two on our bulletin board. Plus, in bad weather those places sometimes send out teams looking for people who need a warm place to sleep. Mostly the teams go down around Hopeville—that's an encampment on the Mississippi, down by Laclede's Landing— or check under the bridges and in the parks, but once in a while they come by the station. I've talked to them a few times. Good people, by and large, doing good work. Living the gospel better than most of us. I did see those two young women talking to them."

Dev rotated his pen end-to-end. Was it possible

Darcy had gone to a shelter? Not on her own, perhaps . . . but if she'd hooked up with a veteran of the streets? Possible.

It was also better than some of the other alternatives she could have chosen.

"That's very helpful. I'll look into that possibility. In case you think of anything else, let me give you my number." He recited it, and the man repeated it back at his request.

"I hope you find that little lady. A girl like her could get into a lot of trouble on the street."

No kidding.

"I'll do my best."

Once he ended the call, Dev wasted no time pulling up the list of homeless shelters in the St. Louis area, concentrating on those that actively recruited in cold weather. If the station agent's suggestion paid off, this might turn out to be a far easier assignment than he'd expected.

Especially if the bad weather continued and Darcy stayed put.

"I can't believe how much food people waste." Star slid into the Burger King booth with the items she'd retrieved from the trash can near the door. "We have a feast."

As Darcy watched, Star set her bounty on the table: two mini blueberry biscuits, half of a sausage muffin with prominent teeth marks, a cardboard pocket containing three hash brown

53

rounds, a French toast stick, a bite-sized cinnamon roll, and the top half of a croissant.

Darcy shrank back in disgust. No way was she going to eat other people's garbage.

"I can see you haven't been on the street long." Star proceeded to cut off the tooth-marked end of the muffin with a plastic knife. "Once you get hungry enough, you'll lose your delicate sensibilities."

"I had a doughnut at the shelter."

Star gave a derisive snort. "You think that food's any better? Most of the stuff at those places is donated 'cause it's out-of-date or going bad. Trust me—this is a lot fresher." She gestured toward her impromptu buffet with one hand and popped a hash brown round in her mouth with the other.

Fresher, maybe, but far less sanitary.

She hoped.

Chowing down on another hash brown, Star returned to the topic Darcy had raised before her new friend's scavenging expedition. "This Mark guy is right about the security check. I've stayed in enough of those places to find out how they work. If he passed it, he's probably safe. But he's taking a big chance. I don't think the volunteers are supposed to get involved with shelter customers."

"They aren't. He kind of implied it was against the rules and asked me not to say anything to anyone." The aroma of the sausage was setting off a rumble in her stomach, and she eased away to remove the temptation. The sandwich she'd had last night had been light on meat and heavy on bread, and the hard doughnut this morning hadn't filled the hole in her stomach. She might have to break down and spend a couple of bucks on a burger.

Star pushed a blueberry biscuit toward her. "Never been touched."

"No thanks." She wasn't going to eat food from a trash can.

Shrugging, Star picked it up and took a bite. "Suit yourself. There's always more where this came from if you change your mind. Now back to Mark. Let's see the card he gave you."

Darcy dug it out of her purse and handed it to the other girl.

After wiping her hands on a paper napkin, Star picked it up. "Looks legit. We could always call directory assistance and see if the number's for real. Then we could call and make sure this really is his extension."

"We don't have a phone."

"I bet there's one at the quick shop we passed on our way here. Do you have any change?"

"Yes."

"Okay. Let me finish my food and we'll see if he checks out." She folded the top of the croissant in half and took a big bite.

"What if he does?"

Star licked her fingers. "I say we go for it. If he'd just asked you, I'd be worried. There are a lot of perverts out there, and you can't be too careful—even with guys who seem on the up-and-up." A shadow crossed her eyes, and Darcy had a feeling her new friend was speaking from experience. "But if he's willing to have me tag along, I doubt he's up to no good—especially if he really does work at this daycare place. And we already know he's a regular volunteer at the shelter, which is a plus. Those places might not be too picky about their clients, but they screen their workers pretty thoroughly. I talked to him quite a bit too, and he seemed okay. The typical do-gooder type."

She finished off her eclectic meal in a few more bites, downed it with water from the discarded cup she'd rinsed out in the ladies' room, and wiped her mouth with a napkin. "Let's roll."

As Star slid from the booth, Darcy scooted to the edge of her seat and stood too. Outside the windows, the snow continued to fall, covering the world with a pristine cloak of white that hid the garbage in the gutters and masked the decay of the rundown buildings in this seedy part of town. But the sordid reality remained underneath.

Things would be better in Chicago, though.

They had to be.

Head bent against the wind, bare fingers tucked deep in the pockets of her coat, Darcy followed

Star into the storm and down the deserted street. No one else had braved the onslaught, either on foot or in vehicle. It felt as if they were alone in the world.

But that was nothing new. She'd felt like this ever since her dad died, even when surrounded by people and activity. And it had been worse at Laura's. They had zilch in common, and her half sister's quiet, predictable life was boring, boring, boring.

Life with Mom, on the other hand, had been one grand adventure.

If only she hadn't died.

Tears blurred her vision as she trudged along. She didn't belong anywhere anymore. Mom was gone. Dad was gone. Laura would be happy to return to her placid, teen-free existence.

That was why Chicago was such a smart idea. A fresh start without a bunch of stupid rules would give her just the boost she needed.

However, with those plans delayed, she needed to focus on conserving her money and waiting out this storm.

But if Mark Hamilton checked out and Star gave the thumbs-up, she might be doing it in a place that was a whole lot safer and more comfortable than a homeless shelter.

3

Arms folded tight against her chest, Laura watched the relentless snow batter the window. The last remnants of light had faded long ago, leaving gloom in their wake.

Where could Darcy be?

Was she warm and safe . . . or cold and at risk?

Had she taken any chances that had put her in danger?

Apparently James Devlin hadn't yet found the answer to any of those questions. In the eight hours that had passed since her visit to the Phoenix offices, he'd called only once—to pass on the surprising news that Darcy was headed to Chicago, not New York. As far as she knew, her half sister had no contacts there, but at his request she'd searched Darcy's room again, looking for anything remotely tied to that city. All to no avail. If there were more clues to be found, they'd eluded her.

So unless her PI had discovered some new information since his call, she wasn't much closer to finding Darcy than she'd been Friday night.

She turned away from the gathering darkness, rubbing her arms to generate some warmth. She needed to eat, hungry or not. The small container of yogurt she'd downed at noon to quiet the protests of her stomach wasn't going to hold her through the evening.

Making her way toward the kitchen of her small bungalow, she switched on every lamp she passed, hoping the light would dispel the shadows and brighten her outlook.

She only got half her wish. The light vanquished only the shadows in the room.

With a sigh, she inventoried the refrigerator. She could nuke the leftover Chinese takeout from last night, but would her unsettled stomach accept such a heavy meal? Iffy. Best to go with a safer option.

As she opened the cabinet and started to pull out a can of chicken noodle soup from a shelf above her head, the phone on the counter beside her gave a sudden, sharp trill. She jerked, losing her grip on the soup. Before she could grab it, the can pitched over the edge of the shelf, ricocheted off her chin, and plummeted to the floor.

Laura ignored both the rolling can and the throbbing pain along her jawline as she grabbed for the phone.

Please let it be James Devlin with good news! Or better yet, let it be Darcy, saying she's had a change of heart.

That plea echoing in her mind, she skimmed the digital display. The number wasn't familiar, but the name was.

Devlin.

Her pulse took a leap—as did her spirits.

She put the phone to her ear. "Any news?" Her words came out in a breathless, hopeful rush.

"Some. Did Brianna's mother call you?"

"Yes. Early this afternoon. She wanted to confirm I'd hired you and promised to talk to her daughter as soon as she got home from school. I never heard back from her."

"I did. Brianna balked at her questions, so she waited for her husband to get home and they double-teamed it. I got the impression they threatened to ground her until she graduated if she didn't talk, but whatever they did, it worked. She gave them the name of the girl Darcy planned to stay with in Chicago. It's someone Brianna met at summer camp two years ago and has kept in touch with through texting and email. Rachel Matthews."

The name rang no bells.

But it was a great lead.

Laura groped for the edge of the table and sank into a chair. "Knowing where she's headed is a huge step forward."

"True—but I'd prefer to find her before she leaves . . . and before Brianna somehow tips her off that you've discovered her destination."

"I agree."

"I also called Rachel's number and left a message. She hasn't gotten back to me yet, but I'll keep trying if I don't hear from her."

Laura gently probed her aching jaw. "What do you suggest in the meantime?"

"I've done some legwork today—figuratively speaking, given the weather."

She listened as he filled her in, suppressing a shudder at his theory that Darcy and the girl she'd met might have gone to a homeless shelter to wait out the storm. It made sense, given her limited funds, but she wouldn't wish that on any sixteen-year-old, no matter how grown-up and street savvy they thought they were.

"Only one downtown winter emergency shelter sent teams to Gateway Station on Friday. I spoke with the director, who reviewed their check-in records for the past two nights. Darcy's name wasn't on the list."

As Dev concluded his recap, Laura's spirits nose-dived. "So it was a dead end."

"Not if she used a fake name."

"Didn't I read somewhere that people have to show IDs to get a bed at a shelter?"

"That's the usual procedure, but temporary overflow emergency facilities might be looser. I'll scope out the place. If Darcy's not there, I'll ask around, see if anyone remembers seeing a girl who fits her description. Even though the director wouldn't violate the privacy of volunteers by giving me their names, he did offer to let me hang around at the shelter and talk to the people on duty. That could be fruitful."

"You're going down there tonight?" Laura stared out the window. The snow hadn't abated, and according to news reports traffic remained at a standstill throughout the metropolitan area.

"That's my plan. I've got sturdy boots, an Explorer with four-wheel drive, and the roads to myself. It'll be a piece of cake."

Would it? Laura stretched out her jeans-clad leg and toed the wayward can of soup out from under the counter. Yeah, probably. James Devlin seemed capable of taking on any challenge, including a megastorm. His confident, decisive manner had no doubt served him well in his ATF days.

Handy guy to have around in this situation too.

"Would it help if I came along?"

As the words left her mouth, Laura froze. Where on earth had that come from? Desperation, perhaps. While battling a blizzard held zero appeal, it was preferable to pacing through her quiet-as-a-tomb house with only worry for company. This way she'd be participating in a productive effort—even if it would tax her coping skills to the limit.

The silence that greeted her offer, however, suggested Dev wasn't keen on the notion. Most likely he figured she'd get in the way—as well she might.

Time to regroup.

"Sorry. Bad suggestion, I guess. I don't want to

cramp your style." She tried to lighten her tone so he wouldn't think she was offended.

"No. It's not that. I was just mulling over your offer. It's not a bad idea. People are often more inclined to open up to a woman—especially a concerned sister. But are you sure you're up for it? Homeless shelters aren't the most . . . refined places."

Laura bent and picked up the soup can, weighing it in her hand as she debated how much to reveal. "I've been exposed to worse environments."

"Okay." His cautious inflection was infused with skepticism.

He wasn't buying her reassurance—and it wasn't hard to figure out why. He'd read her contact sheet, noted her profession, and stereotyped her as a quiet, bookish, stick-in-the-mud who led a sheltered life and whose knowledge of the world came vicariously through the tools of her trade.

So not true.

Still, this stranger didn't need to know that.

Let it go, Laura. No need to open up that can of worms.

Yet even as the admonition sounded in her mind, her mouth opened. "My mother and I once lived in a tenement we shared with rats. The neighbors on our left were drug dealers and the woman on the right—let's just say she had a lot of male visitors who never stayed long. The halls stank of pot and urine, and I never went out alone. That was my life for a year when I was twelve, after my mom blew through my dad's life insurance money."

She set the can carefully on the table and pried her fingers loose, flexing them to restore circulation as she relaxed her too-taut tone. "However, my story had a happy ending. Mom got her act together, landed a decent job, and we left the rats behind—both the human and rodent varieties. Trust me—I can handle a homeless shelter."

After a moment of silence, Devlin cleared his throat. "I guess you can." A rustle came over the line, as if he was consulting a sheet of paper. "You live in Manchester, right?"

"Yes."

"I'm close—Valley Park. But with the weather, give me thirty minutes."

"I'll be ready."

The line went dead.

For several seconds, Laura kept the phone pressed to her ear. Then, brow furrowed, she slowly settled it back in its holder.

Why in the world had she told James Devlin about that terrible year in her life? She'd never, ever shared that sordid chapter of her history with anyone, let alone a man who was little more than a stranger.

Flummoxed, she stood and opened the can of

soup, dumped the contents in a bowl, and slid it into the microwave, moving on autopilot. How had he managed to infiltrate the wall she'd built around those memories?

Retrieving a spoon from the utensil drawer, she inhaled the comforting aroma of the soup as she pondered that question. It wasn't his good looks, even if he did have killer eyes and a deadly dimple that would reduce most women to putty. Rick had been handsome too, and she'd never shared her past with him despite their seven-month dating relationship.

The microwave pinged, and she withdrew the soup. Cradling the bowl in her hands, she settled at the table, wisps of steam tickling her nose. As she backed off to let the broth cool a few degrees, she came to the only possible conclusion.

It was all about character. Bottom line, there was an honorable quality about James Devlin that inspired trust—a trait she'd never fully picked up in Rick. Call it women's intuition, but she had a feeling the PI she'd hired was the kind of man you could count on when the chips were down. A man who stuck to his principles. Who didn't seek fights but never backed away from them if the cause was just.

In other words, the knight-on-a-white-horse type, straight from the pages of the fairy tales she'd devoured as a child.

Her mouth twitched as she picked up her spoon.

Now there was a fanciful notion—one she suspected James Devlin would find amusing on the off chance she ever decided to share it with him.

She dipped her spoon into the soup, lifted it, and blew on the liquid before taking a very cautious sip. The last thing she needed was a burned lip.

And given how easily the handsome Phoenix PI had circumvented her defenses, caution might be a sound strategy with him too.

Because she didn't need a burned heart again, either.

Feeling relaxed for the first time since her flight from Laura's house, Darcy set her half-empty mug of hot chocolate on the coffee table, leaned back on the couch, and smiled at their host. "That was a great dinner."

Mark took a chair across from her. "It's hard to ruin a meal cooked in a Crock-Pot."

"My mom did—regularly. Then again, it's not easy to cook when you're smashed 24/7." Star took a sip of the wine Mark had offered her and slung a jeans-clad leg over the arm of the director's chair she'd claimed.

Darcy snuggled deeper into the soft upholstery, hugging a pillow close to her chest. She'd learned a lot about her new friend's life over the past few days, but far more tonight after the wine loosened her tongue. And none of it was pretty. With an apathetic drunk for a mother and an abusive meth addict for a father, it was no wonder she'd hit the road at fifteen. If she'd been forced to do some questionable things to survive, at least she wasn't getting attacked with broken beer bottles by her father anymore.

As she pictured the long jagged scar on Star's arm, hidden now under the sleeve of her turtleneck sweater but displayed for both her and Mark earlier as they'd cleaned up after dinner, Darcy tightened her grip on the pillow. In light of Star's story, she almost felt guilty for running away. Compared to the aspiring musician's home life, hers was—and had always been—cushy, despite the frequent clashes with her father and Laura. Maybe she ought to rethink her plan to go to Chicago after all.

"A penny for them."

At Mark's comment, she picked up her cocoa again. No way was she ready to admit she was having second thoughts. "Not worth it. Star, why don't you sing us that new song you were working on at the station the first night?"

"It's not done yet." Star swung her leg back and forth and inspected her wineglass, lifting the golden liquid to the light.

"That's okay. Play whatever you have."

With a shrug, she shifted around in her chair. "I guess I could. The refrain's about there, and it might be helpful to get some audience reaction."

She finished off the wine, set the stemmed goblet on the side table, and picked up the guitar that was never far from her side. After a few strums, she launched into a haunting melody, singing in a pop soprano that displayed an impressive range.

As Darcy listened to the words about a young woman searching for love but living a nomadic existence of one-night stands, she wondered how much of the angst and yearning in the music was showmanship and how much reflected actual experience.

Probably more of the latter than she'd want to know.

The hot cocoa soothed her as she sipped, and her eyelids grew heavy. It had been great to take a real shower, and it would be wonderful to sleep in a bed instead of on a cot. Maybe tomorrow Mark would let her do some laundry too, while she debated her future. Listening to Star's stories of life on the road had taken some of the luster off her Chicago adventure.

Stifling a yawn as the song wound down, Darcy set her mug back on the coffee table. "That was great, Star."

"I agree." Mark looked her way. "Tired?"

"A little. Hot chocolate makes me sleepy sometimes. Yours is great, by the way. There's a hint of some flavor I can't quite identify."

"My secret ingredient." He winked at her. "Feel

free to turn in anytime. I tend to be a night owl."
He transferred his attention to Star. "You seem
wide-awake. Would you like another glass of
wine?"

She held out her glass. "I was beginning to think
I'd have to ask for the *second* one too."

"Well, you are underage."

"I'm also in a private house and I'm not
planning to drive anywhere tonight—unless you
want to loan me your Porsche." She giggled,
swallowing a hiccup.

Mark chuckled. "I wish." He rose and started
toward the kitchen, speaking over his shoulder.
"Darcy, would you like anything else?"

"No, thanks. Star . . . are you sure you don't
want to call it a night?" Based on that giggle,
her roommate had already had too much liquor.

"After this last glass of wine."

"Okay." Darcy set the cushion aside and stood,
suddenly bone weary. "I'm heading for bed."

"I'll try not to wake you when I come in."

"Don't worry about it. I can sleep through
anything." That was true enough. Laura had to
bang on the door every morning to rouse her for
school, thanks to her clandestine late-night texting
and surfing. " 'Night, Mark."

"Sleep well."

She left the two of them chatting, yawning again
as she climbed the steps in the two-story brick row
house Mark had gutted and refurbished in the

historic downtown district. She didn't know much about rehabbing, but it looked nice and he seemed proud of the way he'd modernized the interior without changing the character of the exterior. Plus, it was really neat and orderly—even more so than Laura's house, where everything had a place.

But all she cared about was the private, snoreless room where she could fall into bed without worrying about her belongings disappearing.

Ten minutes later, teeth brushed, dressed in her favorite fleece sweatpants and a T-shirt, she crawled under the covers, pulled them up to her neck, and snuggled into the comfy mattress. The voices in the living room below were muted, though Star's higher-pitched laugh floated up through the ceiling as Darcy's eyelids drifted closed. It was nice to hear her laugh, even if her upbeat spirits were wine induced. After the tough life she'd had, she deserved a few pleasant, carefree hours.

And in the final seconds before sleep pulled her into oblivion, Darcy made a mental note to thank their gracious host for giving her newfound friend an evening to remember.

With a glance at his watch, Mark grimaced and twisted on the tap in the master bathroom sink. He'd hoped to be in bed by ten, but Star hadn't cooperated. She'd nursed that last glass of wine forever, growing more garrulous with every sip.

But all was quiet now—and the wine had been better in many ways than other options.

After testing the water, he adjusted the temperature and washed his hands, drying them on a nubby towel. Then he examined them under the light. They weren't as chapped as usual; that was a plus. The cold, dry weather wasn't helping, though. He'd have to put some lotion on before he went to bed or the skin would crack and peel again.

First, though, he'd visit the closet.

Tossing the towel over his shoulder, he walked to the wall in the master bedroom. The closet door slid open noiselessly, and he pushed his own clothes aside to give him access to the long garment bag that hung on the high hook at one end.

His pulse began to pound, and he took a deep breath. Months had passed since he'd had any reason to open the bag, week after week of despair when his search had seemed doomed to failure. But thank goodness caution and logic had triumphed over the temptation to take another chance on the days he'd hit bottom.

A shudder rippled through him as he recalled his previous poor choices. But he'd learned from those mistakes. Hard as it was to accept, the truth was that while redemption was possible, miracles weren't. Some people were beyond saving. The trick was to find a person tottering on the brink. A person about to plunge into the abyss but who could still be pulled back. A person who would be grateful for his intervention and reward him appropriately.

And now, it seemed, his patience may have paid off.

Wiping his palms against the denim fabric of his jeans, he reached up and unzipped the bag.

It was every bit as beautiful as he remembered.

Gently releasing the garment from its protective bag, he draped it over his arms and crossed to his bed. The perfume-saturated sachet in the bottom of the bag had infused the fabric with the subtle but familiar scent of vanilla and jasmine, and he breathed it in. Love, hope, pain, fear, disappointment, hate . . . the emotions swirled around him, jumbled, indistinct, indistinguishable, the memories surging and crashing over him like waves in a storm-agitated sea.

He stopped at the edge of the bed and closed his eyes, waiting for his chaotic thoughts to quiet.

A full minute later, as the clock in the living room emitted a muted bong to mark the half hour, he opened his eyes. Better. He could think again.

He lowered the dress to one side of the queen-sized bed, straightening the skirt so it ran the length of the mattress. Then he hesitated and looked toward the door. Should he lock it?

No need.

No one would bother him this night.

He left the garment to finish his preparations for bed, finally padding back barefoot in his sweatpants and T-shirt. Pausing beside the dress, he traced the scalloped edge of the sweetheart neckline. Stroked his fingers down the long, smooth, white satin skirt studded with glistening beads. Touched the buttons, one by one, at the bottom of the delicate alençon lace sleeve.

The gown was perfect.

And ready.

All it needed was a deserving occupant.

After circling the bed to the other side, Mark slathered lotion on his hands, tugged on a pair of cotton gloves, and turned out the lamp on the nightstand. He slipped under the covers, shifting onto his side to gaze at the gown shimmering beside him in the moonlight from the window.

Maybe this time.

4

The trip to the shelter was a bust.

From his spot at the far end of the room, Dev gave the basement-turned-dormitory a final scan. Every cot had been claimed, and his walk-through with Laura had confirmed Darcy wasn't among the occupants. Not a single guest had professed any recollection of the teen after studying her picture. None of the volunteers on duty had worked either weekend night. And even though he and Laura had hung around for a couple of hours, Darcy hadn't shown.

So much for a quick and easy solution to this case.

Laura rose from the molded plastic chair a few feet from the now-deserted registration desk and joined him, her expression disheartened. "I guess there's no reason to wait any longer."

"No. It's late and they're full up. The chances of her showing at this hour are nil."

"That's what I figured." She sighed and started toward the pegged wall that held their cold-weather gear.

He followed, reaching around her to retrieve her wool coat.

"Thanks." She sent him a weary smile. "Your mother raised you well."

"I'll tell her you said that. She sometimes thinks all her effort to turn me into a gentleman came to naught." He positioned the coat so she could slip her arms into the sleeves.

"One sec." She grabbed for the knitted scarf draped over an adjacent hook and tugged. When it stretched but didn't give, she tipped her chin up to inspect the snag—revealing a purple tinge on her jaw that hadn't been there in his office this morning.

"Hey." Dev caught her arm, and she sent him a

questioning look as she pulled her scarf free. "What's this?" He was tempted to touch her chin, but tapped his own instead.

"Oh." She lifted her hand to the bruise, her lips quirking in a rueful twist. "I was attacked by a can of chicken noodle soup."

Holding up her coat, he arched an eyebrow. "That's a new one. Care to explain?"

She turned her back to him and slid her arms into the sleeves. "I was reaching for the soup when you called this afternoon. The ring startled me, I fumbled, and the can hurtled out at me."

His smile faded. "So this was my fault?"

Tossing the scarf around her neck, she swiveled back to him. "Hardly. Just chalk it up to frayed nerves and my klutziness."

"The nerves I can buy. The klutziness—not a chance."

Their gazes met. Held. Eyes the same hue as her azure scarf and framed by the longest sweep of lashes he'd ever seen sucked him in. His lungs stalled, and the background hum of voices receded.

Somewhere in the recesses of his mind, a warning bell began to ring.

He ignored it.

Lifting his hand to her jaw, he gently angled her head for a better look at the mar on her creamy complexion. Her skin was warm and smooth beneath his fingertips, and a powerful temptation to cup her cheek in his palm swept over him.

Powerful enough to scare him into retreat.

He yanked his hand back, pivoted away, and snagged his fleece-lined jacket from the hook behind him, buying himself a few seconds to regain control.

Off-limits, Devlin. Get a grip.

Exerting every ounce of his self-control, he managed to suppress the urge to touch her again. But it shouldn't have been so hard. He'd mastered those types of impulses long ago, and that self-discipline had saved his life—and his heart—on more than one occasion. Only once had his resolve faltered, and that deadly error had reaffirmed what he'd always known: business and pleasure didn't mix.

He wasn't going to make the same mistake twice.

No matter how lovely the woman.

"You might want to put some ice on that after you get home." He tried for a dispassionate tone—and almost succeeded. "Your jaw's a little puffy."

"Okay." Her response came out scratchy. As if she, too, had been unnerved by the simple touch.

He swiveled back, seeking confirmation of that, but she dipped her head to work on her buttons, hiding her face from his scrutiny. "So what do we do now?"

He knew what he'd like to do—but that wasn't an option. So he shifted gears.

"The storm's not supposed to let up until tomorrow night. I'm betting we have twenty-four hours, minimum, before Darcy leaves town." His tone was cool, polished, professional. Better. "In the meantime, I'll keep calling Rachel in Chicago to see if she's heard from her."

"Do you think Darcy might come back here again?"

"It's possible. That's why I plan to pay a return visit tomorrow night. If she's not here, I'll talk to the volunteers and show her picture around again. If that doesn't pan out, we'll set up round-the-clock surveillance at Gateway Station once buses start running again. I'll also call the other shelters and ask them to review their weekend guest lists, in case Darcy went to a different one under her real name."

Laura tugged on her gloves and moved toward the exit, leaving him to fall in behind. "It sounds like you have all the bases covered. But I wish we could do more."

So did he. Trouble was, they had no more leads to follow—yet.

"Brace yourself." He edged past her at the top of the stairs, turned up his collar, and pushed the door open. A powerful gust of wind rocked her, and he grabbed her arm. "Steady."

"Thanks." Head bent, she dived into the storm.

He stayed by her side, retaining a firm grip on her arm as they plodded through the drifts of snow toward the Explorer. The winter mix felt like sandpaper against his cheeks, and he edged closer to the slender woman beside him, using his body to deflect some of the wind—and wishing he could shield her from both the stinging sleet and the wrenching guilt she carried over Darcy's disappearance.

That wish went deep. Deeper than it should, in view of the fact they'd met mere hours ago. And it was without recent precedent. Years had passed since anyone had triggered his protective instincts in more than a professional capacity.

What in the world was going on?

"Your car is buried."

Laura stopped beside the Explorer, and he gave the vehicle a quick inspection. She was right. In the hour they'd spent at the shelter, it had disappeared beneath a mountain of white. But he'd come prepared.

"It won't take long to clean off." He guided her toward the passenger door. After unlocking it, he pulled it open, holding her back as an avalanche from the roof slid toward their feet. Once the snow settled, he helped her in, circled the vehicle, and took his place behind the wheel. "Buckle up."

"Top of my list." She groped for her seat belt and peered through her side window. "Is it getting worse, or am I imagining things?"

"It's getting worse." He started the engine and cranked up the defroster, then grabbed the ice scraper with the attached brush from behind the front seat. "Sit tight. I'll be back in a minute."

He cleaned the windshield as quickly as he could, pellets of sleet pinging off the exposed glass as fast as he cleared it. Now that ice had been added to the mix, driving would be even trickier.

Time to get this show on the road.

As he brushed himself off and climbed back behind the wheel, Laura sent him a worried look. "Do you think we should be driving in this?"

Putting the engine in gear, he dodged the question with humor. "Since I don't plan to spend the night in my car and the shelter's full, our only other option is to build an igloo."

She tugged off her scarf as the heater kicked in. "I left my igloo-building tools at home. Why don't I just say a few prayers instead?"

From her tone, he couldn't tell if she was joking or serious—but he suspected the latter.

"Can't hurt. And for what it's worth, I grew up in Minnesota." Pressing on the gas, he eased the Explorer toward the middle of the deserted street, leaving a wide berth on either side. "Trust me, if we'd let weather like this stop us, we'd have spent our winters in hibernation. I've driven on plenty of roads in far worse condition and in vehicles far less suited to blizzards."

In the muted glow of a snow-clad street lamp, he caught the brief flicker of her strained smile.

"That's an impressive credential. I'll try to relax."

But it didn't happen. As he drove through the unplowed side streets leading out of downtown, snow crunching under the tires, the tension emanating from the passenger seat in the silent car was as thick as the coating of ice on the pine tree outside his office window—and just as ready to snap.

While navigating the next corner, he sent Laura a surreptitious glance. Her hands were clenched in her lap, her attention riveted on the road ahead, and her back was ramrod straight. It was a repeat performance of the trip down, when his attempts to start a conversation had led to nothing more than monosyllabic answers. And every time he'd reached for the lidded cup of coffee in the holder between their seats, he'd half expected her to slap his fingers and tell him to keep both hands on the wheel.

The lady might be okay visiting homeless shelters, but it was clear she didn't like snow and ice.

A mound of snow appeared in front of him, blocking his way, and his defensive driving skills kicked in with a spurt of adrenaline. Swerving to avoid the obstacle, and anticipating the fishtail that sent his back bumper careening toward a tree near the shoulder, he corrected the skid. Despite his adept handling of the situation, however, Laura gasped and clutched the edge of the seat.

Yep. Totally freaked. It was the kind of reaction he'd expect from a stereotypical sheltered librarian—but not from a woman who'd lived on the seedy side of town for a year and had no doubt been forced to dodge much more dangerous things.

As if reading his mind, she spoke, her subdued voice not quite steady. "Sorry. I'm not normally such a wimp, but I was in an accident years ago in an ice storm during a high school ski trip. Our bus missed a curve on the mountain road and rolled over. Since then, I've avoided driving in ice and snow whenever possible."

No wonder she was gun-shy of slippery roads.

Yet she hadn't let a very legitimate fear stop her from coming with him tonight to help search for Darcy.

Laura Griffith a wimp?

Not even close.

Kicking himself for jumping to conclusions, he lightened his pressure on the gas pedal. He might be used to barreling through this stuff, but there was no reason he couldn't slow things down for the woman beside him. Besides, there was nothing waiting for him in his apartment except mindless TV and a frozen pizza.

"That makes sense." He flexed his fingers on the wheel, debating whether to probe a bit, and decided to go for it. "Were you hurt in that accident?"

"I fractured my arm. But the girl sitting next to me was killed. Broken neck."

A muscle in his jaw clenched. "I'm sorry."

She shrugged and tucked herself into the far corner of her seat. "It's ancient history. I never expected the memories to come back with such a vengeance on the drive down. Sorry if I've been less than communicative."

"Not a problem. Painful memories have a tendency to crop up under the right circumstances. It happens to me sometimes too."

The instant the words left his mouth, he regretted them . . . but he didn't regret the effect they had on Laura.

She angled toward him, her posture more open and approachable. "I guess you've seen some bad stuff in your line of work."

Oh yeah.

He expelled a slow breath and tempered his response. "Enough."

"As a PI—or with the ATF?"

"Mostly with the ATF, in my undercover work."

Frowning, he tightened his grip on the wheel. That was another piece of information he didn't offer clients. Few people knew about his deep cover work—especially his last assignment.

And that was one confidence he had no intention of sharing tonight.

"Wow." Laura's voice was hushed. "I've read

about undercover operatives. That's a tough life. How did you get into that line of work?"

He dodged another pile of drifting snow that had encroached on the road—maneuvering more carefully this time in deference to his skittish passenger—and chose his words with care. "My dad was a cop. I think he passed on the law enforcement genes, because that's all I ever wanted to be. But after a few years, I got restless and decided to ratchet up the action. An ATF agent had done some training for our department once, and I got in touch with him. He walked me through the application process, and the rest is history."

"Did the job have all the action you expected?"

"Yeah." And then some.

"Yet you left to become a PI."

Flashing lights appeared ahead, and he could make out the distinctive metal-against-asphalt rumble of an approaching snowplow. He slowed to a crawl and pulled over as far as possible to let the bulky vehicle pass—and to give himself a moment to compose his response. The bare facts, he decided. Then he'd change the subject.

Once the snowplow lumbered past, making no appreciable dent he could discern, he picked up speed again.

"I had an opportunity to go into business with one of my best friends from college. So tell me how you came to be a librarian."

To his relief, she took the hint and switched gears.

"Simple answer? Books have always been my best friends. They saved my life the year we lived in the tenement. I could lose myself in the pages of a story, pretend I was anywhere but there. Plus, library work is orderly and quiet and predictable—in sharp contrast to life with my mother."

"She was the impulsive type?"

"*Spontaneous* was the word she preferred. She thrived on adventure and was always up for a new escapade. No two days were alike with Carol Griffith. My dad was a moderating influence while he was alive, but once he was gone . . ." Her words trailed off and she turned her head to stare out the passenger-side window into the darkness.

Dev waited her out. There was a lot more to her story, and he wanted to hear it all. But the Explorer's snug, cozy cocoon, which insulated them from the world and created a sense of intimacy, was likely to do a better job of encouraging confidences than the third degree from him.

Thirty seconds later, she proved that theory by continuing her tale without any prompting.

"The truth is, I hated her for a long time after Dad died." Her voice was softer now, and laced with melancholy. "She went on a massive spending spree, blowing all the insurance money on designer clothes and jewelry and first-class trips to exotic locales, dragging me along with her until the funds ran out and we ended up in the tenement. During all that excess, I just wanted to crawl into a hole and grieve. I couldn't under-stand how she could be living the high life with Dad just dead. I knew she loved him, so it didn't make sense to me."

Again, Laura paused, and he heard her take a deep breath. "But as time passed, I realized the spending spree was her way of grieving. She immersed herself in things and experiences until the pain of loss had dulled enough for her to face it. She'd loved my dad since she was fifteen, and his death devastated her, as it did me. She just expressed her grief in a different way. In the end, we mended our fences, but after life with Mom, I craved order and predictability."

"Which you created—and Darcy disrupted."

Another sigh from her dark corner. "Yes. Darcy inherited Mom's spontaneity and sense of adventure, which might explain why we've clashed since she arrived. But I like to think I've learned a few things through the years and that we could make this work if we both tried. Not that present circumstances would suggest that, however."

Once more temptation reared its ugly head, and he fought the urge to reach over, cover her tightly laced fingers with his, and reassure her she'd done her best. Because somehow he knew she had.

Instead, he kept his hands on the wheel and settled for more general words of encouragement. "Maybe she'll learn a thing or two from this experience that will help her understand why living with you is a better alternative—and give her an incentive to do her part to improve the situation at home."

"That would be nice, wouldn't it?" She burrowed deeper into her coat. "Sorry to dump my life history on you. It was probably way more than you wanted to know when you asked why I became a librarian."

"You can never have too much information when you're working a case. Every piece of background helps." True, but not the reason for his interest this time. His motives were far less professional in nature.

A fact he did not intend to share.

"I guess that makes sense." Her tone cooled from personal to polite, breaking the tête-à-tête mood. "You're very adept at building trust and extracting information. I imagine that skill serves you well in your field. So tell me about Phoenix. The website is rather bare bones."

He missed the intimate warmth in her voice—but it was better to keep things professional.

Taking the out she gave him, he moved to safer

ground. He told her how Cal had gotten the idea for the PI firm five years ago and recruited him as a partner. How Connor had joined them a few months later. How they handled a lot of insurance fraud work but also took on missing persons jobs, protection gigs, murders, and cold cases.

He answered her questions about the name— no, it had nothing to do with the city and everything to do with rising from the ashes. Although he cited the murder of Cal's first wife as the reason his partner needed to start over, he left his own situation out of it. And he talked about their motto; of their commitment to putting justice first in every investigation, and of their dedication to taking cases that had fallen between the cracks with official law enforcement.

By the time he regaled her with stories about a few of their more interesting cases—names withheld to protect the innocent . . . or guilty—he was cresting the formidable hill on her street that led to her house.

Exactly how he'd timed it.

"So here you are, safe and sound—as promised." He eased the SUV close to where he thought the curb might be, but in view of the lack of traffic, he could have parked it in the middle of the street for all it mattered.

She released her seat belt and wrapped her scarf back around her neck. "Sorry this trip kept you out so late."

"PIs don't punch time clocks. Believe me, I've burned plenty of midnight oil on surveillance gigs. Sit tight and I'll get your door."

He didn't wait for her to respond. Pushing his door open, he plunged back into the biting, subzero wind and fought his way around the car. She opened her door as he approached, surveying her lawn in dismay.

"I shoveled the walkway before you came, but now I can't even tell where it is."

"Let's stick to the driveway." He took her arm and steadied her as she exited the car. "We know that's level."

They didn't talk as they plowed through the snow. The fierce wind would only snatch their words away.

The drifts on her small front porch weren't too deep, thanks to a sheltering overhang. Once they stepped onto it and sidled past the snow-covered porch swing, a lattice privacy arbor offered a modicum of protection from the storm.

Laura rummaged through her purse for the key, fitting it in the lock before she turned to him. "Thanks for tonight. And for taking the case."

He read the discouragement and worry in her eyes—and in her voice. "We'll find her, you know."

"I know." Her gaze was steady . . . and trusting. "When I talked to your office manager last night, she said you were the best. After meeting with you earlier today at your office and watching you in action tonight, I know that's true."

Nikki had complimented him to Laura?

That was a first.

Assuming she didn't do something to annoy him first, he might have to buy her one of those Starbucks soy, no-whip lattes she liked. The ones he plied her with whenever the pile of files in the corner of his office began to totter.

"I don't know about being the best, but I can promise you we'll all do everything possible to bring Darcy home safe and sound."

A snowflake landed on one of Laura's absurdly long eyelashes, and she blinked it away as a gust of wind whipped a swirl of crystalline snow toward the porch. More icy flakes settled on her gold-streaked brown hair. In the glow of the light she'd left on beside her front door, they sparkled like diamonds.

A lady with diamonds in her hair and eyes the color of a summer sky.

Way too tempting.

He was out of here.

Retreating a step toward the driveway, he gestured to the door. "Go on in before we both freeze to death. I'll be in touch sometime tomorrow. Shall I call you here or on your cell?"

"I don't think I'm going anywhere. I doubt the library will be open for a day or two. My home phone is fine."

"Okay. I'll be in touch." With a brief wave, he bolted for the Explorer.

Only after he climbed behind the wheel and put the SUV in gear did he look back. Laura had disappeared inside, and a soft, warm, welcoming glow shone behind the shades of her front window.

Nice.

Really nice.

Could he think up some excuse to linger in her cozy bungalow for a while before returning to his dark, empty apartment? Maybe he could ask some more questions about Darcy or . . .

Get out of here, Devlin.

Right.

He jerked his attention back to the road and twisted the key in the ignition. If he wanted to live up to Nikki's accolade as well as the trust his new client had placed in him, he needed to focus on the job he'd been hired to do.

Pressing on the gas, he plunged back into the storm and forced himself to think about the task at hand. Competent as he was, the odds of success diminished with each hour that passed. Life on the street was rough—and rougher still if Darcy had picked up with a homeless girl who knew her way around. At the very least, the teen was being exposed to a gritty reality far outside her realm of experience and learning some of life's harsher lessons.

He hoped that was the worst thing that happened to her.

But he wasn't getting positive vibes about this whole situation—and that was never an encouraging sign.

Taking the descent at a prudent speed, he slowed as he approached the intersection at the end of Laura's street and flipped on his blinker. Not that it mattered on this desolate night. Funny how force of habit and ingrained training took over when the mind was otherwise occupied. That had happened to him often in dicey situations and saved his hide on numerous occasions.

Unfortunately, Darcy didn't have any such coping skills to help her survive in the rife-with-risk runaway world, no hard-earned instinctive defensive measures that would automatically kick in when needed.

Dev pulled onto the main road and accelerated, churning up snow in his wake, leaving a set of tracks in the expanse of white behind him.

And hoping the trail leading to Darcy would remain fresh a lot longer than the Explorer's, which was already being obliterated by the storm.

5

As the aroma of frying bacon nudged her awake, Darcy yawned and pried open her eyes.

Boy, did that smell yummy.

Stretching, she examined the framed abstract painting on the wall at the foot of the bed and tried to orient herself. One thing for sure. This wasn't the homeless shelter.

Her gaze still on the painting, she tried to shake off the stubborn fuzziness mucking up her brain. As it slowly receded, yesterday's events clicked into place. She and Star had spent the night at Mark Hamilton's rehabbed house in Soulard.

No wonder she was enjoying the comforts of a real bed, snuggled under a downy comforter.

Giving in to another yawn, she sat up and looked toward the other twin bed in the room she and Star had shared.

It was rumpled but empty.

Darcy smiled. Her new friend must already have succumbed to the lure of the bacon. After rubbing her eyes, she peered at her watch. Nine-fifteen?! No wonder the other girl had beaten her to the kitchen. But she didn't intend to be far behind. After the stale doughnuts in the shelter, she was more than ready for a bacon-and-eggs breakfast. And if Mark wanted to throw in a few pancakes or sausages, he'd get no complaints from her.

Swinging her feet to the floor, she combed her fingers through her unruly long hair and groaned. Just as she figured—frizz city. But she'd been too tired to blow-dry and straighten it after her shower last night, and she wasn't going to take the time to do so before breakfast, either. Her rumbling stomach was already protesting the delay.

She stood, started to walk toward the bathroom—and froze as the room tilted. Groping for the wall, she steadied herself until everything settled into place.

That was weird.

Then again, she'd never had to subsist on one sandwich and a couple of out-of-date doughnuts a day, with long periods of fast in between.

She just needed some real food.

After pulling on jeans and a sweatshirt, she flexed the slats in the miniblinds and found a curtain of white. The reporter on the news last night had called it the storm of the century, and it was living up to its name. The whole city was shut down.

But maybe that was just as well. After listening to Star's stories over the past few days—including the tales she'd told last night under the influence of too much wine—she wasn't quite as keen on the Chicago idea. It might help to have a little more time to think things through, reconsider her plans. She'd do it on the QT, though. Mark and Star didn't need to know about her misgivings. She was old enough to make her own choices. This decision would be hers and hers alone, made without interference from busybodies whose intentions might be good but whose attention could be stifling. Like Laura's.

Leaving her shoes behind, Darcy exited the room, padded down the steps, and crossed the living room in her stocking feet.

The open floor plan of the house gave her a clear view of Mark as she approached the kitchen. His back was to her as he worked at the stove, and she smiled. Lucky thing for her and Star they'd run into someone like him. Laura was always warning her to be careful about trusting people, echoing her dad's advice. She got that. You didn't grow up in New York City without learning to be supercautious around strangers. But this was St. Louis. Middle America. The heartland. If you couldn't trust these people—especially a guy who ran a daycare center and volunteered at a homeless shelter and had gone through security checks for both—who *could* you trust?

She stopped on the threshold of the loosely defined kitchen area. "Good morning."

At her cheery comment, Mark whirled around. The spatula flew out of his hand, clattered to the light-colored wood floor, and pinwheeled across the polished surface, spewing pieces of scrambled egg in its wake. His face flushed crimson, and for a brief moment an intense anger seared across his eyes.

Stumbling back a step, Darcy choked out an apology. "I'm sorry. I-I didn't mean to startle you."

Two beats of silence ticked by, followed by the sonorous bong of a clock behind her marking the quarter hour.

Mark took a deep breath. The flush receded, and he summoned up a stiff-looking smile. "No problem. I'm so used to being here alone that the sound of another voice spooked me." He retrieved the spatula and gestured to the table. "Have a seat. Breakfast is ready."

As he ripped off a paper towel and swiped at the flecks of egg on the floor, she perched on the edge of one of the chairs. Only two places were set.

"Aren't you going to eat?"

With a final scrub of the wood, he stood. "Yes. Why?"

"You only set the table for two people."

"Oh. Right." He deposited the paper towel in the trash can and turned on the faucet. "Star told me last night after you went to bed that she knew someone who might still live here and was toying with the idea of tracking him down. She said she might meet up with him for a few days before continuing on to Nashville." He finished soaping his hands and rinsed them off. "This morning she asked if she could use my phone to make a call, and twenty minutes later she packed up and disappeared."

Star was gone?

The bottom dropped out of Darcy's stomach.

Now she was truly on her own.

Slowly she opened her napkin and placed it on her lap. "She never mentioned she knew anyone here. Why would she go to a homeless shelter if she had a better place to stay?"

"I got the impression she'd just remembered this guy." Mark squirted more soap on his hands and lathered up again. "She spent a few minutes on the phone with directory assistance before she found his number. I think she said she'd run into him in Chicago at some music event last year."

"But she didn't even say good-bye."

He sent her an apologetic look as he dried his hands and dished up the eggs. "Street people are like that, and the ones who move from city to city are the worst. They come and go on a whim, without any real plan in mind, and they don't often make permanent connections. They have a loose network of contacts in different cities, but no one they'd call a real friend. Relationships are expedient, nothing more. She did ask me to tell you good-bye, though."

As he set the plate of food in front of her, Darcy fiddled with the edge of her napkin, trying not to feel hurt. It wasn't as if she and Star had all that

96

much in common or would ever have been BFFs. Their brief liaison had served a purpose for both of them, nothing more. It had been an expedient relationship, like Mark said.

"Hey." He stopped beside her chair. "Don't let it bother you, okay? She's not worth it."

At his flat statement, Darcy frowned and looked up. What an odd comment from a man who worked with the homeless. Had she perhaps misunderstood? "What do you mean?"

He appraised her, as if debating his response, then pulled out a chair and sat. "Darcy, you heard Star's story. Do you approve of all the things she's done?"

She shifted in her seat, suddenly feeling like one of those people in an old movie who was being interrogated under a harsh light in a bare room. "I don't know *everything* she's done."

"You know enough."

"She's had a hard life."

"A lot of people have had hard lives. You've had some tough times too, from what you told me. Does that excuse immoral behavior?"

Did it? A week ago, she'd have said no. Now, knowing Star's story, the answer didn't seem so black-and-white.

Mark scowled at her, and she squirmed under his scrutiny. Clearly he didn't think adversity was an excuse for questionable moral conduct. Why get into a debate? It was obvious he'd given the subject a lot more thought than she had, and he was her host. There was no reason to upset him.

"I guess not. My dad used to tell me people always have choices, no matter their situation."

His scowl vanished. "A smart man."

"Yeah, he was." People did make choices, after all. Like that story the minister had told one of the times Laura dragged her to church, about identical twins separated as children after living with an abusive alcoholic father. One had become a teetotaler, the other a drunk. When asked in later years why they'd ended up that way, both had given the same answer: What else would you expect, given my home environment?

But what if you were young and desperate, with no other resources—like Star? Could that absolve wrong choices?

The ridges on Mark's brow deepened again in disapproval. "You're not certain, are you?"

She shrugged. "It's easier to say certain things are wrong in the abstract than when you see the circumstances that cause them."

"Darcy . . . Star didn't have to steal or sell her body or use drugs. She could have gone to the authorities. There are social service agencies that would have helped her."

"She said she tried that, and they didn't believe her story about the situation at home."

He sighed, as if she was a slow student who couldn't grasp a simple mathematical problem.

"Maybe. But more likely, she was lying. She just wanted to justify her bad choices. People like her don't contribute anything to society, and once they pass a point of no return, you have to give up on them. The trick is to catch them and offer help before they reach that point."

Leaning closer, he caught her gaze and held on. "That's why I like working with children. They're impressionable, and there's great potential to exert a positive influence. But the sad truth is, not everyone has a happy childhood. Some of those children turn bad, and you can't always save them. Like Star. Do you understand?"

It was obvious he wanted her to say yes. So she did.

"Good." He smiled and gestured to her plate. "Go ahead and eat up or everything will get cold."

She picked up her fork and poked at the eggs while he went to dish up his own food. She'd eat, because he'd gone to a lot of effort to make breakfast.

But her appetite had fled.

Dev stamped his boots on the concrete stoop, punched in his access code, pushed through the back door of the Phoenix offices—and ran straight into Connor.

"Hey!" The other man reared back, extended his sloshing mug of coffee to arm's length, and shot him a dark look. "Where's the fire?"

Shoving the steel door closed against the wind, Dev secured it and turned back to the former Secret Service agent. "I saw your car in the lot. What gives? I thought you were on celebrity bodyguard duty."

"I was. But after my charge slipped on some ice and sprained her ankle courtesy of ridiculous spike-heeled boots, she decided she'd had it with blizzard city, chartered a bus with a driver who had more greed than brains, and took off for warmer climes—much to the director's dismay. Last I heard, they were going to pack up and go back to Hollywood as soon as the airport opens, then try the location stuff again here in a month or so."

Dev circled around him, detouring toward the kitchen—and the coffeepot. "Exciting while it lasted though, right?"

"Depends how you define exciting." Connor ambled after him, sipping from his mug. "The director wanted her to learn her lines in her free time. She wanted to drink gin—straight up. I was more referee than bodyguard."

"Sounds like fun and games."

"Not. So what's up here? Nikki tells me you've got a new client."

"Yeah." Dev retrieved his shamrock-bedecked mug from the hook above the coffeemaker and picked up the pot. "Missing person case." He gave him a quick briefing as he poured.

"Sounds interesting. Need any help?"

"I will if we end up doing surveillance at Gateway Station." He set the pot back on the warmer.

"Okay. In the meantime, I've got some new employee background checks and a pending child custody case to keep me busy. We may also be tracking down a high-profile rogue executive who's been cooking the books. Word is he's fled to Costa Rica."

"That last one could be dicey." Balancing his mug in one hand, Dev inspected the refrigerator. The curled-up pieces of pizza were still there—but calling them edible would be a stretch, no matter how hungry he was.

"Tell me about it. He's got plenty of resources to hide out and, as usual, the company wants this kept under the radar. Shareholders wouldn't be too happy to discover the chief financial officer is siphoning off funds."

"No kidding." Dev closed the refrigerator and scanned the countertop. He was hungry enough to eat one of those granola-heavy, heart-healthy muffins Nikki sometimes brought in. "When did all this come up?" He finished his sweep of the counter. No muffins.

"Yesterday. Nikki fielded the calls and kept me in the loop. She said you were tied up with the hot case that just came in—emphasis on hot." Connor propped a shoulder against the door frame, blocking the exit as Dev attempted to pass by.

"I hear that's an accurate description of the client too."

Faint remnants of the annoying blush it had taken him years to beat into submission warmed his cheeks. Most people wouldn't notice it.

Connor wasn't among them.

"Your Irish is showing." One side of his partner's mouth quirked up. "Must be tough, having red hair."

Yeah, it was. How come he couldn't be dark Irish, like Connor, or perennially tanned Irish, like Cal?

Nothing to do but bluff it through.

He lifted one shoulder, feigning nonchalance. "My client is an attractive woman."

"I hear she's also a librarian."

"So?"

"Not your usual type."

He narrowed his eyes. "What's that got to do with anything?"

"Our perceptive office manager says you're smitten."

Nikki's latte was toast.

"I just met this woman yesterday." His reply came out between gritted teeth. "And Nikki's had romance on the brain since she fell for her new husband."

"Maybe. But she pegged Cal and Moira early on too."

He was out of here.

"You want to let me through? I've got work to do." He feinted toward the door.

Connor didn't budge. "I think Nikki's on to something."

Dev moved close. In-your-face close. He and his two partners might be college buddies. They might share an Irish heritage. They might work as a well-oiled team and trust their lives to each other on the job.

But personal topics were off-limits—romance in particular. Even if he was the one who'd led the teasing brigade when Cal started to fall for Moira.

"You want to back off on this?"

"No."

He grabbed Connor's arm, and the black liquid in the other man's mug once again sloshed dangerously close to the rim. "Then you'll be wearing your coffee."

They stared at each other for a moment—until Connor's lips twitched. "Fine. Have it your way. We won't talk about the hot librarian."

Dev released his arm.

Straightening his cable-knit sweater, Connor pushed off from the door and strolled down the hall. But he paused after a few steps to toss a parting remark over his shoulder.

"You know, if you'd joked about it instead of getting mad, you might have convinced me you weren't interested. Score one for Nikki."

Dev grabbed a spoon off the counter to hurl after

him, but Connor ducked in his office, leaving the plastic missive to bounce off the wall.

"More evidence." A laugh lurked beneath the muffled comment that came from inside Connor's office. "You're hanging yourself, buddy."

Heaving a sigh, Dev ignored him and headed for his own office. He had better things to do than engage in a verbal sparring match.

Especially one he wouldn't win.

Slouched on the sofa in Mark's living room, Darcy aimed the remote at the TV and flipped through the channels. There wasn't much selection, since her host didn't have cable. How backward was that? Everyone had cable these days. But Mark had said he wasn't a TV watcher, so he could be trying to save a few bucks.

His lack of Wi-Fi, however, was a different story. Talk about prehistoric. And using his smartphone as a modem for his laptop? According to him, it worked great . . . but what a pain.

"Anything interesting on TV?"

As Mark strolled into the room and deposited a bowl of Hershey's Kisses on the coffee table in front of her, she pressed the off button and reached for a chocolate candy.

"No. The networks are only showing boring talk shows and the local stations are still focused on the storm. Sounds like it might start to let up sometime tonight." She peeled the silver paper off the chocolate, wadded it into a tiny ball, and set it on the coffee table.

Mark leaned down to retrieve it, and she stared at his fingers. They'd seemed a little red at breakfast, but now they looked almost raw. Must be all that hand washing. The man sure had a fetish about cleanliness.

Then again, the spotless condition of his house was far better than the questionable hygiene at the shelter.

As if aware of her scrutiny, Mark retracted his hand and shoved it in the pocket of his jeans. "I'm going to see if I can make some headway on the sidewalk."

Shoveling snow wasn't high on her list of favorite pastimes, but it beat mind-numbing boredom.

"Would you like some help? It would be nice to get some fresh air after being cooped up for the past few days." She started to rise.

"No, thanks. I only have one shovel."

So much for that idea.

She sank back onto the couch as he went to retrieve his coat from the closet. It was only one o'clock, and the whole empty afternoon stretched ahead of her. Yuck.

On the other hand, with Mark occupied outside she'd have some quiet time to rethink her options. He'd been way too distracting for the past few hours, asking her every few minutes if she wanted anything to eat or drink, straightening the CDs in the cabinet, vacuuming the area rug under the dining table, adjusting crooked pictures, picking up specs of dirt from the floor.

And she'd thought Laura was a neat freak just because her half sister asked her to do simple stuff like toss her empty soda cans in the recycling bin and hang up her coat after she got home from school.

If Mark disappeared for an hour, it would also give her a respite from his questions about school and boyfriends—if only!—and the brief forays into pot and truancy and alcohol she'd confessed to him that first night in the shelter, when she'd been desperate for a sympathetic ear.

She wasn't as desperate anymore.

He stopped beside the couch on his way to the back door. "Everything okay?"

Enough already!

"Yeah. Fine. Just going a little stir-crazy."

"I hear you. But the city will be up and running tomorrow, if the weatherpeople are right. Which means I'll have to go back to work and you can get on with your life. If you want to take a few more days to think about your plans, though, you're welcome to stay here. I have plenty of space, and you'll have the place to yourself during the day."

If Star was still around, that would be a tempting offer. But staying here alone?

Maybe not the best idea.

He spoke as if he'd read her mind. "In case you didn't notice, there's a lock on the inside of the guest-room door."

She squirmed on the couch, guilt tugging on her conscience. How could she harbor any suspicious thoughts after he'd gone above and beyond to be nice to her and Star? At least he didn't seem offended by her wariness. On the contrary. For whatever reason, his expression was more pleased than put out.

Nevertheless, she felt obliged to make amends. "It's not that I don't trust you or anything."

"Hey—no apology needed. Prudence is wise. It keeps people from making mistakes." He continued toward the rear door. "I'll be back in a few minutes. Stay out of trouble." With a grin, he disappeared outside.

She took another Hershey's Kiss from the bowl on the coffee table and flopped back against the cushions, surveying the décor in the room. Minimalist, Mark had told her and Star last night. That about summed up the sparse furnishings. The high-ceilinged first floor contained only the low-slung white couch where she sat, a modern-looking beige upholstered chair Mark had occupied last night, the canvas director's chair Star had chosen, a coffee table with a chrome base and glass top, plus a couple of lamps.

The only other furniture was the dinette set

where they'd eaten their meals, adjacent to the kitchen. All the walls were empty except for two posters featuring abstract art, and other than a couple of small, geometric-patterned throw rugs in neutral colors, the hardwood floors were bare. A lone green, leafy plant in the corner next to the entertainment center that housed the TV and other electronic equipment, along with Mark's CD and DVD collection, added the only touch of warmth.

If this was minimalist, he could keep it. The whole place was boring and impersonal, like nobody really lived here. There were no touches that gave a hint of personality, like at Mom and Dad's or Laura's. Not a single souvenir from a vacation or family photo or framed award.

She played with the strip of paper sticking out of the Hershey's Kiss. It had been nice of Laura to display the first-place award she'd gotten for that art-class project last fall. She'd framed the prize-winning collage too, and put both in the hall. It wouldn't have killed her to say thank-you, admit she'd been touched. Except she hadn't exactly had the best attitude four months ago.

Or even four days ago.

Would it be any better if she went back?

Unsure of that answer, she put the question aside for the moment and wandered over to the enter-tainment center. Maybe she could find a movie for later, in case Mark started hovering again.

After peeling the silver paper off the candy, she opened the cabinet, bent down to examine the DVDs—and almost laughed out loud as she read the first few titles.

Leave It to Beaver?
Father Knows Best?
It's a Wonderful Life?

Was this a joke? All of those were prehistoric. For sure too old to have been part of Mark's childhood. He seemed younger than Laura, and those were well before even her half sister's time. If her father hadn't mentioned the old TV shows a few times, she'd have been clueless.

Plus, all the DVDs were alphabetized by title. She examined the CDs on an adjacent shelf. Same there. Even Laura wasn't that particular, and she was a librarian.

No wonder Mark wasn't married. Living with a guy who always wanted everything organized and clean and perfect would be really gnarly.

Was he as fussy about his closets too?

She peeked into the coat closet. Yep, neat as a pin. Same with the pantry in the kitchen. Every can was lined up in military fashion, rows straight, labels facing forward.

Maybe Laura's housekeeping rules hadn't been that extreme after all.

For one thing, she'd never bugged her much about picking the clothes up off the floor in her room. Most of the time she let her do what she wanted in her own space. Laura had cringed a bit at the request to paint the walls purple, but in the end she'd bought the supplies and pitched right in. She'd even gone along with the idea of a silver metallic border.

In hindsight, it really hadn't been so bad at her sister's.

But it was embarrassing to slink back with your tail between your legs. Besides, Laura would probably ground her until she was eighteen for pulling this running-away stunt. And they did fight a lot, just as she and her dad had—and look where that had led. He'd died of a heart attack. Laura was too young for that, but maybe she'd get an ulcer or high blood pressure or some other bad thing people her age could get from stress. She didn't want to have to deal with guilt over that too.

On the other hand, going through with her plan to escape to Chicago was becoming less and less appealing.

She slid onto a stool, rested her elbow on the kitchen counter, and propped her chin in her palm. This decision deserved some careful thought. She didn't want to rush into anything, make a choice she'd regret. It might be better to spend one more night here—with the door locked, just to be safe. She could weigh all the pros and cons today, sleep on them tonight, then think things through one more time while Mark was at work tomorrow and she had the place to herself.

Yeah. That sounded like a plan.

And since she'd already been gone for three days, what could it hurt to wait twenty-four more hours?

6

Laura wiped her palms on her slacks. Picked up the portable phone from the kitchen counter. Hesitated. Set it back in its holder.

All for the third time.

This was nuts.

If Dev had any news to report, he'd call. His job was to find Darcy, not hold her hand . . . even if she could use a little hand-holding.

And Dev's hand would do oh-so-nicely.

Okay. Stop. This is pathetic. You're a strong person and you're coping just fine on your own. Just suck it in.

Pep talk ringing in her mind, Laura turned away and walked toward the living room—only to have the phone ring before she got three steps.

Pulse lurching, she dashed back and snatched it up, scanning caller ID.

It wasn't the number she'd hoped to see.

Reining in her disappointment, she put the phone to her ear. If nothing else, chatting with her boss, who also happened to be her best friend in town, would take her mind off her missing sister and the handsome PI who was looking for her. "Hi, Erin."

"Any sign of her?"

"Not yet."

"I'm sorry, Laura. I hoped she'd gotten some sense and come home on her own by now. How are you holding up?"

Laura paced from the counter to the window and back again as she answered, trying to walk off some of her restless energy. "I've had better days. I think I'm going stir-crazy."

"Try being cooped up with four kids under the age of twelve and you can eliminate stir from that complaint. Which makes me happy to report we're planning to reopen most of the branches tomorrow. If the meteorologists are right, the snow will stop around midnight. That will give the plows a chance to get the main roads clear before rush hour. But we'll open an hour later than usual. If you need to take a few days off for this family emergency, though, that's not a problem. You've hardly used any vacation in the three years you've been with us."

"I appreciate the offer, but there's not much for me to do. My PI is on top of things, and work will help distract me."

"You're sure this guy's on the up-and-up? He doesn't drink cheap whiskey and smoke like a fiend and get his kicks using high-powered binoculars to spy on private activities?"

Laura smothered a laugh. "You've been reading too many gumshoe novels. This isn't a sleazeball operation. Dev was an ATF agent in his prior life, and his partners are all former law enforcement too."

"I guess that sounds legit. So . . . with a name like Dev, could your guy be Irish?"

"I'd say that's a fair bet. His name's James Devlin, he has dark auburn hair, and his coffee mug has shamrocks on it."

"Excellent. I feel much better."

"That wouldn't be because your last name is Clancy, would it?"

"Hey . . . we Irish have to stick together. So is he good-looking?"

As Laura visualized Dev's wavy hair, jade-colored eyes, strong chin, and broad shoulders, her pulse kicked up a notch. Oh yeah.

She cleared her throat and hoped her response didn't come out in a squeak. "Yes."

"Married?"

"Erin—this is a business arrangement."

"Fine—but do yourself a favor. Check for a ring next time."

Might as well admit the truth.

"Already done. No ring. Besides, he told me he's not married."

"Aha! So you are interested."

"I didn't say that. I just said I noticed the absence of a ring. You've trained me well over the past three years in your concerted efforts to improve my lackluster social life."

"You've never followed my advice before. If you've decided to now, you're interested. Listen, once you drag Darcy back home and lock her in her room for the next year or two, why don't you—"

At the sudden beep of call waiting, Laura interrupted her colleague. "Hold on a sec. I have a call coming in from the man in question."

"I'm hanging up. Good luck."

"With Dev or with the search?"

"Take your pick."

Shaking her head, Laura switched over to Dev. Much to her chagrin, her greeting came out a bit too breathless.

Her astute PI noticed. "You sound rushed. Did I catch you in the middle of something?"

Thinking about you.

But her spoken words were different. "No. I've been roaming around the house for hours, waiting to hear from you. Is there any news?"

"Unfortunately, not much, even though I've been hard at it all day. I did hear from Rachel Matthews in Chicago. She said Darcy called and left her a message yesterday morning saying she'd been delayed by the storm and that she'd be back in touch once she was on her way. Rachel hasn't heard from her again, so I think we can assume she's still in St. Louis."

"I'm surprised Rachel was that forthcoming." A cardinal and a tiny wren jockeyed for position on the almost-empty bird feeder in the deepening dusk outside her window, and she made a mental note to refill it soon.

"She wasn't, at first. Once I started spieling off legal lingo about penalties for contributing to the delinquency of a minor, however, she caved. Since she doesn't know Darcy, there wasn't much sense of allegiance. Brianna set this up and told her Darcy was almost eighteen, not sixteen-going-on-seventeen."

"Could you trace the number for the phone Darcy used to make the call?"

"If I had it. Unfortunately, it didn't show up in Rachel's call log."

"Isn't that odd?"

"Not if you tap in the magic code that blocks caller ID. Rachel did promise to let me know immediately when she hears from Darcy and agreed to probe a little about where she was."

"That sounds hopeful."

"It's one lead, anyway. I didn't have as much luck elsewhere. No guests registered over the weekend under Darcy's name at any of the other shelters in town, so that was a dead end. Meaning it's back to the shelter for me tonight."

Another foray into the blizzard? A shudder rippled through her, and she turned away from the window. "What about watching the bus station?

My boss just told me the snow's supposed to stop around midnight. When do you think Greyhound will start running again?"

"Sometime tomorrow, according to my contact at the station. I've worked up a surveillance schedule, and Darcy won't get on a bus without us seeing her. The only other person I still want to talk with is our office manager's brother, since you found his name in Darcy's room. Nikki says he has a crush on her, but that it's one way. If that's the case, he may not have much to offer, but I'm going to swing by her house on the way to the shelter and see what he has to say."

Laura slid onto a stool at the counter, suddenly weary. Her four mostly sleepless nights must be catching up with her. "Darcy's never mentioned him. Then again, she didn't share a whole lot with me. She spent most of her free time hunkered down in her room. I felt like I was trespassing when I searched it after she left."

"Speaking of that—I'd like to stop by your place and take a look too. A fresh eye might catch something helpful."

A visit from Dev? That would add one bright spot to her otherwise depressing day.

"Okay. When?"

"I'd prefer to stop at your place before I go to Nikki's. Forty-five minutes?"

"That's fine." She rose and headed toward her bedroom. The jeans with the hole in the knee and her ratty college sweatshirt with the frayed cuffs might be fine for hanging around at home alone, but she didn't want to look like a refugee from the homeless shelter they'd visited if she was going to have company.

"I know it's early for dinner, but I missed lunch and I'm starving. There won't be any chance to eat once I start rolling tonight, so if I grab a pizza on the way to your house, will you share it with me?"

Her step faltered, and her pulse did an odd little skip as she entered the hall. His suggestion was purely practical, of course. The man had to eat, and this arrangement would save time. Still . . . it would be nice to spend a few extra minutes in his company.

"Sure. I'll provide the drinks."

"Sold. Any pizza topping you don't like?"

"I can do without green peppers."

"Duly noted. I'll see you soon." The line went dead.

Pressing the off button, Laura continued down the hall.

How about that?

Dinner with Dev.

But as appealing as that prospect was, she wished the circumstances were different.

Because until Darcy was back safe and sound, the worry in her heart didn't leave nearly enough room for fanciful thoughts about a handsome PI.

• • •

Mark stirred the pot of soup on the stove and backed up slightly to study Darcy, who was seated on the couch in the living room playing a game on her laptop. She'd dispensed with the heavy-handed makeup she'd worn when she'd shown up that first night in the shelter and looked the way she should—fresh, young, unsullied.

He intended to keep her that way too. She had great potential, despite the mistakes she'd made with pot and alcohol. It was just as he'd told her earlier—the trick was to catch people in time. Before they reached the point of no return. If you did that, you could save them.

That's why he'd failed with the others.

And with Lil.

His hand spasmed, and he tightened his grip on the spoon. He'd tried so hard to help her turn her life around. He'd begged. Pleaded. Done his best to please her. But in the end, he'd failed her. She'd gone over the edge.

Just as the others had after her.

"Mark?"

The soft, tentative voice pulled him back to the present. Setting the spoon aside, he looked up. Darcy stood in the doorway, watching him warily. She must still be spooked from his reaction this morning when she'd startled him. That had to be remedied. He didn't want her to be afraid of him.

He wanted just the opposite.

But first, he needed her to feel safe. Otherwise, with Star gone, she might suggest going back to the homeless shelter.

Smiling, he leaned back against the counter and tried for a relaxed, unintimidating posture. "Sorry. I was lost in thought. Did you ask a question?"

"I wanted to know if I could help with dinner."

"I appreciate the offer, but the soup's about ready and the bread is in the oven. You could set the table, though."

"Okay." She crossed the room toward the utensil drawer.

"Wait!" The word came out too harsh, and he softened his tone. "Did you wash your hands?"

Her gaze darted from her own hands to his and back again. "An hour ago. I'll do it again, though."

"Great. No sense spreading germs around during the flu season."

He watched as she scrubbed her hands. Not long enough to meet his standards—but she'd learn.

As she went about her task, he picked up the spoon and gave the hearty vegetable soup another stir. Some people might call his concern about cleanliness a fetish or an obsession, but they were wrong. It was just sensible hygiene. And volunteering in the shelter these past two winters had made him more conscious than ever of the importance of staying clean.

Mouth compressed, he swallowed past his revulsion. Some of the street people who showed up there were disgusting. That's why he'd only agreed to take registration desk duty, which left him free to walk a wide berth around the dirtiest guests and seek out those who caught his eye. Nevertheless, it had been an unpleasant task.

But if everything worked out as he hoped, he wouldn't have to go back to that place again. It would have served its purpose by leading him to Darcy.

She could be his path to redemption.

He changed position slightly so he could watch her. She was folding the napkins and setting the utensils out, her long blonde hair swinging around her face. The color and length would have to change too. Hair like that was one of the things that had led to Lil's downfall.

Darcy leaned over to straighten a knife, and her waist-skimming top separated from her low-rise jeans in the back, revealing an expanse of skin. His lip curled in distaste. The clothes would have to change as well.

But there would be time for those kinds of cosmetic improvements later.

First, he had to convince her to stay another night or two. Just to make certain she was the one.

Ladling the soup into bowls beside the stove, he gestured toward the oven with his free hand. "Why don't you get the bread out too? There's a cutting board in the cabinet to the right of the sink and knives at the end of the counter. You can put the bread in that." He gestured to a small wicker basket beside the knife rack.

She withdrew the board and set it on the counter, then moved to the oven, opened the door, and gave an appreciate whiff. "Wow. That smells great. And it looks homemade."

"It is, but don't be too impressed—I have a bread machine, so there's no skill involved. All you have to do is follow the directions. I usually bake several loaves at once and pull them out of the freezer as I need them."

"The only homemade bread I ever had, fresh out of the oven, was at Laura's. She made some at Christmas. It was amazing."

Mark frowned. Was there a slight wistful note in Darcy's voice? Every other time she'd spoken about her half sister, he'd gotten the impression neither had liked their living arrangements. That despite their blood tie, they'd been little more than strangers with no real feelings for each other.

Or had he misread her?

He hoped not. He needed a girl no one loved. A girl who wouldn't be missed, who was on a downward spiral and in need of saving.

"Are four pieces enough?"

At Darcy's question, he went back to ladling up the soup. "Yes. We can always cut more if we need it."

She carried the basket to the table and took her place as he served up the soup.

Sliding into his chair, he gestured to her bowl. "Dig in."

After casting a doubtful look at the thick soup, she dipped her spoon in and took a tentative taste. Her expression cleared at once. "Mmm. This is really good. I guess it was worth all those hours you spent chopping in the kitchen today. Is this an old family recipe? Like a dish your mother used to make or something?"

His lips twisted at that ludicrous image. He'd been lucky if she'd opened a can of soup, let alone made it from scratch. "No. She wasn't much of a cook."

"My mom wasn't, either." She helped herself to a piece of the whole wheat bread.

"How about your sister? Does she like to cook?"

Darcy slathered the bread with butter, negating the whole-grain health benefits. He tried not to cringe. "She knows how, but she makes a lot of stuff I don't like. Lots of times I just stick a frozen pizza in the oven. Then I get a lecture about eating healthier. It's one more thing we disagree about. No wonder we argue all the time." She rolled her eyes and dug back into the soup.

"Are you sure she won't miss you, though?" Mark swiped a sparing dab of butter across his own bread, noting a brief flicker of emotion in her eyes at his question. Doubt, perhaps?

She masked it too quickly for him to be certain. "She'll feel guilty. Like she failed at being a guardian. Laura's one of those people with an overdeveloped guilt complex, you know? But I'd always planned to leave the minute I turned eighteen, and she knew that. I'm sure she'll be glad to have her quiet life back a few months sooner than expected. I doubt she'll waste a whole lot of time or effort looking for me."

That was what he'd hoped to hear.

"So you still intend to head for Chicago?" He kept the question casual and conversational.

"I guess." This time there was no mistaking the ripple of uncertainty that swept over her features. "I don't have anywhere else to go. But I might think about it for another day or two. It's not like the buses are running yet anyway."

She'd given him the ideal opening.

"Did you decide if you wanted to stay here tonight? Or would you rather I take you back to the shelter?"

Twin creases appeared on her brow as she played with her soup. "It's a lot nicer here."

"And there's a lock on the bedroom door, remember. Plus, I'll be at work tomorrow. That will give you a chance to think about your options."

"Yeah. That's true. I guess I'll stay. Thanks."

The knot in his stomach relaxed. "Great. Now tell me about New York. I've never been there."

He only half listened as she enthused about her former home, thinking instead about his plans for

123

later in the evening . . . and tomorrow night. Everything was ready.

And unless Darcy said or did something to change his mind in the next twenty-four hours, she would be the chosen one.

7

As the aroma of pepperoni wafted his way from the passenger seat, Dev stopped the Explorer in front of Laura's house, set the brake, and turned off the engine.

A chill settled over the vehicle at once.

An omen?

Could be.

Resting his hands on top of the wheel, he looked at the glow coming from Laura's windows. It was as inviting as it had been last night—the very reason he'd caved and suggested they share dinner. But it was a tactical error. He was used to eating alone and on the run. It would have been smarter and more efficient to snag a drive-through burger . . . assuming he could have found a fast-food place that was open. The whole city still seemed to be in lockdown.

He blew out a breath and raked his fingers through his hair. What was with him, anyway? He never socialized with clients. Oh, sure, he had dinner with them when necessary to discuss business—but this wasn't a business dinner, no matter how hard he might try to convince himself it was. It was a chance to spend more time with Laura. Period.

The temperature in the SUV continued to drop, and he zipped his jacket all the way up to ward off the cold seeping through the Thinsulate outer material and the wool sweater below. Too bad he couldn't as easily protect himself from whatever spell Laura had cast on him.

What was it about her that intrigued—and attracted—him? As Connor had noted, she wasn't his usual share-a-few-laughs-and-forget-the-next-day type. No loose, flowing blonde hair. No flirty manner. No sophisticated makeup. No four-inch heels and flashy clothes.

On the contrary. Laura Griffith was the white-picket-fence, raise-a-family, grow-old-together type.

She was the type a guy married.

His stomach bottomed out.

Now there was a scary thought.

Even scarier than the undercover storefront sting operation that had gone bad in his ATF days, when a convicted-felon-turned-gun-trafficker had paid the store an unfriendly visit with a few of his cohorts. Dev had escaped with his life—barely—by diving behind the counter.

Laura didn't pose a threat to his physical safety. No worries there.

His heart, however, could be at serious risk.

A shadow moved behind the shade in the window near the front door. Paused. Hovered. She must have been watching for him, waiting to open the door when he approached—and was now wondering why it was taking him so long to make the trek to her front porch.

It was too late for escape.

So he'd go with Plan B: ingest the pizza as quickly as possible and get down to business.

Grabbing the box with one hand, he pushed the door open with the other, cringed as a blast of cold air instantly numbed his face, and circled the car. Her front walk was more accessible tonight, meaning she must have made another attempt to shovel it today. With the snow beginning to slacken, they might be able to dig out of this in the next day or two. But inconvenient as the blizzard had been, it had kept Darcy in town. That was a plus—or not, depending on where she'd sought refuge.

No need to worry Laura with possible dire scenarios, though. If fate was kind, Darcy would show at the shelter tonight, safe and sound. Or they'd pick her up at the station once the buses began running again. Between him and Connor and the retired detective he'd recruited in Cal's absence, they should be able to wrap this up within twenty-four hours—unless Darcy had gotten herself into trouble.

But he wasn't going there yet.

The door opened as he approached, and Laura peeked around the edge. "I thought I saw you pull up."

"Sorry I'm later than I said. It took longer than I expected to get here." He stomped the snow off his boots and hefted the pizza. "This was part of the problem. The first two places I tried were closed. The third was barely open. It was staffed by one college kid who lived close enough to walk to work."

She moved aside as he entered in a rush of cold air and a swirl of snow. "I'm sorry you had such a hard time. I could have made omelets or a stir-fry and saved you the trouble."

The lady cooked too. One more reason not to let things get too cozy. His father had always claimed he'd been roped in by his wife's skills in the kitchen—and her great legs. Dev had a feeling Laura had great legs too, though they'd been hidden by trim slacks or jeans in all their encounters.

"It was no trouble." He handed her the box, shrugged out of his coat, and draped it over the back of a wing chair.

"I can hang that up for you."

"Don't bother. I won't be here long. Why don't we eat first, then I'll go through Darcy's room?"

"Okay. I've got everything ready."

As she led the way to the kitchen, he did a quick

inspection. Gas flames burned in the fireplace against the far wall, and a floral-patterned couch was bookended by small tables topped with matching crystal lamps. A glass bowl of candy and what looked like an antique music box rested on the mahogany coffee table. Twin wing chairs in a muted rose color faced the couch. Floor-to-ceiling shelves on either side of the fireplace held books, framed photos, and decorative items. The mantel featured a pair of matching silver candlesticks, one on each end, and a bowl of pinecones in the center. The effect was balanced and restful.

The pale yellow kitchen was just as pleasant. A polished oak table for four occupied one corner, and pot holders hung on hooks below an array of cooking implements on a peg board beside the stove. There was no clutter, but a built-in desk on one side of the room appeared to be well used, with neat piles of bills and other mail that needed attention, and a mixing bowl, measuring cup, and spatula had been left in a dish rack on the counter.

As his hostess slid the pizza box onto the table, he completed his survey by sizing her up too. Her oversized Nordic-style sweater only hinted at the curves beneath, but her snug black leggings left little to the imagination.

Yep. Great legs.

"What would you like to drink?"

He yanked his gaze up as she turned. "Uh . . . whatever you have is fine."

"Diet Coke?"

"Sure."

"Have a seat while I take the brownies out of the oven."

He stared at her. "You baked brownies?"

She shrugged and grabbed a pot holder. "It was the least I could do after you provided dinner."

When she opened the oven, the aroma of chocolate overpowered the smell of the pepperoni, and his salivary glands went into overdrive.

Homemade brownies.

Wow.

Tonight's dessert would be quite an upgrade from his usual Twinkie.

By the time she removed them from the oven, set the pan on a cooling rack, put the pot holders back on their pegs, and poured their sodas, he'd taken a seat at the table and was back in control.

Sort of.

He flipped open the pizza box and slid it in her direction. She took a piece; he took two.

Silence fell in the kitchen as he scarfed down the first piece. He caught her watching him when he picked up his second slice.

"You weren't kidding about being hungry."

"I never kid about important things like food."

She smiled. Full out.

He stopped eating.

Man, she had a great smile. Warm, genuine, straightforward—and charming. Why in the world hadn't some guy marched her down the aisle by now?

"What's wrong?" She sent him a puzzled look.

"Nothing." He thought fast, ad-libbing as he went. "I'm just a little distracted. I've been sorting through what we know so far on this case and planning my strategy for tonight." He took a swig of soda and changed the subject. "By the way, I reviewed your client contact form today and noticed you were born in Dallas. How did you end up in St. Louis?"

She picked a mushroom off her pizza and popped it in her mouth. "I've actually lived in a lot of places. My dad was in sales, and he got transferred every couple of years. For Mom, all the moving around was exciting, but it was too disruptive for me. We were never in one place long enough for me to make many friends—and the few friendships I did form didn't last after we left town. That's another reason I love books. They filled in the lonely gaps in my life."

The notion of Laura as a forlorn, friendless little girl exerted an odd tug on his heart. He ignored it and moved on.

"So once you got out of college, you settled in St. Louis?"

"No." She regarded him over the rim of her glass as she took a sip, her eyes twinkling. "I'd have thought whatever background check you did on me would have turned that up."

It would have if he'd done one, per standard operating procedure. But he'd been too focused on the case since she'd come to the office yesterday to think about it, and since Nikki hadn't been there the task had gone undelegated.

Besides, as he'd told Laura yesterday, background checks were more to verify legitimacy—and there was no question in his mind she was legit.

"No time for that yet." He grabbed a third piece of pizza. "So where else have you lived?"

"I took a job in Charleston after college. Nice town, but very small library. After three years, I was ready for a new challenge. My next stop was Nashville. That was a pleasant job."

The sudden melancholy in her voice piqued his interest. "Why didn't you stay?"

She lifted one shoulder and took another piece of pizza. "It was time for a change of scene. Mom and Dad and I lived in St. Louis for two years when I was a kid and I had fond memories of the city, so when I heard about an opening here, I went for it. It was a smart career move. I think I have a decent shot at the next branch manager slot that opens."

He homed in on her first sentence, sensing a story. "Why did you need a change of scene?"

Instead of answering immediately, she weighed the slice of pizza in her hand, as if weighing her response as well. "Let's just call it personal reasons." She bit into the pizza.

He cocked his head and pursed his lips, keeping his tone conversational. "My guess? A romance gone bad."

She stopped chewing. "Why would you think that?"

"When people upend their lives, there's often a broken heart or two in the rubble."

A few moments of silence passed while she resumed chewing, then swallowed. "My heart was bruised, not broken."

So he'd guessed right. A failed romance had been at least part of the impetus for her move. But if Laura turned out to be half as strong, intelligent, caring, and principled as their short acquaintance suggested she was, the guy she'd been involved with had been an idiot for dumping her—or for letting her get away.

Which was it?

"But my ego took a battering."

Her tacked-on admission gave him his answer. She'd been dumped.

He took another swig of soda. "May I ask what happened?"

"Since when do you ask permission to ask questions?" She finished off her piece of pizza without breaking eye contact.

"Touché." He raised his soda can in salute, relieved she hadn't taken offense at his nosiness. "So are you going to answer?"

"Depends. Why do you want to know?"

Dicey question. Her answer had nothing to do with the case, so he couldn't hide behind that justification. Besides, he'd already used it last night after he'd probed about her background, and he wasn't certain she'd bought it then. Tempered honesty might be the best option.

"I'm a curious guy. I ask questions for a living. If something—or someone—intrigues me, I investigate."

He half expected her to laugh and counter with some flirty, pert remark as most of the women he socialized with would have. Instead, she grew serious and used a finger to gather together the crumbs on her empty plate.

"He said the life I led was too boring and routine." Irony twisted her mouth as she brushed off her finger. "This from a man whose idea of a thrilling date was miniature golf followed by an action movie and Chinese takeout. But after I thought about it, I realized he had a point. Once we broke up and I moved here, I decided to spice things up."

"Now I'm really curious. What did you do?"

"Besides buying a red car?"

"Yeah."

Her expression grew speculative. "Promise you won't laugh?"

"I promise."

"Wait here."

She scooted her chair back and disappeared down the hall.

Dev popped the last bite of pizza in his mouth and picked up his soda. What might someone like Laura do to add some zing to her life? Take a gourmet cooking class? Join a bird-watching group? Go rollerblading?

He tipped back his soda can, took a swig—and almost choked when she came up behind him and laid a blade with a hilt across his plate.

Coughing, he groped for his napkin as he stared at the dangerous-looking object. "That's a sword."

"No. It's a saber."

Saber. His brain started clicking. "You took up fencing?"

She sat back in her chair, bright spots of color in her cheeks. "I know. It's kind of an odd hobby, isn't it? I don't tell many people about it."

He looked back at the saber and tried to wrap his mind around the fact that his librarian client who liked a quiet life participated in a combat sport.

It wasn't computing.

"I took it up right after I moved here. I've always enjoyed watching the Olympic fencing matches. There's a lot of footwork, so I thought I could tie into the ballet training I had as a child. As it turns out, I'm not half bad—and I get a real rush when I win a bout. Plus, the physical action is a great way to relieve stress."

He ran a finger down the flexible steel rod

that served as a blade while he processed all that.

"Careful." She moved the saber to the far side of the table. "It's not sharp, but because it continually knocks against other blades, it develops splinters. I try to keep it smooth, but sometimes I miss a few. Your finger, however, will find them. And trust me, it's no fun digging out slivers of steel. Been there, done that. So . . . are you ready for those brownies now? And how about some coffee to go with them?"

"Yes to both."

She rose and walked over to the counter, reaching up to retrieve mugs, leaning down to scoop up an errant coffee filter as it floated toward the floor, swiveling toward the refrigerator to remove a tub of ice cream.

Okay, he was beginning to see it. She was lithe and graceful, and the footwork part of fencing made sense. The aggressive part of hacking away at an opponent, however, was still giving him trouble. But no one got hurt in fencing. It was more about art and strategy and fitness. Wasn't it?

"You're surprised, aren't you?" She slanted a look at him as she poured water into the top of the coffeemaker.

"Honestly? Yes. It seems kind of . . . violent."

"For a librarian, you mean?" She didn't wait for him to verify her assumption but leaned back against the counter and folded her arms, her posture a bit stiff. "Well, as any librarian will tell you, the old adage about never judging a book by its cover is spot-on. But it took a romance-gone-south to make me realize I was beginning to fall into the classic stereotype. So there was a positive outcome from that experience, after all."

She turned back to the counter and busied herself with dessert preparations while he tried to figure out how to respond. Somehow he felt as if an apology was in order—but he wasn't quite sure how to phrase it.

Half a minute of silence passed as he tried to work through the dilemma, then she swiveled back, plates of brownies in hand. "Sorry about that."

She was apologizing to him?

"For what?"

"Jumping all over you about stereotyping me." She set the plates on the table and went back to the counter to pour the coffee. "I'm overly sensitive to that since my experience with Rick in Nashville, and Darcy's always saying I lead a boring life too, despite the fencing. But that's my issue, not yours."

"If it's any consolation, I don't consider you in the least boring."

She rewarded him with a smile as she rejoined him at the table. "Thanks for that." She picked up her spoon. "These are very warm. Better eat up before all the ice cream melts."

He took her advice with gusto as he dived into brownie nirvana.

"This is amazing." He mumbled the words around a mouthful of molten chocolate.

"I'm glad you like it." She licked some ice cream off her spoon and studied him, her expression thoughtful. "You know, I'm curious about one thing. You said earlier that when people upend their lives, there's often a broken heart involved. Might that be true for you too? I mean, you upended your life when you left the ATF to join Phoenix."

The last bite of brownie got stuck somewhere near his windpipe, and he groped for his coffee to wash it down. He hadn't expected her to turn the tables on him. Yet he was the one who'd started the true confessions session by asking her a lot of personal questions, and she'd been completely open with him. He couldn't fault her for reciprocating.

But he couldn't talk about Cat tonight.

Maybe never.

After a cautious sip of coffee, he set the mug back on the table, wrapped his fingers around it—and hoped his reticence wouldn't offend the woman across from him. "For now, let's just say there is a story there and focus on our priorities for tonight."

She searched his face, then nodded, her manner more subdued. "Okay. If you're finished with your brownie, I'll show you Darcy's room. You can bring your coffee along."

As she began to rise, he reached out and laid his fingers on the back of her hand, an instinctive gesture he couldn't have stopped if his life depended on it. She looked back at him in surprise, and he locked gazes with her. After all she'd shared, he owed her more than that abrupt response.

"The short answer is yes. But I've never talked about it in any detail, even with my partners, who've been my best friends since our college days."

Her blue eyes softened. "I understand. We only met yesterday, and trust takes time to build. My story was easy enough to share because it wasn't tragic. I have a feeling yours is."

Add intuitive to his new client's list of attributes.

"Yeah." The word scraped past his throat.

"Enough said." She covered his fingers with her free hand for one too-fleeting second before gesturing to the hall. "Let me show you Darcy's room."

He followed, coffee mug in hand, grateful for her understanding—and wondering yet again about this woman who'd so quickly touched him in a way no one else ever had. He'd always known that someday, before he could move on with his life, before he could banish the nightmares that still plagued him, he'd have to talk through all that had happened. Only then would he be able to release the demons locked inside, to exorcise the guilt and pain. But it wasn't a journey he'd wanted to make alone, and no one had yet come along who'd given him a reason to tap into that dark place and deal with the pain and sorrow once and for all.

Might Laura be the one, sometime down the road?

It was possible.

But for now, his focus had to be on the present, not the past or the future. He needed to bring Darcy home—ASAP.

Because the longer she stayed on the street, the greater the chance she'd hook up with the wrong kind of person and veer off her planned path.

And if that happened, tracking her down would be a lot more difficult than visiting a homeless shelter or spending a day or two hanging around a bus station.

8

"Would you like to watch a movie?"

As Mark joined her in the living room, Darcy looked up from her laptop. If her computer hadn't been loaded with a bunch of games, the day would have been a total zero. As it was, she was even getting tired of playing The Sims, and that had never happened before.

She cast a doubtful glance toward his DVD collection. "Do you have anything newer than those?"

He walked over to the cabinet and perused the titles. "The old movies and TV shows are the best. Most of what's produced these days is trash." He pulled out a vinyl case and held it up. "Have you ever seen *Stella Dallas*? It's a great movie."

"When was it made?"

"1937."

She stared at him. "That's like . . . ancient."

"But the theme is timeless—a mother's supreme self-sacrifice to give the daughter she loves a better tomorrow." He held the case reverently, like it was made of gold or something.

Darcy tried not to roll her eyes.

B-O-R-I-N-G!

She had to be diplomatic, though. He was feeding and housing her, and she didn't want to hurt his feelings. But she didn't want to watch a movie that was probably in black-and-white, either. Maybe it didn't even have sound.

"Um . . . do you have anything like . . . a little more recent?"

He gave her that disapproving scowl she was beginning to recognize and turned back to his collection. "How about an episode of *Little House on the Prairie*? That ran from the early seventies to the early eighties. Or would you rather watch

The Waltons? That was on for ten years, starting in the seventies."

Both were older than she was. And she doubted whether Mark had been born yet, either, when those programs aired. He couldn't be more than thirty, if he was that old. Why would a guy that age want to watch such old stuff?

"Darcy?" He angled back toward her, a touch of impatience in his inflection.

"*Little House on the Prairie.*" What did it matter? They were both prehistoric.

He withdrew the case, flipped it open, and settled the disc in the player. Then he took a seat on the other side of the couch and sped through the menu as if he'd viewed it many times.

"You'll like this one." He pressed play and the program started.

For the next two hours, as he ran two episodes back-to-back, she divided her attention between her computer game and the programs. The low-action shows moved slow, but the stories were okay. And they had a feel-good quality that was kind of nice. But it was weird to watch a TV program that didn't have any four-letter words or violence or high-tech special effects.

"So what did you think?" As the credits wound down for the second episode, Mark leaned over, grabbed the remote from the coffee table, and pressed the off button.

Those were the first words he'd said since the

programs began, which was fine with her. But the way his attention had been riveted on the screen, almost like he wished he could climb inside and be part of the story, had been a little odd. He was really into this old stuff.

Darcy closed her laptop and tried to be both tactful and truthful. It was a stretch. "They were different than what I usually watch."

"Did you think they were better?"

She shifted under the intensity of his gaze and dispensed with honesty to give him what she knew he wanted to hear. "Yeah. I guess."

"I'm glad." He flashed her a smile, then rose and stretched. "I'm going to turn in early tonight, since my minivacation is about to come to an end. I have to be up at the crack of dawn to open the daycare center. Would you like to join me in a glass of wine before we call it a night?"

She did a double take. He was offering her alcohol? Didn't he remember she was only sixteen?

Then again, he'd let Star drink wine, and she was underage too.

But after those two drinking incidents back home in New York that had left her nauseous and headachy the next day—no thanks.

"Could I have hot chocolate instead?"

"Sure." He beamed at her like she'd just offered him primo tickets to a sold-out concert. "I think I'll have that too. It's perfect for a cold night."

As he headed toward the kitchen, her stomach rumbled. Foraging instincts kicking in, she trailed after him. She hadn't seen any snacks in the cabinets, but he might stash that kind of stuff somewhere else. "Do you have any cookies or chips or anything?"

"Still hungry?" He pulled the milk out of the refrigerator and set it on the counter.

"A little." That was an understatement. Tasty as the soup and bread had been, they hadn't filled her up.

"I don't keep a lot of snack food on hand, but there might be some cookies in the basement. My cabinet space in here is limited, so I store extra supplies down there." He poured the milk into two mugs, replaced the jug in the refrigerator, and crossed to a door on the side of the kitchen. "I'll be back in a minute."

He disappeared, and a few moments later she wandered over to crack the door and peek down. The only illumination was supplied by the light traveling down the steps from the kitchen, but it was obvious despite the dimness that all the work on the house had taken place above the stairs. The unfinished basement appeared to be empty, and it looked old and antiquated enough to have a dirt floor, given the age of the houses around here. Did it? She peered into the shadowy depths. Too dark to tell—but now she was curious.

Grasping the rail, she descended the first two

wooden steps, bent down, and squinted at the floor. Nope. It wasn't dirt. Someone had poured concrete at one time, though it was stained and dark now. So much for her theory.

Just as she started to rise, she caught the outline of a familiar shape leaning against the wall to her right.

Was that a guitar case?

As she peered into the obscuring gloom, a swath of light suddenly illuminated the object.

Yes, it was a guitar case.

Star's guitar case.

She recognized the worn NYC sticker on the front.

"What are you doing down here?"

All at once the basement went dim again as Mark's accusatory voice and the slam of a door jerked her attention his direction.

He rushed toward the stairs from the opposite side of the basement, no more than a shadowy figure in the murky light, as she scrambled back up to the kitchen.

"I-I wondered if the floor was dirt, since this is s-such an old building." She scurried back toward the table as he took the stairs two at a time, a package of Oreos in his hand.

As he emerged into the light of the kitchen, cheeks flushed, he slammed the door shut behind him. Although his mouth was tight and his face looked pinched, when he spoke his voice sounded normal, like they were still talking about the movie or the weather.

"It's not safe down there. Stay out, okay? The floor's not dirt, but it's uneven, and some of the beams are low. You might hit your head. I only use it for storage and my washer and dryer." He deposited the cookies on the table and proceeded to measure out the cocoa.

She rubbed her suddenly chilled arms and kept her distance. "Why is Star's guitar down there?"

A beat of silence ticked by.

"She asked me to keep it for her until she decides whether she's going to stay for a while or move on to Nashville. She didn't want to take it out in the blizzard." He set the mugs in the microwave and pressed the beverage button before he turned to her. "With somebody like Star, there are no guarantees. She might not show up for it for weeks, and I didn't want it cluttering up my house."

The part about clutter she could buy. Mark hated untidiness and dirt more than anyone she'd ever met.

But the part about the guitar didn't quite ring true. Star loved it. At the shelter, she'd slept with it beside her, and it was never more than an arm's reach away when she was awake. That guitar was her most treasured possession—and her ticket to fame.

On the other hand, hauling it around in a

blizzard wasn't ideal. What if she fell on the ice and damaged it?

"I found some Oreos. I remember you mentioning at the shelter they were one of your favorite treats. It's a lot of chocolate on top of that"—he gestured to the mugs rotating in the microwave—"but hey . . . you can splurge if you want."

He sent her a smile, and she did her best to return it. Why get freaked about this? Star had probably just done the smart thing and left her guitar where she knew it would be safe. Maybe she'd even come back for it tomorrow, while Mark was at work. That would be nice. He might not approve of some of the things she'd done, but Darcy liked her despite her mistakes.

As the microwave beeped, she picked up the cookies.

"Grab a plate and take them in the living room. It's more comfortable in there—and I'll splurge and turn on the fireplace. I don't use it often, with the price of gas, but we'll celebrate the end of the blizzard."

He was offering to let her eat in the living room after almost having apoplexy when she'd taken an apple from the bowl on the counter and headed toward the couch earlier in the day?

"Are you sure?"

"Absolutely. I'll be right in."

Maybe he wasn't as rigid as she'd thought.

She took out a dessert plate, helped herself to four cookies, and reclaimed her seat on the sofa. After spreading a paper napkin on her lap to catch any stray crumbs, she dived into the cookies.

When he joined her three minutes later, cocoa in hand, he set her mug on the coffee table and turned on the fireplace. Instantly the room felt more cozy.

"I should use that more often." He settled into the chair he'd sat in last night, sipping his cocoa.

"We had one at our house in New York. Dad used it almost every night." She didn't mention the one at Laura's that was often lit too. Every time she brought up her half sister, he got agitated. "So what time do you have to leave for work tomorrow?"

"Too early—but on the positive side, it's only ten minutes away. We open at seven, but I always get there by six-thirty to make sure everything's ready for the day. Sometimes I stay until six, when the center closes, but if everything is running smoothly, I try to cut out about four."

"That's still a pretty long day." She finished off her third cookie and washed it down with a swig of hot chocolate. The man did make an excellent cup of cocoa, with whipped cream on top and everything.

"I don't mind. It's important for young children to have conscientious, loving care."

"How did you get into that line of work,

anyway? It's kind of different for a guy." She chewed on her last cookie, feeling more relaxed now with the crackling fire, the warm drink, her favorite comfort snack. The same snack Laura had always kept on hand for her.

A twinge of guilt tugged at her. She'd told Mark earlier that Laura wouldn't waste a lot of time or effort looking for her, but she wasn't certain that was true. Her half sister was the type who took responsibilities—like a new ward—seriously. While she might have preferred her previous quiet life, she'd tried her best to open the lines of communication. If the two of them remained strangers, it was her doing, not Laura's.

"Darcy?"

She refocused on Mark. "What?"

"You asked how I got into my line of work, but then you zoned out on me."

"Sorry. I'm kind of tired. Tell me again."

He lifted one shoulder. "Not much to tell. With so many working parents, it seemed like a promising field. And I like kids. They're fresh and innocent and hold such promise." He sipped his hot chocolate and yawned. "I'm getting tired too."

Darcy finished off her drink, set the mug on the coffee table, and glanced at her watch. "I don't usually go to bed before ten, but I think I might turn in."

"I'm right behind you. If you want to go on

up, I'll put the mugs and plate in the dishwasher."

"Sounds like a plan." She stood, grasping the arm of the sofa as the floor shifted a hair. Wow. She was more tired than she'd thought. The stress of the past few days and her restless nights at the shelter must be catching up with her.

Mark rose too. "I expect I'll be gone tomorrow when you get up, but there are eggs and cereal and bagels in the kitchen for breakfast, plus some turkey if you want a sandwich at lunch."

"Thanks. I'll be fine."

"Okay. Sweet dreams."

As he disappeared into the kitchen, mugs in hand, Darcy made a beeline for the stairs. Tomorrow's menu was the last thing on her mind. All she wanted to do was sleep.

After giving her teeth a quick brush, she eyed the shower. Nope. That would have to wait until morning.

Back in her bedroom, she locked the door, kicked off her shoes, and literally fell into bed.

Ten seconds later, she was dead to the world.

"We've talked with all the women. Let's try that group over there." Dev gestured to a small cluster of male homeless-shelter guests gathered around a coffeepot and helping themselves to cookies.

"Okay." Photos of Darcy in hand, Laura followed him across the room, weaving among the cots—and trying to figure out how she'd ended up back in his Explorer, once more trekking through the storm.

Somehow, as she'd watched him go through Darcy's room, the offer had popped out in between answering his questions about items he found—none of which had provided a single additional clue, despite the thoroughness of his search. And he hadn't hesitated to accept, using the same excuse as last night—that people might be more inclined to open up to a concerned sister than to him.

But after that moment in the kitchen, when he'd touched her hand, she suspected the reason was more personal than that.

Then again, that might be wishful thinking . . . just as their hope that Nikki's brother might offer some helpful information had been. According to him, Darcy had rebuffed his offers of assistance with her geometry struggles, even though he'd pressed his name and phone number on her.

Too bad. He was a nice, wholesome, church-going kid—the very kind Darcy needed to befriend.

She was so lost in thought she almost bumped into Dev as he stopped beside a group of five overnight residents, pulling up short just in time.

"Hi, guys." Dev drew her forward, keeping a protective hand on her arm. "We're trying to find my friend's sixteen-year-old sister, and we think she stayed here over the weekend. Were any of you around then?"

When a couple of the men nodded and mumbled their assent, Dev tugged the two photos of Darcy from her grasp and showed both of them. "Here's what she looks like all dressed up and in everyday clothes."

All of the men leaned forward. The two who'd said they'd stayed over the weekend shook their heads.

"Nah. Don't recognize her." A guy who appeared to be in his late thirties and dressed in ragtag clothes licked his lips, sending a shiver down Laura's spine. "I'd a noticed her, though. She's a looker." He grinned, revealing teeth in desperate need of attention. Based on photos she'd seen of meth addicts while helping a library patron with a research project, this guy was into the drug big-time. She suppressed another shudder.

"The women mostly stay to themselves, over there." A middle-aged man motioned to the other side of the room. "The staff here don't like us to fraternize, you know?" He chuckled, but it morphed into a phlegmy cough.

"Never hurts to ask, though. Thanks." As Dev started to pass the pictures back to her, a thin older man with long, stringy hair and a stench that almost made her reel ambled by. He glanced their way, stopped, and homed in on the shot of Darcy looking sixteen instead of twenty-six.

He reached out a trembling finger and touched the image. "Pretty, pretty, pretty."

Laura tried not to recoil.

"Yes, she is." Dev slipped in front of her, the photos still in his hand, and edged away from the man, keeping her behind him.

"She smiled at me. Nice smile." The man took a step toward them, his attention riveted on the photo.

Dev stopped.

Pulse leaping, Laura moved out from behind him. "Did you see her here?"

The man bobbled his head. "Pretty, pretty, pretty. Smiled pretty too. At me, at me."

The lanky guy with the bad teeth guffawed. "In your dreams, Balloon Man."

Dev arched an eyebrow. "Balloon Man?"

"Yeah. That's what everybody calls him down in Hopeville, where we usually hang out, 'cause he's full of hot air. Loco, you know?" He lifted his hand and circled his index finger beside his ear. "Come on, Looney. Time to go to bed." He took the man's arm and spoke over his shoulder as he guided him toward a cot. "That's short for Balloon Man. Cute, huh?"

"Pretty, pretty, pretty." Balloon Man continued to chant the words—but this time he added two more. "Butterfly Girl."

Laura's heart stopped. Raced on.

Dev hadn't missed the reference, either. He was already propelling her after the duo.

As the lanky guy sat Balloon Man down on a cot, Dev handed the photos back to her and addressed the younger guy. "What's his real name?" He indicated the man who was continuing to mutter under his breath.

"He don't answer to it no more, but I seen his ID. It's John."

"Thanks."

"He don't know nothin'. You're wastin' your time."

"I've got all evening."

The man shrugged. "Suit yourself."

As he ambled back toward the tray of cookies, Dev dropped down to balance on the balls of his feet beside the older man. Laura followed his lead, photos in hand, taking shallow breaths to lessen the stench.

"John—my name's Dev, and this is Laura, Butterfly Girl's sister. We're trying hard to find her and we thought you might be able to help us."

"Little sister?" The man focused on her.

"That's right. Butterfly Girl is sixteen."

"Sweet sixteen, sweet sixteen. Sixteen going on seventeen." He said the words in a singsong voice, his smile crinkling the skin at the corners of his eyes and revealing several gaps once occupied by teeth.

"Did you talk to her, John?" Dev's tone was steady but firm, keeping the older man on track.

"No, no, no." He shook his head hard, then began to hum an off-key tune Laura didn't recognize. He tilted his face toward the ceiling and his eyes lost focus.

"John." Dev let three seconds pass. The humming continued. He tried again. "John, can you look at me?" He waved a hand in front of the man's face.

John's vacant eyes swung back to Dev and cleared slightly.

"Did anyone else talk to Butterfly Girl, John?" Dev's words were slow and deliberate.

"Guitar Girl."

Laura caught her breath. That fit with what the agent at the Greyhound station had said.

"Did you talk to her?"

"No, no, no! Not allowed, not allowed." He waved a hand toward the other side of the room. "Girls there. Boys here. Like in school. Sister Mary Martha." He rubbed one index finger back and forth over the other. "Bad boy. Bad boy."

Laura watched Dev, wondering if he'd continue to press the rambling man, keep digging.

He did.

"Do you remember how many nights she was here, John?"

The man drifted again, his gaze wandering past Dev's shoulder. "Cold night. Snow, snow, snow."

Dev tried a different tack. "John—did you see her talk to anyone else?"

If the man heard him, he gave no indication. He began singing another tune, but she could only distinguish every other mumbled word. Something about dirt and grime and grease, plus a reference to a minute and a house. All she could clearly make out was the repetitive last line of his off-key ditty: Mr. Clean, Mr. Clean, Mr. Clean.

Taking her arm, Dev pulled her to her feet. "I don't think we're going to get anything else out of him."

"I don't either. You persisted a lot longer than I would have. But at least he confirmed she was here."

"True." He gestured toward an older man who was relinquishing his registration desk duty to another volunteer. "He's the only one on the staff we haven't talked to tonight. Let's catch him while he's on break."

Once again, they wove through the cots, meeting up with the man as he arrived at the coffeepot.

While the volunteer filled a disposable cup, Dev introduced them and launched into the spiel Laura knew by heart at this point, concluding with the new information—that they had reason to believe Darcy had stayed at the shelter over the weekend. On cue, she passed the photos over, not expecting a lot when Dev asked the man if he'd seen or talked with the teen.

To her surprise, however, the volunteer—whose badge listed his name as Bill—studied the photos with more care than the others had, looking from one to the other.

"I have to say this one rings a bell." He indicated the age-appropriate shot of Darcy. "There was a girl here on Sunday night that reminds me of her. She was more worn around the edges, though, and her hair was pulled back with a rubber band. Still"—he inspected the photo—"it might have been her. But I didn't see her up close. I was on Monday morning cleanup duty and she was getting ready to leave when she caught my eye."

"Did you happen to notice if anyone on the volunteer staff talked to her?"

"Yeah, that's why I spotted her. I needed some help moving a table, and I waved at the guy who usually does registration desk duty. He and the girl were having a very serious conversation. I think his name is Mark, but I'm new here, so don't hold me to that. And I don't know anyone's last name yet."

"That's more than we had before. You've been a big help."

"I hope you find your sister." Bill passed the photos back to her. "This is no place for a teenager—but it's better than the street."

156

"Thanks for your help." Laura tucked the photos back in her purse. As the man moved off, she looked up at Dev. "How are you going to find this Mark guy—assuming that's even his name? I thought the director of the shelter wouldn't give you the names of the volunteers . . . first or last?"

He took her arm and guided her toward their coats. "He won't. For now, we'll go with what we have. I'll ask him to contact anyone named Mark and pass my name and phone number along with a request to call. If that doesn't work, there's always pretexting." He pulled her coat off the hook and held it up. "You ready to get out of here?"

"More than."

She mulled over his answer as they climbed the steps and returned to his car, which once again needed to be cleaned off—though the snow had definitely diminished while they'd been in the shelter.

When he slid into the driver's seat, she shifted toward him. "I'm curious. What's pretexting?"

"Textbook definition? Digging for information using false or misleading pretenses." He twisted the key in the ignition, put the car in gear, and pulled out.

"You mean like . . . lying?" She squirmed in her seat. Was Phoenix a little on the shady side after all?

"I prefer to think of it as pretending—the same

thing undercover law enforcement operatives do. Is that a problem for you?" He spared her a quick look.

She suddenly felt foolish. "Not when you put it that way. From everything I've heard, undercover work is very risky. It's hard to fault people who put their lives on the line every day to combat crime and keep the streets safe."

"That's what we do at Phoenix too. Except we take on cases that fall through the cracks of official law enforcement. And sometimes the only way to catch the bad guys is to use their own tactics against them. Frankly, I don't have any moral issue with that."

He skirted some orange cones delineating an area of buckled pavement, where water company workers were toiling under bright lights amid a frozen sculpture garden.

"Must be a water main break." Laura gave the crew a sympathetic scan as Dev maneuvered the Explorer past.

"Must be." Dev accelerated. "If it helps put your mind at ease, in this case the pretext will be very simple and designed to do nothing more than reveal the name of the guy Darcy may have talked to. He might not know anything even if we find the right guy, but I think it's worth tracking him down and having a conversation. We haven't found anyone else who had contact with her."

"I'm all for that—and watching the bus station."

"On our agenda, starting tomorrow if the buses are running again." He gestured ahead. "And my guess is they will be. The highway ramp is open. They must be making progress in clearing the roads." He turned into the entrance lane. "Are you going to be at work?"

"Yes. I'm on days the rest of the week."

"I assume your cell would be the best way to reach you?"

"Yes. I'll keep it with me. My boss also said I can take time off if I need to."

"I'm hoping we can wrap this up before I might have to ask you to do that."

So was she. But as they headed west on the one lane of the highway that was open, she didn't rely only on hope.

She also prayed.

Mark did a visual sweep of the room. As far as he could see, it was ready for its new occupant. The bed was made, a package of Oreos was on the shelf above the desk, toiletries were stocked in the small private bath/shower annex, and fresh towels were stacked on the linen rack. The small refrigerator was filled with healthy beverages, a bowl of fruit rested on the table next to the wing chair and reading lamp, and the treadmill in the corner was in prime condition.

He just had to add one final touch.

Crossing the room, he unfurled the small banner.

When he reached the far wall, he slid the step-ladder from his shoulder, opened it, and pulled a roll of masking tape from his pocket. Then he climbed the three rungs and taped one end of the banner to his left, the other to his right. After descending, he folded up the ladder and backed off to view his handiwork.

Perfect.

With a final sweep of the room, he flipped off the light, shut the door, and moved to the other side of the basement, the ladder once again hooked on his shoulder. He had one more piece of business to take care of before he went to bed.

He stopped in front of the guitar, set the step-ladder beside it, and expelled an annoyed breath. He should have gotten rid of it immediately, but being housebound by the blizzard had left only the dumpster in the back alley as an option. That had seemed too close to home—and too risky.

Having Darcy spot the stupid thing had been riskier, however. How could he have forgotten it was sitting in plain view? On the other hand, he hadn't expected her to stick her nose in his basement. Fortunately, she'd bought his off-the-cuff explanation.

Tomorrow, however, it was going to disappear. Forever.

He jerked it away from the wall, climbed the stairs, and set it by the back door. There was no chance Darcy would wander down tonight.

Tomorrow he'd drop it in the dumpster in back of the daycare center. He was always the first one there, and it would still be dark at that early hour.

After scrubbing his hands, he turned off the lights on the first floor and climbed the stairs. Darcy's door was closed, and he tested the handle. Locked—and it would stay that way all night. He could sleep in peace.

He took a long, vigorous shower. Washed his hair. Brushed his teeth. Clipped his fingernails and massaged lotion into his hands.

When he was at last ready for bed, he sat on the edge of the mattress and opened the drawer of his nightstand.

The framed photo was on top, as always, next to the faded birthday card. He pulled it out and stared at the image. The edges were yellowing a bit now, after all these years, but the long blonde hair, blue eyes, and winsome smile of the high school senior never changed. She'd been so lovely, had so much promise . . .

Then things had gone very wrong. She'd made bad choices, done bad things. Sought refuge in booze and drugs and sex while turning her back on everything that really mattered. On every*one* that really mattered.

And all the love he'd felt for her hadn't been able to save her.

He'd make up for that, though. He'd save someone else instead, someone who wasn't too far gone. Someone who would appreciate his efforts. Who would thank him and love him.

Darcy.

Carefully he stowed the framed photo back in the nightstand and shut the drawer. After dimming the light to provide a soft illumination that would keep darkness at bay, he lay down and closed his eyes.

Good night, Lil. Sweet dreams.

9

As his radio alarm clock beeped with skull-piercing intensity in the predawn hours, Dev groaned, groped for it, and shoved the switch none too gently into the off position.

Quiet descended, and he flopped on his back, wiping a hand down his face. After tossing and turning until almost three in the morning—thanks to his new client—he was not ready to get up.

The wind whistled around the outside wall of his corner apartment, and he pulled the blankets higher, wishing he had another way to get warm.

Rolling his eyes, he blew out an exasperated breath. That kind of thinking was exactly why sleep had eluded him. Since he'd walked Laura to her door last night at ten-thirty after their second trip to the homeless shelter, images of her big blue eyes, soft lips, and French-braided hair that itched to be released from its plait had dominated his thoughts.

Enough already.

He shoved the blankets back and swung his legs to the floor. This was adolescent stuff. It was the kind of pining he'd done at seventeen when the French exchange student at his high school had kept every guy salivating with her short skirts, exotic accent, and pouty lips. But Laura was nothing like Mary Renee Moreau, and at thirty-five he should be past such immature yearnings.

Too bad he wasn't.

Age and experience, however, had honed his discipline. He might not be able to keep visions of Laura at bay in the dark, empty hours of the night when he should be sleeping, but he knew how to focus on the job during working hours. So the answer to his dilemma was simple: immerse himself in the task at hand.

Even if that meant he had to give up sleeping for the duration.

As he rose, his BlackBerry began to ring and he snatched it from the nightstand, a surge of adrenaline chasing away the last vestiges of sleep. Five-thirty was way too early for social calls.

A quick check of caller ID, however, loosened the snarl of tension in his shoulders. Connor. It figured. The man didn't seem to need more than three hours of shut-eye a night.

"Yeah?"

"Good morning to you too." His partner sounded disgustingly wide-awake and far too cheerful for the early hour.

"Do you know what time it is?"

"What? Did I disturb your beauty sleep?"

"I'll laugh after the sun rises. Whaddya need?" He scrubbed a hand over his face and slogged toward the kitchen, caffeine high on his priority list.

"Since I was up already, I touched base with Greyhound. The buses are going to start running at ten. You still want me on day shift for surveillance?"

"Unless you have something better to do. I was going to call them in about five minutes myself. They told me late last night they wouldn't be back in business until midmorning." He flipped on the switch in the kitchen, squinting against the sudden glare.

"So I saved you a call. You're welcome. And I'm fine with the day shift. I brought the pictures of Darcy home with me. She should be easy to spot."

"Let's hope so." He pulled the pot out from the coffeemaker and continued toward the sink.

"By the way, I also talked to Cal this morning."

Dev frowned, hand on faucet. "You called him on his honeymoon?"

"Give me a break. That's more like a stunt you'd pull."

True—not that he intended to admit it.

"Thanks a lot." He turned on the water. "I always forget about the polish and savoir faire and sensitivity you picked up working with hoity-toity diplomats and politicians all those years in the Secret Service."

"Did you get up on the wrong side of the bed or what?"

"I didn't sleep well, okay?"

"Something on your mind? Like that hot new client, maybe?"

"Connor." The warning came out in a low growl as he twisted off the stream of water and yanked the pot out from under the faucet.

"I guess that's my answer." Dev could hear the grin in his partner's voice. "In any case, Cal called *me*. Their connection from San Francisco was delayed by fog, and Moira was asleep on his shoulder. He said she didn't get much rest on the overnight flight from Hawaii, thanks to a lot of turbulence. He assumed I'd be awake and was using the downtime to check in."

That sounded like Cal. He'd always been Mr. Responsibility.

"I hope you told him we had things under control." He padded back to the coffeemaker, pot in hand.

"More or less. He didn't sound anxious to hear a lot of details."

Dev snorted. "Would you be thinking about

work if you'd just spent ten days honeymooning in a tropical paradise and had a gorgeous woman asleep on your shoulder?"

A chuckle came over the line. "The caffeine must be kicking in."

Dev pulled the bag of ground coffee out of the refrigerator, inhaled the aroma, and shook some into a filter. "Not yet, but close."

"Then I'll make this quick so I don't keep you from that high-priority task. Cal said he'd be in first thing tomorrow. I gave him a topline on your case, but you can fill in the blanks in the office. What's on your agenda today?"

"Working the case, what do you think? And I'll handle anything at the office that can't wait until Cal gets back."

"Okay. I'll be in touch if the girl shows."

"Thanks." Dev set the phone aside, got the coffee brewing, and headed for the bathroom.

A quick shower, a bowl of cereal, several cups of black coffee and he'd be ready to track down the only person so far who might be able to offer them a clue to Darcy's whereabouts.

A man named Mark.

Mark turned into Davis Daycare and eyeballed the parking lot, eerily illuminated in the 6:15 a.m. blackness by overhead pole lights. The crew they contracted to clear snow had already come and gone. Excellent. The lot wasn't pristine, but it was navigable, especially the section at the front where parents parked long enough to dash in and dump their offspring before hurrying off to take care of the important business of the day.

As if raising their own children wasn't important business.

Given the tough economy, though, he ought to cut them a little slack. It was possible some of them needed the two incomes to cover living expenses, not just to stroke their egos and give them cash to buy the latest and greatest flat-screen TV.

Some . . . but not all.

Still, while he might not agree with the priorities of those whose motives were less admirable, they did pay for quality care. And he took the trust they'd placed in him seriously—as did the small family-run Davis chain of daycare centers. Mr. Davis often said that if parents couldn't take care of their kids themselves, they owed them a safe, nurturing environment. That's what the Davis centers provided, and Mark was proud to uphold their high standards of quality care. Children deserved nothing less.

He continued toward the deserted employee parking at the rear of the building, casting a quick glance over his shoulder at the guitar case on the backseat. It was a shame to pitch a musical instrument, but that was the safest option. And what better place than here? By the time the employees finished emptying trash cans at the end of the day, it would be hidden under the kind of refuse even dumpster divers wouldn't want to ferret through. Nobody liked smelly diapers.

Angling in to a spot beside the industrial trash bin, he inched the car forward over a few snow-covered patches and set the brake. No one else should arrive for twenty or thirty minutes, giving him plenty of time to dispose of the guitar and start getting things set up for the day.

Once out of the car, Mark opened the back door, reached in, and grasped the handle of the case. He'd already given it and the guitar a thorough going-over, and there was nothing on either to identify them as Star's. So even if someone by chance found them, there was no way to connect the items to the itinerant teen.

Straightening up, he inspected the parking area once more. It was quiet and dark at this early hour, and the tall bushes at the back hid the lot from the view of the houses on the next street.

There would be no witnesses to his furtive activity.

Guitar in hand, he shut the door, circled behind the car, and headed toward the dumpster.

Too fast.

His foot shot out from under him on a patch of ice, and as he sprawled on the frozen pavement, the guitar slid several feet away.

Gasping for air, he struggled to fill his deflated

lungs as he took a quick inventory. No damage as far as he could tell. Thank goodness. The last thing he needed right now was a sprained ankle or a broken arm. An injury like that wouldn't jibe with his plans.

Back on his feet, he took a second to get his footing before making his way more carefully across the asphalt. Once he retrieved the guitar, he continued toward the dumpster.

Almost done.

He tightened his grip on the handle of the case, reached up, and pushed on the lid of the trash bin.

It didn't budge.

Mark frowned. The lid always gave easily. What was wrong with it today?

He shifted position to take advantage of the light on the other side of the parking lot. Ah. The lid was frozen shut with a thick coating of ice.

A cloud of frosty breath formed in front of his face as he let out a sigh. Was anything ever easy?

He set the guitar down. Using both hands this time, he pushed on the lid as hard as he could. Hammered against it with his fist. Shook it.

Nothing.

Now what was he supposed to do?

Despite the cold, a trickle of sweat inched down his back.

As he tried to think of some other option, he gave the lid one final shove. A cracking sound filled the quiet morning, and all at once the ice shattered, spewing shards in all directions. One of the razor-sharp projectiles clipped his cheek, and he muttered a curse.

At least the dumpster was now accessible.

Hefting the guitar with one hand, he pushed up the lid with the other—just as a pair of headlights arced his direction, pinning him in a spotlight.

What the . . . ?

He swung around, shielding his eyes with one hand as he let the lid drop back into place. The resounding boom echoed like a cannon in the morning stillness.

The headlights swung away from him as a car pulled in beside his. Still blinded by the bright light, he blinked, trying to see who'd interrupted his covert task.

The car lights went out. A door slammed, and a female voice spoke.

"I'm sorry, Mr. Hamilton. I didn't mean to startle you."

It was Faith Bradley, the twenty-two-year-old who worked the front desk. She often came early—but never this early.

She moved closer, her face shadowed in the predawn darkness. "Are you okay?"

"Yes." He shoved the word past his stiff lips, trying to calm his racing pulse. *She doesn't know a thing. Act normal. She's just a dumb kid, and she likes you. She'll buy whatever you say.*

"Can I help you with something?" She glanced toward the guitar in his hand.

"No. I just need to get rid of this old case. It was cluttering up my basement and the dumpster in my alley was full. Why are you here so early?"

"With the center closed for a couple of days, I thought you might be able to use some help getting things ready."

It was hard to fault someone for being a conscientious employee.

"Thanks. Would you mind opening the door and turning on some lights while I finish up out here?" He fished in his pocket for the building key and handed it over. On the plus side, the dim light masked the tremor in his fingers.

"Sure." She leaned closer to examine his cheek, her expression concerned. "I think you're bleeding."

Was he? He tugged off a glove, lifted a hand to his cheek, and swiped his fingers across. Yeah, he was.

"It's nothing. The lid was sealed shut and I had to break the ice to get it loose. A piece flew off in my direction. I'll take care of it when I get inside. It would really help if you'd open up and turn on the lights."

"Right. I'm on it." She trotted toward the door, anxious as always to please.

He waited until she fitted the key in the lock and

disappeared inside before returning to his task. Once more he lifted the lid and hefted the guitar. This time he managed to toss it inside. The lid banged shut.

As he picked his way carefully toward the back door, he let out a long, slow breath. Too bad Faith had shown up. But he'd be extra nice to her today and she'd forget all about this incident— just as he intended to.

Because he had much more important things to think about in the coming days.

As Faith checked in the last batch of arriving children from her position behind the front desk, Mark entered the foyer from the hallway.

Her attention strayed.

Man, was he hot. Even the bandage on his cheek couldn't detract from his appeal.

"Faith?" A woman's impatient voice interrupted her dreamy musing. "Are we set?"

She dragged her gaze back to the harried young mother who was bouncing a crying one-year-old on her hip. "Sorry, Mrs. Vance. Yes. I've got you checked in."

Mark paused beside the desk and scanned the morning melee. "Everything under control?"

"Copasetic." She beamed at him, hoping he was impressed by the big word.

"Great." He sent her a brief smile that set off a flutter in her nerve endings, then moved beside

Mrs. Vance. "I'll take Jillian back. You look like you're in a hurry."

The mother gladly relinquished her grip. "I have an important meeting in an hour and I still have some prep to do."

"Well, don't worry about this little lady." Mark bounced the blonde cherub, who grabbed a fistful of his pressed shirt and hiccupped as she stared at him, her sobs trailing off.

Faith's heart melted. The man had a way with children, no question about it. Despite the muscles hinted at beneath those crisp dress shirts he always wore, he was tender and loving with every child—and expected everyone on the staff to follow his example. Plus, he was clean-cut and had solid values.

Mark Hamilton was perfect husband—and father—material.

If only he'd notice her.

She watched as he disappeared down the hall, Jillian propped on his hip, smothering a sigh as she switched to autopilot and went back to work. It wasn't as if there was that much age difference between them. Six or eight years, tops. That was nothing. And she was smart enough for him. Wasn't she going to night school to get her degree? Plus, she loved kids as much as he did. They would make a nice couple.

But Mark only saw her as an employee.

Moving on to the next parent, she went through

the routine motions. She had to come up with a better strategy to get him to notice her on a personal level. The homemade coffeecake she'd brought a few weeks ago hadn't worked; he'd ended up putting it in the break room to share with the staff. Maybe she could bake him some cookies, but wait until quitting time to give them to him. That might encourage him to take them home—and remind him of her once he got there.

Better yet, why not drop off some sort of treat at his house? She'd driven by there a few times when she'd had nothing better to do. Or would that be too forward?

"Faith?" At Mark's summons, she swiveled toward the hallway that led to the back. "When you're done out here, they could use your help in Room 3."

"No problem."

Once again, he rewarded her with his oh-so-appealing boy-next-door smile.

She had to get him to notice her. Some way, somehow.

And once he did, he might realize what he'd been missing. Then she'd get the happily-ever-after she'd been pining for since the day he'd interviewed her for this job ten months ago.

A girl could dream, couldn't she?

As Laura entered the break room at the library, the muffled trill of her phone sounded from the cavernous depths of her shoulder tote.

A spurt of adrenaline set her nerves jangling, and she lost her grip on the apple in her hand. It fell with a thud and rolled across the floor.

Groping through her tote bag as she chased the wayward red delicious, she yanked out the phone the instant her fingers closed over it, scooping up the apple at the same time. The name she'd hoped to see was displayed in caller ID.

Yes!

Another spurt of adrenaline followed as she put the phone to her ear. "Hi, Dev. Any leads?"

"Not yet, but I wanted to give you a progress report."

"I'm all ears." She sank into one of the molded plastic chairs, propped the phone on her shoulder, and began twisting the stem of her apple.

"I spoke with the director of the emergency shelter first thing this morning. There are two volunteers named Mark, and one of them worked over the weekend. He could be our man. The director promised to call and ask him to contact me, but I haven't heard anything yet. If I don't get a call, I'll find out his name and pay him a visit."

That must be where the pretexting would come in.

The stem of the apple came off in her hand, and she set it aside. "He still might not know anything."

"True. But a competent PI investigates every

lead. One of my partners is also at Gateway Station. Not too many buses are running yet because they're on a limited schedule, but Darcy wasn't on the 10:05 to Chicago that just left. There's another one at 7:10 tonight. He's watching every departure, though, in case she changed her destination. If he spots her, you'll know thirty seconds after I do."

"Is there anything else I can do besides pray?"

"Not at the moment."

The conversation was over—but she didn't want to hang up yet.

She grasped at the first thing that came to mind. "By the way, a missing persons detective called this morning. Mike Butler. He wanted to see if I'd heard anything from Darcy. I mentioned your involvement, and he seemed happy I'd put a PI on the case. He gave Phoenix high marks."

"We've dealt with him before. He and Cal worked together on quite a few cases. Most of the goodwill we have from the police is because of the years my partner spent on the force. He was well liked and well respected."

"Actually, this guy mentioned you by name and referenced a couple of the cases you told me about on our drive home from the shelter the first night. He was quite complimentary."

"Don't put too much stock in that." Dev's tone was dismissive. "Few of our cases are one-man jobs. We work as a team, so the team gets credit."

A man without an ego. Nice.

"So what's next on your agenda for today?" As soon as the words left her mouth, she closed her eyes and shook her head. *Let the man go, Laura. This isn't a social conversation. He has work to do.*

But if he was in a hurry, he gave no indication of it.

"While I wait for Mark to return the call, I've got some intel to dig up on a shady guy who skipped the country. Our business client wants him brought to justice without a lot of publicity. I have a feeling I'll be putting my passport to use."

"I didn't realize you did international work."

"If the case calls for it."

The door to the break room opened and another staff member entered. Wiggling her fingers in greeting, she dropped into a chair at an adjacent table and started to page through a magazine while she drank a soda.

So much for privacy.

But her break time was eroding, anyway. She needed to eat her apple and let Dev get back to work.

"Thanks for keeping me in the loop. Will you call me again later with another update? I'll be sticking close to home tonight."

"Sure." He hesitated, as if he wanted to say more, but instead signed off with a "talk to you soon."

The line went dead, and Laura slipped the phone back in her tote bag, then picked up her apple. She ran her finger over the depressed spot where it had hit the floor. The flesh underneath was soft already. Soon the bruise would spread under the skin, invisible to the eye—kind of like the effects of a failed romance.

It wasn't Rick she had in mind, however. Yes, she'd been disappointed when her relationship fell apart, and her ego had smarted. Yet in hindsight, they hadn't been the best match. He'd been pleasant and attractive, and there'd been a little zing between them. But it had been nothing like the zing she felt with Dev after only a few days.

And that could be dangerous.

Because the Phoenix PI had a tragic romance in his past—one painful enough to make it an off-limits topic. He might not be in the market for another bout with Cupid. And if she let herself get carried away, her heart could end up like the apple in her hand—with a soft spot that hid a great big bruise underneath.

10

Inch by inch, Darcy dragged herself back to consciousness from another deep sleep. Strange. Even after she'd gotten slammed by the flu last year and was wiped out for a month, she hadn't experienced this kind of mind-numbing morning fatigue. It had been the same yesterday. Could spending a few sleepless nights at the bus station and the homeless shelter have been that draining?

Hard to believe.

But facts didn't lie, and convincing her brain to engage and her limbs to cooperate was a huge chore. What other explanation could there be?

It didn't matter, though. She was in no hurry to get up. The only thing on her agenda today was to make a decision about what she wanted to do—and more and more she was leaning toward going back to Laura's. In less than two years, if she stayed the course, she could head off to college and be on her own, anyway—assuming she buckled down and got her grades in shape. Especially geometry. Danny Martin could help her there, though. He might be a Midwest hick, but he wasn't hard on the eyes and he aced every math test.

She readjusted her pillow and snuggled farther into her cocoon of warmth as she turned to the other looming issue. Was it fair to disrupt Laura's life as she'd disrupted her dad's—and risk more bad consequences and stomach-clenching guilt?

Truth be told, however, a lot of the outcome was under her control. All she had to do was follow the house rules—which weren't all that burdensome. Laura wasn't anywhere near as fussy about tidiness as Mark was. And it wouldn't hurt to get rid of the chip on her shoulder, either. After all, if it wasn't for Laura, she'd have ended up in some foster home. Who knows what disaster might have awaited her there?

Darcy yawned, blinking at the blurry numbers on her watch until they came into focus. Was it really past ten? She'd slept for twelve hours? Sheesh. She wouldn't have to sleep again for a week once she went home, after all the hours she'd racked up here.

The room tipped when she stood, but she was starting to get used to that. A hot shower should take care of any lingering fuzziness. Then she'd call Rachel in Chicago to let her know of her change in plans, and phone Laura to ask for a ride home. Her half sister would be at the library today, assuming it was open, but she could hang here until the end of the workday. Knowing Mark, he'd offer to drive her home, but she'd already imposed too much. At the very least she'd have to write him a thank-you note for his hospitality, perhaps even dig into her small cash reserve for a gift certificate to Starbucks.

The house was silent as she traversed the hall. As usual, the door beside the bathroom was closed, and she gave it a curious glance. Mark's room was at the other end of the short passage-way, also behind a closed door. Was this another guest room?

She reached for the knob. Hesitated. Was it

snooping to look behind a closed door? Yeah, it was. But what could it hurt to take a quick peek? It had to just be an office or storage room or another bedroom.

Twisting her wrist, she pushed the door open—and found herself staring at a small but well-equipped gym. Regular exercise and a healthy diet. No wonder her host was in such great shape. Too bad he had such a phobia about neatness and a fixation on old movies and videos. Otherwise, he'd be quite a catch for some woman his age.

Oh, well. Not her problem.

She closed the door and continued toward the shower. Once the haziness in her brain dissipated, she'd grab a bite to eat, make her calls—and get ready to go home.

Mark checked the clock on his office wall, tapped the applications he was reviewing into a neat stack, and stood. It was early for lunch, and in general he never left the premises until the day was over, but he'd been jittery all morning and people were beginning to notice. Especially Faith, who had the annoying habit of watching him whenever they were in the same room.

Leaving for a short time might raise a few eyebrows, but he'd make it through the afternoon much better if he confirmed everything was okay at the house. Now that he'd decided Darcy was the one, he didn't want to risk having her take off on him.

After sliding the applications into a folder, he snagged his coat off the tree in the corner of his office, exited into the hall—and almost ran into Faith hovering outside his door.

She backed up, hand to her throat, and gave a shaky laugh. "Sorry about that. I was just stopping by to see if I could bring you back anything for lunch. I know you usually eat in, but I'm going to Panera in half an hour and I'd be happy to pick you up a sandwich or some soup." She seemed to notice the coat over his arm for the first time. "Oh. I guess you were going out, anyway."

"I have an errand to run." He slid his arms into the sleeves. "I shouldn't be gone more than forty-five minutes. Would you let Vicky know?"

Having Faith pass on his plans would be easier than dealing with the assistant manager in person—not that she'd ask a lot of questions. She did what the job required and kept to herself . . . a great combination. Faith could learn from her on the mind-your-own-business front.

Still, nobody beat the young woman across from him for diligence, reliability, and hard work. She always went the extra mile, and nothing he asked of her was too much trouble. If she didn't have such stellar attributes, he'd have let her go months ago and liberated himself from the constant scrutiny.

"Sure, I'll tell her." She backed up, giving him room to exit. Barely.

"Thanks." He brushed past her and headed for the exit—only to be flagged down by a newer employee.

"Sorry to bother you, Mr. Hamilton, but one of our children is sick."

He detoured into the room to lay a hand against the four-year-old's forehead, examine her flushed face, and listen to a recitation of her other symptoms. "Call the contact person in her file. She's burning up. We don't need to expose the other children to the flu or strep, and both have been going around."

As he began to rise, the little girl clung to his arm and whimpered.

"The kids sure do take to you." The aide patted the girl's head. "I'll go make that call."

He was stuck. Walking out on a child who needed him wasn't an option. He'd have to defer his trip home until the mother or father arrived.

Cuddling the toddler in one arm, he tugged out his phone. Might as well use the delay to check his voice mail—not that there'd be much. There never was. On the few occasions he forgot to run through his messages at night, he never had a backlog. Sometimes there were none for several days in a row.

Phone in hand, he scrolled through the calls. There was only one new one, from the director of the homeless shelter. The man must want to talk about his availability for next weekend. Mark deleted the message.

The little girl in his arms whimpered again, and he stroked her head. "Your mommy will be here soon, honey."

He slipped the phone back in his pocket. Later, he'd take the man's name off his contact list— because he was never going back to the shelter.

It had served its purpose.

Where in the world was Mark's phone?

Bewildered, Darcy padded through the rooms on the main level for a second time. Maybe she'd missed it on the first go-round.

Nothing.

She'd already been through the upper floor twice too, including a quick peek into his bedroom.

The man didn't have a phone.

But wait . . . he did have a phone jack. There, over the kitchen counter, next to a set of electrical outlets.

Weird.

Maybe he'd had it installed as part of the remodeling, in case he ever wanted to move. It wouldn't be easy to sell a house that didn't have a place to plug in a phone. On the other hand, with all the cells around now, people were beginning to get rid of their landlines. Apparently, Mark already had. He was ahead of the curve on that one, even if he was way behind on movies and TV shows.

But how was she supposed to call Rachel and Laura?

Darcy wandered over to the front window, still feeling unsteady. She needed to eat some breakfast. That should help. Then she'd take a walk and find a phone. There were lots of funky restaurants in Soulard, from what she recalled of the city driving tour Laura had taken her on when she'd first arrived. Mostly the excursion had been boring, but she did remember the cool Central West End, which had reminded her of some of the neighborhood enclaves in New York City, and she had a vague recollection of this area. The city hadn't done anything to clean off Mark's street, but the snow had stopped and she had sturdy boots. There had to be a restaurant nearby.

Plus, she was more than ready to breathe some clean, cold air. That might help jump-start her brain too.

But food first.

She wandered back into the spotless kitchen and opened the refrigerator. There was a large mug of cocoa, already mixed and waiting to be nuked. Thoughtful. A package of strawberry cream cheese to go with the promised bagels on the counter. Half a dozen eggs, still in their carton. She bypassed those; too much work. And the box of high-fiber, whole-grain cereal on the counter looked disgusting.

Balancing the cream cheese and cocoa in her hand, she moved to the L-shaped counter and deposited them. Then she toasted a bagel, gathering up stray crumbs and dropping them into the trash can beside the sink after she pulled it out of the oven. Perish the thought she should leave a speck of food on the counter.

While the cocoa heated in the microwave, she spread the cream cheese on the bagel and dived in. Despite the addition of a few Oreos, last night's dinner of soup and bread hadn't cut it. She was starving.

She repeated the procedure with a second bagel, scarfing it down too, before she removed the hot chocolate from the microwave and took a sip. As usual, it was excellent—though she missed the whipped cream. But another search in the refrigerator didn't turn up a can of Reddi-wip. Oh, well. She'd have to suffer.

Smiling at the exaggeration, she toyed with the idea of sitting back at the counter while she drank the cocoa. No, better to do her hair and makeup if she was going to venture out to look for a phone. She could sip while she got ready, since Mark wasn't around to confine her eating and drinking to the kitchen.

That was another thing she liked about Laura— her sister always let her take stuff to her room to eat. She hadn't even gotten mad the time a can of cherry soda exploded and sprayed over everything. A few faint pink spots on her ceiling remained as a souvenir.

Yeah. Living with Laura wasn't all that bad.

And it was a whole lot better than the way Star lived, sleeping in homeless shelters and eating other people's garbage.

Suppressing a shudder, Darcy crossed the living room and started up the steps. It would be better at Laura's from now on. She'd toe the line and be a model sister. In fact, doing her best not to cause waves might make up in a small way for all the grief she'd caused her dad—beginning with the imminent phone call that would include a huge apology and a promise to do better.

After grabbing her toiletries from her suitcase, she carried her hot chocolate to the bathroom and set it on the marble vanity, sipping the rich drink while she combed her hair and did her makeup.

Feeling more upbeat than she had in months, Darcy finished with a swipe of lipstick and headed back to her room, cocoa in hand. As soon as she finished the remaining half cup, she was out of here. She'd find a restaurant, borrow a phone . . . and maybe treat herself to a burger and fries before she came back here and packed up, since she wouldn't need her stash of money.

She picked up her pace, hung a sharp right into the bedroom—and suddenly lost her balance.

Arms flailing, she dropped her toiletries case as she stumbled and groped for a handhold. Her fingers met empty air. Pitching forward, she watched in horror as the contents of the large mug spewed out in an arc and landed in a long, dark swath on the pristine white comforter.

Only after she fell to one knee did she regain her physical balance. Not so with her emotional equilibrium. The dark stain was at eye level—and it was bad.

Mark was going to freak.

Big-time.

She closed her eyes and sank back to sit on the floor. Kind as he'd been to her and Star, he wasn't very tolerant of messes . . . and this was a big one.

Think! There has to be a way to fix this!

Wait . . . hadn't Mark mentioned a washer and dryer in the basement?

Yes!

And surely he had some of that spray-on stain remover down there, along with the laundry detergent. She could have this washed and dried long before the end of the workday. It would delay her going-home plans, but better to take a couple of hours and get this fixed than leave an unhappy host.

Darcy stood carefully, set the empty mug on the dresser, and slipped on her shoes. If she was going to venture into that grungy-looking basement, she wanted some protection for her feet. Who knew what kinds of creepy crawly critters lived in the shadows down there?

After tugging the comforter off the bed, she gathered it in her arms and exited the room.

Halfway down the hall, however, her step faltered as his warning from yesterday echoed in her mind.

It's not safe down there. Stay out, okay?

He wouldn't be happy if he knew she'd gone against his wishes.

But he'd be less happy if he saw the disaster in her arms.

She picked up her pace.

In the kitchen, she shifted the bulky coverlet in her arms and pulled the door that led downstairs fully open to let as much light as possible filter down the stairs. Since there wasn't a light switch on the wall at the top of the steps, she'd have to make do with natural illumination until she got to the washer and dryer. There had to be a light of some kind there.

Still feeling a bit unsteady, she didn't rush her descent on the rough wooden steps. At the bottom, she scanned the dank, dreary space.

The first thing she noticed was that Star's guitar was gone.

Had she come for it this morning?

But Mark had left so early . . . that didn't seem plausible.

So where was it?

And what was in those larger-than-gallon-sized metal containers with screw-top openings that were lined up in military precision against the wall in the far corner?

Puzzling as those questions were, she had a higher priority at the moment—putting the washer and dryer she'd spotted behind the open stairs to use.

Darcy circled around the steps toward them, the light growing dimmer as she approached. A hanging bulb with a pull chain drew her eye, and she swerved toward it and gave a tug. Brightness flooded the area.

Much better. The basement didn't look nearly as spooky in the garish light from the bare bulb. The reflective white of the washer and dryer also added a bright touch, as did the two long white chest freezers that flanked the cleaning appliances.

Strange that Mark would have two freezers. He must bake an awful lot of bread—but who cared as long as she was able to get the comforter clean?

Dumping the dirty coverlet on top of the washer, she surveyed the shelf above it for stain remover. Yep, there it was. She pulled it off, set the nozzle on spray, and gave the dark blemish a thorough soaking. It lightened as she watched—a positive sign . . . she hoped.

Next, she shook some detergent in the washer,

tucked the comforter inside, and started the machine. Hopefully, this would do the trick.

Rubbing her palms on her jeans, she glanced again at the twin freezers. They were awful big for a bachelor pad—but even stranger were the metal straps around them, held in place with industrial-sized locks.

Did Mark use them as safes, maybe? Brianna had told her once her mother kept extra cash in an empty pizza box in their freezer—but how much space would you need for a few extra bucks? And why not just use a safe that was too heavy for a burglar to haul away?

Darcy ambled over to the freezer on her left as the washer continued to fill. She wouldn't mind having some more of Mark's homemade bread. Maybe he'd give her a loaf to take home if she dropped a few hints and he had enough in reserve. Laura would like it too.

There wasn't much chance she'd be able to determine his stash, though, given the locks.

She reached out to weigh the serious-looking piece of hardware in her hand—and an instant later found herself holding it.

Huh.

It must not have been fastened properly.

Dare she peek inside before replacing the lock?

Why not? She'd love to know what Mark kept in these gigantic deep freezes. No way could they be filled with bread.

But if they were, she wouldn't hesitate to ask for a loaf to take home.

Fitting her fingers under the lip of the lid, she lifted it and leaned over.

Instantly, a booming roar thundered through her brain.

Her lungs locked.

The world tilted.

Even as her mind tried to reject what her eyes were seeing, bile rose in her throat.

She gagged.

Dropped the lid.

Staggered back.

No!

The renunciation screamed in her head, but she couldn't erase the image from her mind—or deny the truth.

Mark had killed Star and dumped her in the deep freeze.

She jerked her gaze to the other freezer as her heart slammed into overdrive.

Who else had he killed?

Was she next?

Ohmygodohmygodohmygod!

Black spots crowded into her field of vision. Her legs went rubbery. She swayed.

No!

She couldn't hyperventilate. Couldn't pass out. She had to get out of here.

Now!

With one last look at the freezer that had become Star's tomb, she turned to flee.

And found Mark waiting at the bottom of the steps.

11

She'd ruined everything.

Mark gripped the railing at the bottom of the basement stairs, anger churning in his gut as Darcy stared at him, her eyes wide with terror.

If only he'd gotten out of the center five minutes sooner, this disaster could have been avoided. But a sick child had needed comforting, and he couldn't leave after that without a thorough hand-scrubbing. His chafed fingers still tingled from the meticulous five-minute scouring.

It was too late for regrets, however. The damage was done. The bang of the freezer lid as he'd descended the steps, audible even over the rushing water that was filling the washer, plus the lock lying on the floor, told him that.

Darcy had seen Star—and she'd probably guessed about the others.

She knew what he'd done.

But she didn't know why.

That was the sole saving grace. Because once he explained everything, she'd understand and try hard to prove herself, to live up to his expectations, to step back from the brink and let him help her salvage her life. She had a lot more potential than the others, and he intended to let her know that. It might give her more of an incentive to try hard to be better.

He took a step toward her.

She gasped and veered sideways, closer to the stairs behind him, eyes wild.

"You don't have to be afraid, Darcy."

Her incredulous expression, heaving chest, and the darting glances she was tossing toward the stairs told him she didn't believe that.

But it was true—if she did her part.

All at once she made a break for the stairs, moving faster than he expected.

He beat her there.

When she realized she'd been outmaneuvered, she skidded to a stop several yards away and stared at him. Her throat contracted, and she moistened her lips. "You killed Star." The accusation came out in a horrified whisper.

"She was expendable. And she wasn't part of the plan."

Darcy rubbed her palms on her jeans and retreated a few paces. "W-what plan?"

"I'll tell you all about it in time." Again, he took a step toward her.

She continued to back away—toward the door. Excellent. He didn't want to hurt her more than necessary, but under the circumstances, he doubted she'd go into the soundproof room willingly. Having her in close proximity to the entrance would make things easier.

He reached into his pocket and withdrew the key.

Her gaze dropped to his fingers, and she crouched, every muscle taut, her posture reminding him of a cornered animal about to spring in a last-ditch effort to gain freedom.

Not going to happen.

"I have something to show you." He walked toward her.

She tried to zigzag past him, but he grabbed her arm and dragged her toward the door a few feet away.

"Calm down. I'm not going to hurt you."

If she heard him through the frenzy of her struggle, she gave no indication. Sucking in ragged gasps, she lashed out at him, jerking left and right, clawing at his shirt, kicking his shins, and finally raking her fingers down his face.

For the second time today, he felt a piercing sting on his cheek.

She'd drawn blood.

Enough.

Twisting her arm behind her, he propelled her toward the door and shoved the key in the lock, ignoring her moans as she doubled over.

Once he had the door open, he pushed her inside, yanked the door closed, and relocked the dead bolt. Moving close to the fish-eye peephole, he took in the panoramic, if distorted, view of the room.

Darcy was sprawled on the floor where she'd fallen, staring at the sign on the far wall.

Good.

Maybe now she'd understand he meant her no harm.

Pocketing the key, he crossed the basement to the washer and looked inside. Why was she cleaning the comforter from her bed? He inspected the shelf above. The stain remover was out of position by a couple of inches, and he lifted a hand to straighten it. She must have spilled something on the coverlet and was trying to repair the damage. Breaking his rule about going into the basement had been wrong, but attempting to rectify a mistake was a noble undertaking. He approved.

The lock for the freezer lay several feet away, and he scooped it up and secured it. He must not have latched it properly the night he'd dealt with Star. He'd been in a hurry. That was his fault.

But the discovery was Darcy's. She was too nosy, and she didn't follow instructions. Both were areas she'd have to work on—and there was plenty of time for that.

All the time in the world.

Mark headed back to the stairs. He needed to return to the center. But first he had to take care of whatever damage Darcy had done to his face. Perhaps it was providential he'd been cut by the ice this morning. A larger bandage shouldn't draw all that much attention—except from Faith.

She noticed everything.

As he started up the steps, a faint hammering penetrated the soundproof door of Darcy's new home. And if he listened very closely, he could hear her muted, sobbing plea for release. Neither, however, would be audible from the main house. He'd constructed the room well.

Blocking out the muffled noise, he continued his ascent.

And made a slight change in plans for the evening.

"Do you mind if I cut out early? I have to run an errand."

Dev swiveled away from his computer screen toward Nikki, then cast a pointed look at the growing mound of files in the corner of his office. "Sure. It's not like there's any work to do around here."

She aimed her index finger at him. "Keep that up, and you'll be picking up your own birthday cake."

Birthday cake?

He leaned toward the calendar. February 12. Yeah, tomorrow was the big day. "I forgot all about that."

"We assumed you would. So you want the cake or not? It's a tiramisu from MacArthur's."

His favorite. "I guess. If it's already ordered."

"You're welcome."

"Thanks."

"The thanks is supposed to come first, but I'll take it. Besides, company's paying. I'm just the gofer. Cal says we can't dig into it tomorrow until he gets here, though. Translation—keep your hands to yourself if you happen to get here early . . . like that's going to happen." She started to exit.

"Hey . . . since you're going to the bakery, would you pick me up a caramel pecan coffee cake too?" It was his birthday—he could splurge, couldn't he? It wasn't like anything else special was going to happen, other than calls from his parents and brother in Minnesota.

"Those are loaded with fat and calories." Nikki folded her arms. "Your arteries are gonna fill up with plaque if you eat that kind of stuff."

He dug for his wallet. "I don't care. I like it."

As he pulled out some bills, she waved him off. "Already ordered. My treat, even if I don't approve. See you tomorrow."

Before he could respond, she ducked out and disappeared down the hall.

Bills in hand, Dev settled back in his chair. Nikki was a piece of work, with her sassy mouth and tough-as-nails veneer, but she sure livened things up around the Phoenix offices. Trading barbs with her was one of the highlights of his day.

But he could think of other highlights that would be nice too—like sharing a birthday dinner with a certain librarian.

Unfortunately, that wasn't going to happen. She was an active client. Too bad he didn't have a professional excuse to see her.

Or did he? Not on his birthday, but tonight.

So far, their mystery man Mark hadn't called him. And according to the director of the shelter, neither Mark was scheduled to work again this week. But the man had told him he was still welcome to hang around there, and he had a plan in mind to ferret out the volunteer's name.

Might Laura want to come along? Her presence could be helpful. A guy with a lovely but worried woman on his arm was apt to gain more sympathy and cooperation. Hadn't he used that excuse when he'd taken her along the last two nights to the shelter?

Trouble was, that's exactly what it was—an excuse. He was used to working alone, knew how to push the right buttons to persuade people to cooperate. He didn't need Laura to get the information he was after.

He needed her for entirely different reasons—and pursuing those reasons at this stage wasn't smart.

But even as that caution flag waved in his mind, he was reaching for the phone.

Darcy couldn't stop shaking.

Sitting on the beige carpet in the locked room, back propped against the twin bed that hugged one wall, she shivered, wrapped the throw tighter around her, and did another 180-degree sweep of the 15-by-20 space.

Nightstand with lamp. Dresser. Door leading to a tiny bath that contained a shower and toilet. A small refrigerator stocked with water and juice, a microwave resting on top. A doorless closet containing old-lady clothes on plastic hangers. Treadmill. Round café table with two chairs. Easy chair with an adjacent reading lamp. The twin bed behind her.

It was a room designed for long-term living by a single occupant.

And the "Welcome Darcy" sign on the wall told her she was that occupant.

But she had a feeling she wasn't the first to inhabit this space—nor the coldest.

An image of the second locked freezer on the other side of the washer and dryer flashed across her mind, and another chill convulsed her.

How many girls had Mark killed?

Was she next on his list?

A sob choked off her air.

God, please help me!

Darcy couldn't remember the last time she'd prayed. Not since Mom died, for sure. But who else could extricate her from the mess she'd created for herself? Laura had probably searched for her the first couple of days, but she might have given up by now, relying on prayer herself, asking God to give her stupid half sister some brains so she'd come home.

Well, she'd gotten the brains.

Too late.

The sound of a key turning in the lock sent her pulse skyrocketing, and she jumped to her feet, throwing off the blanket. Too bad she hadn't found some item in the room that would work as a weapon. But the furniture and lamps were bolted in place, the drawers were rigged to keep them from being pulled out all the way, and she didn't have the tools to disassemble the treadmill and use any of the metal tubing that formed the grip bar.

Not that a makeshift weapon would help her all that much. As she'd discovered earlier when Mark had grabbed her arm, his home gym had paid dividends. He had a grip like steel.

He pushed the door open, stepped inside the room, and closed it behind him. A metallic glint drew her attention to his hand, and she sucked in a breath.

Was that a knife?

Frowning, he looked down. After a moment the

201

creases on his brow eased, and he opened his hand so the object rested in his palm.

Scissors?

Stymied, Darcy watched warily as he set a small bag on the table.

"Time for a haircut."

She stared at him as he pulled some plastic sheeting out of the bag, spread it around the base of the chair, and motioned for her to sit.

"I don't want my hair cut." She clenched her hands at her sides and backed away.

The deep creases reappeared on his brow. "Don't make this hard, Darcy. I'm doing this for your own good. You'll thank me for it later."

Not a chance.

The steel blade glinted as he motioned her toward the chair again, and she cringed. Scissors were sharp. They could stab. She didn't want them anywhere near her neck.

She edged farther away, stalling. "Why are you doing this?"

"Long hair leads to temptation."

What was that supposed to mean?

He pointed to the chair. "Come on—let's get this over with and I'll fix you some dinner."

"I'm not hungry."

"Eating is optional. The haircut isn't. Are you going to sit willingly or not?"

The hammering of her heart intensified. What was the best way to play this? Making him angry

202

wouldn't be wise, not with a sharp object in his hand, but neither did she relish watching her long hair end up on the floor . . . nor having the blades of the scissors whispering around her neck in the hands of a man who was clearly certifiable.

Mark set the scissors on the table. "I think we have a little issue with understanding who's in control here."

Before she fathomed his intent, he lunged toward her, lifted his hand, and slapped her hard enough to bring tears to her eyes and leave her gasping.

While she was still reeling from the unexpected blow, he grabbed her arm, dragged her over to the table, and shoved her into the seat. The next thing she knew, he'd pulled her arms behind the back of the chair and slapped handcuffs on her wrists. That task finished, he bent down and got right in her face.

"I don't want to hurt you, Darcy—but I will if you don't cooperate . . . because everything I'm doing is for your benefit. Are we clear on that?"

Hard as she tried, she couldn't get a word past her tight throat. A brief dip of her head was all she could manage.

"That's better."

He stood, picked up the scissors, and began to cut her hair.

As long lengths fluttered down around her, she closed her eyes and tried to keep breathing. *It's okay. Losing your hair isn't the end of the world; what matters is staying alive. Hair will grow back. You just have to do everything you can to survive long enough for someone to find you—and someone will.*

She clung to that belief as the snip-snip of the scissors broke the silence in her prison.

Mark finished in less than three minutes. After stepping back to view his handiwork, he drew her to her feet and led her to the easy chair, the handcuffs still in place.

"Sit while I clean up."

She sat.

He gathered up the plastic, folding it in on itself, until no trace of her long, shorn locks was visible. Then he stuffed the remnants of their haircutting session in a garbage bag and pulled the drawstring top taut.

"There's a vacuum in your closest. Use it after I leave. I expect you to keep the room as clean as when you arrived." He pulled a small box out of the plastic bag he'd deposited on the table earlier and held it up for her to see.

Hair dye.

"I'm going to leave this. Apply it. I'll be back in an hour. If you've followed my instructions, I'll give you dinner. If you haven't, I'll do it for you. Am I clear?"

She nodded.

For a moment he studied her, as if assessing her

sincerity. At last he crossed to her, pulled her shoulder forward, and unlocked the handcuffs. He let them dangle in front of her face from red, chapped fingers as he straightened up. "I hope I won't have to use these again."

He let a few beats of silence pass, then retrieved the trash bag, unlocked the door, and paused on the threshold. "Change out of those clothes too. There are plenty of outfits to pick from in the closet. Put your things in one of the plastic bags in the dresser." With that he exited, clicking the door shut behind him without a backward glance.

For several minutes Darcy was too numb to move. This whole thing was surreal—an alternate universe, like the ones in some of the fantasy books she read.

But the tingling on her cheek was all too real.

Slowly she rose and lurched toward the bathroom, which boasted the only mirror in the room. She flipped on the light—and cringed. All of her long blonde tresses were gone. Her hair was now an uneven chin length.

And the angry red imprint of Mark's hand remained on her cheek.

She touched it gingerly. Heat radiated from the puffy, crimson skin.

But it was better than the cold of a deep freeze.

How many girls were on the other side of the basement? How long had he kept them locked up before they'd displeased him and he'd disposed of them?

Star hadn't lasted one night.

Intuitively, though, Darcy knew that wasn't the norm. She had a sickening feeling the teen who'd served as her guide in the runaway world was what the military called collateral damage—she'd been in the wrong place at the wrong time, and she'd befriended the wrong person.

Once again, someone had suffered because of her.

Darcy squeezed her eyes shut and choked back a sob.

God, I'm so sorry! Please . . . I know I haven't talked to you a whole lot lately, but I need you now. Help me to survive—and to deal with the guilt. I promise I'll be better if you give me another chance!

Fingers gripping the edges of the porcelain sink, she gave in to a torrent of long, choking sobs that left her spent and empty.

But when they subsided, there was a new clarity to her thinking.

Survival was her priority.

Whatever it took.

Drawing in a deep breath, she exited the bathroom, crossed the room, and picked up the package of hair dye.

12

"Is it warm enough for you?"

At Dev's question, Laura transferred her gaze from the passing, moonlight-bathed winter landscape to the driver beside her. "Yes, thanks. Sorry I've been so quiet."

"The roads are clear tonight. I wouldn't have asked you to come with me, otherwise."

She twisted her hands together in her lap, letting his mellow voice soothe her. And she needed a lot of soothing on this frigid night, after beating herself up all day about Darcy's disappearance. Being at work hadn't been as distracting as she'd hoped.

"It's not the roads."

"I didn't think so." He eased out of the one clear lane on the highway, toward the downtown exit ramp. "You've taken all the appropriate steps to find Darcy, you know."

So he'd tapped into her worry and guilt. Why was she not surprised? The man had razor-sharp insights.

The ghost of a smile whispered at her lips. "You must have been a stellar undercover agent. You read people well."

Silence greeted that comment. It was too dark

to make out his features, but his profile was serious and his jaw looked hard.

Just when she decided he wasn't going to respond, he spoke. "I did some things right."

But not all.

She heard that caveat in the subtle nuance of regret in his tone—a tone that also told her this was an off-limits subject. Fair enough. Theirs was a professional relationship . . . even if she was beginning to wish it was more than that. And maybe, if she continued to open up to him, he'd get that message. Besides, she could use a sounding board, and Dev seemed willing to fill that role.

"Can I be honest? In addition to being worried sick about Darcy, I'm also dealing with a boatload of guilt. Wondering if I was too hard on her, if I made the conditions so intolerable she felt her only recourse was to run away."

"You don't strike me as the drill sergeant type."

"I don't think Darcy would agree."

He paused at the bottom of the exit ramp to let a city bus rumble by. "Teens need rules, Laura. If her father was in poor health for a while before he died, she probably had the run of the place, as you suspect. Reining in a kid like that isn't a job for the fainthearted. My guess is you did the best you could with the hand you were dealt."

His succinct assessment of the situation she'd inherited and his matter-of-fact compliment left a warm glow in her heart—even if she wasn't certain the praise was deserved.

"Thanks. But looking back, I could have cut her some slack on a few things. Like, what difference did it make in the big scheme of things whether she put her soda cans in the recycling bin? And so what if she forgot to hang up her coat now and then? I could have compromised on the length of her skirts or the amount of makeup she wore too, instead of taking an all-or-nothing stand."

The knot that had been in her stomach for the past five days tightened another notch, and she found herself fighting back a rush of tears. "If anything happens to her, I'll always feel . . ." Much to her horror, her voice broke. What in the world? She never revealed emotions in public. Thank goodness it was dark in the car and he couldn't see her flaming cheeks. "Sorry."

"Hey." He reached over and touched her jeans-clad leg, keeping a firm grip on the wheel with the other hand. "No apologies, okay? I suspect you're being much too hard on yourself. But if you think you made some mistakes, you can correct them going forward."

"Assuming I get another chance."

"I'm going to do everything I can to make sure you do." With a quick right/left twist of the wheel, he pulled into a parking spot on the street in front of the homeless shelter and shut off the engine. "You ready for round three?"

"I guess so. Same routine as before?"

"For the most part. We'll do a walk-through, show the pictures. Then I'll get a last name for Mark and follow up with him later tonight." He pulled the key out of the ignition.

"You have a plan for how to ferret out that information?"

He grinned. "PIs always have a plan. But it would have been easier if he'd just called me."

"I wonder why he didn't?"

"He might not be our man. Remember, the volunteer we talked with wasn't certain of the guy's name. Or it could be he has nothing to tell me. But it's amazing how often people who think they have no information remember some vital tidbit when asked the right questions. Sit tight. I'll get your door."

With the weather warming slightly, the sidewalk wasn't as icy as they made their way to the door. Nevertheless, Dev took her arm—and she didn't complain.

The shelter wasn't as full, either. Their walk-through took far less time than on past visits, and no one recognized the photos of Darcy. Laura wasn't surprised. Her sister hadn't been here in three nights, and the transient crowd was always in flux.

"On to the next step." Dev took her arm, guided her toward the food table, and lowered his voice. "The woman putting out cookies was here on

Monday night when we visited—but not on Sunday. She's a longtime volunteer. Her name's Nancy."

Laura studied her. No bells of recognition went off. So much for her observation skills. "How do you know all that?"

"I chatted with her for a few minutes while you visited the ladies' room on Monday. Let's hope she remembers me."

Was he kidding? A woman didn't forget a man who looked like James Devlin.

He stopped beside the table and gave the woman a warm smile. "Hi, Nancy. Not quite as busy tonight."

She stopped removing the plastic wrap from a tray of cookies and smiled back. "It always slows down after the weather breaks. Are you any closer to finding the girl?"

"Not much, and I doubt we'll be back. Too much time has elapsed now. But I was hoping to see Mark here tonight." He let his glance skim over the room. "I guess he's not on duty?"

"Neither Mark is here this evening. Which one did you need?"

Dev gave her a rueful look. "I didn't get his last name. He was here on Sunday, though. I had something I wanted to ask him."

"Hmm. That was probably Mark Hamilton. He works weekends. Mark Jacobs volunteers on Fridays." The woman shrugged in apology.

"I'm afraid I don't know his phone number."

"That's okay." He gestured to the tray of cookies. "Your handiwork?"

"The peanut butter ones on your right are. Would you like one?"

"Are you certain you have enough?"

"Plenty. There are trays full in the kitchen."

As he took one, the woman suddenly seemed to remember Laura was standing there. "You're welcome to a cookie too."

"Thanks." She followed Dev's example and picked up one of the peanut butter rounds.

"So do the volunteers here come from all parts of the city?" Dev munched on the cookie, his tone conversational, as if he was just shooting the breeze.

But Laura knew there was a point to every question.

"In normal weather, yes, but during blizzards the director tries to tap into people who live closer. I have a loft on Washington."

"Nice area. And this is delicious." Dev raised the cookie in salute. "I guess Mark Hamilton must live nearby too, then."

"Yes. Over in Soulard. He's not a big talker, but I've gathered he renovated one of those rundown row houses. It's nice to see so many of the older areas in the city being rehabbed."

Masterful. Dev had gotten exactly what he needed without ever deviating from the truth.

Laura wondered if Nancy knew she'd been manipulated . . . or if she'd even care.

"I agree. The revitalization is encouraging." Dev finished the cookie and brushed off his hands. "Well, we're off. Thanks for everything—especially the cookies."

The woman beamed at him. Nope, she wouldn't care. "My pleasure. Good luck with your search."

Laura let Dev guide her out into the cold night air before she spoke. "That was very smooth. I was expecting a pretext."

He opened her door and helped her in. "I only resort to that if the truth doesn't work."

She waited while he circled the car and climbed behind the wheel. "So Mark Hamilton's likely our guy—and he lives nearby."

"Yes. I'm not sure how many Mark Hamiltons I'll find in St. Louis, but knowing he lives in Soulard should narrow down the search."

"I take it we're through with the shelter?"

"Yeah. With the storm letting up and the buses running again, I think there's very little chance we'll find Darcy there."

"Do you think she's still in town?"

His brief hesitation didn't give her a warm and fuzzy feeling.

"My hunch is yes. Rachel hasn't called from Chicago to tell me Darcy's been in touch and is on her way, and we know she didn't leave yet by bus. Hitching a ride in this weather would be tough, unless her guitar-toting friend talked her into it. But that girl bought a ticket too, so I'm thinking she might not have been keen on joining up with a stranger for cross-country travel, either."

His words were reassuring, but the hint of caution in his inflection suggested he was worried —and set off a flurry of butterflies in her stomach. "This isn't looking too encouraging, is it?"

He turned to her, but the darkness hid his expression. "Let's just say the next twenty-four hours will be critical. If she's leaving by bus, there's no reason she should delay much longer, and we'll catch her at the station. In the meantime, I'll also track down this Mark and see if he can shed any light on her whereabouts."

"What if neither of those pan out?"

Once again, he paused. "I have a few other tricks up my sleeve, but let's cross that bridge when we come to it. If we don't have any new information by tomorrow, we'll regroup."

"You wouldn't want to tell me what those other tricks are, would you?"

"Depends on what the situation is in twenty-four hours."

That was too vague for her liking—and it played into her biggest worry. She balled her hands into fists and asked the question that had been troubling her all day. "But what if we haven't found her by then and all the leads have dried up?"

"We'll search as long as you keep us on the case. We won't abandon ship." His steady, confident voice worked its usual magic, and her fingers relaxed a fraction as he continued. "No one disappears off the face of the earth. She's out there somewhere."

But where?

Laura hunched in her seat and stared at the bare branches of the trees whizzing by. Any other time, she'd appreciate the stark beauty of the moonlight-silvered, ice-encrusted limbs. But tonight she saw only bleak, barren landscape.

Was Darcy cold? Hungry? Scared?

Was she in any kind of danger?

A shiver rippled through her, and Dev leaned forward to turn up the heat. The man didn't miss a thing. If there were clues to be found about Darcy's whereabouts, he'd uncover them.

But despite the faith she had in the man beside her, she put even more faith in a higher power. And on this icy winter night, she turned to him with a silent, heartfelt plea.

Lord, please keep Darcy safe.

Juggling a dinner tray, Mark pressed his face close to the peephole. A slow smile curved his mouth.

Darcy was a fast learner.

She'd exchanged the scandalous, low-rise, fitted jeans and revealing cropped top for a pair of loose-fitting sweatpants and an oversized, shape-less sweatshirt. She'd also used the hair dye, transforming the alluring blonde into mousy brown.

In her present state, no man would take a second look at her. All temptation had been removed—thanks to his intervention.

If only Lil had let him do the same for her.

But no. She'd chosen the path of destruction. He'd warned her, begged her, pleaded with her to change her ways, yet she'd paid no heed.

Mark shifted the tray in his hands and closed his eyes as a wistful pang rippled through him. It could have been so different. Lil had loved him in her own way. There had been days when she'd been kind and happy and deeply affectionate. He'd lived for her smiles, done everything he could to win them. And for a while, all would be well—until she fell back to the vices that had ruined her life and made her hateful and angry and abusive.

In the end, he hadn't been able to save her.

But he could save Darcy. Pull her back from the brink and help her lead a productive life free of vice. That would make up for his failure with Lil—and the others who had followed . . . all his lost chances at redemption.

Now he had another opportunity.

And Darcy was showing great promise.

He extracted the key from his pocket, fitted it

in the lock, and pushed through the door. "You look very nice."

Darcy watched him from the table in wary silence as he relocked the door.

"Are you hungry?"

She regarded the tray as he set it in front of her. He'd gone to extra effort for her first dinner in her new home, and he hoped she liked it—Caesar salad, broiled pork chop, roasted sweet potato, steamed broccoli. As a final touch, he'd even baked some low-fat brownies.

When she didn't respond, he gestured to the small refrigerator. "Would you like a beverage with your meal?"

She moistened her lips, her eyes uncertain. As if she was afraid there would be consequences for her answer and she didn't want to make a mistake.

"You seem tense." He laid a hand on her shoulder.

She flinched and pulled herself into a protective tuck, as if she expected him to strike her again.

That wasn't in his plans—as long as she behaved. But perhaps it would be better to keep his distance until she acclimated to her new life and understood the rules. After all these years of waiting, there was no reason to rush the process.

He gentled his voice and removed his hand. "I'll get you some water."

Keeping an eye on her, he moved to the small

refrigerator, reached down to retrieve a bottle, and took a quick inventory. Two waters were missing. Good. She was staying hydrated. Better yet, she hadn't succumbed to temptation. The cans of beer, the bottle of wine, and the joint in the ziplock bag were all untouched.

Then again, it was only the first day.

He grabbed a bottle of water and stood. Angela hadn't caved for a week. Denise, on the other hand, had sucked down all the beers in the first hour, then turned to the pot. And neither girl had improved her behavior, despite his repeated efforts to help them see the light. Both had been bitter disappointments.

Darcy would do better, he was certain of it.

Rejoining her at the table, he twisted off the cap, set the bottle beside the plate, and took the chair across from her. "Go ahead and eat. You must be hungry."

She picked up the plastic knife and fork. They were sturdy, but less dangerous than metal utensils. He'd modified his silverware when Denise went ballistic after downing all those beers.

"If you have any favorite foods, you'll have to let me know. Do you like pork chops?"

"Yes." Her response was barely audible, and her hands were shaking, making it difficult for her to cut the meat.

"Here, let me." He reached toward her to take the utensils.

As his hand brushed hers, she gasped. Dropping her knife and fork, she shot out of her seat and backed away.

He frowned at her. That response wasn't appropriate. He wanted respect and love, not fear—but you couldn't force people to feel those things. He'd just have to be patient with her, and extra kind, until she accepted the truth that he had only her best interest at heart and came to appreciate all he was doing for her.

Slowly he stood. "I'll tell you what. Why don't I leave you alone to enjoy your dinner and come back in half an hour to pick up the tray? Would you prefer that?"

"Yes." Again her reply was whispered, her eyes uncertain.

He forced his mouth into a smile. "Done. I'll bring you an ice pack for that bruise on your cheek too, and some of my special hot chocolate. It will help you sleep. Are those your clothes?" He gestured to a plastic bag with a drawstring top on the bed.

She nodded.

"Why don't you toss them to me? I'll stay over here."

Casting him another guarded look, she complied. Bag in hand, he crossed to the door, let himself out, and locked the dead bolt.

As he watched through the fish-eye lens, Darcy glanced toward him. So she'd spotted the peephole, knew he might be watching her. But with the door between them, perhaps she'd calm down and eat.

Sure enough, she returned to the table, took her seat, and picked up the utensils again. She sampled the potato, moved on to the pork chop, poked at the salad.

Leaving had a been a wise choice—for now.

Mark turned away from the door and started toward the steps. He'd wait half an hour. Then he'd return with the ice pack and hot chocolate. Given her obvious anxiety, tonight he'd add a splash of vodka to the double dose of cherry-flavored Benadryl.

Darcy could use the sleep.

Thirty minutes later, on the dot, Darcy once again heard the key in the lock of her prison.

Mark was back.

The small amount of food she'd managed to ingest suddenly threatened to erupt from her stomach, and she pressed a hand to her abdomen, willing her dinner to stay put. If she was going to have any chance of escaping, she needed to fortify both her physical and mental strength—and that wouldn't happen if she was running on empty.

The door swung open and Mark entered, a small ice pack under one arm and a cup of hot chocolate topped with whipped cream in the other.

She remained sitting cross-legged on the bed as

he approached the table and surveyed her half-eaten dinner. If there'd been anywhere to dispose of the rest, she'd have done so. The first night the three of them had shared dinner, Mark had been clear that he detested wasting food. But she'd choked down as much as she could of the meal he'd prepared, and there was only one trash can in the room. Somehow she sensed it was better to leave the unfinished portion on her plate than make a futile attempt to hide the remains.

Mark set the hot chocolate and ice pack on the table. "I'll be down with your breakfast and lunch tomorrow before I leave for work. Would you like a turkey sandwich or soup for lunch?"

"A sandwich."

"Okay. Sleep well."

With that, he picked up the tray and exited.

Darcy remained where she was. He was probably on the other side of the door, eye glued to the peephole, watching her as if she was an animal in a cage. Was he going to watch her sleep too? How creepy was that?

And what was with the liquor and joint in the refrigerator? Was it a test of some kind? If she gave into temptation, would she end up in the freezer too? What kind of sick game was he playing? And how could she win if she didn't know all the rules?

Once more, her stomach threatened to erupt. Once more she swallowed past the nausea. She wasn't going to get sick again. She'd lost her meager breakfast hours ago, and she couldn't keep doing that. The important thing was to stay strong and lucid and observant. If she did that, maybe she'd have a fighting chance of out-smarting him.

Remote as that possibility was, she clung to that hope. It was the only thing keeping her sane.

She eyed the hot chocolate with its deflating head of whipped cream. Mark had said it would help her sleep, and she didn't doubt that. There had to be something in it that would knock her out. That would explain why she'd been groggy for the past two mornings—and she wasn't going down that road again.

But she didn't intend to let Mark know she was on to him. For all she knew, he was standing there now, waiting to watch her drink the hot chocolate. If she let it sit, he'd get suspicious.

There was a way around that, however.

Rising, she smoothed her damp palms down the fleecy sweatpants, crossed to the table, and fingered the ice pack. How bizarre that the very person who'd inflicted the damage on her throbbing cheek would supply a treatment to make it feel better. And why had he been nice to her on his last couple of visits?

There was no logic to his behavior.

But maybe murderers didn't have to be logical. Maybe tomorrow he'd be an ogre again.

Her stomach knotted, and she drew in a lungful of air. *Don't panic. Take this one day at a time. Learn from each encounter with him. Find a way to outsmart him.*

Deluding him about the hot chocolate was an obvious first step.

Darcy picked up the cocoa in one hand and the ice pack in the other, then retreated to the bed. Setting both items on the nightstand, she drew down the comforter, propped the pillows against the wall, and settled back. With one hand, she picked up the ice pack and pressed it to her tender cheek. With the other, she lifted the mug of cocoa and pretended to take a sip.

She played that charade for a minute before leaning over to flip off the lamp on the bedside table.

The room didn't go black.

She gazed up at the ceiling in dismay, where a low-wattage can light near the door continued to shine, casting faint illumination in the room. It must be controlled from outside. Meaning even at night she couldn't hide from that invasive peep-hole.

Now what?

She reassessed. The light was very dim. There was little chance Mark could tell how much liquid was left in the mug. That could work to her advantage.

She continued to play at sipping.

After five minutes, she rose and headed for the bathroom, mug in hand. As far as she could tell, there was no surveillance of any kind in there, but just to be safe, she left the door cracked rather than turn on the light.

Once inside, she dumped the doctored cocoa down the sink, leaving the residue clinging to the inside of the mug as evidence it had been consumed. But she thoroughly rinsed the porcelain bowl to erase all traces of the chocolate.

She watched the last hint of cocoa disappear down the drain . . . and with it any hope of sleep this night. At least she wouldn't be in a daze tomorrow, though—and that was important.

Because while Mark's plans for her were a mystery, she did know one thing with absolute certainty.

To survive whatever lay ahead, she had to keep her wits about her.

Dev took a swig of coffee, scanned the data on the screen of his laptop, and jotted down Mark Hamilton's phone number and address.

Information brokers were worth their weight in gold.

He leaned back and tapped his fingers in the one uncluttered spot on the dinette table in his apartment. Interesting that Hamilton didn't have a landline, only a cell. More interesting still that he'd ignored the message from the director of the homeless shelter asking that he call him.

Why would he do that?

There were several possible explanations. He wasn't their man. He'd been too busy. It had slipped his mind. Or, as Dev had suggested to Laura earlier in the evening when he'd driven her home, Hamilton was their guy but he didn't think he had information worth passing on.

The other possibility—that Hamilton knew something he didn't *want* to pass on—was less likely . . . but possible.

In any case, now that he had the man's phone number and address, he'd find out for himself. At the very least, Hamilton might have some information about the girl with the guitar who'd befriended Darcy. If he could find her, she could be a font of information.

He pulled his cell off his belt and tapped in *67 to block caller ID, followed by the man's number.

After three rings, it rolled to voice mail.

Dev hung up.

Hamilton had already ignored one message; no reason to think he'd respond to another one. So the next contact would be in person. Tomorrow he'd swing by the man's house during the day, in case he worked an off shift. If no one answered the bell, he'd try again in the evening.

And if that didn't pan out . . . he'd regroup with his partners and discuss next steps. There were other avenues they could pursue to track down the missing teen, but the longer she was gone and the colder the trail became, the less chance they'd succeed in locating her. And despite his promise to Laura that he'd persist, he had a feeling she knew the odds lengthened with each day that passed.

Dev stood, flexed his shoulders, and walked over to the window that looked out on the snow-covered common ground behind his apartment, ticking through all the steps he'd taken to this point. Had he missed anything? No. He was working this case as hard as he could, exploring every possible angle—including one he hadn't mentioned to Laura.

Fortunately, his call to Detective Butler had yielded positive news: there'd been no teenage Jane Doe homicides in the area since Friday night.

Elsewhere . . . that was another story.

As a cloud drifted over the moon, deadening the luminescent glow on the snow, he propped a shoulder against the windowsill. It was possible Darcy had slipped from their grasp and managed to leave town. Yet he hadn't lied to Laura; his gut told him she'd holed up in the city to wait out the storm. But the storm was over—and the unused bus ticket bothered him.

Had she changed her plans?

Or had something—or someone—changed them for her?

Dev hoped it was the former. Because if it was the latter, she'd tangled with the wrong people—and Laura would have a lot more to worry about than whether her half sister was cold or hungry.

13

At six-ten on Thursday morning, Darcy heard the key in the lock. She'd dozed on and off through the night, but she'd been wide-awake since five-thirty, waiting for Mark to show up before he went to work. After positioning herself on her side, her back to the door, she'd been surreptitiously checking her watch every couple of minutes.

As the door opened, she didn't move a muscle. He expected her to be out cold, and she intended to act accordingly. She didn't want to talk to him—nor did she want him to realize she was on to his hot chocolate ploy.

The sound of a tray sliding over the surface of the table broke the stillness. The refrigerator door opened. Closed. The lid of the trash can was lifted off. Replaced.

Then she felt him move beside the bed.

Her lungs stalled, but she forced herself to keep breathing. In. Out. In. Out. Steady and slow, replicating sleep as best she could despite her racing heart.

Please . . . just leave!

After what felt like an eternity, she sensed he'd walked away. The door to the room opened. Shut. The lock clicked.

She was safe.

For now.

Darcy remained unmoving as the hour hand on her watch inched toward seven—opening time at the daycare. Only then did she roll onto her back and sit up.

Rotating the kinks out of her neck, she leaned over and turned on the bedside light.

As promised, Mark had left her food. The covered plate on the tray must hold breakfast, and he'd probably put the sandwich in the refrigerator.

She rose, padded over to the table—and discovered he'd left her a note as well.

Gingerly she picked up the eight-and-a-half-by-eleven sheet of paper and unfolded it. The typewritten words were hard to make out in the dim light, so she returned to the bed and sat on the side as she began to read.

Good morning, Darcy. I hope you slept well. Enjoy your breakfast and lunch. I'll bring you dinner about six. In the meantime, I want you to become familiar with the house rules:

1. Keep your room clean and tidy at all times. Clutter and dirt will not be tolerated.

2. Wash your hands often.
3. Walk two miles on the treadmill every day.
4. Finish all your meals.
5. Do not attempt to block the peephole.
6. Answer when spoken to.

Darcy scanned the rest of the items, a dozen in all, including instructions on how to bundle her laundry and package her trash. But it was the last line that tightened the knot in her stomach.

Never forget: There are consequences for breaking rules.

And she'd complained about *Laura* being too strict.

Slowly Darcy stood and returned to the table, note in hand. She lifted the lid on the covered plate. Scrambled eggs, whole wheat toast, sliced melon.

She didn't want any of it.

Her glance swung back to the note, to rule number four . . . and to the bottom of the page.

She didn't want the consequences, either. She'd already had a sample of those. Her cheek had been so tender all night she hadn't been able to sleep on that side.

Besides, if playing by Mark's rules would buy her time—and an opportunity to plan an escape —she'd follow them to the letter.

Setting the note beside the plate, she sat and began to eat.

"Happy birthday, dear Dev, happy birthday to you."

As the off-key chorus from Cal, Connor, and Nikki died away, Dev gave a mock bow from the doorway of the Phoenix kitchen. "Thank you for that early morning serenade. I think."

"It's about time you got here." Nikki picked up the cake knife. "We've been standing around for five minutes. I thought you were at the McDonald's drive-through when I called you."

"I was." He lifted a white bag with the familiar logo. "Long line."

"Cal's chomping at the bit for a piece of that tiramisu cake." Nikki turned to rummage through the utensil drawer, withdrawing four forks.

"Didn't Moira get up to make breakfast for you?" Dev grinned at his more-tanned-than-usual partner.

"Pulitzer Prize–finalist reporters have more important things to do than cook breakfast—especially when they have a new husband." Cal returned the grin and waggled his eyebrows.

"I take it married life is agreeing with you?" Dev strolled across the room to take a gander at his birthday treat.

Nikki waved the cake knife at him and Connor.

"If either of you would ever get serious about a woman, you might find out for yourself."

"It's two against two, now, you know. Even odds." Connor sent Dev a pointed look as he joined him beside the cake and took a swipe at the icing before Nikki swatted his hand away. "Pre-Moira, only our lovely office manager was on our case about finding a good woman."

"Don't worry. I'm not going to push that agenda. If you guys want to stay single, it's your loss. Nikki and I will just feel sorry for you." Cal winked at the office manager.

"Him, I'll feel sorry for." She pointed the cake knife at Connor, then swiveled Dev's way. "Him . . . not so much."

He made a face at her. "Can't you be nice even on my birthday?"

"Are you going to nag me about those files today?"

"No." He backed away from the knife that was aimed at his heart. "I might have a more interesting project for you to work on soon, anyway."

"Yeah?" She lowered the knife and struck a match. "Then I'll be nice." After lighting the two numeric candles that displayed his age, she backed off and motioned him closer. "Make a wish."

An image of Laura appeared in his mind. Now there was a good woman. Interesting too. There couldn't be many saber-wielding librarians around. And he wasn't getting any younger, as the numbers on his cake reminded him.

"So are you going to blow the candles out or stand around until they melt?"

At Nikki's prompt, he made the wish in his heart. A wish for a future no longer tainted by the past. A future that held joy, not regret. A future that offered love instead of loneliness.

Leaning down, he blew out the candles.

"Finally." Nikki held up the cake knife. "You want to cut?"

"No. Have at it."

She strolled over to the cake. "So what was your wish?"

He managed to tame the annoying blush that had once been the bane of his existence. "If I tell, it won't come true."

"I bet it has something to do with a certain librarian." She smirked at him and leaned forward to cut the cake.

Cal choked on his coffee. "Librarian?" He hacked a couple more times. "What did I miss while I was in Hawaii?"

"Nothing." Dev shot Nikki a dark look.

She ignored him. "His new client is a hot librarian. Right, Connor?"

"I'll have to abstain, since I haven't met the lady in question."

"Chicken." Nikki shoved a plate of cake at him.

"Prudent." Connor took the generous slice, grabbed his coffee mug from the counter, and made a fast exit.

"If you ask me—" The kitchen extension from Nikki's desk began to ring, cutting her off, and she huffed out a sigh. "Talk about rotten timing." She snatched up her own cake and dashed down the hall.

"I guess we're on our own here." Cal cut himself a piece of cake.

"I'm going to eat my breakfast first."

"You're looking at mine." Cal grabbed a fork and used the edge to break off a large bite. "Moira and I had to choose between bed or breakfast. Guess which won?" He smiled and speared the bite of cake. "So what's with the librarian? And is she really hot?"

Dev snagged his mug from the hook on the wall, keeping his back to his partner. "She's a client. It's a business relationship. But yes, she's nice looking." He filled his mug to the brim and turned to face Cal.

His partner was still grinning.

"What?"

"Moira was a client too."

"That's different. I met Laura four days ago. You worked on Moira's case for weeks."

"But I knew she was special from the get-go— as you reminded me ad nauseum at the time." He licked the icing off his fork, and Dev didn't like the sudden gleam in his eyes. "You know, this could be a lot of fun."

"Don't even go there." His warning came out as a growl.

"What? Are you going to fire me?"

"Very funny."

Cal chuckled. "On a more serious note, you want to tell me about the case? Connor just gave me the highlights on the phone."

"Yeah. Your office or mine?"

"Yours. My desk is piled high with two weeks' worth of stuff." He started toward the door but turned back halfway there. "On second thought—when's the last time Nikki filed in your office?"

"A week ago."

"A whole week? We'll use my office." Cal hung a left at the door.

Dev stuck his head out and called after him. "I'll be with you in a minute. I want to cut a piece of cake for myself and stash it for later."

Cal continued to chow down on his own cake and waved an acknowledgment.

After helping himself to a sizeable chunk of the cake and stowing it, plus the remaining cake, in the refrigerator, Dev grabbed the mug and white bag he'd deposited on the table and followed his partner.

He'd fill Cal in on the case . . . but he intended to leave the personal stuff out.

• • •

Faith stopped outside the closed door of Mark's office and bit her lip as she gazed down at the small gift bag in her hands. Was she overstepping? Being too pushy? Maybe. But how else was she going to get him to notice her? She needed to show him how thoughtful and caring she was. If today's gesture went over okay, she'd follow up with part two of her plan tomorrow.

Taking a deep breath, she knocked.

"Come in."

She pushed into the office, closing the door halfway behind her. He was angled away, facing his computer screen, and twin creases were embedded above his nose—the kind that came from worry or stress. The man worked far too hard. She hoped Mr. Davis appreciated Mark's commitment to his business. "Am I disturbing you? This will only take a minute."

He gestured her in. "No. What did you need?"

"I know you're busy. I just wanted to give you this." She crossed to his desk and set the small bag on top.

He tipped his head, his expression confused. "What is it?"

"Open it and see."

"Is this from you?"

"Yes."

"What's the occasion?" He swiveled around and rolled his chair closer to his desk.

"There isn't one. I just ran across this and thought you might find it useful. It's no big deal."

That was a lie. She'd spent two hours on the net searching for a product like this. And at the price per ounce, it was also a big deal for her budget. But Mark didn't need to know that.

He tugged the bag toward him and peeked inside. The grooves on his forehead returned as he pulled out the small bottle of lotion.

"I've watched how conscientious you are with the children, always washing your hands so no germs are passed around. I think that's really admirable—but in this weather, that can take a toll. I thought this might help your chapped hands a little." Her words came out in a gush, and she twisted her fingers together in front of her.

His lips compressed as he stared at the bottle. Was he moved—and trying not to get emotional— or angry that she'd called attention to his red, cracked hands?

It was impossible to tell.

But as the seconds ticked by, she had a feeling it might be the latter . . . and that she'd made a huge mistake.

Now what was she supposed to do?

And then Mark surprised her. He looked up and smiled. "That was a very considerate thing to do, Faith. You're an observant woman. This winter has been tough on my hands, especially the past few days. I'm sure this will help a lot."

She hadn't blown it. Thank goodness.

"I hope so. Well . . ." She backed toward the door, her legs suddenly shaky. "I'll get back to work now."

Once in the hall, she paused and gave her pulse a chance to moderate. That had gone well. Mark seemed to appreciate the gift, and he'd paid her a personal compliment. He thought she was considerate. That was a promising start.

Saturday morning, she'd implement part two. And before she was through, Mark Hamilton would know how interested she was in him.

As she walked back toward her room assignment for the day, her spirits took a decided uptick. Maybe her romantic notions about Mark weren't pie-in-the-sky after all. He'd been receptive a few minutes ago. Perhaps he would be on Saturday too. She had other ideas to get him to notice her as well—and she'd try them all, if necessary.

After that, the ball would be in his court.

And if she was lucky, he'd decide to play.

Dev started to reach for the phone on his desk. Turned back to his computer. Aimed another look at the phone.

"What's with you?" Nikki grunted and stood, a large stack of files in her arms. The pile had dwindled while he'd driven down to Soulard to pay a visit to Mark Hamilton's house, and she was still hard at it. "Do you know how many times you've gone through that routine in the past ten minutes?"

There was nothing wrong with their office manager's observation skills. She had eyes like an eagle.

"What's it to you?"

She cocked her head and ignored his question. "This new indecisive mode is different. Must be related to your librarian."

Yeah, she was way too observant.

"I'm not going to dignify that with an answer." He swung away and focused on his computer screen, hoping she'd let it drop.

Fat chance.

"That means I'm right." She rested a hip on the edge of his desk, apparently in no hurry to leave. "You know, since it's your birthday, I doubt anyone would give you a lot of trouble for fudging the rules a tad and inviting her out for a drink."

"Not on the agenda."

"Then have dinner with us. Danny would love it, and I could tolerate your presence for one night."

He looked at her over his shoulder. "That's the most backhanded invitation I've ever received."

"Take it or leave it." She stood, shifted the files to her other arm, and cleared her throat. "But seriously, you'd be welcome. We have plenty of food, and birthdays should be celebrated with people who care."

He caught the fleeting melancholy that passed over her eyes, reminding him that once upon a time, in the abusive home she'd exchanged for life on the street at fifteen, birthdays had passed unnoticed. And that despite her sassy attitude, she still carried scars from those days. It was a tribute to her perseverance that she'd created a better life not only for herself but for her younger brother.

Mollified, he smiled at her. "I appreciate the thought, but I have to work tonight."

For a few seconds she studied him, as if assessing the truth of that statement. Then she shrugged, her usual impertinent demeanor back in place. "Fine." She moseyed over to the door, where she turned. "But do yourself a favor. Call the lady and end your birthday with a few pleasant moments."

As she disappeared down the hall, Dev leaned back in his chair and eyed the phone. Socializing with clients was verboten—but could he bend the rules a touch? After all, hadn't he been doing that all along, by inviting Laura to go with him to the shelter?

Maybe.

And his work plans for tonight did involve a return visit to Mark Hamilton's, where he hoped to catch the man at home, since no one had answered the door today. He'd handle the questioning alone, but what could it hurt to have Laura ride along? There wasn't much chance he'd spend more than ten minutes with the man, tops. Then the two of them could stop for coffee, if she was willing. Besides, he owed her an update. Rachel hadn't heard from Darcy today, nor had the teen shown at the station. He was about to throw in the towel on Greyhound, and she needed to know that too.

Besides, it was his birthday, as Nikki had pointed out.

Once more he scooted toward the phone, reached for it—and didn't pull back.

Mark opened the back door of his house, stepped inside, and set the locks behind him. After depositing his briefcase on the bare top of the built-in desk, he dropped Faith's offering beside it.

His lip curled in disgust as he regarded the smiley-face pattern on the gift bag. He'd begun to suspect she had a crush on him, and this clinched it. The last thing he needed was another female complication in his life. He had his hands full with Darcy—and Darcy was all that mattered.

On the other hand, he didn't want to hurt Faith's feelings. She was an excellent, reliable, flexible worker who was always willing to fill in wherever needed when they were short-staffed—a frequent occurrence. What had happened to people's work ethic, anyway? These days, they just up and quit with no notice, despite the bad economy. He couldn't afford to lose an employee as conscientious as Faith.

But he sure didn't want her pursuing him, either.

That, however, was a dilemma for another day. He was home now, and he had an agenda for the evening. All day he'd been trying to think of some way to demonstrate to Darcy that he didn't mean her any harm. She needed to understand that he had plans for her, that she had happier days to look forward to.

And he'd come up with an inspired idea as he drove home.

He stopped at the sink, turned on the faucet, and sudsed his hands. After a thorough rinse, he evaluated them under the light.

Faith was right. They were a lot worse than usual. That was due in part to the washing he did at work to keep germs at bay, but more because of the washing he'd been doing at home since Darcy had come into his life. The same thing had happened with Angela and Denise too, but their stays had been short. Darcy, however, would be here for the long term if everything went as he hoped—meaning his hands could become an ongoing issue.

He sudsed up again, casting a glance at the desk. The lotion Faith had given him was high-end stuff. He'd tried plenty of products like that over the years. Once, when he'd gotten a raise, he'd even splurged and bought a bottle of the very product Faith had bought him. But he couldn't afford it on a regular basis—and neither could she.

As long as she'd given it to him, though, why not use it? He didn't want his hands to raise questions, and he'd noticed several of the aides at work today giving them the once-over. This stuff would help minimize the redness and cracking.

After drying his hands, he crossed to the desk, pulled the lotion from the bag, and removed the cap. He put a dab on each palm and rubbed it in, liking the silky feel. Taking his time, he headed for the stairs to the second level.

He'd give the lotion a few minutes to soak in.

And then he'd pay Darcy a visit with his little surprise.

14

"That's it, up ahead on the left. The one with the iron fence in front."

As Dev pointed out Mark Hamilton's row house, Laura leaned forward in the front seat of the Explorer. "There are lights on."

"A positive sign." Dev slowed, as if he intended to pull up to the curb, then suddenly picked up speed and passed the house.

Laura shot him a surprised look. "What's wrong?"

"Maybe nothing. But there's a woman sitting in a blue Ford Focus across the street who seems to be watching Hamilton's house."

Craning her neck, Laura looked through the back window. Even with the moonlight reflecting off the snow, she had no idea how Dev had spotted a person in a dark car.

The man was a total pro.

"Do you think that's important?"

"Not likely. She could be looking for an address, or she might have spotted a stray dog and is waiting for the coast to clear before she heads for her own house. On the other hand, I've learned never to make assumptions in this business. We'll give her a few minutes and drive by again."

Laura settled back in her seat as he turned at the corner. "What if she's there when we come back?"

"We wait her out—unless you need to be some-where. I don't want to monopolize your evening."

"It's only six o'clock—and finding Darcy is my top priority. Besides, other than putting in some practice time on my fencing, I have no plans for the night. But I bet you do." A guy like Dev probably had a black book an inch thick. He might not be over the tragic romance in his past, but she doubted he was averse to female companionship. "These kinds of assignments must play havoc with your social life."

"Sometimes. But I didn't have plans for tonight, either."

His prompt reply was good news—for her, anyway.

He swung around another corner, and she gripped the armrest as they skidded slightly on a slick spot.

"Steady." His hand shot out to rest on her knee. "We're fine."

He might be, but she wasn't. Not with the warmth of his fingers seeping through the denim fabric of her jeans and shooting straight to her heart. Nevertheless, she preferred that to the chill left behind when he retracted his hand.

Dev circled a few more blocks, then once more turned onto Hamilton's street, flipping open the storage compartment between their seats. "There's a notebook and pencil in there. If she's still parked in front of the house, I'll read her license as we drive by. Would you jot it down?"

"Sure." She dug around for the pad of paper and the pencil.

Half a minute later, he recited the letters and numbers as they passed the woman's car. After pulling into an empty spot by the curb a few cars ahead of her, he flipped off his lights but left the engine running and the heater cranked up.

"Was she still watching the house?" Laura twisted in her seat, but the shadows of the night continued to hide the woman from her view.

"Intently." Dev's gaze was fixed on his rear-view mirror, and he adjusted it from inside for a better view.

"That's kind of odd, isn't it?"

"Interesting, at least. I'll check her out later."

"You have access to car license data?"

"Yes." He remained focused on the rearview mirror. "Licensed PIs can get into REJIS—the Regional Justice Information Service. It's the same system patrol officers use for traffic stops. We have legal entrée to almost everything law enforcement does, except the FBI's National Crime Information Center." He shifted in his seat to alter his line of sight. "She's leaving."

A sudden arc of headlights followed his comment, and a few seconds later the Focus rolled by on the snow-packed road. She caught only a quick glimpse of the driver's curly black hair and pixie profile before the young woman turned their direction to look back at Hamilton's house. Laura shrank back in her seat, but Dev touched her arm.

"Don't worry. The dark windows make us invisible."

"Oh." She straightened up. "A tool of the trade?"

"A critical tool." He did a fast sweep of the deserted street. "I won't be long. I'd prefer to shut the engine off so we don't attract attention. Will you get too cold?"

She held up her gloves, then slipped them on. "Thermal. I'll be fine."

"Lock the doors after I get out. This isn't the safest neighborhood. If you have any problem at all, don't hesitate to lay on the horn."

"Got it."

"Okay. Let's see what Hamilton has to say." He exited the vehicle, waiting beside the door until she hit the locks. Once they clicked, he gave her a thumbs-up and walked down the street, turning in at the short iron fence. From her vantage point, she could watch through the side windows as he crossed the front lawn, climbed the three steps to the small stoop, and pressed the bell.

After thirty seconds, he pressed the bell again.

Still no response.

That was odd, since lights on both floors were lit.

After a full minute passed, Dev retraced his steps down the path, left through the iron gate, and slid in beside her once she released the locks.

"It seems Mr. Hamilton isn't in the mood for company." He rested his hands on the wheel, the light from the street lamp casting the twin crevices in his brow into sharp relief.

"Maybe he just leaves a lot of lights on for security when he isn't home."

"He's home. Or someone is. I could hear a muffled sound, like a heavy pot dropping on the floor, after the doorbell rang the first time."

"If his wife is there alone, she might not open the door for strangers. As you pointed out, it's not the best neighborhood."

"That's possible. But he hasn't returned my calls, either. I'll run some background on him tonight when I get home and have Nikki dig deeper tomorrow." He put the car in gear and pulled away from the curb.

While Laura was glad Dev was thorough, odds were the man would be of little use to them. There was probably a valid reason he hadn't returned calls or answered the door—one that had nothing to do with Darcy.

To make matters worse, the other leads were drying up too. As Dev had told her on the drive down, Rachel hadn't heard from Darcy. Neither had Brianna in New York. He'd also recommended they pull surveillance from the Gateway Station after tonight. That meant Hamilton was their last hope—and he didn't appear to be panning out.

Her spirits nose-dived, and the view of the snowy street in front of her blurred as moisture clouded her vision. She groped in her pocket for a tissue but came up empty.

"You okay?"

"Yeah." But the tremor in her response to Dev's quiet question belied her assurance.

"Don't give up."

A tear spilled out of one eye and started to track down her cheek. She dug deeper in her pocket and remained silent, not trusting her traitorous voice.

"There are usually a few napkins from fast-food places in the glove compartment." He took one hand off the wheel and released the catch for her.

So much for hiding her sudden display of emotion.

She leaned forward, reached in—and yanked her hand back with a startled exclamation.

"What's wrong?" His tone sharpened as he pressed on the brake.

"There's something soft and . . . sticky . . . in there." She leaned toward the storage compartment again, keeping her hand a safe distance away from her body. "It looks like . . . a piece of cake?" Hard to tell now, since she'd mashed whatever it was and a napkin covered part of it. But when she lifted her fingers to her nose and took a sniff, she got an unmistakable whiff of sugar—as in icing.

"Oh. I forgot all about that. Sorry. I stuck it in there so it wouldn't roll around on the backseat and get all over the upholstery." Dev fumbled in his pocket and handed her a handkerchief. "It's clean."

She took it and wiped the gooey residue off her fingers. "You keep cake in your glove compartment?"

"Not usually." He hesitated, then shrugged.

"They brought me a cake at work today for my birthday, and I was taking a piece home."

"Today's your birthday?" She stared at his profile in the darkness.

"Yeah."

"And you spent it chasing a lead on my case?"

"I often end up working on my birthday. It's not an issue."

"My mom wouldn't have agreed with you. I can still hear her saying, 'Laura, most days in life are ordinary. When special ones roll around, celebrate and make happy memories to carry you through the dull days.'" She finished wiping off her fingers, wadded the handkerchief into a small ball, and stuffed it in her pocket for later laundering. "That's one of the few things we agreed on. I'll always remember the elaborate cakes and clowns and ponies and face painters she used to round up for my birthdays."

"I think I've outgrown that kind of stuff." She could hear the smile in his voice.

"There are other ways to celebrate—and I feel bad I kept you from enjoying any of them."

After a slight hesitation, he responded. "How bad?"

"What do you mean?"

"Bad enough to join me for dinner so I don't have to eat alone on my birthday?"

He was asking her to dinner?

"Unless you already ate." He tacked on the

caveat as she grappled with the surprising invitation.

"No." There was no hesitation in *her* response.

"Then how about it? I won't keep you out late. I have more work to do later on Hamilton. And it would make my mom happy too. When I talked to her earlier, she wasn't pleased about my birthday plans. She'll be glad to know I didn't end up eating a frozen dinner and a piece of leftover cake."

It would make my mom happy too.

That last little three-letter word perked up her spirits.

"Since I smashed the cake in question, it's the least I can do."

"True." His smile was caught for an instant in the glow of a streetlight before it disappeared in the shadows. "But I get a real birthday dinner in return, so you're actually doing me a favor."

She gave his strong profile a quick inspection as she braced herself while he turned onto the highway entrance ramp. He thought she'd done *him* a favor?

No way.

When it came to sharing dinner, she was definitely the one on the receiving end.

Darcy gripped the back of the upholstered chair in front of her, fingers clenching the velour fabric as the key rattled in the lock. Mark had said he'd be here at six. It was now quarter past, and with every minute that had ticked by after the hour, her tension had mounted.

Would he be in a good mood or a bad mood tonight?

She cast another quick glance around the room. Everything was in its place. She'd eaten all her food. Done her two miles on the treadmill. Followed all the rules.

But maybe that wasn't enough to keep you safe if you were dealing with a crazy person.

He pushed through the door, a long garment bag draped over his arm. "Hello, Darcy. Did you have a nice day?"

"Yes."

"Excellent." He checked the odometer on the treadmill. Gave the room a scan. Noted the laundry she'd bundled up, per his instructions. Looked in the refrigerator. "You've done well—and admirable behavior should be rewarded. I have a surprise for you."

He crossed to the closet and hung the bag on the clothes rod. Smiling at her, he pulled down the zipper and carefully removed the garment inside.

It was a . . . wedding dress?

She stared at the satin and lace confection as he turned toward her and let the fabric of the skirt float down to sweep over the carpet in a graceful arc.

"Do you like it?"

Tightening her grip on the back of the chair, she tried to keep breathing. "It's very pretty."

"It is, isn't it?" He straightened a fold in the skirt. "I've had it a long time, just waiting for the right person to come along. I think she has at last." He fingered the lace at the neckline. "How would you like to wear this?"

A wave of revulsion shuddered through her as panic clawed at her throat. "I'm only s-sixteen."

"Almost seventeen, according to your driver's license. And eighteen is the magic age. A year isn't that long to wait. It will give us time to get to know one another better."

The breath whooshed out of her lungs.

He was going to keep her locked in this base- ment prison for a *year?*

"I wanted you to have something to look forward to. That's why I showed you this. You have great promise. I never let Angela or Denise see it."

Angela and Denise?

Her gaze flicked in the direction of the freezers on the other side of the basement.

There must be two more girls over there.

Girls who'd made a mistake—and paid for it with their life.

Just as she would.

Because the truth was, no matter how hard she tried, the longer she stayed down here, the greater the probability she'd run afoul of his rules and end up like her predecessors.

She had to figure out some way to outmaneuver him and get out of this place ASAP!

"Would you like to touch it?"

His question drew her back to the moment. Yes or no—which was the right answer?

"I don't want to get it dirty." Her words came out in a whisper.

"Admirable. So wash your hands first." He gestured toward the bathroom.

She followed his instructions, lathering up, taking her time with the process, as he always did. When she rejoined him, he indicated the sleeve. "You can touch that."

Keeping as much distance between them as possible, she gingerly fingered the lace at the edge of the cuff.

"Do you like it?"

"Yes." Amazing how easy it was to lie once your survival instincts took over.

"I thought you would. Someday soon I might let you try it on." As he zipped the dress into the bag, she edged back to her defensive position behind the chair. "Now I'll go get your dinner. It's just your leftovers from last night, but if you eat them all, I'll make fresh salmon tomorrow. How does that sound?"

She gritted her teeth, trying not to barf. "Fine."

He opened the door and exited. She waited as long as she dared once it clicked shut, in case he was watching her through the peephole.

Then she raced to the bathroom and lost her lunch.

"Would you like some dessert?" Dev indicated the menu the waiter had deposited as he'd cleared their plates. He hoped Laura would say yes; even though it was past eight and he'd promised to get her home early, this had been the nicest evening he'd spent in a very long while. It would be better yet if he could extend it another half hour.

Laura took a sip of her coffee and gave him a quick smile. "What about the cake in your glove compartment?"

He perused the menu. "The apple tart sounds better—and it won't be squashed."

"True." She studied the offerings. "I've always been a sucker for chocolate mousse."

"Sold." He signaled to the waiter.

She cradled her cup in her hands and looked around the intimate French-country-themed restaurant from the tucked-in-the-corner table he'd requested. "I'm surprised I've never heard of this place."

"It's more a local spot, but it has a big following."

"I can see that—and I'm not surprised. The food is great. Do you come here often?"

"No." Quiet, intimate spots like this were designed for more serious, in-depth, let's-get-to-know-each-other conversations, and he'd had no interest in setting that kind of tone with any of his dates—until now.

But that was a tidbit he did not intend to share.

She added another splash of cream to her coffee. "I'm honored, then. And I'm glad you introduced me to it."

So was he—another fact he intended to keep to himself.

The waiter returned, and once he'd given their dessert orders, Dev settled back in his chair, coffee in hand. Since the moment they'd met, Laura had been taut as a bowstring with worry, and the dark circles under her eyes told him she'd clocked little sleep during the past week.

Tonight, though, the rigid line of her shoulders had eased and her lips had softened a fraction.

He didn't flatter himself the change was due to his company, much as he wished it was. More likely it was the soothing ambiance of the restaurant, the lighthearted conversation he'd initiated, and a decent meal . . . not that she'd eaten all of it.

"You seem deep in thought." She regarded him over the flickering candle that rested in the middle of the linen-covered café table.

He refocused. "I was just thinking how some people eat when they're stressed; my guess is you do the opposite."

"Guilty as charged. Stress may not be healthy for my heart, but it benefits my waistline."

"As if you need to worry." *Too personal, Devlin. Watch it.*

"Thanks, but trust me, I do watch my weight. Those unforgiving fencing outfits give me an excellent incentive to stay in shape."

An image of her in white, form-fitting fencing gear, saber in hand, appeared in his mind—and elevated his pulse.

He quashed it at once . . . or tried to.

"So what about you? Do you eat or fast when you're stressed?" She took a sip of her coffee, watching him over the rim of the cup. The waiter appeared with their desserts, giving him a few seconds to frame a response that was vague but truthful. "Usually stress doesn't affect my appetite one way or the other."

Unfortunately, Laura homed in on the vague part as she spooned up a bite of her mousse. "Implying there are exceptions?"

Oh yeah.

He looked down at his dessert. The warmth from the apple pastry was melting the scoop of vanilla bean ice cream, and he edged it away. But he couldn't move it far enough, and the ice cream continued to thaw.

Kind of like his heart did when he was around Laura.

"I'm sorry." Her voice was soft, her expression apologetic, as she reached over to touch the back of his hand. "I didn't mean to pry. Forgive me?"

In the glow of the candlelight, her blue eyes reminded him of the summer skies of his Minnesota youth—clear and vast, filled with wonder and welcome and possibilities. They called to him, seeming to offer release and freedom, just as those endless heavens once had.

All at once he was transported back to his seventeenth summer, to the day he and a buddy had forked out a chunk of their hard-earned summer-job money to go hang gliding. They'd wanted to soar above the world, leave all its cares behind. And the feeling of exhilaration and freedom had been everything he'd expected. Even though his parents had later gotten wind of his escapade and grounded him for a month, he'd never regretted taking that risk.

Did he have the courage to do the same now?

As he debated that question, distress etched Laura's features, and the tension that had dissipated during dinner crept back into her posture.

Time for damage control.

"There's nothing to forgive." The words came out stiffer than he intended, and she dropped her gaze.

He poked his fork into a piece of tart, swirled it in the melted ice cream, and put it in his mouth. But his taste buds had shut down, just as they had five and a half years ago during the darkest period of his life, when he'd lost twenty pounds in ten weeks.

No longer hungry, he set the fork down and picked up his coffee instead.

Laura set her spoon down too.

Great. Now he'd ruined what up till a minute ago had been an enjoyable evening.

He took a deep breath and slowly let it out. "I think it's my turn to apologize. I didn't mean to cast a pall over the evening. Your question just brought back some unpleasant memories."

"I gathered that." With a fingertip, she traced the trail from a bead of condensation down the side of her water glass. "It goes back to that comment you made the night we had the pizza, doesn't it? About how people often upend their life because of a romance gone bad."

He swallowed past the lump that rose in his throat. "Yeah."

"I should have remembered that and not pressed. But if . . ." She hesitated, biting her lip. "Look, I don't want to sound pushy or invade your turf. But if you ever need a sounding board, I've been told I'm a decent listener—not by Darcy, but by others." She flashed him the barest hint of a smile.

He tried to respond in kind. Couldn't get his lips to cooperate. "You have enough on your plate without listening to my tale of woe."

A beat of silence passed as she appraised him. "I'm not sure if that's a brush-off or if you're just being thoughtful, but if it's the latter, there's still room on my plate. You've listened to my angst over the past few days, and I'd be happy to return the favor. You could think of it as a birthday present, if you like."

His breath jammed in his throat, the same way it had the day he'd stood at the edge of the cliff, preparing to put his trust in the flimsy gliding rig attached to his body while he jumped into an abyss. There had been danger then. A risk to his physical safety.

And there was danger now too—except this leap would put his heart at risk.

That was even scarier.

The waiter stopped beside their table, pitcher of water in hand. "Is there anything else you need?"

Laura laid her napkin on the table beside her barely touched dessert. "You could point me to the ladies' room."

"Straight back, past the kitchen, on your left."

"Thanks." She rose as the waiter moved off, giving him a smile that seemed forced. "I'll be back in a couple of minutes."

He stood too, but she didn't wait for a response.

As she wove through the tables, he slowly sat again. The ladies' room was a ruse. She'd sensed his indecision, picked up on his turbulent emotions, and was giving him space to work things out in his mind. He also knew she'd let him take the lead on the conversation after she returned, giving him the choice to accept her offer or simply change the subject.

The lady was one class act.

As for those empathetic eyes . . . they sucked him in, undermining his resolve to refrain from burdening her with his problems while she was in the midst of her own. How odd was that, when no one else—not his family, not his buddies, not the counselor he'd met with for a while after the incident—had managed to persuade him to spill his guts? Yet Laura had won his trust without even trying.

It had to be due to the potent chemistry thing going on between them. Despite their short acquaintance, he felt linked to her in a way he never had with anyone else—including Cat. He'd lay odds Laura felt it too. And because of it, he had a feeling she could be the catalyst that would help him let go of the past and move on . . . a task that had taken on a much higher priority since she'd entered his life—for reasons he wasn't ready to examine.

He picked up his coffee, frowning at the slight tremor in his fingers. He was always steady under pressure. Always. Nothing made him lose his cool. Ever.

Then again, there weren't many times in a man's life when he was called on to put his heart on the line.

But this night was one of them.

15

You idiot!

Laura stared in disgust at her reflection in the ladies' room mirror. How could she have been so stupid? Dev had referenced a tragic incident just days ago. She should have realized his ambiguous answer to her question about his behavior under stress might be vague for a reason and backed off.

Now she'd ruined his birthday dinner.

Way to go, Laura.

Too bad she couldn't slink out and catch a cab home.

But that would be cowardly. So she'd march back out there, change the subject . . . and hope he didn't hold her faux pas against her.

Straightening her shoulders, she tucked a few rebellious wisps of hair into her French braid and headed back to the table.

Dev smiled and rose as she approached—an encouraging sign.

She forced her own lips up and adopted a bright tone. "You know, I feel like I've gone to France without ever leaving St. Louis. This place seems very authentic. Of course, I wouldn't know for sure, since I've never been overseas. How about you?" Not the smoothest segue, and the words

261

had come out a bit breathless, but it definitely moved the conversation to a safer topic.

Except much to her surprise, Dev didn't take her cue. Instead, his expression sobered as he sat.

"I've made a few trips to Europe. But if you haven't changed your mind, I'd rather take advantage of those listening skills you mentioned than talk about foreign travel."

Her pulse gave a little flutter at the unexpected turn of events. "I haven't changed my mind."

"There's one small caveat, though. You have to finish your dessert. It would be a crime to let that mousse go to waste."

She looked at his place. The plate of apple tart and ice cream had disappeared during her absence. Had he finished it . . . or asked the waiter to take it away?

This time she left her question unasked.

Transferring her attention to her own dessert, she inspected the generous serving. "I can try." It was the best she could promise.

"Fair enough." He waited until she picked up her spoon, then rested his elbows on the table and linked his fingers. "I told you a few days ago that I used to be an undercover ATF agent, but in the beginning I was a regular agent. I only did undercover work during my last two years with the Bureau."

He lifted his coffee, took a sip, and assessed her

progress. She spooned up another bite of her chocolate mousse as he continued.

"During my first six months undercover, I worked a storefront sting operation. That's a decent place to get your feet wet, see if you're comfortable with that type of work. We were targeting gunrunners, illegal gun purchasers, and felons who were carrying guns. Even though we had a few dicey moments, the operation was clean overall and successful. We got sixty-five indictments, removed a lot of guns and drugs from the streets, and all the ATF agents walked away whole."

He paused again, and Laura had a hard time swallowing the bite of mousse she'd just taken. Whatever he was going to tell her next, she had a feeling *clean, successful,* and *walking away whole* weren't going to be part of the story.

His subsequent words confirmed that. "My second assignment didn't have the same kind of ending. Are you still certain you want to hear this? It's not pretty."

In truth, she wasn't. But the fact that Dev was willing to trust her with details he'd never revealed to anyone else awed—and touched—her. And while his story might be disturbing, the sharing of it would also forge a stronger bond between them. One she hoped would long outlive their professional relationship.

Taking a deep breath, she tried to prepare herself

for an emotional avalanche. "Yes, I'd still like to hear it."

He dipped his head in acknowledgment, then looked off toward a shadowy corner of the restaurant. She doubted he was seeing the racks of wine stored there. Rather, his gaze seemed aimed on the past. So much so, he didn't notice when she slipped her spoon back onto the table and set aside the remainder of her mousse.

"Another agent and I were assigned to infiltrate a new gang operating in the Southwest. The job was supposed to last about a year, and our mission was to befriend them, get inside the organization, and see what they were up to. I won't go into the details of how we got inside, but let's just say it involved lots of black hair dye for me and the faked murder of a rival start-up gang member."

He picked up his glass of water. After taking a long sip, he refocused on the shadowy wall. "The group was every bit as bad as we suspected. During the nine months we were inside, we saw it all—drugs, gun trafficking, violence, intimidation, extortion. We lived in seedy trailer parks, watched people zone out on meth, saw enough needles and heroin to last a lifetime. There was zero glamour in the work, despite what you see on TV. But Cat and I believed we could bring the bad guys to justice and that the world would be better because of our sacrifices." His throat worked as he swallowed. "I've never met anyone more passionate about their work than she was."

She?

A wave of shock rippled through Laura as she digested that news. "Your partner was a woman?"

He seemed to pull himself back from some faraway place. "Yes. Catalina. She was Hispanic, and she knew her way around the streets of Phoenix. I speak fluent Spanish and looked the part once I finished with the dye and some temporary tattoos, but she's the main reason we got into the group. I posed as her boyfriend, which allowed both of us to avoid any . . . personal involvement with gang members."

Laura began to get a glimmer of where this was headed. "But you didn't manage to avoid personal involvement with each other."

"No." His Adam's apple bobbed again, and he cleared his throat. "Living in forced proximity, playing the part of lovers in public . . ." He gave a stiff shrug. "Somewhere along the way, the line between acting and real life faded. We fell in love. Cat handled it better than I did. She was able to separate personal feelings from professional duties, but for me, it was a struggle. I started to worry about her too much—and that was our undoing. What happened in the end was totally my fault." His voice choked, and he took another sip of water.

Laura's fingers clenched the napkin in her lap. Was it possible the consummate professional sitting across from her had slipped and made a mistake that put someone at risk?

Maybe.

When you loved someone—spouse, parent, child . . . sister—and they were in danger, fear could cloud your judgment. Her own turmoil over Darcy had taught her that. That's why she'd been relieved to have an impartial, clear-thinking pro handling the case.

Yet mistakes could happen on both sides, couldn't they? Especially in a high-risk under-cover assignment. Was Dev shouldering all the blame for a situation that might have had multiple causes?

"You once told me I was being too hard on myself about Darcy." She spoke quietly, choosing her words with care. "Do you think the same might be true in your case?"

"No." His jaw hardened, and his lips flattened into an unforgiving line. "I wish it was. I was the one who stepped over the line. I wanted Cat out of the assignment, despite the fact we were getting close to wrapping things up. We had a huge argument about it, and she refused to back down no matter how hard I pushed. She'd seen her own brother die of an overdose after getting involved with a similar gang, and I suspect she looked upon this assignment as a way to avenge his death—though she never admitted that. The disagreement strained our relationship and compromised our communication. And when you aren't in sync in a situation like that, people die."

He stopped—but Laura knew where the story would end, even if he decided not to continue. Knew, also, that he'd borne a heavy burden of guilt every single day since the tragedy that had taken the life of his partner . . . and the woman he'd loved.

As he lifted the glass of water once more, the sight of the ever-so-slight tremble in his fingers tightened her throat. Without thinking, she leaned forward and placed her hand on his as he set the glass down.

He dropped his chin and concentrated on her fingers as he finished the story.

"Three weeks after our argument, the take down opportunity we'd been waiting for came up. A major transaction with some European gun-runners was scheduled. It was a tailor-made scenario for the Bureau and our other law enforcement partners to move in and make multiple arrests. We had enough evidence on that group to send dozens of them to prison for a very long time. But nothing went according to plan." He expelled a long breath and wiped a hand down his face.

When he continued, his words were steadier, but they were more clinical and devoid of emotion. "For whatever reason, the gang leader got suspicious and backed out of the meeting at the very last minute. He sent me and one of his right-hand men instead. I was worried, but there was no way I could get a message at that point to my contacts without arousing further suspicion. I hoped I was wrong—and I hoped Cat would pick up on the bad vibes and find a way to alert our people things might have gone south. But I wasn't—and she didn't. If we'd been sticking tighter together, though, she'd have been with me when the gang leader backed out. Her guard would have been up, and the outcome might have been very different."

He twined his fingers with hers, holding on tight as if he needed an anchor to get through this final part. "We did end up making a lot of arrests that day, even though the gang had scattered. I managed to avoid the bullets that were flying—but they got Cat. They shot her up with heroin and left her locked in a bathroom in a dumpy trailer they sometimes used for meetings. She died of an overdose, just like her brother . . . except his heroin was self-administered."

Laura closed her eyes, squeezing back tears as Dev clung to her hand. What could she say that would let him know how much her heart ached for him? That would console and comfort him? That would mitigate his guilt and sorrow and the burden he'd shouldered for five and a half long years?

No words came to mind except the ones she

uttered, which were trite and lame. "I'm so sorry, Dev."

He looked at her with eyes as bleak as the winter landscape outside. "So am I."

Desperately she searched for something—anything—else she could say to ease his burden of grief and guilt.

"A lot of those people were prosecuted though, right?" It was the sole consolation she could think to offer. "Some good came out of the bad, didn't it?"

A muscle in his cheek clenched. "Very little. The ATF and US Attorneys' Office got into a dispute over evidence, and the majority of the serious charges were dropped. Only a couple of the gang members were tried for RICO violations. So in the end, Cat died for nothing."

There was no response to that—nor did Dev seem to expect one.

He took a sip of coffee and carefully set the cup back on the saucer. "I took a leave of absence after the case fell apart, and six months later, when Cal approached me about opening Phoenix, I chucked the ATF and all the protocol garbage and endless red tape. That was five years ago, and I've never looked back—until tonight."

As he locked gazes with her, Laura searched his eyes. Past the pain, past the regret, past the self-recrimination, she saw a tiny glimmer of . . . hope? Longing? A plea for understanding?

Whatever it was, she knew her response had to be spot-on. That what she said in the next few seconds could have a huge impact on both of their futures.

Please, Lord . . . give me the right words.

Leaning closer, she placed her free hand atop their joined fingers. "I haven't known you very long, but my sense is that you're a man of integrity and character, and that any culpability you bear for what happened to your partner has been atoned for by the burden of guilt and grief you've carried all these years. The other thing to remember is that God doesn't expect perfection. All he asks is that we learn from our mistakes and try to do better in the future. He forgives us far more easily than we often forgive ourselves. He also heals the brokenhearted and saves those whose spirit is crushed."

"Psalms."

Laura blinked. Somehow, she hadn't expected Dev to have a close enough acquaintance with the Bible to be able to identify an ad-libbed passage.

"I can quote an applicable verse from Isaiah too. 'Remember not the events of the past, the things of long ago consider not.' I searched for consolation for a long time, in a lot of places."

His knowledge of Scripture was impressive. But his weary inflection suggested the good book had given him little comfort.

"Your forays into the Bible didn't help, though,

did they?" She kept her tone gentle and non-judgmental.

"The truth? No. I grew up in a faith-filled home, and my belief in God has never wavered. That's why I turned to his book in those dark days. But I've seen the worst the world has to offer, and I've come to believe God may have given up on the human race and walked away in disgust. To be honest, I wouldn't blame him if he did. We've made a royal mess of things."

"I felt like that a lot too, during the year Mom and I lived in the tenement."

"But you don't anymore."

She heard the query underneath his statement.

"No. When things got really bad back then, I tried to remember what my father had always told me whenever I got mad at God or complained he wasn't paying attention to my prayers. He said the tougher things got, the harder I had to look to see God. But if I did look hard, I'd find him."

Dev's expression grew skeptical. "Even in a tenement?"

"That's what I thought at first too, but you know what? It worked. Bad as things were there, I did see God. In the woman at the corner grocery store who always saved me the out-of-date Hostess cupcakes because she knew I didn't have the money to buy fresh ones. In the librarian at school who went out of her way to find special books for me so I could escape to a different world through the pages of a story instead of through the drugs that were rampant in our neighborhood. In the janitor of our building, who hung around when the school bus dropped me off to make sure none of the bigger kids harassed me in the hall."

She studied the lean fingers twined with hers. "Much as I didn't want to admit it at the time, I saw him in my mother too. I might have been mad at her, but I knew she loved me. She went without dinner a lot of nights so I'd have enough to eat."

A few beats of silence passed as Dev regarded her. "That's an interesting take on how to find God."

She gave him a small smile. "Sometimes he's most evident in small gestures of kindness. And those gestures can be found even in the worst situations."

The waiter reappeared and discreetly slipped the bill on the table. Laura reached for it, but her companion beat her.

"Please . . . let me cover this, Dev. Consider it a birthday present."

"No way." He dug his credit card out of his wallet and handed it to the waiter. "You've already given me the best possible present." He touched her hand again for a brief moment, then sent her a rueful look. "But I'm afraid I reneged on my promise about getting you home early. It will be close to nine before I drop you off."

"My fencing practice can wait until tomorrow night."

"Not the most romantic activity for Valentine's Day."

That's right. Tomorrow was Valentine's Day. But even without Darcy's disappearance, it would have been a day like any other for her, as usual. Even last year's celebration had been less than memorable. Rick had taken her to a crowded restaurant where they'd had to shout to be heard and the fixed-price menu had tasted like banquet fare. Being home alone would be better—unless she happened to have a date with a man like the one across from her.

But that wasn't going to happen this year.

She summoned up a smile. "That's not a holiday most guys remember without prompting."

The half-hitch grin he gave her produced a distracting dimple in one cheek. "They do if their birthday is the day before and their mother baked them a heart-shaped cake every year, complete with pink icing and curlicues." He signed the slip the waiter slid in front of him and pocketed the receipt. "By the time I was twelve, I'd had it and asked for a cake shaped like a football instead. I don't think Mom ever forgave me. She didn't have any girls to fuss over, and the timing of my birthday gave her an excuse to do froufrou stuff."

Laura chuckled and picked up her purse. "I think the football suited you better."

"Much. Ready?"

"Yes."

They retrieved their coats, and within a few minutes were on their way back to her house. He kept the conversation light during the drive, only growing serious again when he walked her to her door.

While she fitted the key in the lock, he angled toward her, the warm glow from the porch light bronzing his skin. "Thanks for a memorable birthday."

Slipping the key back in her purse, she faced him. "Thanks for trusting me with your story."

As Dev looked at her, the distant, plaintive whistle of a train sounded. A crisp breeze whispered past her cheeks, bringing with it the tangy scent of his aftershave. A tiny fleck of crust from the apple cobbler clung to his jaw, and without thinking she reached up to brush it off, the stubble of his nine o'clock shadow scratchy against her fingertips.

The instant her fingers connected with his skin, a spark of electricity zipped through her—and based on the sudden darkening of his eyes, the phenomenon wasn't one-sided.

Her mouth went dry, and she froze.

He wanted to kiss her.

And she wanted him to.

But this was nuts.

They'd only met four days ago, and she wasn't

a fast mover. Never had been, never would be—despite the adrenaline pinging through her nerve endings. Tempting as it might be, moving fast was dangerous. She needed to step back, literally and figuratively. Now.

Except she didn't.

But Dev did.

"I need to go." His words came out hoarse . . . and gruff.

"Okay."

"I'll call you as soon as I have any new information."

"Okay." She was starting to sound like a parrot. "Happy birthday again."

"Thanks."

With a lift of his hand, he pivoted and strode down the sidewalk toward the Explorer.

If he looked back once he was inside the vehicle, she couldn't tell. He was right about the tinted windows. They offered no clue about the identity or behavior of occupants. Still, she raised her hand in farewell in case he was watching her. Then she slipped inside, locked the door, and let out a slow breath.

This evening had turned out nothing like she expected.

Leaning back against the sturdy oak panels, she stared into the empty living room.

Who could have known, when Dev had invited her along on the drive to Mark Hamilton's, that they'd end up in a cozy restaurant and that he'd share his most closely guarded secret with her?

For that matter, who could have known Darcy's disappearance would put her on a collision course with the most intriguing man she'd ever met, a man who dominated her thoughts whenever they weren't centered on her sister?

Guilt tugged at her conscience, and she folded her arms tight over her chest. With Darcy missing, was it wrong to have enjoyed her evening with Dev? She'd actually forgotten, for a few minutes, the worry that had plagued her day and night since last Friday, when she'd arrived home from work and discovered Darcy's note.

Yet worry wasn't going to bring her sister home any sooner. She'd done everything possible to locate her, and she knew Dev was giving the search top priority too. For now, all she could do was put her sister's welfare in God's hands.

And pray for her safety.

Mark scrubbed his face dry with a towel and picked up the watch he'd left on the vanity before stepping into the shower. Nine-thirty. He was right on schedule to be in bed by ten—a half hour earlier than his pre-Darcy routine.

But that was fine. Going to bed earlier to compensate for getting up earlier so he could make her lunch and breakfast before he left for work wasn't a chore. You were supposed to do things like that for people who were important in your life.

He folded the towel, draped it neatly back over the bar, and padded into the bedroom toward his nightstand. The lotion Faith had given him was already beginning to work, and he squeezed a dab onto his palms as he examined his hands. In another few days, after things settled into more of a routine and he didn't feel the urge to wash his hands as often, the redness should fade and he wouldn't need high-priced ointments anymore. In the meantime, why not take advantage of Faith's generosity?

Once the lotion soaked in, he opened the nightstand and removed Lil's picture. Cradling it in his hands, he examined the fresh, smiling face—so different from the image that lingered in his mind. But this photo represented the real Lil. The woman she was supposed to be. The woman she was before the world led her astray. Before she discovered drugs and alcohol and resorted to other immoral activities. Before her priorities became twisted.

Before she stopped loving him.

He tightened his grip on the gold-edged frame that had tarnished through the years, just as Lil had, and sucked in a breath. "I tried so hard to help you . . . but you wouldn't let me."

She smiled back at him, as deaf to his voice

now as she'd been at the end. But still he continued to speak, as he had then.

"You could have changed. You could have saved yourself. But you made bad choices, and you wouldn't mend your ways. I could see how it would end even if you couldn't."

His fingers started to itch, but he resisted the urge to get up and wash his hands again. That would negate the effect of the expensive lotion he'd just applied.

Instead, he concentrated on the photo. "There's a young woman downstairs who reminds me of you. She's a runaway too, on the brink of making the wrong choices. I didn't want to mention her until I was sure she was the one. Now I think she is—and I also think I got to her in time. So I'll save her instead of you. With her, I'll wipe the slate clean, make amends, and start fresh."

For several more seconds, he examined the photo. Then he slipped it back in the nightstand, closed the drawer, and dimmed the bedside light.

Silence descended, and he began to drift off. But the muffled slam of a car door from outside pulled him back from the edge of sleep.

The car was close to his house.

He lay in the darkness, listening. Car doors slammed at all hours in this neighborhood; you learned to tune them out. After that unexpected ring on his doorbell tonight, however, every single one had registered.

Because no one ever rang his bell, except an occasional derelict looking for a handout. No wonder he'd dropped that frying pan at the sudden peal. And who could blame him for creeping to the door, staying in the shadows along the wall of the living room to avoid detection as he checked out the intruder?

But the guy on the other side of the peephole hadn't been a derelict. He'd been dressed too well for that, and he'd gone away after the second ring. Most likely he'd just come to the wrong address; the house numbers were hard to read with all the snow. There was no reason for him to come back. Probably one of the college students who lived in the house next door had slammed the door. They were a wild bunch, with their loud weekend parties.

Still . . . Mark rose and moved to the front window. Just in case.

The street was deserted. Whoever had made the noise must have scurried inside on this cold night.

He started back toward his bed but halfway there detoured to the bathroom.

There was no way he'd go to sleep if he didn't wash his hands again—and he had to get enough sleep to be at the top of his game for the children in his charge at daycare . . . and the girl in his charge in the basement.

16

"I'd ask if you had a nice evening, but I already know the answer."

Frowning at the interruption, Dev transferred his attention from his computer screen to Phoenix's senior partner, who'd propped his shoulder against the door frame and was regarding him with an amused expression. "What are you talking about?"

"Your intimate dinner for two at Café Provencal looked very cozy."

Dev switched on blush control and resorted to evasive maneuvers as he contemplated his strategy. "You were there?"

"Yep. With my beautiful bride."

"An early Valentine's Day celebration?"

"I just got married. Every day is Valentine's Day at our house."

Dev rolled his eyes. "Give me a break."

"I'm serious." Cal strolled in and dropped into the chair across from the desk, making it clear he was in no hurry to leave.

Great.

"Moira was giving me a hard time last night about not inviting you out for your birthday, but I told her I was sure you had the evening covered, as usual. Thanks for getting me off the hook."

"My pleasure."

"So I noted."

Could Cal's grin get any bigger?

His partner stretched out his legs and settled in. "So who's the lovely lady?"

Continue to evade until you come up with a better plan.

"Where were you, anyway? I looked the place over as we were being seated and I didn't see you."

"You were already at your table when we arrived. Deep in conversation, with eyes only for your companion. I'm not surprised you neglected to notice us. And you didn't answer my question."

No kidding.

"What question?" Stalling was only going to buy him a few more seconds. Max. *Think fast, Devlin.*

"Who's asking questions?" Nikki strolled in and dropped a bunch of papers in his in-box.

"I am." Cal tossed the reply over his shoulder. "About who he was with last night at Café Provencal."

As Nikki's expression morphed from curious to smug, Dev stifled a groan. Things were going from bad to worse.

"You took my advice, didn't you?"

Connor stopped midstride as he passed in the hall. "What advice?" He poked his head in and did a sweep of the office. "Is this a party or what?"

"No, but it sounds like Dev had his own party last night." Nikki sat on the edge of his desk. "Dinner with the lovely librarian, right?"

"Your client?" Cal squinted at him.

"It was his birthday," Nikki pointed out. "Extenuating circumstances."

"You're dating a client?" Connor moved into the office too, which was suddenly feeling claustrophobic.

Dev rolled his chair a few inches farther away from the growing mob. "Before this gets out of hand . . ."

"Too late for that, based on the evidence." Cal shifted sideways to better address Connor and Nikki. "They were holding hands."

"No, we weren't." At the skeptical twist of his partner's mouth, he backpedaled. "Not like you mean, anyway."

"There's more than one way to hold hands?" Nikki's raised eyebrow said "get real."

"As a matter of fact, yes. This was not a romantic rendezvous. Cal's conclusion is based on circumstantial evidence that happens to be faulty."

"I can buy that."

Dev sent Connor a grateful look. "Thank you."

"But I'm guessing this smoke might lead to fire."

Three against one. Not the best odds he'd ever faced.

"You can leave now." Dev sent Connor a dark look. "I need allies, not subversives."

"Hey . . . I'm fine with whatever you did on your birthday." The other man ambled back toward the hall. "I can't see any harm in suspending the no-socializing-with-clients rule one day a year."

"I'm with Connor." Nikki sent a meaningful glance toward Cal, then retreated to the hall in Connor's wake.

That left Cal, who crossed an ankle over his knee and regarded him. "You want to talk about this?"

No. But he was going to have to. None of them took the house rules lightly, and he owed Cal an explanation for the lapse.

Rising, he circled his desk, shut the door, and dropped into the chair beside his partner. "I want to make it clear I would never do anything to compromise the integrity of Phoenix."

"I know that."

At Cal's steady look, Dev's throat tightened. He was closer to his college buddies than anyone else on this planet. Cal and Connor were more like brothers to him than his blood brother. He had trusted them with his life on numerous occasions—and would no doubt do so again. They might all kid around in the office, but each of them was a consummate professional who knew his stuff and could be counted on to pull his weight under fire. He would never—ever—do anything to jeopardize the respect his partners had for him.

He was glad Cal understood that.

"The truth is, I like Laura Griffith." He twined his fingers together. "We were together early last evening for business reasons. Did I need to invite her to dinner afterward? No. Am I sorry I did? No. Am I going to take this any further while she's a client? No. Afterward? Probably."

"That works for me." Cal rose. "I know what it's like to fall for a client. I married one. And if Laura is even half the woman my wife is, I'll be in your corner once this case is closed."

"Thanks."

With a thumbs-up, Cal exited.

Left blessedly alone once more, Dev returned to his desk and took a sip of his coffee. He was on his third cup, and he could use another. After tossing for the better part of the night, thanks to a certain librarian whose image kept flitting across his mind, and then getting up in the wee hours to do a little surveillance on the elusive Mark Hamilton, he needed all the caffeine he could get.

But his early morning stakeout in the back alley of the man's house, where most residents seemed to park, hadn't been all that productive. Before the sun ever rose, Hamilton had come out the back door and climbed into a slate-colored Nissan Maxima. He'd driven straight to his job at Davis Daycare Center ten minutes away, validating the employment info in the short news item about his promotion last year that a Google search had unearthed. No detours. Nothing out of the ordinary.

Dev gulped down the last of his coffee. By the time he drove back downtown, it would be close to nine-thirty—well past the morning drop-off rush at a child care center. Hamilton might be able to ignore his doorbell at home, as he'd done last night, but he'd have more difficulty hiding out at work.

As soon as he got with Nikki, gave her the basics he'd uncovered on Mark Hamilton last night after his dinner with Laura, and turned her loose to dig deeper, he'd head back down there.

And hope Hamilton had information that would shed some light on Darcy's whereabouts so he could wrap up this case as soon as possible—for personal as well as professional reasons.

Elbow on desk, Laura propped her head in her hand and stifled a yawn, hoping none of the nearby patrons in the reference room would notice. One of these nights, maybe she'd manage more than three or four hours of fitful shut-eye.

But probably not until Darcy was back, safe and sound.

Truth be told, though, worry over Darcy was only part of the reason for her restless night. Dev shared the blame. Long after he'd driven away, the electric charge that had passed between them on her porch had continued to pulse through her. In fact, she could still feel the remnants of it this morning.

And that staying power scared her. Chemistry that potent could carry a person away, lead to foolish mistakes, even when you knew any relationship with a future had to be based on much more than hormones.

The potential with Dev was there, though. No doubt about it. But she had to give this a lot more time before she entertained any serious thoughts about the appealing PI. It was the smart, prudent thing to do.

And in the interim, she needed to concentrate on finding Darcy.

"Any news?" Erin stopped beside her desk and set a fruit cup and granola bar in front of her.

"No. What's this?" She gestured to the food.

"Your breakfast. I'm guessing you didn't bother to eat. Again."

Her boss knew her too well. "I had a great dinner, though."

"Yeah? Let me guess. Soup and crackers. Again."

"No. Salad, lamb shank, mashed potatoes, fresh asparagus, and chocolate mousse."

Erin grabbed a nearby chair and dragged it beside the desk. "Okay. Spill it."

Turning her back on the patrons, Laura gave

her a recap of the evening—leaving out Dev's personal disclosures and downplaying the intimate nature of the evening.

When she finished, Erin sized her up. "Are you suggesting that having dinner with your handsome, single PI was an act of mercy because you didn't want him to eat dinner alone on his birthday?"

"If I said yes, would you buy it?"

"Not a chance. Eat your fruit. So did you have fun?"

Laura pried off the lid of the plastic container and speared a chunk of pineapple. "It was a nice evening."

"I'm hearing a *but* in there."

The sweet burst of flavor as she bit into the pineapple wasn't enough to offset the sour taste of guilt.

"The thing is, I actually forgot about Darcy for a few minutes and enjoyed myself. That feels wrong." She toyed with a grape, but it eluded the tines of the fork.

"Laura . . . you're doing everything possible to find her. It could be she doesn't want to be found. You told me yourself she's intelligent and has some street smarts. For all you know, she's perfectly fine and hanging out with that girl she met who was also waiting for the storm to pass. She might have decided to stick around town for a while, stay under the radar, rethink her plans."

"Then why didn't she call Rachel in Chicago to tell her that?"

Erin shrugged. "You said she was smart, not considerate."

She captured the grape at last. "I think she would have called, if she could. We might have clashed, but she had decent manners with other people. And Rachel was doing her a favor. I don't think she'd have left her hanging. She hasn't gotten in touch with her best friend from New York, either."

"Maybe she's afraid you could trace her if she called them."

"Or maybe she *can't* call." A drop of juice dripped out of the grape, leaving a dark spot on the polished surface of the desk.

It looked like blood.

She swiped it away. "I'm afraid she might have made mistakes, trusted the wrong people. I just have this lurking sense of unease that she needs help. So instead of worrying, what do I do? I go out to dinner with a handsome man."

"Who's also trying to find Darcy."

"Not during dinner."

"The man has to eat—and you do too." Erin stood and tapped the granola bar. "This is breakfast, not lunch. Eat it now. And if you ask me, you have nothing to feel guilty about over last night. You took Darcy in when she had no place else to go. You bent over backward to make her feel welcome. You've got dark circles under your eyes that weren't there a week ago, thanks to constant worry and no sleep. If you had a respite from that anxiety for a few minutes over dinner, I say you deserve it."

Laura gave her boss a tired smile. "Thanks for the pep talk."

"Did it help?"

"A little."

"If you need another one, call me." She moved the chair back into position against the wall and gentled her voice. "I'm praying for her every day too, you know."

"I appreciate that."

Pointing once more at the food, Erin headed back toward the front desk.

Laura fished out another pineapple chunk, letting the sweet flavor linger on her tongue as she replayed Erin's comments. It was possible her friend was right. Darcy might be safe and hanging out somewhere in town while she revised the plans that had been altered by the blizzard.

But the unexpected tartness of the blueberry she chose next chased away the fleeting sweetness.

Dev had offered her no such reassurances. Just two days ago he'd acknowledged that the next twenty-four hours were critical. Forty-eight hours had now passed with no sign of Darcy.

Yet he'd also said he wouldn't abandon ship,

that he'd keep searching. And Laura intended to hold him to that promise.

Because despite Erin's attempt to reassure her, she had a sinking feeling Darcy was in big trouble.

"Mr. Hamilton? May I speak with you for a moment?"

At Faith's question, Mark looked up in irritation from the castle he was building out of blocks with a group of four-year-olds. She knew the one hour a day he spent interacting with the children was sacrosanct. Interruptions were supposed to be confined to emergencies.

This better qualify.

Patting one of the youngsters on the head, he stood. "I'll be back in a few minutes, and we'll add the towers on the corners, okay?"

A chorus of okays followed him to the door, where Faith waited for him.

"What's up?"

She tucked one of those annoying flyaway curls behind her ear. "There's a man in the lobby who says he needs to speak with you about an urgent personal matter. His name is James Devlin, and he looks kind of . . . official. Otherwise I wouldn't have bothered you."

Mark frowned. "What do you mean, official?"

"I don't know exactly. Kind of like he's used to being in charge."

An image of the guy he'd viewed through the

peephole on his front door appeared in Mark's mind. He'd been dressed in casual attire, but he'd seemed like the confident, in-charge type.

Could it be the same guy?

"Did you ask for a card?"

"Yes." Faith scrubbed her palms down her slacks. "He said he'd be happy to give you one when you talked with him."

Why wouldn't the guy give his card to Faith to pass on?

And could this have anything to do with the message he'd erased on his voice mail? The one with blocked caller ID he hadn't bothered to play back?

Faith shifted from one foot to the other as the silence between them lengthened. "So, um, do you want to talk with him?"

Did he? Mark's hands started to itch. He needed to wash them. Now. His breath stalled in his lungs, and he charged toward the hall.

"Give me five minutes, then send him back to my office." He was almost jogging as he called the instruction over his shoulder.

He didn't wait for Faith to respond. Instead, he turned the corner and pushed through the door into the men's room. Lucky thing he was one of the few males who worked on the premises. The bathroom was rarely occupied when he needed it.

After twisting on the faucet, he lathered up his hands, working the soap between his fingers, around his cuticles, scrubbing the palms and backs.

Better.

His lungs resumed their regular rhythm, and he forced himself to take steady breaths as he thought through the situation.

What were the odds this guy was the one he'd seen on his doorstep? And even if he was, there was no way he could have any connection to Darcy. Hadn't the girl told him she wouldn't be missed? That she and her half sister . . . Laura, that was her name . . . were almost strangers, that they'd clashed constantly, and that her librarian sibling would be happy to get rid of her?

So who was his official-looking visitor? Not a cop. He wasn't in trouble with the law. Not a bill collector. He wasn't behind on any of his payments for the house or utilities or car. Not a lawyer. He hadn't been involved in a car accident or had any legal-related issues at the daycare center.

Mark rinsed his hands and yanked off a length of paper towel from the automatic dispenser. Maybe the guy was an insurance salesman or some forgotten acquaintance from his past who'd tracked him down. If so, he could blow him off. Why not have one of the aides tell Faith to inform the man he'd been called into a meeting and wasn't available?

On the other hand, if his visitor was here in

some sort of official capacity, he didn't want to make waves by refusing to talk with him. Given his present circumstances, it was important to stay as far under the radar as possible.

He wadded up the paper towel, hurled it in the trash, and inspected his hands. They still itched, and he was tempted to wash them again. But the hot water had already turned the skin redder than usual; another round would make them even more conspicuous.

Better to head back to his office and find out what James Devlin wanted. Maybe dealing with him would be a simple matter.

But as he pushed through the door with his shoulder and walked down the hall, a sudden, familiar feeling of unease swept over him. The same one he'd always felt as he'd walked toward the door of the apartment he'd called home, wondering what kind of mood Lil would be in. Would she greet him with a kiss—or lash out at him with a string of obscenities for imagined transgressions?

Mark's stomach knotted, and his heart began to pound. He hated this feeling. Hated the sense of looming threat, of impending doom.

Why had this stranger resurrected it?

He scratched the back of one hand, then the other, as he rounded the corner in the hall and entered his office. He had to remain calm. After all, no one knew what he'd done. No one. How could they? He'd been careful. This guy, who-ever he turned out to be, was probably here on mundane business of some kind. Fifteen minutes from now, he'd be chiding himself for over-reacting.

Feeling better, Mark circled his desk and settled in his chair. This was his world. His turf. He was in charge and in control.

There was no reason to be concerned.

Dev folded his hands over his stomach, main-taining a relaxed posture as the woman behind the reception desk in the Davis Daycare lobby pretended to be busy while she cast surreptitious glances his direction. Faith Bradley, according to the name tag pinned to her shirt—the same woman who'd been watching Hamilton's house last night from behind the wheel of her car, according to the license check he'd run.

Interesting.

She flicked a glance at her watch, then motioned to the door behind her that led to the offices. "Mr. Hamilton will see you now. He's in the second room on the left."

Dev rose and followed her, waiting as she entered a security code and moved aside.

"Thanks." He smiled, but she simply edged away and returned to the desk.

Not the friendliest place he'd ever visited.

Once in the hall, he could hear the high-pitched

voices of children from behind the doors lining the corridor. He stopped in front of the office with Hamilton's nameplate beside it and knocked.

"Come in."

At the invitation, he pushed through and stepped inside. As Hamilton rose from behind the desk, Dev did a rapid assessment. Midthirtyish, five-nine or ten, neatly trimmed brown hair, crisp button-down shirt and dress slacks. Very preppy. But the bandage on his cheek raised questions, as did the chapped, red hand the man extended as he closed the distance between them.

"Mark Hamilton. How can I help you?"

Dev took his hand. It might be abnormally ruddy, but his grip was firm. A little too firm.

Nerves could do that to a person.

But why was he nervous?

"James Devlin." He released the man's hand and withdrew a card from his pocket, which he handed over. "I'm hoping you can answer a few questions for me."

Twin crevices appeared on the man's forehead as he read the card, and a faint crimson stain crept across his cheeks. "Are you a private eye?"

"That's the popular terminology."

The man's lips tilted into the facsimile of a smile, but there was no humor in his eyes. "My only experience with private investigators up to this point is Paul Drake on TV."

It took Dev a moment to dredge up the name

from the recesses of his memory. "You mean the PI from those old Perry Mason shows?"

"Yeah. Did you ever see any?"

"My dad used to watch the reruns when I was a kid. I caught a few."

"It was a great show. As I recall, Perry got the glory, but Paul did the work." Again, the man tried for a smile but barely managed a stretch of the lips.

"It happens that way sometimes." Nervous energy was pinging around the room, and Dev's antennas went up another notch. Hamilton was trying to be genial, but he wasn't happy about a visit from a PI. Because he didn't want to waste his time—or because he had something to hide?

A little behavior test was in order before he got to the important questions.

"Do you remember the name of the secretary in that show?" He kept his tone casual and conversational.

Hamilton looked up and slightly to the right. "Della Street."

"I'm impressed. Wasn't there a hard-nosed district attorney in the cast too?"

"Yeah." Once more, Hamilton shifted his focus a bit to the right, then shook his head. "I'm blanking out on that one. Please, have a seat. I'm sure you didn't come to play Trivial Pursuit about old TV shows." He gestured to the chair across from his desk and lowered himself into his own seat. "How can I help you?"

Dev assessed the office as he settled into the chair. The room was pristine, unlike his own working space. Other than a few items in the in-box and a neat stack of files on one corner of the desk, all the surfaces were empty. Nor did the office contain any family pictures. There was nothing to latch on to as a conversation starter except for a framed photo of a tropical beach on the wall.

He'd have to work with that.

"Nice picture on a day like this." He gestured toward it. "A favorite vacation spot?"

Hamilton gave it a quick, dismissive glance. "No. It was on the wall when I moved in last year and I never took it down."

"Makes me think about vacation, though." Dev kept his inflection friendly and chatty. "If I could be anywhere right now, I'd pick a place like that. Hawaii would be nice. What about you?"

The man squinted at him, as if trying to figure out what vacations had to do with this visit, then lifted his gaze and flitted his eyes a hair to the left.

Mission accomplished.

Body language wasn't foolproof, but nine times out of ten it was accurate. When Hamilton was remembering facts, he looked up and right. When he was creating an answer, he looked up and left.

"Florida might be nice. I've always wanted to

visit there in the winter." He shrugged. "Maybe someday. So what can I do for you today?"

Dev pulled the two shots of Darcy from the inside pocket of his jacket. "I'm investigating the disappearance of a sixteen-year-old girl who ran away a week ago. We believe she spent a couple of nights at the temporary homeless shelter where you volunteer. One of the other volunteers thinks he saw you speaking with her. I was hoping she might have made some remark to you that would give us a clue about her plans and help us track her down."

The man's color surged slightly. "I talk to a lot of people there."

Dev laid the two shots on the desk, facing Hamilton. "It never hurts to ask, though. You might recognize her."

The man's demeanor didn't change as he studied the photos, but a muscle clenched in his jaw and his nostrils flared.

He knew something.

Yet when he looked up, he shook his head. "Sorry. She doesn't ring any bells."

That was a lie.

"I was hoping for better news." Dev rested his elbows on the arms of his chair and linked his fingers, maintaining a casual posture. "As I said, one of the other volunteers was certain he saw you talking with this girl on Monday morning. Are you sure you don't recognize her?"

"I'm sure." The daycare manager didn't even bother to scan the photos again.

"I wonder who your fellow volunteer saw you talking with?" He picked up the photos but kept his focus on Hamilton.

The other man looked up and to the left.

Another fabrication was coming.

"You know, there was a young woman at the shelter over the weekend who had a faint resemblance to the runaway you're looking for. From a distance I can see how someone might confuse them."

All lies.

Why?

What was the man hiding?

Those were questions that would have to be answered through more discreet tactics, however. And he intended to implement them immediately.

Tucking the photos back into his jacket, Dev rose. "I appreciate your time."

Hamilton stood too. "No problem. Best of luck with your search."

"Thanks." Dev walked toward the door. When he turned at the threshold, he caught Hamilton scratching his fingers. The man stopped instantly and shoved both hands into his pockets. "If you think of anything that might be helpful, I'd appreciate a call."

"Sure."

The word was cooperative; the man's demeanor wasn't.

Dev retraced his steps down the hall, nodded to a somber-faced Faith Bradley at the front desk, and pushed through the outside door. The cold air that hit him in the face was balmy compared to the chilly reception he'd just received.

Why was the receptionist so nervous? Why had she been watching the daycare manager's house last night? And what did Hamilton know about Darcy?

Pressing the autolock button on his key chain, he crossed the plowed parking lot, salt crunching under his shoes. He had no answers to those questions.

But before this day ended, he intended to be a lot closer to finding them.

17

At the sound of a key being inserted in the door, Darcy jerked her head to the right and froze, her hand halfway into the refrigerator.

Why was Mark home in the middle of the day?

Her pulse spiked, and she closed the refrigerator without retrieving her lunch.

This wasn't good.

The knob turned. An instant later, the door crashed against the wall, leaving Mark framed on the threshold, his face mottled with angry spots of color.

Fear clawing at her throat, she backed away and groped for the wing chair, seeking refuge behind it.

Mark slammed the door shut behind him, and she flinched as the noise reverberated through the room. After shoving the key into his pocket, he advanced toward the chair, his eyes scorching her with the heat of his anger.

He stopped mere inches away, his fists clenching and unclenching at his sides. "You said no one would miss you." The accusation came out in a hiss.

She stared at him, trying to regroup. This wasn't about some transgression she'd made? Some inadvertent breaking of rules?

When she didn't respond, he got in her face and wrapped his fingers around her upper arm in a crushing grip. She gasped and tried to shrink back, but his fingers tightened, cutting off the circulation and holding her in place.

"You said no one would miss you."

As he repeated the words through clenched teeth, her brain clicked into gear. Had Laura been searching for her? But if so, how could she possibly have known where to look?

Mark shook her. Hard. "Why did you lie?"

"I d-didn't. No one cares about m-me."

The punch in the stomach came so fast and so hard she didn't have a chance to prepare for it. If he hadn't had her arm in such a tight grip, she'd have doubled over and fallen to her knees. As it was, she groaned and sagged against him as a sharp wave of pain radiated outward from her core.

"You're lying." He bared his teeth, reminding her of a video she'd once seen on the nature channel of a snarling wolf about to pounce on its trapped prey. "You've been lying all along."

The scent of the lotion he used on his hands infiltrated her nostrils, and nausea rolled through her.

Don't puke! Don't puke!

"No." She gasped the word past the pain in her midsection. "I'm not lying."

He shook her again. Her teeth rattled, and her eyes began to water. "I don't believe you!"

This time he yelled, directly in her ear. She flinched and once more tried to shrink back.

He didn't let her.

Instead, he yanked her toward the wing chair and shoved her into the seat. Planting his hands on the arms, he leaned into her face, close enough for her to feel the heat of his breath.

"Who else cares about you other than your half sister?"

She pressed her head against the cushioned back, trying to put as much distance as possible between them. "No one." Her reply came out in a quavering whisper.

For a long moment he watched her, his eyes boring into hers. She tried not to cringe as she looked back at him, willing him to believe her.

Her life could depend on it.

After a century of agonizing seconds dragged by, he straightened up, flexing his fingers as he scrutinized her.

Her gaze dropped to his hands, straight in front of her at eye level. She already knew they were strong. Were they also lethal? Had he used those fingers to crush the breath out of the girls resting in their cold tombs on the other side of the wall?

Her heart stumbled.

Please, don't let him reach for my throat!

Her lungs stalled, the ominous quiet broken only by a sudden mechanical hum as the motor on the dorm-sized refrigerator kicked on.

Finally he reached into his pocket, pulled out a business card, and flipped it into her lap.

She picked up the rectangular piece of heavy stock. Her hand was shaking so badly it was hard to read the lettering, but she could make out Phoenix Inc. The man's name was unfamiliar, but her eyes widened as she read the words underneath.

Private investigator?

Laura had hired a PI to find her?

She hadn't expected extreme measures like that. A few circuits of her hangouts, a few calls to friends, maybe, but not this all-out effort.

Her half sister obviously cared a lot more about her than she'd let herself believe.

Warmth ignited in her heart, chasing away some of the chill—but in its wake came regret. Once again her actions had created trauma for someone who cared about her—perhaps even loved her.

Would she never learn?

Darcy's throat tightened, and tears blurred her vision.

"Is there anyone besides your half sister who might have hired this PI?"

Forcing herself to refocus, she considered Mark's question, unsure of the safest answer. In the end, she went with honesty. "No."

"Do either of you have any other relatives you haven't told me about?"

"No."

He studied her, his eyes measuring, assessing. Finally he exhaled, as if he'd accepted the truth of her answers. "Then I guess I have some work to do." He snatched the card back, yanked her lunch from the fridge, and stomped to the door.

Work to do?

Heart thudding, Darcy scrambled to her feet, not certain what he meant but not liking the undertones of his cryptic comment. "Wait."

He paused on the threshold, key in hand, and looked at her over his shoulder.

"What kind of work?"

"When you have a problem, you eliminate it."

The knot in Darcy's stomach squeezed tighter. Laura was a problem, and Mark was going to take care of her—the same way he'd taken care of Angela and Denise and Star.

She clasped her hands in front of her, squeezing them tight, desperation drumming a staccato beat in her chest. "You don't have to worry about Laura. She'll lose interest w-when she doesn't find me. She'll s-stop looking. I know she will."

"I'm not going to take that chance. Don't expect dinner tonight." With that, he exited.

As the lock clicked into position, her legs began to shake and she collapsed back into the wing chair. Drawing up her knees, she huddled into a protective tuck around her aching stomach as shudders rippled through her body.

Mark was going to hurt Laura. Maybe he'd even kill her.

All because her ungrateful younger half sister had been stupid, stupid, stupid.

A sob tore at her throat. She didn't care if Mark was watching from the other side of the peephole. She didn't even care at this point if he killed her. She deserved to be punished after causing nothing but trouble for the people who loved her. And better her than Laura, who'd opened up her home and disrupted her life for a half sister she barely knew. That kind of sacrifice shouldn't be rewarded with the boatload of grief that had been heaped on her.

Despair settled over her like a shroud, and in the tomblike quiet of her prison, she continued to weep.

But when at last her tears were spent and her shaking subsided, one clear thought emerged.

Keeping Laura safe had to be her first priority.

She might not survive whatever Mark had in store for her, but she couldn't let him hurt the sister who'd taken her in. Before another day passed, she had to come up with a plan to thwart whatever he might be plotting.

No matter the risk to herself.

"You want to talk about Mark Hamilton and Faith Bradley?"

At Nikki's question, Dev looked away from his computer screen and waved her in. "Yeah. Have a seat. I'll be done in a sec."

As she dropped into the chair across from his desk, he expelled a frustrated breath and went back to the email he was composing. With Cal caught up in a defense attorney client meeting in a neighboring suburb, and Connor staking out Davis Daycare in case Hamilton decided to take another impromptu trip—as he'd done soon after their meeting two hours ago to make a fast visit to his house—he'd drawn the short straw when an urgent call came in from the corporate client in search of its rogue executive. Things were heating up fast on that front. Fortunately, all three of them kept their passports in order. This would be a three-man job.

So instead of helping Nikki research Hamilton and Bradley, he'd been exchanging phone calls and emails with the corporate security chief as they hammered out logistics for the Costa Rica trip. He'd be glad to turn this baby back over to Connor tomorrow. Foreign assignments were more his buddy's forte, thanks to his years of foreign travel with the Secret Service.

After hitting the send button, Dev swung toward Nikki. "Sorry to dump most of the research on you."

She cocked an eyebrow.

"Okay. All of the research. I owe you a latte. What have you got?"

She opened the folder. "You owe me two lattes. Your Mark Hamilton is an under-the-radar kind of guy. The man has no social media presence—my favorite place to scavenge. I had to dig pretty deep and turn on the charm."

"But you found some stuff to supplement the paltry facts I came up with last night."

"Yeah." She consulted the file in her lap. "He was born twenty-nine years ago. That fact courtesy of the DMV. Property records show he bought the house in Soulard three years ago. He got it for a song since it's in a historic district and was badly in need of renovation. You already know he volunteers at a homeless shelter. He's worked at Davis Daycare for seven years, the last year as a manager, as you discovered in that bare-bones news story you stumbled on about his promotion. I found the original press release, which also listed his impressive accreditation in his field. I verified those credentials with the appropriate professional organizations."

"Any luck on his earlier history?"

"That was harder. I scoured a couple of our best proprietary databases and public records, plus talked with our primo information broker. The earliest address that shows up for him from any of those sources is Columbia, Missouri, when he was eighteen. So I pieced together his social security number and gave Mizzou a call. They confirmed he was a student there. He graduated in three years with a degree in early childhood education."

"Fast track."

"Yeah. The guy's no slouch, that's for sure. While I had the clerk at Mizzou on the phone, I chatted her up a bit. I told her we were doing a background check, and asked if she'd mind confirming his address at the time of his application."

Dev grinned. When it came to finagling information out of people, Nikki had all three of the Phoenix PIs beat. "You got it, right?"

"Yep. Holyoke, Mass."

"A state with open access to vital records. Finally something goes our way with this case."

"We lucked out on that one, for sure. According

to the birth certificate, our guy's mother was Lillian Hamilton, age eighteen. No father was listed. I dug into death certificates too. Lillian died at age thirty. Suffocation was listed as cause of death, but it wasn't ruled as suspicious."

"Why not?"

"Same question I had—so I did a little digging in the local newspaper archives. From what I was able to cobble together based on articles that quoted police reports, she was a drug addict who made her living as a hooker. She was found ODed on coke in bed, lying on her stomach, face buried in a pillow. BAC was high too. I couldn't find any mention of family other than a son."

Dev leaned back in his chair, rested his elbows on the arms, and steepled his fingers. "Hamilton must have ended up in the foster care system."

"That would be my assumption—not that we'll be able to prove our theory."

"Yeah." Juvenile records weren't even available to law enforcement personnel in most cases, a fact that had grated on him in his former career whenever he'd had to deal with punks who had the law on their side. No way could a PI get access to those records.

He picked up his mug, took a sip of coffee, and made a face as the cold liquid sluiced down his throat.

"Looks like you could use a warm-up." Nikki glanced over at him.

"On the coffee and on the case." He set the mug down and pushed it away.

"Nothing I found is going to help you much on the latter score. Hamilton comes across as squeaky clean."

Clean.

An image of Hamilton's hands, along with Balloon Man's ditty about Mr. Clean, suddenly replayed in his mind. The homeless man had started singing it after Dev asked him whether he'd seen anyone talking to Darcy. He'd dismissed the tune as the rantings of a man whose brain was no longer firing on all cylinders, but there might be more to it than that. The red, chapped condition of Hamilton's hands suggested he washed them a lot. Was that because he worked among children all day and wanted to avoid passing germs—or for more dysfunctional psychological reasons?

In any case, he'd been wrong to write off Balloon Man's tune. His little song helped validate the volunteer's claim that he'd seen Hamilton talking to Darcy.

All the more reason to target the guy.

"Hey . . . are you still with me?"

At Nikki's prod, he refocused on her. "Yeah. Just making some connections."

"Helpful ones?"

"Maybe."

"As I said, we're looking at a Boy Scout here.

There aren't even any traffic citations on his record. No family ties, though, as far as I can tell." She lowered the file. "Quite an impressive life in view of his less-than-ideal childhood."

Dev drummed his fingers on his desk, frowning. "What about Faith Bradley?"

She closed the first file and opened the second one. "She was easy. Great Facebook presence. Age twenty-two. Born in Chicago, moved here for college. Dropped out two years ago but reenrolled in night school last fall. Lives in an apartment in South City. No problems with the law, either."

"Any connection between the two?"

"Other than working at the same place, nothing that I could find."

"Okay. Thanks."

Nikki closed the file and slid both onto his desk. "This doesn't help much, does it?"

He leaned back in his chair. "No. But my gut tells me Hamilton has information he's not sharing. And his background is interesting—a drug addict hooker for a mother and no father figure."

"Sounds to me like he overcame those impediments." Nikki leveled a direct look at him. "Some people do. Sometimes that kind of background is an incentive to create a better life."

He'd put his foot in that one. "Not everyone rises above their upbringing like you did. That takes a lot of strength and fortitude."

Her eyes widened, then thinned. "Is that on the level?"

"Yeah. I admire your accomplishments, even if I don't say it very often."

"Like never."

"I don't want you to get a swelled head."

She snorted. "Like that's gonna happen. Raising a teenager, even if he's my brother, is a constant reminder of my shortcomings." She stood. "If you need me to do anything else, let me know. In the meantime, I'll surf some more as time permits and see if I can dig up a few more facts."

Without giving him a chance to respond, she turned and disappeared into the hall.

Rocking forward in his chair, Dev pulled the files in front of him and tapped his finger against the top. Nikki was the best database searcher he knew. If this was all she'd come up with, there wasn't much else to be found aside from a piece or two of stray information. There was nothing here to suggest the man was involved in anything nefarious.

Yet the Mr. Clean connection, combined with his own instincts, was enough to convince him Phoenix's time would be well spent further investigating the man.

That left only one option.

Surveillance.

Putting someone on Hamilton's tail 24/7 was going to be expensive, however, and would require client consent. Might obtaining that consent justify a visit with Laura?

No. A phone call would suffice. He needed to honor his promise to Cal and keep his distance from his client for now.

But as he reached for the phone to tap in her number, he couldn't help wishing he was just a tad less conscientious.

At the vibration of her phone, Laura jerked and snatched it off her belt.

Dev.

The patron she'd been helping gave her a startled look.

"Sorry. I've been waiting for this call."

"Go ahead and take it. I'd like to page through some of these books."

With a nod, she retreated a few steps.

"Hi." She kept her voice low in the hushed quiet of the library and put some more distance between herself and the man in search of books on woodworking. "Any news?"

She listened as he briefed her on his visit with Hamilton and his discovery that the woman who'd been watching the man's house was a co-worker.

"What do you make of that?" She sent a quick look toward the white-haired man, who'd gone back to perusing the shelf of books she'd pointed out to him. He seemed absorbed for the moment.

"I don't know. But I've been in this business

long enough to know when someone's trying to cover up something—and Hamilton's behavior says cover-up loud and clear. That's the main reason I called you. I think it's worth putting round-the-clock surveillance on him for a few days, but that's pricey and I wanted to get your approval."

Laura didn't hesitate. After seeing Dev in action, she trusted his instincts. "I'm fine with that."

"Okay. Connor's on him now at work, and I'll take over later when he goes home. There's a spot on a side street that will give us a view of both the exit for the dead-end alley in back, where Hamilton parks, and the front of the house. It would be easier to have two people on the job, but I don't want to waste your money. If I think we need broader coverage at any point, I can always call in reinforcements."

"That sounds reasonable." She straightened a book about macramé on the shelf in front of her, noting the title on the spine. *Tied Up in Knots*. How appropriate, given the situation with Darcy—and her feelings about the man on the other end of the line.

"So is there anything else I can do to help? I'm off tomorrow, and other than running a few typical Saturday-morning errands, I'm free. I know Nikki is a whiz at database searches, but I've done a fair amount of those in my work too.

Would you like me to see if I can find out anything more about Hamilton or Faith too?"

"It can't hurt. The more eyes on this, the better."

Silence fell between them, and she adjusted a bookend. He hadn't mentioned the birthday dinner last night—nor suggested any further in-person contact. Was that because he was sorry he'd told her so much . . . or because he was simply too busy with the case?

She chose to believe the latter, even though his tone was far more professional than personal today.

"I guess I'll hear from you if you have any news, then."

"Of course. I always keep my client informed."

Client.

That put her in her place.

Maybe he *was* regretting their intimate little interlude last night.

When the silence lengthened again, she realized it was her turn to speak. "All right. Thanks." Her reply came out stiffer and more abrupt than she intended.

He noticed.

"Look, Laura, I need to keep some distance while this is an active investigation. Company policy. But once Darcy is home and the case is over, that rule won't apply . . . unless you want it to."

Meaning he wanted to see her after this was

resolved—in a nonprofessional capacity. Her spirits lifted a notch. "I think we could dispense with the rule at that point."

"I'll look forward to that. Now, I'm off to relieve Connor, who no doubt has a hot date tonight."

That's right. It was Valentine's Day.

"I'm sorry you have to spend the evening sitting in a cold car."

She heard him sigh. "Me too. I can think of other places I'd rather be." A spark of energy crackled over the line, and Laura's heart skipped a beat. "However, I'll console myself with the hope of a better Valentine's Day next year. I'll be in touch."

"Okay. I'll keep my cell with me at all times in case you have any news."

The line went dead, and Laura slowly depressed the end button, visions of cupid dancing in her head.

"Excuse me . . ."

Clearing her throat, she composed her face and turned toward the patron, who held up a book with a porch swing on the cover.

"I wanted to thank you for helping me find this. I had no idea what project might catch my fancy, but this"—he tapped the photo of the swing—"will be the perfect gift for my wife's birthday. We courted on a swing just like this." The tips of the man's ears pinkened as he tucked the book under his arm. "Next stop—pick up a bouquet of roses for my valentine." With a wave, he headed toward the checkout desk.

Laura smiled as she watched him disappear. Ten minutes ago, she would have felt melancholy—and sorry for herself—at such an expression of sentiment. Now, she felt hopeful.

This year's Valentine's Day might be a bust.

But with a certain PI waiting in the wings, next year might be a whole different story.

18

Stifling a yawn, Dev shook a handful of smoked almonds into his hand and tossed them into his mouth.

Some Valentine's Day dinner.

He snagged the bottle of water from the Explorer's cup holder, took a swig, and watched a cloud of breath form in front of his face. Too bad he hadn't included a second thermos of hot coffee in his gear for the night—or rationed the one he'd brought instead of finishing it off forty-five minutes ago. He angled his wrist until the LED display on his watch came into view. Four hours since he'd relieved Connor of surveillance duty, eight to go.

It was going to be a long, cold night, even with the heat packs in his pockets, the Gore-Tex clothing, and the electric blanket plugged into the cigarette lighter.

Leaning to his right, he grabbed the night-vision binoculars from the seat beside him and fitted them to his eyes. All was quiet, which seemed to be par for the course. He'd recorded zero activity all evening in the case log beside him. According to Connor, the man had arrived home about four-thirty, and he hadn't budged or had any visitors since.

Their subject was spending a quiet Valentine's Day too.

As Dev swept the binoculars toward the alley, headlights suddenly appeared. A moment later, a slate-colored Nissan Maxima rolled into view. He focused on the license plate.

Hamilton.

Dev's pulse took an uptick as he set the binoculars back on the passenger seat, flipped the switch that would cut off all exterior lights on the SUV, and turned the key in the ignition. It was possible the daycare manager had a late-night rendezvous with a Valentine's Day date, but he'd lay odds the man with the chapped hands didn't have romance on his mind at this hour of the night. Most people who'd put in a full week of work were thinking sleep by eleven o'clock, not going out to start an evening of socializing.

The Maxima paused at the exit of the alley, then moved onto the street, heading west.

Dev shoved the blanket out of his way and fell in behind him, keeping a prudent distance between them on the deserted, snow-packed side streets. If Hamilton spotted him, future surveillance would prove fruitless. The man would be on guard constantly.

After several turns, Hamilton emerged onto Jefferson Avenue. Was he heading for the highway access point a short distance away?

Dev had his answer a few minutes later when the man edged into the lane for the entrance ramp of westbound I-44.

This was getting interesting.

Once Hamilton turned left and accelerated onto the ramp, Dev increased the pressure on his gas pedal and flipped on his lights. It would be more difficult to keep the man in view on the highway, but with the additional traffic there'd also be less risk of getting spotted.

At the top of the ramp, Dev caught sight of the Maxima two cars ahead, traveling at a fast clip. The man either had a heavy foot or was in a hurry to get somewhere.

As they traveled west, Dev varied the distance between them, keeping one or two cars as a buffer. Whenever the traffic thinned, he dropped back.

Five minutes out of downtown, flashing lights caught his attention ahead. Most likely it was a spinout on the still-icy roads. He slowed his speed to match that of the cars around him.

Flares and cones reduced the traffic flow to a single lane, but with just one car separating him from Hamilton, Dev had no problem keeping him in sight as they approached the floodlit accident site.

At least he didn't until one of the cops working the scene stepped in front of the car preceding him, held up a hand, and motioned the wrecker with a mangled car attached to it into the traffic lane.

Muttering a word that wasn't pretty, Dev tightened his grip on the wheel as the taillights on Hamilton's car melted into the night and disappeared.

Talk about rotten timing.

A full minute passed while the driver of the wrecker jockeyed the vehicle back and forth, and Dev felt his blood pressure inch toward combustion level. Could the man move any slower?

He drummed his fingers on the wheel, compressing his lips into a thin line. For someone who'd once tailed a suspected terrorist bomber through the teeming streets of New York City without losing him, he'd made a pathetic showing tonight.

But maybe, just maybe, he'd be able to catch up to Hamilton.

By the time the cop waved the traffic through and Dev could pick up speed, however, he knew it was a lost cause. The road was deserted, and Hamilton had been pushing the speed limit. He was probably long gone.

Still, he continued west for five more minutes . . . hoping.

But the daycare center manager had vanished.

Giving up the chase at last, he exited and retraced his route to Hamilton's house to await the man's return. If nothing else, he could determine how long their subject was gone.

Unfortunately, that wasn't going to answer the key question.

Where had Mark Hamilton gone at such a late hour on this cold winter night?

"Turn right, one hundred yards."

As the British-accented voice of his GPS guided him the last quarter of a mile to his destination, Mark surveyed the snow-covered terrain. The quiet neighborhood was exactly what he'd expected after studying the aerial and street views on Google maps.

"Turn right."

Following the GPS prod, he discovered that the hill he'd seen on his computer screen was longer and steeper than the imagery had suggested. It also contained patches of ice. No other drivers were on the road, and only a few cars were parked on either side.

Perfect.

He made the climb slowly, as if he was just being a cautious driver.

"You have reached your destination."

Mark slowed even more as he approached the small bungalow on his left with the attached one-car garage—the one the address on Darcy's driver's permit had guided him to. There was no external lighting except for low-wattage dawn-to-dusk lanterns on either side of the front door, and the house was dark inside; her half sister must be asleep.

Also perfect.

He passed Laura's house, drove to the end of the cul-de-sac, and started back. Two houses before hers, he eased onto the side of the road, parked, and killed his lights.

Once more, he inspected the slumbering neighborhood. He'd wait awhile, perhaps as long as an hour, to be certain there was no unexpected activity.

Then he'd make his move.

He turned off the engine, reached for the thermos beside him, and poured a cup of tea. The unaccustomed late night and delayed bedtime would take a toll tomorrow, but it was Saturday; he could compensate by sleeping in. After all the trouble she'd caused, Darcy could wait an extra couple of hours for her breakfast.

Resting one arm on the wheel as he drank his tea, he thought through his plan again, twisting around to eyeball the equipment on the seat behind him. No matter which form of entry he chose after he scoped out the place, he was covered. Once inside, he'd do the job and get out fast.

A mirthless grin twisted his lips. There wasn't much he was grateful for from his old life, but he'd picked up a few questionable skills in his younger years that came in handy on occasion.

He settled back in his seat as the cold outside air began to seep inside, stealing the warmth from the car.

But that wasn't a problem.

After setting his tea in the cup holder, he zipped his thermal jacket all the way to the neck and tugged on fleece-lined gloves. He'd been cold many times in the past, with only a red nose and the sniffles to show for it.

Tonight's payoff, however, would be worth the discomfort.

Because come tomorrow, if all went as he hoped, Laura would either be far too distracted to bother him anymore and would let the search for Darcy lapse—or she'd be out of the picture altogether.

Either alternative suited him just fine.

Where was Mark?

Darcy wiped her damp palms down her baggy slacks as she paced.

Ten feet one way.

Ten feet the other way.

Repeat.

Why hadn't he delivered her breakfast and lunch? He always came through the door with food by six-ten. It was now eight-thirty. Nor had she heard the muted sound of running water in the pipes that always signaled his rising.

What was going on? Had he decided to . . .

Wait.

She stopped, frowning. It was hard to keep track of the days down here, but this was Saturday, wasn't it? Maybe he followed a different routine on the weekends.

Combing her fingers through her hair, she fought back a wave of panic. Two hours ago, she'd been psyched up to carry out her plan. When he hadn't shown, however, the adrenaline rush had subsided. Now she was just plain scared.

But fear was her enemy. She had to keep it at bay. Had to be positive. Had to continue believing the plan would work despite the delay.

Because this was her only chance of escape.

It *had* to work.

Forcing down the flutters in her stomach, she resumed pacing and listening.

Five minutes later, she heard the muffled sound of water rushing through the pipes. A toilet was flushing.

Her adrenaline surged.

This was it.

Heart hammering, she scurried toward the bathroom. Once inside, she turned on the shower, raised the water temperature to hot, and exited, pulling the door closed behind her except for a six-inch crack. Then she took up her position beside the door that led into the main part of the basement, crouching down as far as possible, flattening herself against the wall, praying she was hidden from the peephole lens. She had to be invisible to him for this to work.

As the minutes ticked by, steam began to seep through the bathroom door, just as she'd planned.

If all went well, Mark would see the steam through the peephole and assume she was taking a shower. He'd never think she was lying in wait, ready to spring at his legs, knock him to the floor, and sprint toward safety.

Please, God, let this work so I can save Laura—and maybe myself.

Faith edged into a parking spot in front of Mark's house, shut off the engine, and shoved the pan of fresh-baked cinnamon rolls on the seat beside her farther away. Normally the savory aroma would set off a rumble in her stomach, but this morning it made her more nauseous than hungry.

What if Mark didn't appreciate her early visit, despite the homemade offering she'd risen at 5:00 a.m. to bake?

What if he was sleeping in and she woke him up?

What if he thought she was being too forward?

But what else could she do? No matter what she tried at work, to him she was nothing more than an employee. Even the hand lotion hadn't helped change that perception, though he was using it. She could smell the faint fragrance whenever he passed her in the hall. Since a personal gift like that hadn't worked, however, this was her only option.

She picked up the pan of rolls and juggled it in her hands. Best case, he'd invite her in to share them over a cup of coffee. That would be a great way to start a Saturday morning.

If he wasn't pleased . . . well, she'd be no worse off than she was now.

Weighing the pan in her hands, she took a deep breath.

Just do it!

Following that prompt, she reached for the door handle—but when her pulse leapt, she dropped her hand. She needed to let her heart settle down and get her respiration under control.

Once she calmed down, though, she was going to march right up to that door and deliver her gift.

Come what may.

Laura stifled a yawn, slid behind the wheel of her car, and tossed her purse on the seat beside her.

It was only nine in the morning, and already she felt as if she'd put in a full day.

But that's what you got when you tossed most of the night, every night, for more than a week.

Fortunately, she didn't have anything more pressing on her agenda today than a trip to the grocery store and dry cleaner. Then she'd put in a few hours on the web, doing her own search for information on Mark Hamilton and Faith Bradley. There wasn't much chance she'd unearth anything Nikki hadn't already found, but it was better than sitting around doing nothing while others searched for Darcy.

She turned the key in the ignition, pressed the button for the garage opener, and waited while the door rolled up. Sun streamed in the opening, reflecting off the snow, and she squinted against the glare as she backed out slow and easy. With all the icy patches on her driveway, she could find herself sliding into the mailbox and having to deal with a dented fender if she wasn't careful. That was one complication she didn't need, with everything else going on.

A glance in both directions confirmed the street was deserted, and she backed onto the pavement, swinging the wheel to her left at the end of the drive. A flicker on the dashboard caught her eye as she applied her brakes, and she dropped her gaze to the brake warning light, frowning. Now what?

Pausing in the middle of the street, she regarded

the light. It could be an electronic glitch, like when the alternator light had begun blinking on and off last year for no apparent reason. Still . . . she'd have to get it checked out, just in case.

One more chore to add to her list.

With a sigh, she shifted from reverse to drive. The best plan might be to swing by the garage on the way to the grocery store, see if they could take a quick look. If the fates were kind, it would be some minor connection thing, similar to the alternator light problem—a minor nuisance that could be ignored until she was ready to have it fixed.

Accelerating slowly on the flat stretch of the street at the top of the hill, she started and stopped a few times. The light came on whenever she applied pressure to the brakes, but as far as she could tell, they were working fine.

The tension in her shoulders eased a notch, and she moved forward, doing her best to avoid the icy patches on the road. That was the one downside to her off-the-beaten-path neighborhood —the snowplows and salt trucks gave it low priority. A couple of quick passes, that's all they'd made during the blizzard. On the plus side, her cul-de-sac was in far better shape than the untouched residential streets in the city like the one Mark Hamilton called home.

She dodged another patch of ice as her thoughts drifted to Dev. Was he still there, or had he handed off the surveillance to one of his partners? She hoped it was the latter. But since she hadn't heard from him, he must have spent a long, cold night with nothing to show for it. She hoped he was now asleep under a thick comforter, all warm and toasty.

A smile flirted with her lips as that image materialized in her mind . . . but she forced herself to erase it. There'd be time for that kind of daydreaming down the road, once Darcy was home and the case was closed.

After skirting a slippery-looking spot, she looked down the hill toward the main road. There were a few more patches of ice to negotiate, but in general it was clearer than the upper section by her house.

She started down the hill, picking up too much speed too quickly, given the marginal driving conditions. Pressing on the brake, she waited for the car to slow.

Instead, it continued to accelerate.

Her pulse ratcheted up, and she tightened her grip on the wheel, pushing as hard as she could on the brake.

The car slowed a tiny bit this time—but not enough.

Apparently the warning light had been significant after all.

As her speed continued to increase, panic squeezed the air from her lungs. In less than ten seconds, she was going to shoot past the stop sign at the end of her street and onto the busy thoroughfare below—straight into traffic.

People could be killed.

Including her.

Think, Laura!

Heart pounding, she forced her brain to engage.

What about pumping the brakes, or slowly applying the emergency brake?

She tried both.

Pumping did nothing. The emergency brake had a small impact, but there was no way the car was going to stop before she reached the bottom.

Now what?

If she jerked the wheel to the left, she might be able to get the car to rotate around and face the opposite, uphill direction. Or she could aim for the empty lot near the bottom of the street and hope she didn't plow into the house on the far side of it.

Neither option was optimal—but both were better than barreling onto the main road.

The lot was coming up fast on her right. Twist the wheel and hope to reverse the direction of the car, or head for the open ground?

Wait . . . the lot wasn't an option. There was too much snow and ice piled along the edge of the road, blocking her access. If she went that way, it would be like plowing into a brick wall.

That left her one choice.

She jerked the wheel hard to the left. The back of the car swung around toward the bottom of the hill, just as she'd hoped.

Except it kept going, even as she straightened out the wheel.

The car was sliding on a patch of ice.

Laura tried to counter the spin, calling up every defensive driving tip she'd ever learned. But nothing worked as her Civic careened across the road, directly toward a telephone pole.

She sucked in a deep breath and did her best to brace for the impact.

Yet she still wasn't prepared for the heart-jarring jolt of the impact or the cacophony of crushing metal and splintering glass or the sudden explosion in her face.

But the chaos was short-lived.

Because everything suddenly went black.

Mark added a sprig of parsley to the scrambled eggs and set the plate on the tray next to a small bowl of fresh fruit. He'd fix Darcy's lunch later, since he'd be home all day. He might even eat with her. She needed more time to adjust to her new situation, but leaving her locked up and alone for too long wasn't wise. Solitary confinement could mess with a person's mind, and that wasn't his goal. He just wanted to keep her from making any more mistakes and falling into the kind of destructive lifestyle that had killed Lil.

He retrieved the key from the hook on the wall, picked up the tray, and started down the steps, sparing the freezers behind him a quick glance as he reached the bottom. Those were his failures.

Darcy would be his redemption.

At the entrance to her room, he stopped to look through the peephole. The bathroom door was cracked open, and steam was seeping out. She must be in the shower. No problem. Clean was good. He'd leave her breakfast so it was waiting when she came out.

Balancing the tray in one hand, he fitted the key in the lock, turned it, then tucked it away. At least he was calmer today. After the visit from that PI yesterday, he'd been furious at Darcy, convinced she'd lied to him. But when he'd confronted her and recounted what had happened, he'd seen surprise, not deceit, in her eyes . . . giving credence to her claim that she hadn't expected anyone to expend a lot of effort searching for her.

That was a huge relief. He hated being lied to. Hated having his trust violated. Hated having his hopes dashed time and again.

But Darcy hadn't done that.

Everything was going to be okay.

He twisted the knob, stepped into the room—and suddenly found himself pitching forward, eggs and fruit flying in all directions.

What the . . . !

He reached forward, arms flailing, his brain processing what had happened even as he fell.

Darcy had ambushed him—and once again shattered his dream of redemption.

As he slammed against the floor, one hand landing in a mass of slippery scrambled egg, he spewed out his anger and anguish in the bellow of a single word.

"N-o-o-o-!"

Mark's furious roar echoing in her ears, Darcy took off for the basement stairs, running as fast as her shaky legs could carry her.

She had to get to the first floor. Had to slam the door and secure the flip-type safety lock at the top of the basement stairs. Had to run for the front door, escape, and sprint for the nearest car, person, or major street she could find.

Everything had to work perfectly—or she was dead.

She clambered up the stairs, missing one, her breath coming in short, choppy gasps. Behind her, a spew of vulgarity burned her ears as Mark scrambled to regain his footing.

Adrenaline pumping, she increased her speed.

At the top of the stairs, she pushed through the door, spun around—and found Mark taking the steps two at a time.

She slammed the door. Fumbled with the lock.

Please, God, please help me!

The mechanism slipped into place.

As Mark tried the knob and began pounding on the door, she took off for the living room.

The pounding gave way to kicking.

Fear humming through her nerve endings, Darcy reached the front door, grasped the handle, and pulled.

The door didn't budge.

She flipped the lock and tried again.

Nothing.

There must be a dead bolt too.

Wood splinted behind her, and she jerked around. He'd kicked through the bottom of the door.

At this rate, he'd be free in moments.

She hesitated. The only other exit was the back door, and she'd have to go directly past Mark to get there. Plus, it could be dead bolted too. Should she risk it?

The decision was taken out of her hands an instant later when the bottom panel of the door splintered.

A sob caught in her throat.

No!

She couldn't come this close and fail.

What about the living room window? Maybe she could open it and climb through. It wasn't much of a drop to the ground.

She ran to the middle of the front wall and yanked at the cord on the miniblinds that hid the interior of the house from the eyes of the world. She had them halfway up the tall, narrow living room window when more wood splintered behind her.

With a gasp, she spun around to find Mark climbing through the lower half of the door. He'd be on her in seconds.

There was no time to get the window up.

But she might be able to break it and yell for help.

Desperation tightening her chest, she scanned the room. It was bare of clutter and ornamentation except for the decorative fireplace tools that had never touched a fleck of ash, set to one side of the mantel. Her gaze locked in on the poker. That would work.

She let go of the cord on the blinds. They crashed down behind her as she dashed for the poker.

But by the time she grabbed it and turned, he was already on the threshold of the room, mere steps away.

She raised the poker above her head as she faced him.

His chest was heaving, just as hers was. His shirt was torn, and an angry gash on his arm was seeping blood as he glared at her from across the room.

"Put down the poker, Darcy." His tone was icy. Controlled.

"No." He walked toward her, and she tightened her grip. "Stay back."

He kept coming, circling around the couch, toward the fireplace where she stood.

She edged away, moving backward toward the front door.

He stopped.

So did she.

"You're just like all the others." His voice was flat. "Too stubborn to let anyone help you. Just like Lil."

Darcy stared at him. Lil? Was there another girl down in the freezers?

Her mouth went dry, and she moistened her lips. Mark might be crazy, but his eyes had always seemed lucid. Not anymore. Now they looked . . . odd. Disconnected from reality. Focused on some view only he could see.

She had to get out of here. Fast.

Swallowing past her fear, she tightened her grip on the poker. She was only going to get one swing at him; it had to do the job. Even if she merely stunned him, it would give her a chance to open or break the window. After that, she'd . . .

His next move was so sudden, so unexpected there was no way she could have guessed his intent.

One second, he was staring at her, hands at his sides.

Then, in the blink of an eye, he bent down,

grabbed the corner of the throw rug where she stood, and yanked.

Her feet went out from under her and she crashed to the floor, falling hard on her back.

And as the poker flew from her grasp, as Mark loomed over her, Darcy knew she was going to die.

19

When the BlackBerry on his nightstand began to beep with the piercing, high-pitched ring tone he always used while sleeping after an all-night surveillance gig, Dev groaned, groped for the phone with one hand, and squinted at his watch with the other. Nine-thirty in the morning.

Meaning he'd logged all of two hours' sleep since falling into bed.

He tried to focus on caller ID. Connor? The very man who'd relieved him of surveillance duty two and a half hours ago?

This better be good.

Stabbing the talk button, he rolled onto his back. "Yeah?"

"Good morning to you too."

"I was up all night, remember? You may be able to survive on three hours' sleep, but not all of us are wired that way. What's up?"

"There's been some activity down here I thought you might find interesting."

"Okay." He stared at the ceiling, trying to kick-start his brain, wishing he had a cup of coffee in hand.

"You awake enough to hear about it?"

"Yeah." That was a lie. He forced himself to sit up, hoping the change in position would accelerate the flow of blood to his brain. "Go ahead."

"Faith Bradley showed up this morning, bearing gifts. I recognized her from the shot Nikki found on her Facebook page."

That helped wake him up. "Go on."

"She sat in her car in front of the house for about ten minutes. I figured she was going to pull the same stunt you observed—watch for a while, then drive away. But this time she got out carrying what looked like a plate of homemade cinnamon rolls. I zeroed in on them with the telephoto lens while I snapped a few shots of her. Man, did they make my mouth water."

Dev rolled his eyes. "You want to stick to the story?"

His colleague's chuckle came over the line. "I always forget what a grouch you are when you're tired."

"Yeah, well, I'm reminding you. Go on."

"She started up the walk. I was snapping some close-ups—of her, not the cinnamon rolls—when she stopped all of a sudden. She was staring straight ahead, and I switched over to the house to see what had grabbed her attention. I caught the tail end of the blinds dropping down in the front window—blinds that hadn't been open moments before. She did a 180 and almost ran back toward her car."

Dev swung his legs to the floor and stood, his mind now firing on all cylinders. "She saw something that startled her."

"That would be my guess. So, top-notch PI that I am, I decided to try a little pretext."

Knowing Connor, this ought to be entertaining. "You have my full attention."

"I tore a page out of my surveillance log and hotfooted it down the street. She was nearly to her car by the time I intercepted her. Up close, it was obvious she was shaken and upset."

Dev planted a fist on his hip. "What did you say?"

"I told her I was trying to track down my sister, who was supposed to be at a party in the neighborhood last night but hadn't come home yet and my mom was worried. Except I couldn't read my mom's handwriting and I wasn't sure I had the last digit right. So did she happen to know if there'd been a party at Hamilton's house, since I'd seen her coming down the walk?"

Dev tried to follow the logic of his approach. Failed. "And the point was . . . ?"

"The truth? It was a stab in the dark. I said the first thing that came to mind, hoping she might drop me a few crumbs about Hamilton or mention what she'd seen in the window."

"Did she?"

"Yep. On both counts. She said she hadn't thought the guy who lived there socialized a lot or had many parties, but she must be wrong because she'd just seen a girl at the window. That's why she was leaving. She didn't want to disturb him."

Dev's pulse spiked. "Did you get a description of the girl?"

"I did, on the excuse it might be my sister. No go. The girl in the window had short dark hair."

Not what he wanted to hear. "Sounds like Hamilton might have a girlfriend."

"I could run plates for the cars in the alley near his house and in front, then track down the driver's license info and photos of the owners. We might find a young woman who fits Faith's description of the person she saw."

"Not a bad idea." IDing the girl in the window would give them another avenue to pursue for more info on the reticent daycare center manager. "But we'll lose surveillance on the front or back while you're getting numbers on the opposite side of the house."

"You want to come back down and do the recon?"

"No." He wiped a hand down his face. "I need some shut-eye. What's Cal doing today?"

"He and Moira were planning to extend their

Valentine's celebration by sleeping late, going to a brunch in the Central West End, and taking in the new exhibit at the art museum."

"When did he tell you all this?"

"He didn't. I overheard Nikki asking him about his weekend plans."

Dev paced to the window and frowned at the snow. He was still chilled from his all-night stint in the Explorer. Going back out into the cold held zero appeal. "Why don't you call and ask him if he could spare an hour to run down there before they go to brunch? It wouldn't be that much of a detour."

"Uh-uh. This is your case, and I want to stay on friendly terms with him—and his new wife. You call."

Dev huffed out a breath. "He just got back from his honeymoon. They've been together for almost two weeks. You don't think he could tear himself away from Moira for an hour?"

"Let's see. Spend the day with a gorgeous woman doing fun things or wander around slushy streets reading license plates? I can understand how that might be a hard choice."

"Very funny." He crossed the room toward his closet. "Fine. I'll check the plates. Look for me in thirty minutes. Maybe forty-five."

"Get some coffee on the way."

"Trust me, it's on the top of my list. Is Faith still there?"

341

"No. She made a fast exit after we talked."

He pulled a pair of jeans off a hanger. "What's your take on her visit—and her reaction to the other woman?"

"The same as yours, I assume. She's got the hots for Hamilton, was trying to impress him with the way-to-a-man's-heart-is-through-his-stomach ploy, and got blindsided when she found another female in his house at this hour of the morning."

"Yeah." He pulled a sweatshirt out of his dresser. Gave it a sniff. Passable. But one of these days—soon—he had to do some laundry. "That means she's been noticing Hamilton, paying attention to stuff an ordinary co-worker wouldn't. I wonder if she'd offer us any interesting insights if Cal paid her a visit on some pretext and did a little digging?"

"Couldn't hurt to give it a shot . . . but wait until later today, okay?"

"Yeah, yeah." He pawed through his sock drawer, looking for two that matched. "I'll call you with the license numbers."

"I'll be here. I've already got the ones I can see with the binoculars on the street in front of his house. I just need a few that are blocked and the ones in the alley that are in reasonable proximity to his place."

"I'm on it."

After dumping the phone and his clothes on the bed, Dev padded toward the bathroom, rubbing his jaw. He needed a shave, but niceties like that would have to wait. The cars parked in front of and behind Hamilton's place could disappear at any moment, and if one of them held a clue to the identity of the woman inside his house, he didn't want to risk missing it. If she was close enough friends with Hamilton to be in his house early on Saturday morning—or had perhaps been there all night—she might also know what he knew about Darcy.

And with eight days elapsed since Laura's half sister had run away . . . with the trail growing colder by the hour . . . they needed every bit of information they could dredge up if they wanted to find the missing teen and bring this case to the best possible conclusion.

Mark pounded the edge of the snow shovel against the patch of ice on his front sidewalk. Once. Twice. Three times. Hard. Harder. Hardest.

When it finally cracked, he jammed the shovel under the ice, hefted the jagged chunks, and hurled them onto the lawn.

Ice, he could break.

People and habits . . . much more difficult to handle.

He'd failed with Lil. Failed with Angela. Failed with Denise. Now he'd failed with Darcy.

He couldn't save anybody.

Lifting the shovel, he tightened his grip and

slammed the edge against another patch of ice. The impact reverberated through his body—just like the ramifications of his latest failure.

Because this failure, unlike the others, had complications.

If Laura had survived her trip down the hill this morning, she might eventually come looking for her sister again, despite what Darcy seemed to believe. On the flip side, other than the busybody volunteer who'd noticed him talking to the girl at the homeless shelter, there was nothing to tie them together and no reason for anyone to suspect she was, at this very moment, locked in his basement apartment.

Besides, she wouldn't be there long—only until he decided how to handle the situation. She might still serve a purpose if he needed to deal with the sister.

Once again, he scooped up the shattered fragments of ice and flung them onto the lawn. The abraded skin on his arm stung as the edges peeking out under the bandage rubbed against the sleeve of his shirt, and he clenched his teeth. When his vision blurred, he froze.

Were those tears in his eyes?

Yes.

And they had nothing to do with the pain in his arm.

Their source was much, much older than that.

He lifted a gloved hand and swiped the back of

it across his eyes as his legs grew shaky. What was going on? He'd stopped crying two decades ago, after learning the harsh lesson that tears never helped. Ever. Instead, they'd made things worse. That's why he'd learned to control them, to cultivate logic and pragmatism over emotions and feelings. And that approach had served him well, allowed him to survive. Changing course now would leave him adrift.

Yet he felt as if he was drifting, anyway.

Fear snaked through him, and he forced himself to take some deep breaths. Things would be okay. He'd get through this, just like he'd gotten through all the other bad stuff in his life. He'd do what he had to do to survive and never look back. And someday, down the road, he'd find the one he could save—and who would, in turn, save him.

In the meantime, he'd do what he always did. He'd focus on the children at Davis Daycare. They depended on him, and he'd do everything he could to make certain they got a happy, nurturing start in life. He'd see that they were cuddled and cared for and listened to and fed and covered with a warm blanket when they slept— all the things that gave a child comfort and security and a sense of safety.

All the things he'd never been able to count on Lil to provide.

A gust of icy wind swept past, and he began to tremble. But the cold wasn't to blame for his case of the shakes. The shudders rolling through him were Lil's fault.

Just as they'd been in the old days.

He clung to the handle of the shovel, using it for support as the memories he'd locked away began to crash over him, seeping around the edges of the door he'd sealed shut years ago.

Lil in his face, yelling at the top of her voice, telling him he was a worthless piece of garbage.

Lil locking him in the dark closet for every tiny mistake, ranting at his ineptitude, ignoring his hysterical pleas for release.

Lil sending him out to huddle on the back stoop for hours at a time whenever a man showed up with money in his pockets, oblivious as he baked in blistering heat or cowered during torrential, lightning-laced downpours or shivered in frigid winds that whitened his nose and fingers with frostbite.

Lil forcing him to eat dog food after he complained about being hungry.

Lil ordering him to clean up the vomit and urine in the bathroom following particularly wild sessions with one of her men.

He closed his eyes and swallowed, trying to ignore the itching in his fingers as he rode out the wave of nausea.

Just like in the old days.

But that wasn't the real Lil. He knew that. Had always known that. She hadn't been mean and vindictive and heartless deep inside. On the rare days she wasn't drunk or high or entertaining men, she'd been a loving mother.

He'd lived for those days.

Treasured them.

Especially his eighth birthday.

A smile flickered at his lips. That had been his best day ever. She'd remembered to get him a cake and a present. The baseball cards had disintegrated through the years from too much handling, but the greeting card that said "Happy Birthday to My Dear Son" had survived.

Moisture gathered in his eyes again, distorting his view of the world, and he swiped it away. All of his days would have been like that one if he could have saved her, if he could have convinced her she didn't need the booze or the drugs or the sex. They were the real culprit.

But she'd never listened.

And so she'd died—unredeemed.

He straightened up, lifted the shovel, and circled around the house toward the garage in the back. The path was restored now and in excellent condition, thanks to his efforts.

And somewhere, some misguided girl who was about the age Lil had been when she made her first mistakes, would be too. Also thanks to him.

It wasn't going to be Darcy—but he'd start looking again soon.

After he took care of his latest error in judgment.

Dev punched in Connor's number as he approached Hamilton's street. His partner picked up on the first ring. "You have a pen and paper handy? I'm a block away. I'll read off license plates as I drive by."

"Yeah. By the way, you just missed our friend. He came out to tackle the snow on the walk—and I do mean tackle. I'm surprised the shovel survived. The ice he was hacking at sure didn't."

"You picked up anger?"

"His body language spelled it in capital letters. And there were a couple of very nasty scratches on his face. I took a few tight shots of him and downloaded them to my computer. It looks like someone dragged fingernails over his cheek."

Suspicious.

Dev swung onto Hamilton's street and slowed as he approached the house. "Any sign of the girl?"

"No."

"Get ready to write."

After reading off the plate numbers for the cars near Hamilton's house, he turned the corner and passed the white van with the magnetic Sullivan Heating and Cooling sign on the side—Connor's home for the day.

He peered in as he drove past, but his partner was hidden behind the privacy windows tinted even darker than those in the Explorer. "I'd wave, but you wouldn't see me."

"I appreciate the thought, though."

"I'm doing the alley on foot. I'll call you after I have the numbers."

Dev slipped the phone back into its holster and passed the alley, parking half a block away. After setting the brake, he reached for the hard hat and clipboard props on the passenger seat. Once he'd donned the hat and a pair of dark sunglasses, he slid out of the car, locked it, and took the short hike to the alley, periodically pausing to look up at the electric poles and scribble gibberish on his clipboard.

Ten minutes later, he was back in the Explorer. Once again, Connor answered on the first ring.

"I only saw one car parked anywhere close to Hamilton's." He recited the number and set the clipboard beside him. "I think it was parked too far away to be relevant, but it can't hurt to run it."

"I'll add it to the list. The first two I ran weren't a match. I got a twenty-year-old male and a seventy-two-year-old woman. I'll run the rest and let you know what I find. You still thinking about asking Cal to contact Faith?"

"Unless I can figure out a way to do it myself. But I'll wait until later to call him."

"Smart man. So are you heading home to crash again?"

"The sooner the better. Call me if anything else

interesting . . ." A double beep sounded on the line. "Gotta run. I have a call coming in. Talk to you later."

He scanned the unfamiliar number. Take it, or let the call roll to voice mail? As he debated the question, he pulled onto Jefferson and aimed for the highway, following the same route Hamilton had taken last night. Might as well answer. It would save him having to return the call later.

He put the phone to his ear. "Devlin."

"James Devlin?" A woman's voice.

"Yes."

"This is Carolyn Mitchell from St. Luke's Hospital emergency room. A patient was brought in about forty-five minutes ago who doesn't seem to have any next of kin available, but she mentioned your name. We found your card in her purse. Do you know a Laura Griffith?"

Dev's pulse kicked into high gear, and he pressed harder on the accelerator. "Yes. What happened?"

"She was in a car accident."

Dev sucked in a breath. "How bad is it?"

"The doctor's still evaluating her."

At the woman's evasive answer, his lips settled into a grim line. Unfortunately, that was the best he was going to get, thanks to HIPAA rules. If he wanted more information, he'd have to show up in person.

His new top priority.

"I'll be there in thirty minutes."

Tossing the phone on the seat beside him, he swung onto the highway entrance ramp, merged into traffic, and floored it.

As he dodged around cars, he forced the left side of his brain to engage. If the accident was bad enough to send her to the hospital, it was more than a fender bender. But the fact that Laura had mentioned his name meant she was conscious—and perhaps a sign her injuries weren't serious.

Barreling west, he clung to that hope during his twenty-nine-minute race to St. Luke's ER.

Once in the parking lot, he made a hard right into a space near the entrance and strode inside. Before the woman behind the intake desk had a chance to launch into her usual spiel, he glowered at her and cut to the chase.

"Carolyn Mitchell called me about a patient who was brought in a little over an hour ago. Laura Griffith. I need to see her. The name's Devlin."

As a PI, he didn't often pull the intimidating stance he'd perfected in his ATF days out of mothballs, but it came in handy when he needed fast action . . . and cooperation.

As usual, it worked.

The woman rose and took a step back. "I'll get Carolyn for you."

Sixty seconds later, another woman with short, black hair appeared and held out her hand. "Mr. Devlin, I'm—"

"Carolyn Mitchell." He squeezed her fingers as he finished the introduction for her, motioning with his free hand to the secure door that led to the treatment rooms. "I need to see Laura."

She gave him a quick once-over, then pressed a button on the wall beside her. The door swung open. "She's in room four. We told her you were on the way."

"Thanks."

The door to room four was partly closed as he approached, and he stopped at the threshold to take a long, slow breath before he knocked. "Laura?"

"Come in." Her voice sounded strong and alert.

The tension in his shoulders ebbed.

Thank you, God.

But once he pushed through the door and rounded the curtain that hid her from view, the uptick in his mood dropped back a few notches.

Her pallor was alarming. There was also an angry red burn mark on the left side of her face and traces of white powder in her hair, suggesting a frontal collision strong enough to deploy her airbag. Her left wrist sported an elastic bandage. A sheet covered the rest of her, hiding any additional damage.

She managed a strained smile. "Hi."

He moved beside the bed, trying to mask his concern with an answering smile of his own. Too bad his lips wouldn't cooperate. "You don't look as if you've had the best Saturday morning of your life."

"Not even close. I'm just sorry you got dragged into this. I know you want to keep our personal and professional lives separate until Darcy's found." She tugged the sheet higher and played with the edge. "I was kind of out of it after the crash, and I guess I mentioned your name. The hospital called you before I could stop them."

"I'm glad they did." He gestured toward her prone form and braced for bad news. "So what's the verdict?"

"Not too bad. Slightly sprained wrist, assorted bruises, small burn from the air bag." She lifted her hand to indicate her face. "The doctor did say I might be achy for a few days too."

No maybe about it. If the air bag had deployed, she'd sustained a sizeable jolt. But she'd recover from that. The news was much better than he'd expected. "Tylenol will help."

"That's what the doctor said." She shifted in the bed and grimaced. "A double dose."

She was hurting . . . and the urge to touch her, to soothe away her pain, to sweep his fingers over her forehead and brush aside the tendrils of hair that had worked loose from her French braid was strong.

Too strong.

Clearing his throat, he jammed his hands in his

pockets to make certain they behaved. "So what happened?"

She sighed. "I wish I knew. My brakes just stopped working as I started down the hill on my street, and I ran into a telephone pole."

Dev frowned. That wasn't what he'd expected to hear. He'd assumed bad roads had been to blame for the accident, that she might have slid on ice and rear-ended another car. This put a different spin on things.

An alert began to beep in his mind.

"Brakes don't give out all of a sudden. Has your warning light been coming on?"

"Not until this morning. I thought it might be another short, like I had with my alternator a couple of years ago. This time it was the real thing."

"Is the car still on the street?"

"As far as I know. It wasn't blocking traffic, so I doubt the police towed it, and I haven't called anyone to haul it away yet. Why?"

"I can recommend a competent body shop. I'd like to have a mechanic I know there look it over, anyway."

She caught her lower lip between her teeth. "What aren't you telling me?"

He hesitated. The last thing he wanted to do was worry her unnecessarily—but the timing of recent events was troublesome. If someone was after her, she needed to be on her guard . . . and a whole lot more careful than usual.

"Let's just say I'm not liking the sequence of events. First Darcy disappears. Then you hire Phoenix to find her. Now your brakes fail on a formidable hill. Attributing that succession of developments to coincidence seems like a stretch. So I'd like to have the mechanic I know check out your brakes with an eye to tampering."

Her complexion went a shade paler, and she wadded the sheet in her fists. "That's a scary thought. You're going to make me paranoid."

"I'll settle for careful rather than paranoid. I hope I'm wrong, but I'd rather err on the side of caution. Is it all right if I call him and have your car towed there?"

"I'll defer to your judgment on this."

"I'd also like to take a look at your garage door after I drive you home."

The offer of a lift seemed to surprise her. "You don't have to drive me home. I can call a friend to come pick me up."

This time he had no trouble summoning up a genuine smile. "I'd like to think I might be in that category soon."

Some color seeped back into her face. "You already are."

"That's the best news I've had all day." At his wink, a soft, appealing blush crept over her cheeks and he cleared his throat. "While they're tending to you, I'm going to call my contact at the body shop and arrange to have your car picked up, check in with my colleague on surveillance duty, and hunt down a megadose of caffeine."

Her eyes widened as she studied him. "I forgot all about the surveillance. You were sleeping when the hospital called, weren't you? They woke you up."

"No, they didn't. I was actually in my car." He could fill her in on the details of his morning excursion later. "How long before they spring you?"

"Less than an hour, according to the nurse who stopped in right before you arrived."

"That will give me plenty of time for a major infusion of caffeine."

"I'm sorry about this, Dev."

"Don't be." His hand came out of his pocket, headed for hers—and there wasn't a thing he could do to stop it. Twining their fingers together, he gave hers a brief squeeze. "There isn't anywhere else I'd rather be. Keep hanging in, okay?"

At the warm smile she gave him in response, his gaze dropped to her lips. Lingered. They were soft . . . full . . . distracting—and they were playing havoc with his self-discipline.

He had to get out of here.

Now.

Tugging his hand free, he moved toward the door, putting a safe distance between them. "I'll be back shortly." Without waiting for a response, he retraced his steps down the hall, pushed through the security door, and aimed for the outside exit, telling himself he'd get better cell reception there.

That was true.

But he also hoped a few lungfuls of the fresh, cold air would clear his mind, help him remember his promise to Cal that he wouldn't get involved with Laura while she was a client. He intended to honor it—but it was getting harder with each day that passed.

Giving him an even more compelling incentive to solve this case and bring Darcy home ASAP.

20

Mark added the last ingredient to the ground beef, shaped it into a patty, sealed it in plastic wrap, and deposited it in the refrigerator. It would last three or four days—long enough for him to determine whether Laura Griffith was still going to be a problem. Either way, the burger would serve his purposes.

He closed the door of the fridge and crossed to the sink. After squirting a liberal amount of soap onto his palm, he cleansed his hands. Then he repeated the ritual and examined them, front and back, in the light from the window.

Thanks to Darcy, the skin was redder and more cracked than it had been in years.

He clenched his fists and pressed his lips together.

The girl had turned out to be nothing but trouble.

But he had a plan now to deal with her—and her sister, if necessary. It had come to him in the shower, where he'd headed as soon as he'd finished shoveling the sidewalk. They had no other family, no one to badger police or hire PIs on their behalf if they both went missing. The plan would take some careful preparation and coordination, but he could do this.

He *had* to do this.

There was no other way to make this problem go away.

He squeezed out some of Faith's lotion and began to massage it into the chapped skin. Within seconds his hands felt better. The stuff might be expensive, but it was worth every penny she'd spent.

Wrinkling his brow, he continued to work the lotion between his fingers. Had he thanked her for the gift? Maybe not. At the time she'd given it to him, he'd been more annoyed than grateful. Tomorrow he'd have to make amends. He'd also have to indulge the stupid crush she had on him just enough to satisfy her silly romantic notions without encouraging her attention. Davis Daycare prided itself on low turnover, and he intended to do his part to maintain that record. It wouldn't kill him to be extra nice to her for a few days.

Besides, depending on how the sister thing played out, he might need her help this week to cover a few absences—and a little attention would ensure her cooperation. Not that he needed to worry a whole lot about that. She already liked him—too much.

Funny how an annoyance had suddenly become an asset.

A tiny smile played at his lips.

Monday was going to be Faith Bradley's lucky day.

"Wow. It's even worse than I thought." Laura stared through the window of the Explorer at the crumpled hood of her car, still wrapped around the telephone pole, as Dev drove past.

He slowed, and she turned toward him in time to see a muscle twitch in his jaw as he inspected the wreck.

"You were very lucky to walk away from that with minor injuries."

"I know." She spared the car one more brief glance, then faced forward. "When is the body shop you called going to tow it away?"

"Within the hour." He crested the hill and a few moments later pulled into her driveway.

"My garage door opener is in my car. We'll have to go in through the front door."

"Okay." He set the brake. "Sit tight while I get your door."

Before she could respond, he was out of the Explorer and circling the hood. Just as well. Aches were already beginning to settle in, and she wasn't averse to a strong arm to hold on to until she was safely inside.

And Dev's arm was too appealing to turn down.

Her door opened, and he held out a hand. "We'll take it slow and easy. Feel free to lean on me."

She put her hand in his. "I'm not usually a leaner."

One side of his mouth hitched up. "I already knew that—but I won't hold it against you if you make an exception today. Ready?"

With a nod, she slid to the ground and tucked her arm in his. As they navigated her frosty walkway, she somehow managed to resist the urge to lean into his solid strength.

At the door, she dug her key out of her purse and inserted it in the lock.

"You need rest, so I'm not going to linger. I'll just take a quick look at your garage, if you'll open the door for me."

He wasn't staying.

She fought down a surge of disappointment and composed her face before she turned to him. "Sure. Do you want to come through this way?"

"No." He stepped back and inclined his head toward the driveway. "I'll wait in front."

"Give me two minutes."

"Don't rush."

With that, he did a 180 and strode back down the walk as if he couldn't get away fast enough. Because he was tired and wanted to go home and sleep . . . or because he was tempted to stay but didn't want to cross the professional/personal line any more than he already had today?

Laura chose to believe the latter.

After closing and locking the front door behind her, she made her way gingerly through the living room and across the kitchen to open the door to the garage. Entering the freezing space, she shivered as she pushed the button for the garage door opener.

Three seconds later Dev's shoes came into view as the door rolled up. The instant it was high enough, he ducked inside, did a quick sweep, and crossed to the small window at the rear.

"Want to tell me what you're looking for?"

"Evidence of forced entry."

A shudder rippled through her that had nothing to do with the frigid air in the garage. "You're thinking someone broke in here and tampered with my brakes?"

"The thought crossed my mind. Brakes don't usually go bad overnight." He stopped in front of the window and examined the latch on the lower sash as she joined him. "Did you know this was unlocked—and not fully closed?"

Did she?

Digging deep, Laura tried to recall the last time she'd paid any attention to the window. Last summer, perhaps? On that hot day when she'd been using her garage as a potting shed for her patio planters?

"I remember opening it back in May to get a cross breeze while I did some gardening stuff. When it started to rain, I lowered the sash. I guess I forgot to lock it." She smoothed a hand over her mangled French braid, feeling like an idiot. "Not too smart, huh?"

She felt even worse when he didn't attempt to reassure her.

"I'm going to take a look outside. Sit tight for a minute."

He disappeared around the side of the garage, appearing a few moments later outside the window. After bending down to examine the ground, he inspected the frame of the window before rejoining her.

"What's the verdict?"

"Inconclusive. The snow along the base of the house is frozen solid, so there aren't any foot-prints. Do your gutters leak?"

"No. But they overflow when they're in desperate need of being cleaned out—which they are. With all my Darcy issues, I never got around to it after the leaves fell in the fall."

"That would explain the icy perimeter. The open

window would provide easy access, and once inside it wouldn't take someone who knew what he was doing very long to tamper with the brakes."

The whole scenario was taking on an air of unreality. "But why would someone do that?"

"Maybe to sideline you—and prevent you from looking for Darcy."

A chill snaked through her, and she wrapped her arms around her body. "Why would someone think a car problem would stop me from searching for my sister?"

He exhaled, his breath creating a ghostlike cloud in the dank, numbing cold of the garage. "It would stop you if you were dead." His voice was quiet, his tone solemn, his expression somber. "That hill could be lethal without brakes."

Laura's heart stuttered as she tried to wrap her mind around the notion that someone might have been trying to kill her.

It didn't compute.

She moistened her lips, fighting the headache beginning to throb in her temples. "Assuming there is a connection between my accident and Darcy's disappearance, there would be no guarantee I'd be . . . killed. Or even have serious injuries. I walked away."

"Sometimes desperate people take chances. They don't always pay off. This one easily could have."

She tried to control the sudden chattering of her

teeth. "I feel like I'm in an old m-melodramatic B movie or something." She swallowed and balled her hands into fists. "Do you think we might be overreacting? I mean, even if someone does have Darcy, it's not like we have any clues to his identity at this point. He's n-not in imminent danger of being discovered."

Dev studied her, as if debating his next move. "I'll tell you what. Let's see what my mechanic friend has to say about the car and we'll go from there. How does that sound?"

"Reasonable."

"Then that's our game plan. I'll have an answer Monday morning. In the meantime, be cautious, keep your doors—and windows—locked, and get some rest. I'll check in periodically, but call me with any concerns or if you need anything."

"Okay."

He crossed to the window and locked it. "Close the door behind me."

Once he stepped outside, she pushed the button to activate the door. As it glided down, she followed his progress down the driveway until he disappeared from view, the quiet drone of the electric motor the only sound in the silent garage.

When at last the door clicked into place and the hum ceased, she returned to the kitchen, closed the door, and flipped the lock. By the time she got to the front window and looked out, Dev was already gone.

But the fear he'd planted in her mind remained —mostly because he'd never answered her question about whether they could be over-reacting.

And if Dev was worried, there was reason for concern . . . even if she didn't want to believe that.

So she'd follow his advice and be extra cautious until they had the results from his mechanic friend. Hopefully, the man would rule out tamper-ing and they could refocus on finding Darcy.

If he didn't . . .

She double-checked the locks on her front door, cradled her aching wrist in her other hand, and headed for the medicine chest in search of Tylenol. She wasn't going to go there yet. For now, she'd remain optimistic.

And do a whole lot of praying.

As the doorbell in her apartment pealed, Faith dropped the basket of laundry she'd lugged upstairs from the community washer and dryer, shoved her hair out of her eyes, and surveyed her spic-and-span living room. Her morning visit to Mark's might have been a disaster, but her apartment had benefited with an early spring cleaning. Her grandmother had been right—the best way to work off strong emotions was to scrub the floor, beat the rugs, and banish the dirt. The sick disappointment prompted by her discovery of Mark's early morning visitor was dissipating, though she was still working out the anger. Another couple of hours of hard cleaning should help.

The apartment was more than presentable enough for an unexpected visitor, however.

Wiping her hands on her jeans, she slid the security chain into the catch and cracked the door.

A tall, attractive guy with dark hair stood on the other side. For some reason he reminded her of the man who'd stopped at work yesterday to talk to Mark. Not in appearance; there was no resemblance between the two men. It was more the way they carried themselves, like they were in charge.

And, like yesterday, that authoritative aura made her nervous for some reason.

"Can I help you?" She wrapped her fingers around the edge of the door.

The guy flashed a glance at her white-knuckled grip, then smiled. "I hope so. I'm sorry to interrupt your Saturday, but my firm is doing some consulting work involving the daycare industry and we're talking with people in the field as part of our research. I understand you work for Davis Daycare, and I hoped you might be able to spare about twenty minutes to answer a few general questions about the industry. My firm is paying seventy-five dollars in cash to every-one who participates."

He passed a business card through the opening. She pried her fingers off the door and took it. According to the card, Jack Ferguson was a senior director of CCD Consulting, based in Chicago.

It seemed legit . . . but it could be a scam. And she wasn't some gullible teenager. She watched the news, read the paper. There were bad characters everywhere, sometimes right under people's noses. Like that story she'd read a few months ago, about the kindly old man who was arrested for molesting children. He'd fooled everyone, even his neighbors. You just never knew these days.

Still . . . seventy-five bucks would be really nice. It would give her Jimmy Choo shoe fund a nice boost. She'd had her eye on those budget-breaking open-toed red spikes for months. At the glacial rate her fund was growing, they'd be discontinued before she could order them.

She fingered the card. "How did you get my name and address?"

"All of the people we're talking with are referrals. Someone must have given your name and phone number to one of our people, and I was asked to contact you. Normally I'd call in advance to set up an interview, but I found your address in the phone directory and since I was in the area, I decided to take a chance you'd be home. I hoped you'd be willing to pick up a few dollars for twenty minutes of shooting the breeze." He gave her that megawatt smile again.

Seventy-five bucks was compelling, no question about it. Why not talk to the man—as long as it was on her terms?

"I'm game. But could we meet at the coffee shop at the corner? It's half a block down on the left. I could be there in ten minutes."

"That works for me. I do a lot of interviews in public places. People often feel more secure there. See you shortly."

With that, he turned away and retraced his steps toward the street.

Faith watched him disappear down the walkway in front of the four-family flat she called home, then read his card again before she tucked it in the pocket of her jeans. Seventy-five bucks for twenty minutes. Not bad.

If she was lucky, maybe he'd spring for a latte too.

She was still alive—but for how long?

From her seated position on the floor, back against the wall, Darcy drew her legs up, wrapped her arms around her knees, and stared at the shackle on her left ankle. Her gaze followed the attached chain six feet to the metal ring tucked in behind the now-empty refrigerator, which had been pulled away from the wall. The ring had been there all along; she'd just never noticed it.

The other girls probably hadn't, either—until the end.

Another wave of nausea rolled through her, and she tensed, ready to spring toward the bathroom if necessary. The chain was long enough to allow her to reach the toilet—good thing, because she'd thrown up twice in the seven hours and ten minutes since Mark had left her here—but not long enough to reach the bed or chair. That was deliberate, she was certain. The man was methodical and precise.

He'd also stopped communicating with her. He hadn't said one word as he'd dragged her back down the steps after her escape attempt, pausing only to slap her into submission when she resisted. And he hadn't returned.

But she wasn't in any hurry to hear his key in the lock, either. The next time he appeared might be the end.

She let out an unsteady breath, fighting back tears. Her whole face ached. So did her stomach. But those injuries would heal.

You didn't recover from death.

And that's where she was headed.

She'd read it in Mark's eyes. He'd disengaged from her—probably the same way he'd disengaged from Angela and Denise before he killed them. And who was that third person he'd mentioned? Lil. Had death been her fate too?

The acrid taste of fear and vomit coalesced in

her mouth, and she pulled herself to her feet and lurched into the bathroom. Twisting the tap, she bent down, slurped up a mouthful of water, swished it around, then spit it out. A piece of hard candy would help dispel the unpleasant flavor, but the few provisions in the room were out of reach.

Bracing herself on the edge of the sink, she forced herself to swallow some of the water. Dehydration would be debilitating, and she needed to stay alert. Laura was at risk, and if there was anything she could still do to keep her sister safe, she intended to attempt it—no matter the risk.

Because at this point, she had nothing to lose.

For the second time in one day, Dev woke to the piercing, high-pitched ring tone of the BlackBerry on his nightstand.

Pulling himself back from the dark abyss of exhaustion, he forced his eyelids open. The room was pitch-black, meaning he'd been out cold since he'd arrived home from Laura's at one and fallen face-first onto the bed, fully clothed. It had to be past five now—and he had a feeling he hadn't moved an inch.

After groping for the cell, he peered at caller ID until the readout came into focus. Cal. "What've you got?"

"I had a fruitful talk with Faith Bradley."

He pushed himself into a sitting position. "I take it the consulting pretext worked?"

"Like a charm. Those generic cards we had printed last year, and the phone line that rolls to an answering service, are worth their weight in gold. Long story short, I hit pay dirt on my question about what qualities she thought were important for a daycare manager, and could she single anyone out at her own operation who exemplified those."

"She mentioned Hamilton."

"Yep. She sang his praises for a full minute. Talked about how kind and caring he was with the children, how meticulous he was about cleanliness, how he always came in early and stayed late, how he had strict, very old-fashioned moral standards. But after I dug a little deeper, she also mentioned he was hard to get to know, seemed to be a loner since he never talked about family or friends or his social life, and that he'd been acting very preoccupied lately. She speculated it might be due to a brand-new girlfriend—because when she'd probed a few weeks ago about whether he had any romantic interests, he'd told her he didn't have time for personal relationships."

Dev rubbed the grit from his eyes. "How did you get her to talk about all that stuff?"

"I'm a very sympathetic listener—or so Moira tells me. Women find undivided attention appealing, in case you haven't figured that out by now."

"Thanks for the tip."

"No charge. Back on subject, I don't think she knows anything about Hamilton's personal life. It sounds like their relationship is totally employer/ employee, much to her regret. Other than the few insights she offered about his character today, I'd say she's a dead end in terms of your case."

Dev stood and started to pace. There was a disconnect somewhere in the information Faith had offered . . . some inconsistency that hovered just out of reach . . . wait.

He stopped. "You know, if Faith is right about Mark having such high moral standards, doesn't it strike you as odd he'd have a brand-new girlfriend spending the night or maybe even living with him? As far as I know, she's still there. Connor hasn't called to say she left."

"She is. I talked to Connor half an hour ago. I don't know if I buy your theory, though. Hamilton could just be one of those people who presents one face in public and a very different one in private. Working with young children, it wouldn't behoove him to advertise a promiscuous life-style."

"My gut tells me it's more than that." Dev shoved his fingers through his hair. "There's something not right about this guy. I can feel it."

"Well, I'm not going to dispute your instincts. They've saved my hide on more than one occasion. But I don't think Faith is going to be of any help. By the way, Connor said to let you know none of the plates he ran on the cars parked near Hamilton's house produced anyone who remotely fit the description of the woman Faith saw in his window."

Another dead end.

"Then where did she come from?"

"Maybe Hamilton picked her up at her place or she took a cab. She might even be a neighbor who popped in the back door."

Dev frowned. "I don't think she's a neighbor. This guy isn't Mr. Sociability. Besides, he might be a recluse off the job, but I doubt his neighbors are hermits. They all come and go, and none of us has spotted anyone at his front door or in a car pulling out of the alley who fits the description Faith provided."

"Maybe she'll leave Monday, while Hamilton's at work."

He started pacing again. "Yeah. And I'll be cooling my heels at the daycare center, watching his car." He scrubbed a hand down his face. "One set of eyes on the house is fine when he's home, because if she leaves with him, we can follow, and if she leaves by cab or car, we can get a license. But we need another set on the house while Hamilton's at work."

"Is your client willing to pick up the extra expense?"

"I'll ask. It can't be for long, because the woman has to leave sometime."

"Sounds like a plan. Meanwhile, I'm going home to share supper with my wife."

"Sorry again about interrupting your day with Moira."

"Not a problem. Two minutes after you called, she got a hot lead on a big story she's working on and had to take off anyway. With the unpredictability of both of our professions, I think that's going to be the story of our life."

One side of Dev's mouth rose. "Would you rather go back to being single?"

"Not a chance. Thanks for the perspective check."

"Anytime. Talk to you later."

With one last, longing look at the bed, Dev headed for the kitchen to nuke a frozen dinner. Then he'd take a shower, throw in some laundry, and call Laura to see if she was on board with the additional surveillance.

All the while trying not to envy Cal his much-deserved second chance at love.

It was time.

Heart hammering, Mark crept into his mother's bedroom. Lil was out cold, arms flung to the sides, head half off the pillow and tilted back, mouth open. With all the liquor she'd downed—not to mention whatever the drug of choice had been last night—it would be hours before she

374

roused from the stupor. But the crushed Ambien he'd stirred into her drink while she wasn't looking gave him extra insurance. He didn't want her waking up in the middle of everything.

If she opened her eyes, he'd lose his nerve.

Mark tiptoed next to the bed, the faint, familiar scent of vanilla and jasmine from her perfume drifting his way. Sometimes it was hard to see Lil's resemblance to the high school graduation photo she kept tucked in her dresser. The one he liked to look at when he needed to remind himself who she really was, underneath the booze and sex and drugs.

But time—and her dissipated lifestyle—hadn't been kind to her. Free of makeup, her skin was mottled and shadows hung under her eyes. The meth she'd begun using was also taking a toll, aging her beyond her years. She looked like the mother of the young woman in the photo taken just twelve years ago—the woman she'd been before she'd given herself to a man she'd known less than three days, gotten pregnant, been disowned by her family, and gone down the path of destruction.

Now she'd reached the end of that unhappy road.

Sweat broke out on his brow as he picked up one of the extra pillows on the bed, his fingers clenching around the edge as a tsunami of doubts suddenly crashed over him.

He fought them back, knuckles whitening, heart pounding. He'd thought this through for weeks while shivering out on the freezing stoop whenever his mother entertained clients. Disgust had left a bitter taste in his mouth as he'd sat there thinking about what was happening inside. He wasn't a kid anymore. He knew what was going on. Knew what his classmates' sneers about his mother meant.

And he couldn't argue with them. The things she did were wrong. So he'd tried to get her to change. Tried to make her see that her life could be different. Pleaded with her. Begged. All to no avail—until finally he'd accepted the truth.

It was too late for Lil.

There was only one way to remove her from the sinful life she'd chosen.

Mark moved beside the bed, braced himself on one knee on the mattress, and pressed the pillow over his mother's face. Hard.

He'd done his research. It would take about five minutes, but he planned on eight, just to be certain.

Keeping his gaze on the bedside clock, he counted off the minutes. His arms began to ache, but he didn't lessen the pressure. Three more to go. Two. One.

Done.

Slowly he eased back on the pressure and lifted the pillow. Her chest wasn't moving anymore, and when he averted his face and leaned down, he felt no warmth on his cheek from her breath.

It was over.

And it had been far easier than he'd expected.

His arms were shaking as he turned her onto her stomach, face pressed into the pillow, then set more pillows around her head. He lifted one of her arms and tucked a pillow in, as if she'd been clutching it to her head. Blocking off her air. It was too bad it had come to this, that she hadn't seen the light and changed her ways. But it was better this way—for everyone.

"I did it for you, Mom." He whispered the words as he touched her hair. "To keep you from making any more mistakes. You understand, don't you?"

All at once, she flipped back over and glared at him, anger glinting in her eyes.

His lungs stopped working as he gaped at her.

No! She was dead!

"I'm not dead." She spoke as if she'd read his mind. "I'll never be dead. You may be a murderer, but you can never kill me." She lunged at him then, her hands finding his neck, filth spewing from her mouth as she squeezed. He tugged at her fingers, but her grip was too tight. He couldn't dislodge them. Nor could he manage to draw in even one gasp of air.

She was sucking the life out of him.

He was going to die.

"No!"

As the cry ripped past his lips, Mark shot bolt upright in bed, chest heaving, forehead clammy, T-shirt damp with sweat, legs tangled in the covers. Bunching the sheet in his fists, he gave the dimly lit room a frantic sweep, half expecting to see Lil emerge from the shadows.

But no. She'd died seventeen years ago.

It was a dream.

Nothing more.

The same dream he had every time he was preparing to keep another young woman from making more mistakes.

This one, however, had been more vivid than usual. And his mother had never spoken to him in past dreams. Her vitriolic words continued to burn in his ear no matter how hard he tried to block them out.

His hands started to itch.

Then his whole body began to itch.

He needed a shower. Now. Even if it was two in the morning.

Mark threw the covers back, swung his feet to the floor, and jogged toward the bathroom, shivering in the sweat-drenched clothing plastered to his body. He'd feel better after a shower. He always did.

No matter what his mother had said in that dream, he wasn't a murderer. She and the others had died as a result of their bad choices. They should be grateful he'd stopped them from sinking further into the abyss of debauchery.

He leaned into the shower and turned on the water, letting his hand linger under the cleansing spray.

One day soon, though, he'd save a girl on the brink, rescue her before she ruined her life and the lives of those around her. Then he'd be vindicated—and redeemed. He didn't remember much from his few long-ago forays to Sunday school, but the Bible story about God rejoicing more over one sinner who repented than ninety-nine righteous people had stuck with him. If that was true, God would approve of his noble quest to save a lost sheep.

As for those with whom he'd failed . . . he'd done all he could.

Now they were in God's hands.

Just as Darcy—and perhaps her sister—soon would be too.

21

Was he planning to starve her to death?

Is that how he'd killed the other girls?

As her stomach growled again, Darcy curled into a fetal position and wrapped herself tighter in the blanket she'd managed to snag off the bed.

She hadn't eaten since . . . when? Friday breakfast. Two and a half days ago.

She shifted, trying to find a more comfortable position on the thin carpet that covered the concrete floor. A few days without food—even a week or two—wouldn't kill her . . . but eventually she'd die. Was he going to watch the show through the peephole in the door as some kind of sick entertainment?

Squeezing her eyes shut, she drew in a shuddering breath. Whatever he had in mind, her fate was sealed. She had no chance of escaping the shackle—or this room. But she'd brought it on herself by running away and taking foolish chances.

Laura, however, didn't deserve whatever Mark had in store for her.

A tear trickled out of the corner of her eye, down her aching cheek, and she sniffled. There was only one person who could save her sister now. One power mighty enough to foil her captor. So she turned to him, placing her anguish and despair and need in his hands.

Lord, I'm sorry for all the trouble I've caused. Please . . . please keep Laura safe. Protect her. Send someone to help her if danger gets too close. And if you could somehow let her know how much I appreciate all she tried to do for me—and how much I love her—I'd be forever grateful.

∙ ∙ ∙

Mark consulted the piece of paper with Laura's cell number on it and punched the seven digits into the throwaway, pay-as-you-go phone he'd registered months ago under a false name—just in case he ever needed an untraceable number.

Meticulous planning always paid off.

As the call went through, he checked on the bread baking in the oven. Almost done. It would go well with the roast chicken breast and green beans he was having for dinner. A healthy, balanced diet was as important for adults as it was for children.

The phone began to ring, and he dropped onto a stool at the counter. How many hospitals had he called before trying her direct lines? Ten? Twelve? He scanned the list in front of him. All the major ones, that was for sure. But she wasn't a patient at any of them, according to the operators who'd searched their rosters when he'd asked them to ring her room. That could mean she hadn't been badly hurt.

On the other hand, she hadn't answered his last call, to her landline. If she didn't pick up on the cell number he'd found in Darcy's backpack, either, it could mean the failed brakes had proven fatal.

Having an accident remove her from the picture would be so much easier.

On the third ring, just as he expected the

answering machine to kick in as it had on her landline, a breathless female voice answered.

"Hello?"

She was home—and well enough to answer the phone.

He stifled a curse.

"Hello?" Her inflection was hesitant now.

"Sorry." He mumbled the apology, finger poised over the end button. "Wrong number." Mashing it down, he cut off the call and tossed the phone on the counter.

The brake job might have been a piece of cake, but it hadn't produced an optimal result.

Had it injured or distracted her sufficiently to relegate the search for Darcy to the back burner, though?

He crossed to the built-in desk in the kitchen and extracted his regular cell from his briefcase, along with James Devlin's card. Might as well go right to the source and find out the status of the investigation. He'd play it empathetic and helpful, giving the PI no reason to suspect there was anything more to the call than genuine concern.

But he wasn't hanging up until he had the answer he needed.

Dev pulled into the empty spot behind the white utility van, today posing as Walden Electronics, and punched in Connor's number. "Your replacement is here."

"I noticed. All quiet on the western front. No sign of life, and Hamilton's car never left the alley. The dark-haired girl never came out, either."

"That's what I assumed, since I didn't hear from you all day."

The van pulled out as Dev cut the SUV's engine and did a sweep of the neighborhood. "This spot gives us great lines of sight to the alley and Hamilton's front door, but we're going to have to find a different location if we're still on surveillance in a few days. Someone's going to notice the same cars rotating through here 24/7." He picked up the Starbucks cup next to his seat and took a swig. He was going to need plenty of caffeine to make it through the cold, dark hours ahead.

"Let's hope this wraps up before we have to worry about that. With the corporate fraud case heating up, we might need to hop a plane to Costa Rica later in the week. I've whiled away the hours here talking with my contacts and dealing with on-the-ground logistics and possible itineraries." The van disappeared around the corner.

Dev sighed. The Costa Rica gig would be another killer case requiring long hours.

Maybe one of these days he'd catch up on his sleep.

"The sooner we put this one to bed, the better, as far as I'm concerned."

"I'm sure . . . considering you have a vested interested in tying up all the loose ends."

He heard the grin in his partner's voice. Ignored it. "Did you manage to get a sub lined up to watch the house while Hamilton's at work, in case the dark-haired girl leaves?"

"Yeah. I followed your advice and tapped Dale to double up on the day shift, since he helped out with the bus station surveillance. But the meter is beginning to rack up some serious numbers. You certain your client is okay with another body on this?"

"For a few days at least. Enjoy your Sunday night."

"What's left of it."

"You'll be more comfortable than me."

"No argument there. Have fun." The line went dead.

Dev started to put the phone back in its holster, only to have it vibrate as it slid into place. He pulled it out again, eyebrows rising at the name in the display.

Mark Hamilton?

A caution sign began to flash in his mind as he answered. "Devlin."

"Mr. Devlin, Mark Hamilton. You stopped in to see me at Davis Daycare on Friday, hoping I might remember something about the missing teen you're trying to track down. You had the impression my path had crossed with hers at the homeless shelter."

"That's right." Dev stared at the light seeping

around the edges of the blinds in Hamilton's front window. What was the guy up to?

"The thing is, I haven't been able to get your visit off my mind. A teenage girl on the streets in today's world—that's a recipe for disaster. So I've been racking my brain, trying to recall her. As I told you the other day, I did remember talking to a girl who bore a faint resemblance to your runaway. But last night, I was thinking about one of the other girls at the shelter during the storm. I noticed her because she had a guitar case she never let out of her sight, and I wondered if she might be a struggling musician. The thing is, there was a blonde girl hanging around with her who stayed in the background and didn't do much talking. We exchanged a few words, and I think she might have been a match for those photos you showed me. I don't know how much that helps, but I thought I'd pass it on, for what it's worth. Unless you've already found her?"

"Not yet." Could this be on the level?

"Her family must be very worried."

"Yes."

Silence.

Dev waited him out.

"Well . . . if I think of anything else that might be useful, would you be the person to call? Or is someone else handling the case now?"

"I'm still the main contact."

"Okay. I'll keep your number handy."

"Thanks for calling."

Dev slipped his phone back onto his belt and tapped his finger against the steering wheel.

That was bizarre.

There could be only two reasons for a call from Hamilton. Either he was sincerely concerned and was telling the truth about suddenly remembering Darcy—or he'd been fishing for information, trying to determine if the case was still active.

If it was the former, they were wasting their time—and Laura's money—on this surveillance gig.

If it was the latter, Hamilton was in this thing up to his neck.

And the red alert pinging in his head told him it was the latter.

So far, however, they had zero proof he'd had any contact with Darcy beyond the homeless shelter. But the connection was there somewhere, and if they hung in long enough, they'd find it.

He hoped before it was too late.

What was up with Faith?

Mark watched her from the doorway as she helped pass snacks out in the two-year-old room. She'd barely said hello to him when they passed in the hall earlier, had given him a clipped answer as he stopped by the front desk and asked how her weekend had been, and now she was refusing to look at him.

Was she mad because he'd been less than gracious about the gift she'd given him? No. That didn't ring true. She'd been fine on Friday.

Then again, she'd had a whole weekend to brood about his tepid response. That could have put her in a snit.

He sighed.

Why did women have to be such complicated creatures?

Whatever the problem, however, he had to fix it. His plan depended on her unwitting cooperation.

"Faith?" When she looked his way—with obvious reluctance—he summoned up a smile. "After you finish in here, would you stop by my office?"

She shrugged. "Sure." She turned her back and continued to help with the children.

Talk about being out of sorts.

This was going to be a challenge.

But it had to be done. Getting back in her good graces for the next thirty-six hours was essential. He'd just have to suck it in and pull out the charm—distasteful as that prospect was.

By the time she knocked on his open door a few minutes later, he was psyched up for the encounter.

He swiveled around in his chair to find her hovering on the threshold, her expression wary. Stretching his lips into a smile, he motioned her toward the chair across from his desk. "Have a seat."

After a momentary hesitation, she entered and perched on the edge of the cushion.

"Last week was very busy, and it occurred to me over the weekend that I hadn't thanked you properly for your gift on Thursday. I've been using it, and it's great stuff. I want you to know how much I appreciate it. I haven't had anyone do anything that thoughtful for me in a long time."

Her taut posture relaxed a fraction, and some of the tension ebbed from her features.

Better.

"I'm glad you liked it."

He opened his desk drawer and withdrew the eight-piece box of Godiva chocolate one of the parents had given him last Christmas. It had been sitting there for almost two months, and it wasn't getting better with age. Might as well put it to productive use.

Her eyes widened as he held it out to her. "A small token of my thanks."

"For me?" Her voice actually came out in a squeak.

How pathetic.

"Who else? I hope you enjoy it."

"Oh, I will!" She hugged it to her chest and tucked one of those annoying curls behind her ear, her face softening as the last of her wariness melted away. "After Saturday, I never expected anything like this."

At the non sequitur, he frowned. "Saturday?"

A flush rose on her cheeks, and she clutched the candy tighter—as if she was afraid he was going to snatch it back. "I shouldn't have let that slip, I guess." She chewed on her bottom lip and took a deep breath. "The thing is . . . I baked some homemade cinnamon rolls on Saturday morning and decided to bring a few to your house. But as I was walking up toward the door, I caught a glimpse of a girl at the window, so I turned around and left."

Faith had been at his house?

She'd seen Darcy?

A roar filled his head.

"Mr. Hamilton?" Faith leaned forward, the color fading from her cheeks. "I'm sorry. I didn't mean to upset you. I shouldn't have said anything."

"I'm not upset." Somehow he managed to get the words out. *Stay calm, stay calm, stay calm. If you spook her, she'll clam up before you find out what else she might have seen.* "I was just surprised. You should have rung the bell."

"I didn't want to . . . interrupt." Her fingers picked at the ribbon on the box of candy. "I thought maybe she was a girlfriend, especially after that guy stopped me on the way back to my car."

The roar swelled.

"What guy?"

"I don't know who he was. He said he was looking for his sister, who'd been at a party in your neighborhood the night before—maybe at your house. Didn't he ring your bell and ask about her? He said he was going to."

His hands started to itch, and he clenched them into fists in his lap.

"No. And I didn't have a party Friday night. Nor do I have a girlfriend. A bunch of college kids live next door, and sometimes a couple of them stop by on Saturday morning for my hot chocolate. It's famous in the neighborhood." The glib words tumbled out of his mouth. He had no idea where they'd come from.

Relief smoothed the renewed tension from her features. "It just goes to show how jumping to conclusions can lead to all sorts of misunderstandings. I should have known you weren't the wild party type. But even though I was kind of upset most of the weekend, I still said nice things about you to that consultant who came by Saturday afternoon."

Mark's heart stuttered as he tried to keep up with her rapid changes of subject. "What consultant?"

She lifted one shoulder. "Some guy from Chicago. He said his company was doing research on the daycare industry and they were paying people who worked in the field seventy-five bucks to answer twenty minutes' worth of questions."

"This guy asked about me?" The itching in his hands intensified.

"No, I was the one who brought up your name. At the end, he asked me what qualities I thought made an effective daycare manager, and I used you as an example." She chewed on her lip again. "I hope that was all right. I said all positive things."

"What was the name of this company?"

She scrunched up her face. "It had letters in it . . ." She shook her head. "I can't remember. He gave me a card, though."

"Do you have it with you?"

"No. I think it's in the pocket of my jeans at home. Why?"

It was hard to talk over the roar in his head.

"I'm sure Mr. Davis would be interested to know one of his employees has been interviewed for a study."

She leaned forward, concern etching her features. "He didn't ask anything about our center. Just general questions. I'd never say anything bad about Davis Daycare, anyway."

"I know that." He coaxed the corners of his lips up a fraction and gripped the arms of his chair, trying to ignore the fierce urge to scratch his hands. "He might be curious about the research they're doing, though. Could you bring the card in tomorrow?"

"Sure."

"Great." He rolled his chair toward his computer. "I'll let you get back to work now. And thank you again for the gift."

"You're welcome." She rose, hugging the Godiva box as she backed away. "And thank you again for the candy. I love chocolate."

"My pleasure. Now . . . work calls." He gestured to his desk, hoping she didn't notice the tremble in his fingers. "Would you shut the door as you leave?"

"Sure. Talk to you later." She beamed at him and slipped through, closing it behind her.

The instant it clicked, Mark rose and began to pace, raking his clipped nails over the back of one hand, then the other.

Something was going on.

And it wasn't good.

The story about the guy looking for his sister sounded fishy—especially since he'd never followed through on his conversation with Faith and rung the doorbell to ask about his supposed missing sibling.

The consultant was even fishier, despite the card the guy had given Faith. He'd check that out first thing tomorrow, once he had the name and phone number—but he had a strong suspicion it would turn out to be phony.

Because given Devlin's confirmation yesterday that Phoenix was still on the case, he'd be willing to bet the guys who'd talked to Faith were connected to the investigation.

He was still in their sights.

Maybe they were even tailing him, watching his house.

His pulse spiked, and he froze.

Was that possible—or was he being paranoid?

No matter. He couldn't take a chance. He'd have to adjust his plans slightly.

But the end result would be the same.

As Dev swung into her driveway, Laura stepped onto the front porch, turned her key in the lock, and started down the walk.

He opened his door and slid out, smiling as she drew close. "You must have been watching for me."

"I was. I thought I'd save you a walk in light of your all-night surveillance stint."

"After being cooped up for twelve hours, I don't mind stretching my legs." He reached for her tote bag and took her arm as they circled the Explorer. "I even bypassed the drive-through and went inside to get my double cheeseburger and fries."

"At eight-thirty in the morning?"

"It's dinnertime for me."

"I guess that's true." He shut the door behind her, and she secured her seat belt as he retraced his steps, then slid in beside her. "Thanks again for the offer of a lift. My boss would have picked me up, but she's got several little ones at home and it's tough to get everyone moving early in the morning."

"Do you need a ride home too?"

"No—but thanks for asking. The rental car place is going to drop off a car for me at the library."

"In that case, I plan to sleep all afternoon."

As he backed out, she studied the faint purple tinge beneath his lashes and the fine lines at the corners of his eyes. The all-nighters were taking a toll—and as far as she could tell, they weren't producing much.

"So how long do you plan to continue the surveillance?"

"Tough to say. We don't have any real evidence pointing to Hamilton's involvement in Darcy's disappearance, but I'm getting bad vibes about him. We'll regroup midweek. The double set of eyes during the day is expensive, and I don't want to waste your money if we don't turn up some definite connection by then."

They passed the freshly marred telephone pole at the side of the road, and she asked the question she'd been dreading since he'd inspected her garage Saturday afternoon. "Did you hear from your mechanic friend?"

"Yes. He gave your car a thorough going-over first thing this morning and called me a few minutes ago. The brake lines weren't cut, but there was a sizeable hole in the front line—and the front brakes provide 70 percent of stopping power on a rear-wheel-drive vehicle."

She tightened her grip on the handle of the tote bag in her lap and braced herself. "Was it a man-made hole?"

"He couldn't confirm that. The best he'd give me was fifty-fifty."

Some of the tension in her shoulders dissolved. "So there's a strong possibility it truly was an accident."

The Explorer slowed as they approached the bottom of her hill. "Strong might be pushing it."

Her shoulders tightened again. "You still think it was deliberate?"

"The way this case has been going, let's just say I'm suspicious. But we can't prove it." He looked over at her, his intent gaze lingering on the burn on her face. "How are you feeling today?"

"Still achy, but the Tylenol is helping, and the salve they gave me for this"—she gestured to the burn—"is great."

"Did you think about calling in sick?"

"Yes, but sitting home worrying about Darcy all day wasn't appealing. At work I'll be forced to focus on other things for a few hours."

"Makes sense, as long as you're up to it."

She angled toward him as she gathered her courage to broach the next question. "Dev . . . it's been almost ten days since she disappeared. I did some reading about teen runaways on the Net yesterday. The stuff they can encounter is very scary. Drugs, gangs, exploitation, violence, assault, suicide . . ."

When her words trailed off, he gave her an apologetic glance. "The street isn't a pretty place, Laura. Runaways do face a lot of dangers."

Her tiny hope he'd downplay what she'd read deflated.

She moistened her lips and steeled herself. "One article I read said a third of the teens who don't return within forty-eight hours are lured into prostitution, and within two weeks 75 percent are involved in theft, drugs, or pornography." Her voice broke, and she cleared her throat. "You've spent a lot of time on the street. What do you think the odds are Darcy's still okay?"

His jaw hardened, and he flexed his fingers on the steering wheel. As he swung onto the main road and accelerated, he kept his face in profile instead of looking at her.

Bad sign.

"I think we shouldn't jump to conclusions." His tone was careful, reasoned, matter-of-fact. "The stats are daunting—but not everyone becomes a statistic. Darcy might be headstrong and too cocky, but from everything you've said over the past week, she's bright and basically a good kid. She might be fine and coming to her senses as we speak. For all we know, you'll either get a call one of these days from her saying she's had a change of heart and wants to come home, or she'll just show up at your house."

Laura desperately wanted to believe that.

"You're not saying that to placate me, are you?"

This time he did look at her. "No. I've seen it happen before. It's a possibility. But in our business, we always operate under the worst assumptions. That keeps our investigation focused and helps us maintain a sense of urgency."

She scrutinized him, searching for any sign of deceit, but found none. As far as she knew, he'd been honest with her all along. There was no reason to think he'd change course at this point. If he believed there was a chance Darcy could reappear on her own, there was—however slim.

Settling back in the seat, she cradled her wrist as they drove through the snow-covered landscape. The roads were clear now, except for a few icy patches on side streets, and Dev made excellent time to the library. He also managed to elicit a few smiles from her with stories about his childhood —a purposeful distraction, she knew, but she appreciated the effort in light of his obvious fatigue.

As he pulled up in front of the main entrance and came around to open her door, he took her hand . . . and held onto it once she slid out.

Lifting her chin, she gave him a surprised look.

"We're working this as hard as we can, Laura."

She nodded. "I know."

"Something will break soon."

"I'm holding on to that thought."

With a final squeeze, he released her fingers. "I'll call you later, after I catch up on sleep, and give you an update. In the meantime, try not to worry too much."

"I can try."

She watched while he took his place behind the wheel again and pulled away from the curb. Sixty seconds later, as the Explorer disappeared into traffic and she turned toward the library, she resolved to do her best to live up to her promise.

But until Darcy showed up at her door, or called to say she was okay, or Dev tracked her down, she had a feeling that keeping her worry at bay was going to be a losing battle no matter how hard she tried.

22

"CCD Consulting. All lines are busy at the moment. Please leave your name, number, and a brief message and we'll return your call as soon as possible."

A beep sounded on the toll-free number.

So the company had an active business line.

Could it be legit after all?

Jack Ferguson's business card in hand, Mark

hung up, swung around to his computer, and Googled the company.

Nothing came up in Chicago with the firm's name, and there was no address on the business card.

CCD Consulting was a fake, as he'd suspected . . . meaning Darcy's sister had to be dealt with ASAP. Once she was out of the picture and the PIs were no longer being paid, they'd drop the case. The police would step in to investigate her disappearance, but with their stretched resources and no relatives clamoring for action, they weren't going to stay on it long without any leads.

And there wouldn't be any. He'd make certain of that. Long before the spring thaw set in next month, the case would be as cold as the piles of ice on his lawn. Laura Griffith would be just another missing person on the police department's long list.

Plus, after spending most of yesterday refining his contingency plan, he knew how to make her disappear. Fast.

A soft knock sounded on his door, and Faith stuck her head inside.

The very person he wanted to see.

"Did you find the . . . oh." Her gaze homed in on the CCD card in his hand. "I guess you did. Was it helpful?"

"Yes. Very." He set it on his desk and motioned her in, then folded his hands to disguise the tremble in his fingers. "Would you close the door for a minute?"

She sent him an uncertain look but did as he asked.

"I know you have work to do and I won't keep you, but I wanted to ask if you'd like to stop by my place tonight and try some of that famous hot chocolate I mentioned yesterday."

Her eyes widened. "Seriously?"

"Why not? I have a nice fireplace, it's cold outside—can you think of a better way to spend an evening?"

From her expression, you'd think she'd won the lottery. "No. That sounds wonderful! What time would you like me to come?"

"How about seven-thirty?"

"I'll be there."

He conjured up a smile. "And I'll have the hot chocolate waiting." As she started to turn away, he spoke again, as if it was an afterthought. "Oh . . . it'll be better if you park on the street behind me and cut between the houses. The frat boys next door have a lot of drinking parties, and they damaged a car parked in front of my house over the weekend. I wouldn't want that to happen to yours. If you'll call me on your cell when you arrive, I'll escort you over."

Her eyes lit up. "Thank you for that offer. It's hard to find a gentleman these days. Your mother must have raised you right."

His smile turned so brittle he was afraid his lips would crack. "I'm sure she'd appreciate you saying that." He gestured to his desk. "Sorry to rush things, but I'm snowed today."

"That's okay. We have tonight to look forward to." Her smile held a hint of suggestiveness as she slipped through the door and closed it behind her.

His mouth flattened in disgust. This charade couldn't be over fast enough to suit him.

On the other hand, he'd found a way to take advantage of her silly schoolgirl crush. How else would he have managed to implement his plan? It wasn't as if he had any buddies he could use. Making and maintaining friends took a lot of effort. Plus, they expected you to share your opinions, your feelings, your history. And girlfriends were worse, from everything he'd heard. They wanted to know every little thing about a guy—including his secrets.

Not going to happen.

Even when he did find the right girl . . . the one who would redeem him . . . he didn't intend to share any of those things with her. His past would truly be past then, and it would never rear its ugly head again.

In the meantime, his pseudo, one-night girlfriend was more than sufficient for his needs.

And tomorrow, after Faith had served her purpose? It would be back to business as usual for both of them.

Even if dealing with the fallout from her side wasn't going to be fun.

Dev stretched, yawned, and looked over at the bedside clock.

Had he really been out for seven hours?

Amazing.

He'd hoped for five at best, with the Costa Rica trip heating up and a new insurance fraud case on the docket. Either Connor had done double duty this afternoon at the office or he'd slept through the ringing phone. In any case, the extra sleep would help set him up for another long, cold night. That, plus a double-sized thermos of coffee and some soup.

Stifling another yawn, he swung his legs to the floor, grabbed his BlackBerry off the nightstand, and tapped in Cal's number.

His partner answered on the first ring. "Tell me you're planning to relieve me early so I can eat dinner with Moira."

"Don't push it, buddy." He rose and stretched. Man, these long sedentary surveillance gigs were a pain. One of these days soon, he was going to have to squeeze in a workout or his fitness routine would be shot. "You already owe me for my magnanimous offer to take all the night shifts as a concession to your newlywed status. My body clock is going to be out of whack for weeks."

"It was a noble gesture, and you have my

undying gratitude. Moira's too. In fact, she's talking about inviting you to the house for a home-cooked meal after this is all over as a thank-you."

"Yeah?" He padded toward the bathroom, following the path of clothes he'd shed en route to bed after his all-nighter. "If she makes that pot roast she cooked for our company Christmas party, I'll consider the sacrifice worthwhile and the debt fully paid."

"I'll pass your menu request along."

"Anything going on down there?" He picked up the worn jeans from the floor and gave them a cursory inspection. They'd last another day.

"Nope. I followed him home from work. He didn't stop anywhere. No fast-food place, no grocery store, no bar for a quick beer. Does this guy have a life?"

"I'm beginning to wonder. He hasn't left the house since we began surveillance, except to go to work. Have you talked to Dale?"

"Yeah. About twenty minutes ago, as we did the handoff at the corner. He said there was zero activity at the house all day and no sign of the girl."

"She must be a hermit too." He detoured to the closet and rooted through the sweaters dumped in a pile on the floor. If things ever calmed down, he was going to have to do some serious straightening up around here. Laura would think he was a slob if she saw his apartment in its present state.

"Hey . . . you still there?"

"Yeah. Sorry. I got distracted for a sec." He snagged a sweater.

"Would the distraction's name be Laura?"

He stifled a sigh. Sometimes the cons of working with longtime friends who knew you well outweighed the pros.

"I'll take the fifth."

Cal's chuckle came over the line. "That's what I thought. Maybe you'll get lucky and there'll be a break tonight so you can wrap up this case."

"Wouldn't that be nice? See you in a couple of hours."

As he tossed the phone on the bed and shoved his legs into the jeans, Dev hoped his partner was right.

But the way things were going, he'd most likely put in another long, cold night with nothing to show for it.

As the key rattled in the lock, Darcy jerked and raised her head from her drawn-up knees. For a moment the room swam. No surprise there in light of her meager menu over the past two days, since Mark had begun feeding her again. A scrambled egg, slice of toast, apple, bowl of soup, half a turkey sandwich, and two Gatorades might be enough for one day, but spread out over almost five? They'd barely put a dent in her hunger.

On the other hand, if he was trying to starve her to death, why was he feeding her at all?

The door opened and he crossed the room, a plate in his hand. On his previous visits, he'd neither looked at her nor spoken. This one was no different. He set the food on the floor at the outer limits of her reach and retreated, pulling the door closed behind him.

As the lock clicked into place and the room fell silent, Darcy stared at the plate.

Was that a *cheeseburger?*

Despite the weakness in her legs and a relentless pounding in her temples, she crawled toward it, extended her hand to grasp the edge of the plate, and pulled it toward her.

It wasn't a mirage. The savory aroma wafting up to her nose confirmed the burger was real.

Yet as her salivary glands kicked into overdrive, so did her apprehension.

Why this sudden feast after her sparse diet of the previous five days?

The answer eluded her—but her brain hadn't been working at 100 percent for the past two or three days. Putting some substantial food in her stomach would kick it back into gear. At least her worries about being poisoned had diminished. He'd had plenty of chances to spike her food with some lethal toxin if that had been his plan.

She picked up the burger, took a bite—and closed her eyes.

Nirvana.

Her survival instincts clamored for her to scarf it down, but she forced herself to eat slowly. Hadn't she read somewhere once that if you'd been on a fast, a heavy meal was a no-no? And a burger qualified as heavy. It might shock her stomach.

Not eating it, however, wasn't an option.

As she devoured it one tiny bite at a time, Darcy felt strength seeping back into her limbs—and the clarity of her thinking also began to improve.

But that had a downside.

Because as she washed the last bite down with some slurps of water from the bathroom sink, a terrifying explanation for the hearty dinner suddenly occurred to her.

Perhaps, like a prisoner on death row, she'd just been served her last meal.

If she swallowed more than another mouthful or two of Mark's famous hot chocolate, Faith was going to lose her dinner.

"Do you like it?"

She pretended to take another sip as she debated how to answer her host's question. If she lied and said yes, he might offer her more. But if she told the truth, she might jinx their very first date. Better to go with noncommittal.

Cradling the oversized mug in her hands, she

leaned back on the couch. "I've never had any-thing quite like it. Do I detect a slight cherry flavor?"

His eyes widened slightly. "You must have amazing taste buds to pick that up. The cherry-flavored syrup I use is very subtle."

The words were complimentary . . . but he didn't look pleased she'd identified his secret ingredient. Most people probably wouldn't have been able to pinpoint it. But overindulging on chocolate-covered cherries the Christmas Eve when she was ten—and puking all night—had left her with an acute ability to detect even a drop of the detested flavor. And it never failed to turn her stomach.

No way did she intend to share that piece of her history, however.

"I've been able to pick up cherry flavor ever since I was a kid. One of those freaky idio-syncrasies, I guess. I can see why this is famous in the neighborhood." She lifted the mug to her lips and faked another sip, trying not to gag.

"I'm glad you're enjoying it."

She wished.

The question was, how could she get rid of the rest of it before she repeated her performance at age ten?

She scanned the living room, searching for possible spots to dump the hot chocolate. "This is a really nice house." What about the fireplace?

No; that would only work if it was real rather than gas. She kept looking. "Did it need a lot of rehabbing?" A plant beside the entertainment center caught her eye. Was it real? If so, the soil in the decorative pot would be a perfect disposal medium.

"Yes. It's been a lot of work, but the end result was worth it."

She held her breath so she wouldn't have to smell the cherry aroma and pretended to sip again. "You know, hot chocolate always makes me thirsty. Could I have a glass of water?"

A flash of . . . irritation? . . . streaked across his face, but he rose from the upholstered chair he'd chosen, his own hot chocolate in hand. "Sure. I'll be back in a minute."

As he walked toward the kitchen, she stood and crossed the room. While he retrieved a glass from the cabinet, she pretended to study the titles of his DVDs, keeping watch on him out of the corner of her eye. The instant he turned his back to stick the glass under the ice maker, she verified that the pot contained real dirt, then dumped the remainder of the hot chocolate in the soil.

Whew. That had been close.

When Mark started back, she tipped up the mug and pretended to drain it as he approached.

"All done?" He handed over the water and a paper napkin, then took the mug from her.

"Yes. Thanks again." She gulped the water,

trying to wash away the lingering cherry flavor in her mouth.

"So . . . would you like to watch an old movie? I have quite a collection."

"Sure." She wandered back to the couch, leaving plenty of room for him to join her. It wasn't going to be much of an evening if he stayed a coffee table away in that chair.

"Give me a sec to get rid of this in the kitchen"—he lifted the mug—"and I'll pull a few titles for you to choose from."

Faith settled on the sofa, set the glass on the paper napkin on the coffee table, and scooted toward the corner to open up even more space.

A minute later, Mark detoured toward the entertainment center as he returned, quickly selecting three DVDs. He handed them over with a smile. If he'd been miffed at her discovery of his secret ingredient, he seemed over it now.

She read the titles, examined the dated hair-styles and cover photos on the jackets. These weren't just old, they were antique. Only one title rang any bells—distant ones, at that—but it was clear these were very old-fashioned stories.

Different.

But kind of cute.

And truth be told, they looked better than the violence-drenched flicks her past dates had typically taken her to.

"How about this one?" She held up *Meet Me in*

St. Louis. At least she recognized the name of one of the stars. She was pretty certain Judy Garland had been the chick in *The Wizard of Oz* —another oldie but goodie.

"Nice choice." Mark took the DVDs from her, popped in the disc she'd chosen, and picked up the remote. Then he joined her on the sofa, sitting mere inches away.

Yes!

As the opening credits began to roll, she glanced at the fire in the hearth, let out a soft, contented sigh, and settled in.

This was going to be a great evening.

23

Faith was asleep.

Finally.

Easing off the couch, Mark watched the even rise and fall of the afghan he'd draped over her when she'd grown sleepy. Odd that it had taken an hour for the double dose of Benadryl to kick in—especially since he'd also added some pulverized Ambien from the stockpile he kept on hand for the nights when sleep wouldn't come. Then again, Faith had stretched out the drink as long as possible. She might also have a high tolerance for sleep aids.

Whatever.

She was out now, that was all that mattered. And, she should stay that way for several hours, though two would suffice if all went well.

In any case, by the time she woke up and he sent her on her way, everything would be in place for the final act.

He turned off the lamp and the fireplace, leaving the room in darkness. The crepe soles of his shoes were silent on the floor as he walked toward the kitchen, snagging her bulging purse from the dining table as he passed.

Once at the counter next to the sink, he zipped it open—too fast. Her keys, lipstick, hand mirror, comb, and a tube of mascara spilled out, clattering onto the hard surface.

Pulse surging, he muttered an oath and backed up until she was in sight. Still out cold. He exhaled. The drugs might have taken awhile to kick in, but they seemed to be doing their job now.

He returned to the counter and surveyed the personal items, his lips curling in disgust at the evidence of her last-minute primping before she'd called him from the next street. Like it mattered.

After retrieving a pair of rubber gloves from beneath the sink, he picked the items up one by one and shoved them back into the purse, leaving only her keys on the counter.

His fingers started to itch as he removed the gloves, and he eyed the sink, fighting the urge to wash his hands. There wasn't time. Every minute had to count, in case Faith didn't stay out for as long as he expected.

But he'd make up for it later, after everything was over, by taking a long, hot shower—an appropriate symbol for a fresh, clean start.

With one more glance at his guest, he slid his arms into the sleeves of his black jacket, pulled a dark knit cap over his head, and tugged on a pair of wool gloves. Pocketing Faith's keys, he moved beside the knife rack on the counter, running his fingers across the handles. Which would work best?

In the end, he chose a sharp, thin-bladed paring knife. It wasn't as impressive as the bigger knives, but it would be easy to hold . . . and the four-inch blade would be more than adequate.

After retrieving the case from a drawer, he slid the blade inside, tucked the knife inside his jacket, and crossed to the basement door. Checking on Faith once more over his shoulder, he turned the handle slow and easy, pulled open the door, and descended the stairs.

At the bottom he paused, giving his eyes a chance to adjust to the dim light before approaching the soundproof room. Once he reached the door, he bent and retrieved Darcy's jacket, a neck warmer, and a hat from the floor where he'd dropped them earlier in preparation for this moment. He shoved a second neck warmer and the extra pair of gloves into the pockets of his jacket.

Planning was everything.

As he pulled out the key, he fitted his eye to the peephole.

The plate with the burger was empty. She'd probably scarfed it down in three minutes flat after the subsistence diet he'd fed her for the past few days. Hunger had surely dulled her senses, but even if she'd been more alert, she would never have tasted the crushed Ambien in the meat. The extra seasonings he'd added would have masked the flavor.

And it appeared the drug had kicked in. She was lying on the floor, her back to him, unmoving. Asleep but not comatose, if his guess on dosage had been correct. He needed her awake but groggy.

With a twist of the key in the lock, he entered, shut the door behind him, and approached her carefully. She'd fooled him once; he wasn't about to take another chance.

Staying on guard, he dumped the clothing items on her bed and moved close enough to nudge her in the back with the toe of his shoe.

No response.

He prodded her harder.

She moaned and curled into a protective tuck.

Unless she was a better actress than he thought, she was in the exact state he wanted her.

Poised to react in case he was wrong, he extracted another key from his pocket and unlocked the shackle. Once her leg was free, he positioned himself behind her, bent down to grab her under the arms, and lifted her to her feet.

She wobbled and collapsed against him.

Grunting, he absorbed her full weight. "Darcy . . . stand up."

Her eyelids flickered open at his terse command, and she managed to regain her footing, though she was swaying so much she'd have fallen again if he wasn't supporting her.

He half dragged, half guided her to the bed and lowered her to the side. Even sitting, she had difficulty staying upright.

Holding on to her shoulder with one hand, he maneuvered the jacket onto first one arm, then the other. As he leaned down to zip it up, she gaped at him through dilated pupils.

"Ish not cole in here."

"We're taking a little trip."

He rummaged through the pocket of his own jacket and pulled out the strip of cloth he'd prepared. "Open your mouth."

She looked up at him dully, her eyes uncomprehending.

"Darcy . . . open your mouth." He enunciated each word.

"Why?"

The instant she spoke, he whipped the strip of

cloth between her teeth and tugged it taut as she weakly flailed against him.

Once it was tied behind her head, he grasped her shoulders and shook her. Hard.

"Stop struggling. Do you hear me? Stop struggling!"

When she continued to writhe, he grabbed her arm and twisted it behind her back.

She took a sharp breath and went still.

Better.

"Do what I tell you, or you'll be hurting a lot worse than this." He increased the upward pressure on her arm to reinforce his message, letting her moan for a moment before releasing her.

He worked the gloves onto her fingers, then yanked the neck warmer over her head, covering her nose and mouth, hiding the gag from view. Finally, he pulled the hat over her hair, tugging it down over her ears.

Stepping back, he gave her a swift perusal. Excellent. She looked like someone bundled up for the cold.

"Stand up."

She whimpered and tried to follow his instruction, but her legs folded under her and she dropped back to the bed.

No problem. He was prepared for this contingency.

After pulling her back to her feet, he bent down

and hefted her over his shoulder. Once they were outside, the cold air should wake her up enough to let her get to the car on her own, with some assistance.

Shrugging her into a more comfortable position, he exited, shutting the door behind him before he started up the steps.

He took it slow, but by the time he reached the top, his heart was pounding. He'd never have made it without his diligent workouts and regular weight lifting.

Again, it all came down to planning. To being ready for every possible outcome. To covering all the bases. And he was a master at that.

He stopped to catch his breath on the top step, then peeked around the door. As near as he could tell, Faith hadn't budged from her spot on the couch.

So far, so good.

He closed the basement door behind him and crossed the kitchen to the back door. Gently he turned the knob and exited onto the small, covered stoop, the salt he'd strewn on the wooden decking crunching under his feet as he emerged.

A quick sweep of the area confirmed his expectations. The alley was deserted on this dark, cold, Tuesday night—and it should be even quieter around ten-thirty, when he returned.

Lowering Darcy to her feet, he waited while she regained her equilibrium. As he'd hoped, the cold air was bringing her around, and she was able to stand on her own with minimal assistance.

Nevertheless, he wrapped one arm around her waist, pressed close beside her, and took her arm in a firm grip.

"Walk with me." He spoke the quiet but firm words into her ear and urged her forward.

She complied, her gait halting. Looking like someone who'd had one too many hot toddies on a cold winter night—his very story on the off chance they encountered anyone or were stopped for some reason.

Tucking his chin into the collar of his coat, he struck out for the narrow passageway between the row houses on the other side of the alley, heading for Faith's car. In less than five minutes, they'd be inside, Darcy's hands would be bound, and he'd be on his way to step two.

When they got back, he'd send Faith home and complete the third and final step of his plan.

The ice-crusted snow crackled under their feet as they walked, and a shiver passed through him. From cold, not anxiety.

Well . . . maybe a little anxiety.

This was the most ambitious and intricate plan he'd ever developed. But everything would work out. He was thorough and meticulous and careful. That's why no one had ever discovered the truth about Lil's death. Or Angela's. Or Denise's. Star would never be missed, either.

Too bad Darcy had complicated things. She'd been nothing but trouble from day one. Choosing her had been a mistake, and he regretted it.

But he wouldn't make a mistake disposing of her—and her sister. Nor would he harbor one iota of regret over their demise. They'd brought it on themselves by misleading and hounding him. Transgressions like that had to be punished.

And before this night was over, they would be.

Dev finished off the last cupful of chicken noodle soup from his thermos, replaced the cap, and did another sweep of Hamilton's neighborhood. Talk about dead. Only four cars had rolled down the street since he'd relieved Cal two and a half hours ago, and none had pulled in or out of the alley. Nor had he seen a single person wandering around.

Looked like it was going to be another boring, unproductive night.

A call to Laura would liven things up, though. And updating her was the professional thing to do—even if he didn't brief most clients every day.

He plugged the small fan unit into his lighter and flipped it on, along with the optional heat element, and aimed it at the front window. It did a better job defogging his sight line than keeping him warm, but if the cold got too bad, he could always plug in the electric blanket for a while.

Meanwhile, he'd find another way to add some warmth to his life.

Settling back into his seat, he pulled his cell from his belt and tapped in Laura's speed dial number. It rang three times before she answered, and when she greeted him, she sounded breathless.

"Did I catch you at a bad time?"

"No. Sorry it took me a minute to reach the phone. I just got out of a hot bath, and I was dripping water everywhere."

Hot bath.

Laura.

That combination warmed him up real fine. Much better than an electric blanket.

He cleared his throat. "I could call you back."

"That's okay. The towel will do for a few minutes. Is anything going on down there?"

Laura was wearing a towel.

He cracked the window and forced himself to refocus on her question.

"No. There were some lights on in the front of the house awhile ago, but they're out now. I think he's gone to bed."

"Have you given any more thought to how long we should keep this up?"

"Until the weekend, if you can manage the fees. Did Nikki call you with the charges to date?"

"Yes. I had to sit down when I heard the total. But it's worth every penny if we find Darcy."

And if we don't?

He didn't voice that question, but it had been on his mind all day. He'd played his hunch on Hamilton, partly because his gut told him the man was involved, partly because it was the only viable lead they had.

But at some point soon, he'd have to back off. He couldn't continue to charge Laura based on nothing more than Hamilton's one encounter with Darcy and his own intuition.

As the silence lengthened, she spoke again, her words laced with trepidation. "Dev? You aren't giving up, are you?"

"Not yet." It was the best he could offer.

"Soon, though." It wasn't a question this time, just a disheartened statement.

"No. We'll keep working this case as long as you want us to. We can't sustain the surveillance forever, but we'll continue to track down and follow up any leads we can find."

"Leads haven't been all that plentiful."

"Trust me, they can come up when you least expect them. We could discover a new piece of information any day that will be helpful. But let's table this discussion until later in the week. We've only been on the case nine days. Have you heard anything from the police recently?"

"I was just going to mention that I heard from Detective Butler again today. It was more a courtesy call. They haven't found a thing—if they're even looking."

Despite her discouraged tone, he didn't try to reassure her. She was right. Police resources were stretched thin investigating far more serious cases than teen runaways. Darcy wouldn't merit any special attention.

"Well, we're looking. And we'll keep looking. Darcy's out there, and . . ." His phone beeped twice, and he pulled it away from his ear. Connor. There must be a new development on the Costa Rica case. "Laura, I need to take this call from one of my partners. Can I call you back?"

"You don't have to do that. It's late."

"Not for me. Are you planning to go to bed soon?"

"I'll be up until ten or ten-thirty."

"I don't think this call will last that long. I'll try to get back to you before then." He switched to Connor's call. "What's up?"

"You weren't sleeping, were you?"

"Very funny. I was on another call."

"And how is your lovely client?"

Did both his partners have ESP?

Dev flipped off the heater. It was plenty hot in the Explorer now. "Did you have a reason for this call?" He didn't try to disguise his irritation.

"Touchy, touchy. But yeah, I did. Looks like it's wheels up on Friday for Costa Rica. I want to get Cal on a conference call so we can talk through a few of the logistics. What about your case? We're going to have to pull in a lot of reinforcements if you want to continue the surveillance past Friday morning."

"I was just talking to Laura about that."

"Aha. I was right about your phone call."

"You want to stick with the subject?"

"She is the subject. What do you want to do about her case?"

"I'm not sure yet." He massaged the bridge of his nose. "Let's give it twenty-four more hours. Then we can regroup."

"Okay. Hang tight while I get Cal on the line."

As Connor put him on hold, Dev stared at Hamilton's dark house. If the man was involved in Darcy's disappearance, he was doing an excellent job of disguising that fact. More often than not, however, if you watched and investigated perps long enough and hard enough, they slipped up somewhere.

But time was running out with this one.

They needed Hamilton to slip.

And they needed him to do it soon.

Mark turned onto Laura's street, slowing as he drove past the empty lot on his left. It was pitch-black. The few streetlights on her cul-de-sac were better at creating atmosphere than illuminating, and there were none close to the dark lot. Nor were there any cars parked on the street in front of it.

Excellent.

Slowly he drove up the long, steep hill toward Laura's house. Only one car had been left curbside on the whole block.

Also excellent.

He didn't want any witnesses nearby.

A garbled sound came from the passenger seat, and he transferred his gaze to Darcy. She was more alert now, her eyes wide with fear in the band of her face visible between the bottom of the cap and the top of the neck warmer.

"Good. You're awake just in time to play your role."

She lifted her bound hands, aiming for the neck warmer, and he reached over and yanked them down, squeezing hard on her forearm. When she whimpered and tried to pull away, he squeezed harder.

"Keep your hands in your lap. Got it?"

She gave a jerky nod.

After maintaining his grip for another five seconds, he released her and continued toward Laura's house, scrutinizing it as he passed.

There were no cars in front or in the driveway, and a single light was burning in one of the rooms on the far left. Her bedroom, perhaps.

She was home alone and still up—the exact situation he'd hoped to find. At almost ten on a weeknight, there wasn't much chance she'd be entertaining company. The odds had been in his favor.

Thankfully, they'd played out.

He drove around the circle at the end of the cul-de-sac and retraced his route. At the bottom of the hill, he pulled close to the curb in front of the empty lot, turned off his lights and engine, and scanned the street again. It was still deserted.

The ideal setting for what he had in mind.

He slipped out of the car, went around to the front passenger door, and tugged Darcy to her feet. Then he opened the back door and shoved her in.

It was reunion time.

24

Was that her phone?

Laura shut off the blow-dryer and cocked her head.

A second later, a muffled trill seeped through the bathroom door.

Wow. If she'd known Dev was going to get back to her this fast, she'd have brought the phone with her into the bathroom.

She set the dryer on the counter and dashed for the kitchen. There wasn't much chance she'd be able to intercept the call before it rolled to voice mail, but it was worth a try.

As the third ring trailed off, she skidded to a stop beside the phone and managed to snatch it out of its cradle before the recorded greeting kicked in. "Sorry, Dev." The apology came out in a breath-less rush. "I had the blow-dryer going and could barely hear the phone."

Silence.

She frowned. "Dev?"

"No." The male voice was muffled—and unfamiliar. "Is this Laura Griffith?"

"Yes." A tingle of unease crept up her spine. "Who is this?"

"A friend of your sister."

Her heart skipped a beat, and her fingers clenched around the phone. "Do you know where she is?"

"Yeah. With me. Here's the thing. She got in with some bad dudes and she's real sick. I was gonna dump her off in front of your house, but I was afraid she might lay there all night and freeze to death."

A surge of adrenaline set her nerve endings thrumming. "I can come and get her. That's no problem. Just tell me where you are."

"At the bottom of your street, by that empty lot. I'll leave her on the sidewalk. But make it fast or she might wander off."

Dear heaven, how sick was she?

Pulse pounding, Laura raced toward the living room. "Look . . . I can be there in sixty seconds. Can you wait until then?" She jammed her feet into her boots and grabbed her coat.

"I don't want no trouble, lady."

"I promise, I won't even ask your name. I just want Darcy back."

Silence.

"Please!"

"Okay. I guess I can wait."

A muffled sob sounded in the background, and her heart lurched again. "Is that Darcy?"

"Yeah. I'll put her on."

A few moments later, a sniffle sounded on the line, and Laura's grip tightened. "Darcy, sweetie . . . is that you?"

"Y-yes. Laura, d-don't—"

The words ended in a gasp, but she'd heard enough. It was Darcy. No question about that, despite the shakiness in her voice. And she was able to talk coherently. Maybe she wasn't as sick as the man had suggested.

She heard a fumbling sound, then the man spoke again. "You've got one minute. After that, I dump her."

The line went dead.

Laura tossed the phone onto the couch and raced for the door. Rather than waste time detouring down the cleared driveway, she tore diagonally across the lawn, stumbling through the piles of snow.

Darcy was home!

That joyful refrain echoed and reechoed in her mind as she flew down the sidewalk, her spirits soaring. Dev had been right. After all their efforts, her sister had shown up on her own. And no matter what was wrong with her, she'd fix it. Whatever it took.

When the lone car in front of the vacant lot came into view, she picked up her speed.

The back door opened as she approached, and she slid to a stop beside it.

The first thing she saw in the recesses of the dark interior was Darcy's terrified eyes.

The second thing she saw was the glint of the knife blade pressed against her sister's throat.

The third thing she saw was the rope binding Darcy's gloved hands.

She gaped at the scene, shock and disbelief reverberating through her.

"If you want your sister to continue breathing, you'll do exactly as I say."

It was the same voice that had spoken to her on the phone—but the tone had changed. Nervousness and uncertainty had been replaced by cold, deliberate calculation.

The man pressed the knife more firmly against Darcy's neck, and her sister stiffened and gasped.

"Who are you?" Laura's voice hoarsened as she struggled to get the words past her tight throat. "What's going on?"

Instead of answering, he tossed a pair of knit gloves toward her. She caught them on reflex.

"Put those on and get in the driver's seat."

Panic surged through her, and her hands began to shake. She couldn't get into the car. Couldn't let him force them away from here. If she did, they'd be at his mercy. He could . . .

The man yanked up Darcy's chin, and even though her sister was wearing a neck warmer, Laura knew the knife was aimed at her windpipe.

One plunge, and it was all over.

Her lungs froze. He wouldn't kill her in cold blood . . . would he?

She looked into his eyes, and the strange glitter in their depths gave her the answer to her question . . . and left her no option.

As if sensing her acquiescence, he nodded toward the front passenger seat. "Get in on that side and slide over."

God, please help me! Show me what to do!
"Now."

Numbly, she straightened up and scanned the neighborhood for any sign of life, any passerby who might come to their assistance.

No one was out at this late hour on this cold night.

She could bolt, bang on a door, plead for help.

But then Darcy would die. There was no doubt in her mind the man would carry out his threat.

Slowly she pulled on the gloves, opened the front door, and slid onto the seat.

"I see you follow instructions better than your

sister. Very good. Close the door and move behind the wheel. I'll give you directions."

She scooted across the seat. Behind her, she heard the back door slam.

"Start the engine and make a left at the stop sign."

Somehow she managed to turn the key in the ignition and put the car in gear.

As she followed his directions, she cast frequent glances in the rearview mirror. He still had Darcy in a death grip. Still had the knife pressed against her throat. Still had that odd glitter in his eyes.

Mind racing, she ran through her options. If she rear-ended a car in front of her, the knife could slip from the impact and Darcy would die. Same for swerving suddenly, or aiming the car at a streetlight. And with her hands gripping the wheel and her foot on the pedals, she was powerless to use either to attack the man as long as she was driving.

He had all the physical advantages.

That left her only one tool—and she wasn't optimistic it would work. Darcy's captor didn't seem like the type who could be dissuaded by words.

But she had to try.

"Look, this really isn't a great idea." She did her best to sound logical and persuasive. "If you get caught, you could be charged with kidnapping and sent to prison. But if you let us go, things will go a lot easier for you."

Silence.

Her mouth went dry, making it difficult to swallow. "Could you at least tell me why you're doing this?"

"Turn onto the eastbound I-44 ramp."

She complied.

The car remained quiet except for the sound of Darcy's ragged breathing and muffled sobs.

Laura's stomach clenched. She could feel her sister's fear. Could taste her own. The terror inside the car was almost palpable as questions tumbled through her mind.

Where was he taking them?

Why had he targeted Darcy?

What had he done to her sister in the days she'd been missing?

A wave of nausea swept over her as a parade of dire possibilities strobed through her brain.

No! Don't go there! Stay focused on the present, or you and Darcy won't have a future. Don't waste time and energy wondering about what's already happened. You need to analyze this situation and think about what you're going to do next!

She inhaled. Held her breath. Slowly exhaled. Repeated the process once. Twice. Three times. Her pulse rate decelerated slightly, and her brain kicked in enough to do some topline analysis.

Fact one. There wasn't much, if any, chance she

was going to get the upper hand on the man in the backseat while she was driving.

Fact two. Her best opportunity to engineer an escape would be after they reached their destination and were out of the car. On her feet, facing Darcy's captor, she might find a tiny window of opportunity to distract him, throw him off balance, and pull her sister free. He'd still have the knife —but as long as it wasn't pressed to Darcy's throat, she'd be far less timid about lunging for his legs or delivering a well-placed kick, no matter the risks to herself.

Fact three. The chances of success for that plan were very small.

But the chances of escaping if she did nothing were zero.

"Get off here and turn right."

She read the exit sign. Jefferson.

As the significance of the name and their location registered, three additional facts clicked into place in rapid succession.

They were heading for Soulard.

The man in the backseat was Mark Hamilton.

And Dev's hunch had been right all along.

"Make a left at the next corner."

She put on the blinker, her hope surging. Dev was close by. Once they stopped, all she had to do was get his attention. Hamilton wasn't likely to park on the street, but she could kill the motor at the entrance to the alley, then flood the engine and hope it didn't start again. Dev would notice the stalled vehicle. And if they had to get out and hoof it down the alley to Hamilton's house, Dev would figure out what was happening. With his training and experience, he'd be all over the man before Hamilton knew what was happening.

Maybe . . . just maybe . . . there was a way out of this after all.

Three minutes later, Hamilton spoke again. "Turn left."

Hands trembling on the wheel, Laura read the street sign as she complied. It wasn't the name Dev had mentioned, but perhaps they were still a block or two away.

"Park on the right. By the big tree."

Here? She furrowed her brow. This wasn't his street.

What was the man up to?

"Did you hear me? I said park on the right!"

There was a taut edge to his voice now, as if he might be getting nervous. No surprise there. Once they were out of the car, the risk of discovery would increase exponentially—and he knew it.

That also meant he'd be more on alert.

But why hadn't he gone to his own house?

Edging into the spot adjacent to the sidewalk, she examined the structure beside her. It looked empty. Abandoned, even.

A strip of cloth fluttered onto the seat beside her, and she glanced down.

"Put that between your teeth and tie it at the back of your head. Tight."

She picked it up.

He wanted her to gag herself?

She stared at the cloth. Was Darcy gagged too? Was that why she hadn't spoken?

"Now, Laura."

Her sister gasped, and she swiveled to look over her shoulder. Hamilton held up the knife until the blade glinted in the glow from a streetlight. The tip was red.

Once again, her heart slammed into overdrive.

"Just a nick—but there'll be a lot more blood if you don't follow my instructions."

Darcy's terrified eyes met hers.

Laura did as he told her with the cloth.

"Put your hands on the wheel, where I can see them."

Again, she followed his instructions.

She felt a tug on her gag, as if he was testing whether she'd tied it tight. Then a dark blob dropped over the seat.

"Pull that over your head and cover your nose and mouth."

She picked up the knitted object. It was a neck warmer, like Darcy's.

So she wasn't going to have her voice. But she had her arms and legs—and before she went into any building with this man, she intended to use both . . . even if Dev wasn't around to help her.

A door opened behind her, and then Hamilton and Darcy appeared outside her window. He gestured her to exit.

When she opened the door, he spoke again. "Bring the keys."

She pulled them out and wrapped her fist around them, maneuvering one key so the end with teeth was pointing out. It wasn't as sharp as a knife, but it could do some serious damage to a face—or eyes.

"That way." Hamilton unzipped Darcy's coat and pulled her close beside him, indicating the narrow walkway between the empty structure and the house beside it, where a light shone in the upper window. "And remember . . . I have a knife aimed at your sister's heart from below her rib cage. One wrong move, I shove it in."

She started down the passage, walking as slow as she dared, buying herself every possible second to think. From what she'd been able to see, the knife blade wasn't that long. Would it reach Darcy's heart? Maybe not.

But she couldn't take the chance.

As she emerged into an alley at the back of the buildings, Hamilton spoke again.

"Keep going. Straight ahead."

She continued toward a two-story row house. Hamilton's? If so, they were entering through the back door.

Out of Dev's sight.

A suffocating wave of panic crashed over her. This was going to be up to her, after all. And she had to make her move out here. Once they went inside, they'd disappear from the eyes of the world.

Perhaps forever.

Her heart began to pound as she approached the small stoop.

Please, God . . . give me strength.

"Step up to the door."

As she did so, he reached over and placed a single key on the wooden railing that rimmed the small space.

"Put it in the lock and turn it."

Her fingers were trembling so badly it took her three tries, but at last she managed to insert it. One soft click, and the lock released.

"Now here's what we're going to do. There's a door to your left when you enter. Open it slow and easy. Go down the steps. Make a left and walk to the door on the far wall. Is that clear?"

She angled toward him. Assessed the situation in one swift glance. Her best bet was to lunge off the stoop. Shove Darcy back. Kick Hamilton with her right leg.

But as her muscles tensed in preparation, he somehow read her intent.

Before she could move an inch, he shoved Darcy to the ground, leapt onto the stoop, and slammed a fist into her face.

Her chin jerked up as shafts of pain pierced her head. She staggered. Lost her balance. Felt herself falling backward. Heard a crack.

Then the world went dark.

As Laura crumpled in a heap on the stoop, Mark spat out a curse.

Everything had gone so well until now.

But he wasn't surprised she'd tried a stunt like that. Darcy had too, and they were related. Similar traits often ran in families. He'd seen it in siblings at daycare. Thank goodness he'd been on alert.

Behind him, he heard Darcy scrambling to her feet. Or trying to. He turned. She still wasn't steady, and she wouldn't get far even if she did manage to stand without falling again. But she had a strong pair of lungs—and as her bound hands rose toward the gag, he shot toward her. A scream would carry in the silent night air, and there were lights on in the house they'd passed on the other side of the alley.

He grabbed for her hands, hauled her to her feet, and dragged her toward the back door. Once on the stoop, he got in her face and put the point of the knife an inch from her eyes.

"I told your sister I'd kill you if she didn't do what I said." He spoke through clenched teeth, keeping his voice low and menacing. "I'm telling you the same thing. You make one sound when we get inside, your sister dies. Got it?"

A tear spilled down her cheek, but she nodded.

He wasn't certain she'd comply, but he couldn't delay entry. Laura had knocked her head hard on the porch railing as she'd fallen, but unless she was seriously injured, she wouldn't stay out long. He needed to dispose of Darcy and get back here fast.

Sliding the knife into the case he'd shoved inside his boot at Laura's house, he once more hefted Darcy onto his shoulder.

She whimpered.

"Shut up."

When she quieted, he twisted the knob on the back door and eased through. The lack of lights in the house was a positive sign. Faith must still be sleeping it off.

A quick look into the living room confirmed that conclusion. She was right where he'd left her, curled on the couch under the afghan.

That part of his plan had worked flawlessly, anyway.

He opened the basement door and started down the stairs. He could feel Darcy shaking, but she wasn't making a sound. And going down was much easier than going up.

Once he reached her room, he dumped her on the bed and exited without looking back, locking the door behind him.

One down, one to go.

At the top of the stairs, he again checked on Faith.

No change.

Continuing to the back door, he pulled the knife out again—just in case. But when he emerged, Laura was slumped where he'd left her.

Was it possible the knock on the head had killed her, saving him the trouble?

But there'd be time to find out once he had her stowed in the basement, away from prying eyes.

He put the knife back in its case and knelt on one knee. It took some maneuvering, but he finally managed to hoist her over his shoulder. She groaned and stirred as he stood, and his lips flattened.

So much for his hope she might already be dead.

With one final scan to confirm no one was about, he moved to the door and slipped inside. The house remained dark. Faith was still out cold. And in sixty seconds, his two biggest problems would be locked away tight until he was ready to deal with them.

Once and for all.

As he started toward the basement stairs, Laura gave another muffled groan and began to writhe on his shoulder.

He picked up his pace.

Two steps down, something snagged, bringing him up short. He looked over his shoulder.

Laura had grabbed the door frame with one hand.

Taking a firm grip on the railing, he jerked her forward. Her hand pulled away with minimal resistance.

The fist in her face and the blow to the head had clearly weakened her, but she could work the gag loose if she tried—and that would be a disaster. The last thing he needed was for Faith to get wind of the drama playing out one floor below.

Descending the remaining stairs as fast as he dared, he pulled the key out of his pocket and half jogged toward Darcy's room, Laura bouncing on his shoulder. A fast peek through the peephole confirmed the teen had remained where he'd dropped her on the bed.

The lock clicked and he pulled the door open. Three steps into the room, he dumped Laura onto the floor. Darcy gasped as her sister fell, but Laura lay unmoving except for the blood oozing out of her nose now that the neck warmer had slipped down.

With one last glance at the duo, he backed toward the door, the knot of tension in his stomach beginning to uncoil.

He'd pulled it off.

The hardest part was over.

As for the two women in his basement, he could take care of their final disposal at his leisure. Maybe he'd leave them down here for a few days without food. They'd be easier to manage then.

Weaker. Less likely to struggle when he pressed the pillow to their—

All at once, Darcy's sister came to life. She rolled toward him, grabbed his leg, and tugged.

Thrown off balance, he fell backward, surprise giving way to anger even before he slammed onto the floor.

How could he have let himself be fooled a second time? Was he stupid after all, just like his mother used to say when drugs or alcohol stirred up the venom inside her and she spewed out hateful things?

No!

He had a college degree and a responsible, important job. People respected him. He was smart. Smart enough to fix this problem.

Besides, he had the advantage.

As his body absorbed the impact, he reached for the knife in his boot.

Coming slowly awake, Faith rubbed her eyes and stared into the darkness.

Where was she?

And what was that odd muffled, scuffling noise?

She forced herself upright, fighting back a wave of dizziness and an odd lethargy in her limbs.

Man. You'd think she'd downed half a bottle of wine instead of a mug of hot chocolate. She must have been a lot more tired than she'd thought to fall into such a deep sleep.

Closing her eyes, she gripped the edge of the couch until her head stopped swimming, then focused on getting the lay of the land.

She was still on the couch at Mark's house. They'd been watching that old movie, the one with the chick from *The Wizard of Oz*, and she'd gotten sleepy. The last thing she remembered before drifting off was Mark draping an afghan over her.

Rotating her wrist toward the blank, illuminated screen, she peered at her watch. Was it really ten-forty? She'd been asleep for two hours?!

Warmth rose on her cheeks and she closed her eyes again. Talk about embarrassing. Falling asleep on a first date was the kiss of death. Mark would never ask her out again. Why, oh why, had she stayed up last night watching MTV?

The muted noise intruded on her thoughts again, and she looked toward the back of the house. It seemed to be coming from the basement—but what was it?

She rose, and the floor tilted.

Whoa!

She groped for the arm of the couch and held on tight until the room settled down. What in the world was going on?

Once she felt steady enough to walk, she carefully worked her way down the length of the couch in the dark. Had Mark gone to bed rather than disturb her? That would be like him. Everyone at work was impressed with his kindness and caring toward the children. Knowing him, he'd left a note by her purse telling her to wake him when she was ready to leave and he'd walk her back to her car.

Not a chance. After falling asleep on him, she'd rather slink out and hope he didn't hold it against her tomorrow. Could she spin her faux pas in some positive way? Tell him she'd drifted off because she felt so relaxed and at home here, and that it was actually a compliment?

Lame . . . but it would have to do unless she came up with a better excuse.

Pausing at the dining table, she frowned and surveyed the empty top. She'd left her purse here, hadn't she? Maybe Mark had moved it. If so, where had he put it?

She needed light.

Retracing her steps to the living room, she felt around the base of the lamp that had been on earlier, searching for the switch. Too bad her keys were inside her purse. Otherwise, she could leave it and let Mark bring it with him to work tomorrow.

Her fingers closed over the switch and she flipped it on. Soft light flooded the room—but her purse was nowhere to be seen.

Had he taken it to the kitchen, perhaps?

Still plagued with a weird unsteadiness, she concentrated on walking a straight line to the back of the house.

It wasn't easy.

On the threshold of the kitchen, she stopped and gripped the door frame, searching the wall for a light switch. There. Over by the back door. Near where she'd left her boots when they arrived.

Stifling a yawn, she padded across the light-colored wood floor in her socks, groped for the switch, and flipped it on. Success. Her purse was front and center, smack in the middle of the bare counter.

She started toward it . . . then froze midstride.

What were those red splotches on the other-wise spotless floor? The ones that began halfway across the room and led to the open basement door? They hadn't been there earlier.

She moved close to the first one and bent down. Was that . . . blood?

More muffled noises came from the basement —and one of them sounded like a moan. Followed by a grunt.

She straightened up and backed off a step, visually following the trail of spots that ended at the basement door.

She lifted her gaze.

Stopped breathing.

Were those bloody fingerprints on the white door frame?

A thump sounded below her and she jumped.

The vibes in the house were suddenly getting bad.

Very bad.

"No!" The faint, muted cry from below was female.

A door slammed.

She jumped, gripping her hands in front of her as she strained to listen for more sounds.

All was quiet for half a minute—until one of the stairs creaked.

Someone was coming up!

Mark?

An intruder?

An ax murderer?

Pulse surging, she dashed toward the back door. Maybe there was a simple explanation for what she'd seen and heard. The red stuff might be paint. The voice might not have been a voice at all, but a cat or a CD or . . . something. Mark might have a workshop in the basement, and maybe he'd been watching a spooky DVD while he waited for her to wake up.

But she wasn't waiting around to find out.

Tomorrow, she'd make her apologies and listen to explanations.

Tonight, she was out of here.

Swinging around, she grabbed her boots, reached for the door handle, and prepared to bolt.

25

Mark stopped two steps up on the basement stairs and double-checked his hands in the light spilling down through the door to the kitchen.

No blood.

Good.

But there was plenty of it in the room. It would take him weeks to clean and restore the space for the next girl.

Not that he'd had any choice, once the floor-board squeaked overhead. Knocking Darcy's sister around, like Lil used to do to him when he got out of line, would have taken too long with Faith wandering around. He couldn't risk having his "date" hear noises, get curious, and come downstairs to investigate.

Funny thing, though. While he'd never been the violent sort, driving the blade into flesh had been much easier than he'd expected. Satisfying too. With every thrust, his anger had dissipated and he'd felt more energized and powerful.

Maybe he'd rethink his plans for finishing the two of them off. Forget about the pillow method. Shake things up a little—if he could stand the mess. And that was a big if. Blood was a bear to clean up.

But he could make that decision later. First, he needed to get rid of Faith.

Scratching the back of his hand, he continued up the steps.

Three seconds later, as his eyes came level with the floor, red spots appeared in his field of vision, neon-like against the pristine polished oak.

He froze.

Laura's nose must have dripped on the floor.

Had Faith seen it?

He took the last steps two at a time, arriving at the top just as his date for the night disappeared out the back door.

A roar filled his head, rising to a crescendo.

She'd seen the blood. There was a trail of spots halfway across the floor. No wonder she'd freaked.

But he could explain it. There were lots of reasons for red splotches on a floor. He could say he cut his finger on a knife in the kitchen. Or had suffered a nosebleed himself. Or that he'd spilled some tomato soup while fixing himself a snack.

Those were all logical explanations. Any of them could be true. Plus, she liked him. Trusted him. Once he caught up with her, it would be an easy sell. And it wasn't as if she was going anywhere until he spoke with her. He had her keys. The ones he'd wrestled from Laura after she'd tried to jab one of them into his eye.

He crossed the kitchen in several long strides, pulled the door open, and exited onto the stoop.

Voices next door caught his attention, and he paused in the shadows. One of the frat boys was in the alley, by the dumpster. Probably getting rid of another trash bag full of beer cans. His lips curled in disgust. No wonder they were in a drunken stupor every weekend.

The kid was listening to Faith, though, as she gestured behind her, toward his house. He couldn't make out her words, but the hysterical pitch of her voice carried in the quiet air.

He needed to stop this before it went any further.

Rubbing his palms down his slacks, he stepped off the stoop and started toward them. Too bad he'd ditched his jacket, hat, and gloves on the basement floor before coming upstairs. It was freezing out here.

The kid looked his way as he approached, and Faith spun toward him. Her eyes widened, and she edged behind the guy, swaying slightly as she grabbed his arm.

"Faith . . . what's wrong?" He tried for a solicitous tone. "Are you feeling okay?"

She just stared at him.

"She said there was blood in your house." The muscular kid with the build of a quarterback hefted a bulging plastic bag into the dumpster and faced him.

"Yeah." He managed a rueful laugh and went for the nosebleed explanation as he addressed Faith. "After you conked out on me, I went downstairs to fiddle around with the hot water heater. It's been acting up the past few days. Sometimes if I bend over for too long, I get nosebleeds. It happens now and then. I'm sorry you got scared."

Faith edged out a fraction from behind the guy, her expression shifting from fear to uncertainty.

She was buying his explanation.

"Why don't you come back to the house and we'll gather up your things? Then I'll walk you to your car."

Super Jock looked at her and decided to play Galahad. "I can walk you to your car if you'd rather."

Faith bit her lip, tucked her hair behind her ear, and studied him across the frozen expanse. When she dropped her gaze and angled toward his neighbor, Mark knew she'd decided to accept the guy's offer.

"Thank you. I'd appreciate the escort. But I need my stuff from the house. My keys are in my purse."

They both looked his way.

He was stuck. Refusing to hand over her things would only add to their suspicions. He'd have to smooth things out with Faith tomorrow at work. Convince her it really had been a nosebleed. In the daylight, back in familiar surroundings, she'd accept that explanation. Right now she was drugged, cold, and standing in a strange, dark alley. Her imagination would be playing tricks on her—or so he'd tell her tomorrow.

Unfortunately, he'd also have to play out this romance thing a little longer, until tonight was forgotten. An unappealing prospect, but necessary.

"Fine. I'll get your things."

He turned away, but when she gasped he swung back. "What's wrong?"

The guy spoke. "There's blood on the back of your shirt."

He smothered a curse.

He'd been wearing his jacket when he'd grappled with Laura in the basement room. Some of the blood must have gotten on it, then rubbed off on the back of his shirt as he'd shed his outerwear.

And a bloody nose wouldn't explain stains on the back of his shirt.

But how much could there be? A few streaks? And in the dark, they wouldn't be able to tell for sure if it was blood.

Staring the two of them down, he lifted his chin. "I don't like your insinuations. Faith, I'll put your things on the back porch, since you prefer the company of your new friend." He shot the guy a quick, scornful look, then refocused on her. "I'll see you at work tomorrow."

With that, he walked back to his house, pushed through the door, and closed it behind him.

Only then did he allow his shoulders to sag.

He was going to have to do some serious damage control at work tomorrow.

Closer to home, he'd also have to undermine Faith's credibility. That should be easier. He'd watch for Super Jock, then happen to run into him in the alley. The guy would surely notice Faith's unsteadiness if he walked her to her car tonight, and a couple of remarks about drinking should punch a lot of holes in her story. The crew next door had firsthand knowledge about the mind-muddling effects of alcohol.

For now, though, he'd gather up her stuff, hand it over, and scrub the kitchen until there wasn't a speck of blood left, even if it kept him up past midnight. The basement room would require a much bigger effort, but since he never allowed anyone downstairs, it could wait.

Mark pushed off from the door and went in search of Faith's coat and purse, scrutinizing her keys for any sign of blood before he dropped them in one of the side compartments on her bag.

She and the college guy were still standing in the distance when he set her things at the edge of the stoop—and neither approached until he retreated inside.

He watched from a slit in the blinds as her protector retrieved the items, then rejoined her.

But instead of heading down the walkway between the buildings on the other side of the alley, they disappeared in the direction of the house next door.

Had he offered her a drink? Was he trying to pick her up? Did he intend to take advantage of her tipsy, vulnerable state?

Who cared? She was old enough to fend for herself.

And he had other, more important things to worry about.

"Lie still, sweetie. You're going to be fine." Laura tried for an encouraging tone, hoping the assurance was true. But she didn't like the location of Darcy's abdominal wound, even if it wasn't bleeding nearly as much as the puncture on her own leg.

Lord, please don't let one of her vital organs be damaged!

Tears trickled out of the corners of her sister's eyes. "I'm s-so sorry."

"There's nothing to be sorry about. You saved my life. If you hadn't lunged for him when he raised the knife over me, I'd be dead. Instead, you got the brunt of it."

"We wouldn't b-be in this mess if it w-wasn't for me."

As Laura fought back another wave of mind-numbing dizziness, she tried to think of a way to refute that. Failed. Darcy was right.

Except *mess* was far too mild a word.

Tightening the makeshift bandage on her leg, fighting the near-debilitating weakness in her limbs, she glanced around the room from her kneeling position on the floor beside her sister.

Pure carnage.

There were streaks and splotches of blood everywhere—and more was being added by the minute. In addition to the ever-widening circumference on the towel she'd secured to her leg by knotting the sleeves of one of the blouses in the closet around it, she could also feel warmth trickling down her shoulder from the wound at the top of her left arm that she hadn't been able to bandage. On the plus side, the blood from the stabs on her arms was no longer seeping through the washcloths she'd tied around them. Her nose had also stopped bleeding.

"Laura?"

At Darcy's soft summons, she refocused on her sister. Her head was throbbing, and her vision was going in and out of focus, but she could see clearly enough to discern that her sister had been through hell over the past ten days. Her face was one giant bruise, her blonde hair had been hacked off and dyed, and she'd lost a significant amount of weight. Now she'd sustained a possible life-threatening wound that needed professional medical attention.

The specter of death was an almost palpable presence.

Her throat constricted, and she tried to swallow past her panic. She couldn't lose Darcy now. *Please, God, no! Not after all we've both been through!*

"What is it, sweetie?" Despite her best efforts to sound calm and in control, a tremor ran through her words.

"I w-want you to know I appreciate all you d-did for me."

"You can thank me later, after this is over."

"He's going to k-kill us." Darcy's voice was dull now—and resigned. "Just like the o-others."

A cold chill settled in the pit of Laura's stomach. "What others?"

Darcy drew a shuddering breath. "Star and Angela and Denise. Maybe Lil too."

Hamilton had killed four women already?

The pounding in her head intensified.

If they were dealing with a serial killer, he wouldn't hesitate to kill again—and he'd had a lot of practice.

Her estimate of their odds of survival plummeted.

But she wasn't going to give up yet. Hamilton might be smart and physically strong, but no one was unbeatable. She'd cling to that thought and focus every ounce of her diminished brainpower on coming up with a plan to outwit him.

"That doesn't mean we have to be his next victims." The words came out sounding much more confident than she felt.

"There's no way out of this room. And he's not going to let us jump him again."

That was true—but they weren't in any condition to attempt a repeat performance of that in any case.

"Then we'll think of something else." Laura scooted up and set to work on the rope binding Darcy's wrists.

"Like what?"

"I don't know yet. I'm working on it—but it wouldn't be a bad idea to ask for some help. Will you pray with me once I get your hands free?"

Her sister gave a soft sigh. "I guess. I've been doing a lot of that since I've been down here, but I didn't talk to God much before this and you always had to drag me to services, so I don't know if he's been listening. Still, where two or three are gathered and all that."

Apparently a few things from the sermons her sister had claimed were lame and boring had stuck.

"He always listens to us, no matter how long it's been since we last spoke with him. It's just that we don't always get the answer we want." Giving Darcy's hand a squeeze, Laura closed her eyes. "Lord, we need your strength and your wisdom and your fortitude. Please inspire our thinking and help us find a way out of this situation. Give us courage and fill our minds with the serenity that comes from knowing no matter what happens, you are with us always. But if it's your will, please save us from this danger so we can have many years together to discover all the blessings of sisterhood. Amen."

As Darcy's hushed amen echoed hers in the silent room, Laura squeezed her fingers again and added one more silent plea for help.

Because despite the brave face she was trying to maintain for her sister's sake, in her heart she knew it would take a miracle for them to escape whatever fate Hamilton had planned for them.

Insulated mug poised halfway to his mouth, Dev watched the police car pull up to the curb and stop in front of the house next to Hamilton's.

Interesting. During all his hours of surveillance, he'd seen a few cops drive by—but none had ever stopped.

He took a sip of coffee and watched the car.

Two minutes later, the officer got out and started up the walkway toward the front door of Hamilton's neighbor.

Dev straightened in his seat, grabbed his night-vision binoculars, and fitted them to his eyes. With the tiny front yards in Soulard, he had no problem keeping the officer in sight as the man made the short trek to the door and rang the bell.

Almost at once, a tall, broad-shouldered college-age kid answered. After talking for less than a minute, the officer disappeared inside with him.

Dev lowered the binoculars. It was possible a police visit to Hamilton's neighbor didn't have any bearing on his case, but it was a peculiar coincidence.

Too peculiar.

Something relevant to his investigation was going on. He could feel it in his bones.

Fifteen minutes later, the officer emerged. Instead of returning to his car, however, he detoured toward Hamilton's house, went up the walkway, and rang his bell.

Just as Dev prepared to put the binoculars to use again, he caught a movement in the upper window, out of sight of the officer. A thin, very faint band of light appeared for a moment, as if someone had cracked the blinds. Then it was gone.

The officer waited a full minute, but when no one answered he descended the steps and walked back to his car.

Frowning, Dev set the binoculars on the seat and tapped a finger on the wheel. He knew how this was going to play out. The officer would make a note of the call and code it a dead end.

But perhaps he could offer some additional information that would pique the man's interest—and pick up some info for himself as well.

Turning up the collar of his jacket, Dev

untangled himself from the electric blanket and pulled a cap over his hair. If Hamilton decided to peek out the window again, he preferred to remain anonymous, and the auburn hair would be a dead giveaway.

After flipping off the dome light, he dug his PI license out of his wallet and palmed it. Then he swept the windows in Hamilton's house to verify the man wasn't watching, opened the door, and hustled down the street, crossing at the corner.

As he approached the police car from the front, he kept his hands at his sides. In this neighborhood, at this hour, it wouldn't hurt to let the officer know he wasn't holding a weapon.

On the other hand, the man didn't need to know about the compact Sig Sauer in the concealed holster on his belt.

The officer cracked his window as he approached. The forty-something guy had the look of a seasoned street cop. That was a plus. "Can I help you?"

"Possibly. I'm James Devlin with Phoenix Inc., a private investigation firm. We've had this house under surveillance for the past week." He indicated Hamilton's place and handed the officer his license through the window.

"Phoenix . . . that's Cal Burke's outfit, isn't it?"

"You know Cal?"

"Our paths crossed a few times while he was a street cop with County, before his detective days.

Good guy. Are you the ATF partner or the Secret Service partner?"

"ATF. I see our reputation has preceded us."

"Word gets around. Most of the PIs we tangle with aren't in your league." The officer slid out of the car and returned the license as he introduced himself. "Ken Larson. So what's going on here?" He gestured to the house.

"I'm hoping you can offer *me* some insights. Here's what I know." Dev gave the man a rapid briefing on the case. "And FYI, while you were ringing the bell, someone was checking you out through the blinds on the second floor."

The man raised an eyebrow, then shrugged. "Unfortunately, we can't force people to answer the door."

"I know. I've been in your shoes. What can you tell me about your call here tonight?"

"One of the college kids next door said a woman rushed out of Hamilton's back door while he was taking some trash to the dumpster. She told him she was visiting Hamilton for the evening and fell asleep while they were watching a movie."

Dev frowned. "That can't be. I've been watching the house all night. No one went in or out the front door, and no young woman has been in any of the cars that entered or exited the alley."

"She says Hamilton told her to park on the next street because there'd been some vandalism to cars in front of his house."

"Is that true?"

"Not that I know of. Anyway, she claims that when she woke up she saw drops of blood on the kitchen floor and a bloody handprint, plus heard odd noises in the basement. The college kid said there was also a stain on the back of Hamilton's shirt that looked like blood. Hamilton told them it was from a nosebleed."

Dev's pulse spiked. This was getting weirder and weirder. "You don't get blood on the back of your shirt from a nosebleed."

"That occurred to me too." The man folded his arms. "Here's another interesting tidbit. The woman whose statement I just took is the same one you mentioned in your case recap. Faith Bradley."

His adrenaline surged as he processed that unexpected piece of news. "She'd have to have been really rattled to bolt during a long-coveted date."

"Rattled would be an apt way to describe her condition."

Dev blew out a breath, a cloud of vapor forming in front of his face, obscuring his view for a moment. "So what's your take?"

The man leaned back against the side of the car. "I'm not sure what to make of it. We've had several complaints in the past few months about the occupants of that house." He gestured toward the two-story brick next to Hamilton's, where

Faith had taken refuge. "Loud parties. Disorderly conduct. Beer cans littering the alley. You name it. They all seemed sober tonight, though. To be honest, I was planning to code it as a dead end, but now that we've talked, I'll swing by a couple more times during my shift. I can also try ringing the bell again tomorrow night, earlier in my shift. Maybe he'll answer then."

"Tomorrow's a long time away if there's fresh blood in the house."

"*If* being the operative word. When I pressed, neither the girl or the kid could confirm that the stain on the back of Hamilton's shirt was blood. It was too dark in the alley. So the blood in the house could have been from a nosebleed. As for the noises in the basement . . . the girl admitted they could have come from a radio or DVD."

Dev surveyed Hamilton's house. "I might buy that if I didn't already suspect this guy was up to his neck in trouble."

"You said the background check you did was clean." The officer lifted his hands, palms up. "I can't arrest a law-abiding citizen or demand entry based on a hunch."

"I know that."

A car drove by, wheels crunching on the remnants of ice in the street, and Dev moved closer to the police car as a brutal blast of cold air whipped past.

"I'll tell you what." The officer gave the passing

car a practiced sweep, then refocused on him. "I'll put in a call to my supervisor while I continue my patrol. She might want to get one of the detectives to pay a visit to your guy at his place of business tomorrow. Maybe talk to a few of the neighbors at a more reasonable hour."

It wasn't enough. Dev knew that deep in his gut. But he also knew the officer's hands were tied. Police were constrained both by staffing levels and red tape.

Fortunately, he didn't have to deal with either of those problems anymore.

"Whatever you can do would be helpful. We might talk to some neighbors too."

As the officer's radio sprang to life, he handed over a card. "I assume you'll be here for a while?"

"All night." Dev took the card and gestured to the Explorer parked around the corner.

"If anything looks suspicious, call it in. Or call me on my cell. Number's on the card. I won't be far away."

"Thanks."

As the officer slid back into the car and Dev started to turn away, he glanced up at the second floor . . . just in time to once again catch a thin, faint bar of light before the window went dark.

Hamilton was still keeping tabs on them.

The man was spooked. Why else would he be watching the activity on the street? Why else would he have refused to answer the door for the police?

If there had, indeed, been blood on the floor and on the door frame, however, it was gone by now. Hamilton had had plenty of time to clean it up. But if the nosebleed story was a lie, as Dev suspected, the source of that blood was still inside.

And that person needed help.

Dev continued down the street and hung a right at the corner—away from his vehicle. Once he was out of sight of Hamilton's window, he crossed to the other side, staying in the shadows. He'd give it ten minutes, then skulk his way back to the Explorer and slip inside as unobtrusively as possible.

In the meantime, he pulled his cell off his belt. Given Faith's report and Hamilton's circumspect spying from the second-floor window, the day-care manager was getting nervous about what-ever he had to hide. And nervous people made mistakes.

If he made one tonight, Dev didn't intend to miss it. But he needed more eyes on Hamilton's house—and he wanted backup in place.

It was time to call for reinforcements.

26

The cop was finally leaving.

And the other guy had disappeared too—whoever he was.

Mark let the slat in the blinds drop back into place, backed away from his bedroom window, and began to pace.

So there'd been a few glitches in his plan. Faith should have slept longer. And he hadn't expected Laura to bleed all over his kitchen floor or attack him in the basement.

But none of that was the end of the world. For all he knew, the police hadn't believed a word anyone next door had said. The college kids were known troublemakers, and Faith was still trying to shake off the effects of the sleeping drugs. The cop might have taken one look at her, figured she was tipsy, and dismissed the story. After all, he'd done nothing more than ring the doorbell.

And now he was gone.

Mark's hands began to itch, and he detoured to the bathroom, turned on the faucet, and lathered up. The blood in the kitchen had been cleaned up, and he'd cut up the stained shirt for disposal in the trash—all except for the bloodstained section, which he'd drop into one of the soiled-diaper bins at the daycare center tomorrow. No one would ever see it again.

Drying his hands on the towel, he walked back to the front window and peeked through the blinds again. Everything appeared quiet. No cops. No strangers. No activity.

He let out a long, slow breath.

All he had to do was act normal for the next few days. Go about his usual routine. The PIs would stop looking for Darcy as soon as the payments from Laura dried up. Even when they found out she was missing, why would they care? They didn't do investigations out of the goodness of their hearts. Sure, they might wonder about her, but they'd move on to the next paying job. And suppose they did mention to the police that she'd been their client? There was no hard evidence to link him to her—or her sister. Nor would there be. Everything else he had planned for them would take place inside the constitutionally protected privacy of his house.

There was no need to worry.

A sudden, heavy weariness settled over him, and he checked the time. Groaned. Five-thirty was going to come way too fast, and six hours of sleep wasn't nearly enough. However, he'd get less than that if he tried to deal with the two spitfires in the basement tonight. Better to let them go hungry for a few days. The weaker they became, the easier they'd be to finish off.

He did have to take a shower, though. Otherwise he'd never get to sleep. But he'd only give himself five minutes instead of his usual ten to fifteen.

Flexing a slat in the blinds, he took one more look outside. The street remained deserted—its typical condition at eleven-thirty on a weeknight. Still, there was no harm in confirming that once more, after he was clean. But cops were busy. They weren't going to waste time on some cockeyed story from documented troublemakers. He wouldn't be surprised if the officer had already forgotten about the encounter.

Mark crossed toward the bathroom, flipping on another light in the bedroom as he passed to dispel the shadows lurking in the corners. The soft illumination from the lamp on the nightstand wasn't cutting it tonight.

A relaxing hot shower, one more scan of the street, and then he'd call it a night.

The excitement for this day was over.

As Dev's BlackBerry began to vibrate, he pulled it out of the holster . . . and expelled a frustrated breath. Connor—not Laura. He needed to talk to his partner, but why hadn't Laura returned the message he'd left after the shorter-than-expected Costa Rica conference call? Why had her phone rolled to voice mail every time he'd tried to call her since? Had she forgotten to press end after their last call and fallen asleep? His mom did that a lot.

He hoped the explanation was that simple—but he was beginning to get uneasy.

Putting the phone to his ear, he kept his attention focused on Hamilton's house. "Where were you when I called fifteen minutes ago?"

A moment of silence ticked by. "Not that it's any of your business, but I was taking a shower." As usual, Connor sounded wide-awake and chipper despite the late hour.

"At eleven-thirty at night? Do you ever sleep?"

"On occasion."

"Well, tonight's not going to be one of them."

Another beat of silence. "Something going on down there?"

"Maybe." The windows in the Explorer began to fog up, and he flipped on the small fan while he brought Connor up to speed on the events of the evening. "Also, based on the bright lights on the second floor, Hamilton's still roaming around. That's out of pattern. The man gets up at the crack of dawn, so he's an early-to-bed type. My gut tells me things are close to breaking here, and I want another set of eyes positioned to see down the alley toward the back of the house while I watch the front."

"I'll be there in thirty."

That was it. No questions. No complaints. No doubting his partner's instincts. Just "I'll be there."

But that was how Phoenix worked. That was *why* it worked. They trusted each other. Period.

Partners didn't come any finer than Connor and Cal.

He changed the angle of the fan on the front window as the glass started to fog up on the right. "Thanks."

"You bringing Cal into this?"

Dev hesitated. That hadn't been part of his plan . . . but the more he thought about Laura's MIA status, the more worried he became.

"I know it's late, but I might ask him to run by Laura's place. I left her a message almost two hours ago and she never returned it. She's not answering her home phone, and her cell's rolling to voice mail immediately."

"Maybe she's on the line."

"At eleven-thirty at night? For two hours?"

"Could be a family emergency."

"She doesn't have any family except Darcy."

"In that case, it might not hurt to check out her house."

"Yeah, that's what I'm thinking. I'll look for you in thirty." He ended the call, then tapped in Cal's speed dial number. Unlike Connor, his other colleague would be asleep. But he wouldn't complain about the request, either. They all respected each other's instincts too much.

At the same time, this might be a wild goose chase. Laura could very well be safe in her bed, sound asleep. He hoped she was. But any ribbing Cal might dole out tomorrow about hormones short-circuiting brain cells would be endurable as long as she was okay.

Yet as he stared at the bright light shining around the edges of the blinds in Hamilton's upstairs window, as he pulled up the collar of his coat to keep the numbing chill in the SUV at bay, as he filled Cal in on the situation and made his request, he couldn't shake the unsettling feeling that something was amiss at Laura's.

Laura adjusted the blanket she'd draped over Darcy and smoothed the hair back from her sister's forehead. Despite the small amount of bleeding from her abdominal wound, her skin felt cool and clammy, and her eyes were becoming glazed.

Shock was setting in.

And shock could be deadly.

Fighting down yet another wave of panic, Laura drew a shaky breath. At least she'd come up with a plan. The odds weren't great it would work, but it was better than sitting around waiting for Hamilton to come back and finish them off.

She crawled to the side of the room and climbed to her feet, steadying herself with a hand against the wall as the floor shifted. She could tell the wound had started to bleed again beneath the bandage on her thigh. But there was nothing to be done about that. She had to keep moving or her plan would fizzle.

Once the dizziness passed, she crossed to the door. The punctures on her arms were beginning to crust over, but she picked away the dried blood from one until it began to ooze again. After dipping her finger in, she smeared the blood over the peephole in a thick layer.

If Hamilton wanted to see what they were up to now, he'd have to come in.

But she hoped he didn't—not for at least several hours. Best case, he'd gone to bed and relegated the disposition of the two females in his basement until tomorrow. That would give her time to get everything set up.

Once the peephole was covered, she mustered her strength and moved the microwave from the top of the small refrigerator to the floor, ignoring the ache in her sprained wrist. Then she unplugged the fridge, tugged it into the center of the room and climbed on top, praying her balance wouldn't fail her. When she felt steady enough to stand, she began pushing up the tiles in the drop ceiling.

Under the third one, she found what she was looking for. Concentrating on remaining upright, she shifted the tile aside to expose the full length of ductwork.

After climbing down, she maneuvered the refrigerator in front of the door.

"Laura?" Darcy turned her head. "What are you doing?"

"Working on a plan to get us out of here. Do you think you're up to helping?"

"I'll try."

"I've got a few things to do first. You rest for a while. Once I have everything ready, I'll tell you all about it and explain what I need you to do. You don't even have to move from the floor, okay?"

" 'Kay." Her eyelids drifted shut again.

Please, God, let her stay conscious long enough for me to pull this off! I can't do it without her.

Fighting back panic, Laura fisted her hands. She was *not* going to cave. Not. Going. To. Cave. If she did, Hamilton would win without a fight. She had to keep working on her plan, had to keep believing there was a chance it could succeed.

Despite the insidious doubts undermining her composure, she crossed to the bed and began stripping off the blanket. Every movement brought a fresh wave of pain, and it was slow going. But at last she managed to tug it free.

After putting the blanket beside the refrigerator, she limped back to the bed and pulled off the top sheet. Then she sat on the edge of the mattress, and with the plastic saw-toothed knife she'd scavenged from a drawer in the desk, she worked it against the fabric to create a slit. Once she made several parallel cuts, the fabric should rip into strips without too much difficulty. Tied together, they'd work well for her purposes.

She hoped.

As she labored over the slits, she checked her watch. Just past midnight. Surely Hamilton would have come back down by now if he'd intended to kill them tonight. That must mean he'd gone to bed, as she'd hoped. Dev had told her he was always in his room by ten and rose before dawn. That should buy her a few hours.

But he wasn't going to sleep until dawn on this new day. She planned to rudely awaken him long before that—as soon as everything was in place.

And if all went well, in a handful of hours, she and Darcy would be free.

"I'm not liking what I'm seeing here."

As Cal dispensed with a greeting and cut to the chase in a sober tone, Dev gripped the steering wheel and braced himself. "What did you find?"

"Signs of a hasty departure. There were lights on in the house when I arrived, so I went up to ring the bell and found the door cracked open. I invited myself in. Your client wasn't there, but I did find her phone on the couch. It was still on. The coat closet door was open. The blow-dryer on the bathroom counter looks as if it had been in use and suddenly set down. Neither bed has been slept in."

"Is her car in the garage?"

"Yes. So I nosed around outside. There was a single set of footsteps cutting diagonally across the snow on the front lawn toward the sidewalk. A lot of people have cleared their walks, but I was able to pick up a few of her prints in the uncleared areas and follow them down the hill, to an empty lot. There's some tramped-down snow where they disappear. That's where I am now. I do see tire treads in the snow at the curb, as if someone pulled over, but it's impossible to tell how recent they are in this weather. They could have been frozen here for days. Give me a minute while I look around for more footprints."

As the line went silent and Dev processed this new information, everything clicked into place with a sickening thud. If Hamilton had suspected he was being watched, he could gain access to a car without detection by inviting Faith over, telling her to park on the next block, then giving her some kind of drug to knock her out for a few hours.

It was brilliant.

The man was even smarter than they'd given him credit for.

Dev's stomach clenched, the same way it had when things had gone south on his last undercover ATF job.

The day Cat had disappeared—and later been found murdered.

Please, God, no! Don't let Laura die!

The prayer came unbidden, torn from the recesses of his soul. It was the same plea he'd uttered on that fateful day five and a half years ago—to no avail. The day he'd stopped believing that God took an active interest in the human race.

Laura didn't believe that, though, despite her own hard times. She'd still managed to find evidence of God's presence in her world. Still believed he listened.

Maybe he should give prayer another shot.

Closing his eyes, he took a deep breath. *Lord, I'm sorry if I failed you. But please don't fail me tonight. I need your help—and your strength. Keep Laura safe and . . .*

"You still there?" A door slammed in the background as Cal spoke.

Dev opened his eyes and cleared his throat. "Yeah."

"No more footprints."

"That's what I figured." He related the story the cop had told him about where Faith had parked, as well as his theory. "If he lured Laura to his car and brought her back to his house, that would explain why he refused to answer the door when the officer rang—and the presence of blood."

"What about Darcy?"

"She may be in there too. Maybe that's how he convinced Laura to go with him. Proved he had her, then threatened her if Laura refused to cooperate."

Dev heard an engine start. "Pushing it . . . but possible."

"I need to get in there." He tapped the steering wheel and did a sweep of Hamilton's house as a plan began to take shape.

"Do you have a ruse in mind? A *legal* ruse?"

"Ruse, yes. Legal . . . let's just say it's worth the risk if it saves lives."

"You gonna let me in on this?"

"It might be better if I don't."

"Forget it. I like to know what I'm facing before I dive into a situation—and I'll be there in half an hour."

"Connor's here already, covering the alley."

"If this goes down tonight, you may need all hands on deck. So what's your plan?"

As Dev talked him through it, making up a lot of the details as he went along, Cal remained silent. That wasn't usually a positive sign. "So what do you think?"

"It's risky. Hamilton may not react the way you expect. You could find yourself facing charges if he doesn't."

"I know. But I can't think of any other tactic to flush him out quickly, force him to show his hand. It will look very suspicious if he refuses to cooperate."

"It could also make him panic."

"I know that too." And that was the risk that was churning up his insides, not the danger to himself. If Hamilton thought he was cornered, he could go off the deep end. Dev had seen it happen on plenty of occasions during his years in law enforcement.

Except he was pretty certain Hamilton had already gone off the deep end. And with Laura now missing too, letting this thing play out over an extended period wasn't tenable.

"Based on what we know so far about what's happened tonight, I think waiting is riskier." He sucked in a breath. "Someone's bleeding in there, Cal."

At the uncharacteristic thread of desperation in the last sentence, he frowned. What was that all about? He was always cool under pressure.

Cal's next comment told him he'd noticed the anomaly too. "Listen—hang in there. I'm with you. And Larson's a sharp guy. He'll push this as hard as he can within legal limits."

"Good to know. Expect some action when you get here—but stay on the sidelines unless things start popping. No sense everyone getting their hands dirty if this goes south. See you soon."

Connor wasn't all that enthusiastic about his plan, either, when he called to brief him, but he didn't balk. Just promised to be close at hand in case backup was needed.

Once he got squared away with Connor, Dev

pulled out the officer's card. Without hesitating, he punched in the man's number.

"I had a feeling I might hear from you before the night was over." The police radio crackled to life in the background as Larson answered. "What's happening?"

"Nothing yet, but I'm getting ready to place a call to 911 about a broken window at Hamilton's. If you head back now, you might catch the perpetrator—and get a chance to talk with the owner while he decides whether to file a report."

Two beats of silence passed.

"This doesn't sound like Phoenix's usual modus operandi."

"It's not. This is a personal decision. But lives may be hanging in the balance."

"I'm on my way—and I'll bring some backup. Two cars are always more impressive than one."

Nice to know the officer was on his side.

Once he got the dial tone again, Dev tapped in *67 followed by 911.

"911. Please state the nature of your emergency."

"I want to report some suspicious activity. My guess is a rock's about to be thrown through a window of a house." He recited the address.

"Can you—"

He cut off the call in the middle of the operator's question.

Seconds later, after verifying no one was peeking out of the upstairs window, he slipped from the SUV and jogged toward Hamilton's house. He'd already scoped out the front with the night-vision binoculars while formulating his plan, and he headed straight for the rock-rimmed flower bed abutting Hamilton's property.

After a quick scan of his choices, he picked up one of the larger rocks and weighed it in his hand. Yeah. That should do some serious damage to the tall window in front.

For the space of a few heartbeats, he hesitated. He'd walked a fine line at times in his PI career, but he'd never strayed over it, never broken the law. If he'd guessed wrong on this whole thing, the glass wasn't the only thing that would shatter this night.

So would his career.

But he trusted his instincts—and they told him Hamilton was up to his eyeballs in trouble. He was 99 percent certain the man would react as he expected.

He wasn't going to worry about that other 1 percent.

Moving closer to the house, he reared back and lobbed the rock. At least he'd finally found some practical use for all those years of college football.

The sound of breaking glass exploded in the quiet of the night. The rock also played havoc with the blinds. One side dropped, and they swung to and fro inside the window, dangling from a hook at the top.

Within fifteen seconds, a first-floor light came on. Dev stepped back into the shadow of a pine tree on the neighbor's property.

Through the broken window, he watched as Hamilton examined the damage. A couple of minutes later, he came to the door, threw it open, and stepped onto the stoop—just as a police car turned the corner and rolled to a stop on the other side of the street. Larson got out.

While the officer approached the house, Dev kept his focus on Hamilton. The man backed up, and as the light from the window illuminated his face, Dev read his emotions.

Panic and terror.

Any doubts about the wisdom of his plan evaporated.

"I got a 911 call about breaking glass. Looks like this is the place." Larson stopped a few feet away from Hamilton. "Any idea who did this?"

"No." Hamilton edged toward the door. "But my insurance will cover the damage. Forget it."

Larson matched him step for step, keeping the space between them consistent. "Vandalism is a crime. We like to catch people who damage property." He planted a foot on the bottom step of Hamilton's tiny porch.

"I doubt you'll catch anyone at this hour. People can melt into the night. Don't worry about it, Officer."

This was his cue.

Dev stepped out of the shadows and walked toward the duo. "I'll make it easy for you and turn myself in."

Both men shifted toward him.

As Hamilton looked his way, Dev pulled his hat off. If the man had any doubts about his identity, they'd be erased now. His red hair was a give-away. Might as well play all his cards at once.

Hamilton's eyes widened. "What the . . . What are you trying to pull?"

Playing dumb, Larson swiveled his head back and forth between them. "You two know each other?"

Dev remained silent.

"We've met." Hamilton glared at him as Dev stopped beside the officer.

"Well, now that we have the perpetrator, I'm sure you'll want to file a report." Larson started to reach for his notebook.

"Look . . . it's late. Can we do this tomorrow?" Hamilton scratched the back of his hand.

The gesture was at eye level for Larson, and Dev noted his almost imperceptible squint as the man took in Hamilton's red, chapped hands.

"If you prefer. But while I have you, Mr. Hamilton, I'd like to ask a few questions about a report I took earlier tonight from your neighbor and the woman who was your guest for the evening. When I stopped by at the time to talk with you, no one answered."

Hamilton's gaze shifted up and left. "I might have been in the shower."

If Dev hadn't already known he was lying, the body language would have confirmed it.

Larson let a beat of "yeah, sure" silence pass. "The woman says she saw blood in your kitchen."

"As I told her, I had a nosebleed while she was sleeping off the three glasses of wine she drank."

"She said she didn't have any alcohol."

The corners of Hamilton's lips lifted, but the stiff smile didn't reach his eyes. "You must have noticed she was a bit unsteady, Officer."

"People can be unsteady for a lot of reasons." Larson didn't blink. "She also said she saw a bloody handprint on the basement door and heard suspicious noises. I wonder if you might let me come in and take a quick look around, as long as you're up."

In his peripheral vision, Dev saw a second patrol car pull up. Hamilton saw it too. His nostrils flared and his mouth flattened.

"It's the middle of the night, Officer. I'm going to bed." He backed through the door and grasped the edge, as if he intended to slam it in their faces.

"This won't take long."

"Not tonight." Hamilton eased the door toward the closed position.

"Then I'll swing by again tomorrow night, earlier in the evening. And I believe a detective will also be stopping by your workplace to have a chat. Are you certain you don't want to give us a few minutes tonight, save yourself all that hassle?" He gave the last word a subtle emphasis.

Hamilton's knuckles whitened on the door even as his complexion reddened. "I'm sure. Good night."

As the door shut, Larson inclined his head toward the front sidewalk. Dev fell in behind him.

The officer in the other car got out as they approached.

Dev waited while Larson gave a topline to the new arrival, who had rookie written all over him. Lucky thing he hadn't responded to the first call.

Maybe God was watching out for them after all.

Once he briefed his colleague, Larson gestured toward the house. "Check out the perimeter."

The younger guy nodded, grabbed a flashlight from the car, and jogged toward the side of the structure.

"The guy's hiding something." Larson planted his fists on his hips. "But my guess is we're not going to find anything outside that will give us a basis to get inside. Our best bet might be to confront him at work tomorrow and keep the pressure on. Eventually, most guilty people crack."

"Eventually might not be good enough."

Larson didn't respond to that comment. He didn't have to. They both knew the risks of the situation—as well as the legal constraints.

"I assume you're going to continue hanging around?"

"Yeah. I called my two partners in too. Hamilton has to be panicking. He knows he's being watched by PIs. Knows the police are interested in talking with him. Knows his behavior a few minutes ago was suspicious. People who are afraid often do rash things."

"No argument there." The man pulled his radio off his belt to respond to a call.

By the time he finished, the younger cop had completed his circuit of the house and rejoined them. "Nothing suspicious. I couldn't even find any footprints, with the frozen ground."

"Okay. No reason to hang around." As the rookie returned to his car, Larson slid the radio back on his belt. "You have my card, and I know how to reach you on the remote chance Hamilton decides to press charges. I'll swing by several more times before my shift ends."

"Thanks."

With a lift of his hand, the man headed back to his cruiser.

Dev waited while the two cops drove away. Then he walked directly back to the Explorer. It didn't matter if Hamilton was peeking through the blinds again. The gig was up on the clandestine surveillance. The man now knew he was being watched.

And even though he was smart, he wasn't going

to outwit three experienced law enforcement professionals. Phoenix would crack this case soon.

Dev just hoped it was soon enough to save whoever had been bleeding on Hamilton's floor.

27

Mark dropped his head in his hands at the kitchen table, the weight of his failure crushing the breath from his lungs.

The cops might be gone for now—including the one who'd nosed around his house with a flashlight—but they were coming back tomorrow. Here, or at work. He hadn't missed the implied threat the older one had thrown out with the word *hassle*. Eventually, he'd have to talk with them . . . and they'd be a lot harder to fool than Faith. If they got interested enough, they could make his life miserable.

The PI wasn't going away anytime soon, either. The hard set of Devlin's jaw and the steel in his eyes had told him that. Plus, the guy had two other colleagues, according to their website. They might all be watching his house at this very moment. And based on what had just happened, he had a feeling they'd keep watching it—with or without a steady stream of checks from Darcy's sister.

Run!

That single word strobed across his mind, followed by a surge of adrenaline. The temptation to flee was so strong he half rose from his chair.

But after a few seconds, he sank back down. That kind of right-brain response would make everyone even more suspicious. And where would he go? It was tough to disappear in today's world.

Yet if he stayed, and if the cops managed to get a search warrant, he'd end up in prison. That would be worse than the death of his dream. Worse than death itself. He'd never be able to stay clean in a place like that. The very thought of it made his skin itch.

Besides, even if everything he'd done up until now remained a secret, his plan for redemption was ruined. Searching for another girl, bringing her here—the risk was too high now. He was on too many people's radar.

And what was the point of living if he couldn't save someone else . . . and thereby save himself?

None.

He froze as the truth slammed into him with all the force of one of Lil's backhanded blows: his well-plotted quest was over.

As he grappled with that reality, as the pounding of his pulse roared in his ears, he clenched his fists and sucked in a breath. Counted to five. Released it.

After several methodical reps of that exercise, his brain began to function again.

The facts were clear.

Things had fallen apart.

He'd always known there was a chance this could happen. That's why he had the necessary materials on hand.

But he'd never expected to need them.

Tears pricked his eyes, blurring the room as he struggled to accept the inevitable, to acknowledge that there was no choice.

When at last he wrestled the last remnants of resistance into submission, he placed his palms on the table. He could do this. But he had to do it right. Succeed at this if nothing else. And it shouldn't be difficult. All he had to do was follow the plan he'd laid out long ago.

The outcome wouldn't be all bad, either. His skin wouldn't itch anymore. The nightmares would end. His fear of the dark would be history. The gnawing sense of inadequacy, the constant worry someone would discover he was a worthless piece of trash, would disappear.

That was a salvation of sorts, even if he'd lost the chance for redemption.

Salvation.

He let the word resonate in his mind. It had a nice sound. Hopeful and upbeat. Plus, the path he was about to embark on was easier in a lot of ways than continuing his quest. There would be no more pressure. No more stress. No more tilting at the windmill of redemption. Just release . . . and freedom.

As his pulse slowed, a sense of utter peace settled over him.

Everything was going to be okay.

He was going to be okay.

And he'd never have to be afraid again. Of anything—or anyone.

Resolved, he pushed himself to his feet, crossed the room, and descended the basement stairs. The four two-gallon metal cans were lined up in a straight row against the wall, near the corner, far from the furnace—right where they'd been since he'd placed them there, one by one, during the first few weeks he'd lived in the house. There was more than enough to do the job, according to his research. Petroleum-based products caused fires to burn fast and hot.

Just the way he wanted it.

He hauled the cans to the second floor, two at a time, then retrieved the Ambien from the drawer in his vanity. He didn't need all of the remaining pills. Five or six would be more than sufficient when downed with a glass of wine.

After pocketing the pills, he put on a pair of plastic gloves and went through the upstairs, opening the metal containers one by one, splattering the liquid on the upholstered furniture, drapes, bedding, carpets, and rugs. He splashed it on the walls, the floors, the ceilings, and created drip paths from room to room and down the hall.

Last can in hand, he descended the steps, pouring a zigzag line behind him on the carpet. He also drizzled a generous amount on the rug by the front door.

No way would anyone get past those barriers and foil his plan.

The house began to reek of the pungent smell, and he wrinkled his nose. At least he wouldn't have to put up with the caustic stink for long.

In the kitchen, he wadded up sheets of newspaper from his recycle bin, forming several balls. Then he pulled the box of extra sturdy matches from the top shelf of the cabinet where he'd placed them after the rehab was finished. Bending, he opened a lower cabinet and withdrew the bottle of chardonnay Star had enjoyed less than two weeks ago.

Hard to believe so much had changed in such a short time.

A brief wave of melancholy swept over him, but he quashed it ruthlessly. It was too late for regrets.

Forcing himself to focus on the task at hand, he did some calculations. One Ambien took thirty to forty-five minutes to kick in. Five pills? Maybe ten minutes—and the alcohol would exacerbate the effect. He'd have to move fast once he swallowed them.

He retrieved a wineglass from the cabinet and

filled it to the brim. Not a drop sloshed out, and a smile whispered at his lips. He was calm, cool, collected. And why not? This was his choice. He was still in control of his destiny.

One by one, he downed the pills. After draining the wineglass, he slipped the matches into his pocket. Then he picked up the newspaper balls and descended the basement stairs, the final metal can in hand.

Moving through the space, he splashed the remaining liquid on the outside walls of the sound-proof room, the concrete floor, and the steps, leaving a wide swath clear around the furnace. He didn't want the place to blow too soon. He also soaked the newspaper balls with gasoline and placed them around the basement.

It was time to start the show.

Matches in hand, he examined his fingers. Not a tremor. Lil might have called him a spineless, brainless twit on her bad days, but she'd been wrong. He was strong. And smart. And brave.

Circling the room, he lit the wads of gasoline-soaked newspaper. By the time he backed up the stairs, flames were licking up throughout the basement.

At the front door, he tossed a match onto the rug. It whooshed into flames as he retreated up the steps.

On the second floor, he threw a match onto the gas-splattered carpet on the steps, backing away as flames erupted in the stairwell. Before entering his bedroom, he ignited the end of the gasoline path in the hall, watching as flames zipped along the trail he'd created, heading for the guest room and exercise room.

Smoke was already rolling toward the ceiling, and he began to cough. Too soon for that. He had one more task to complete.

Slipping inside his room, he closed the door behind him and stripped off his gloves, tossing them onto the floor as he walked over to the closet. From the garment bag, he gently extracted the wedding gown.

The dress was beautiful. Pristine. Pure and white, like a bride should be.

Too bad it would never be worn.

His vision blurred as he crossed toward the bed, the dress draped over his arm, and he grabbed the corner post to steady himself. The drugs and alcohol were kicking in. He had to hurry.

Moving to the edge of the bed, he spread the gown on one side, fluffing the lace, straightening the skirt.

The room tipped.

Hurry, hurry.

He wove toward the door and opened it. Smoke billowed in, and he backed away, coughing.

Hurry!

Eyes watering, he touched a match to the circle of gasoline he'd poured in an arc around his bed. Flames scuttled along the protective ring.

Finished, he sat on the bed and opened the nightstand. As always, Lil smiled back at him from the frame. The real Lil. The sweet, innocent girl who should have worn a dress like the one beside him, given him a father, and created a family like the ones in those old movies and TV shows.

The room began to spin, and he laid back on the bed. Pressed the photo and the birthday card to his chest, next to his heart. Closed his eyes.

And the world faded away.

Standing under the exposed duct, Laura did one final sweep of the room. Despite the throbbing in her head and the searing pain from her stab wounds, she couldn't afford to miss one single detail. Their lives depended on her getting this right.

The blanket was caught above the door—barely—in the framework of the drop ceiling, positioned to land on top of Hamilton's head when he entered the room.

Darcy was now lying closer to the door so the rope fashioned out of sheeting and attached to one corner of the suspended blanket would be less noticeable. But to better disguise it, Laura had broken all the lightbulbs except the one in the bathroom.

The small ball made of sheeting was in her hand, ready to roll across the floor toward the door as Hamilton entered. Hopefully he'd be distracted and look down. Then, with one tug from Darcy, the blanket would drop over his head.

They'd done a dry run, and it had all worked flawlessly—in rehearsal, anyway.

The sturdy metal support rod she'd wrestled from under the mattresses wasn't a saber, but it could do some serious damage if she got in a few thrusts and whacks before he untangled himself from the bedding.

They were as prepared as they were going to be.

Time to bang on the duct.

She limped to Darcy and knelt beside her. "I think we're set. Are you ready?"

Her sister groped for her hand, her voice faint—and fading. "I love you, Laura."

Pressure built in her throat. "I love you too. But we'll have plenty of time for this sappy stuff later. Hang in a few more minutes, okay?"

"Okay." It was more breath than word.

Forcing herself back to her feet, Laura gritted her teeth and fought back a powerful wave of dizziness. She couldn't pass out now! *God, please keep me conscious. Please!*

The world steadied, the floor under her feet firmed, and she moved under the exposed duct-work. Tightening her grip on the metal support rod, she moistened her lips, lifted it, and . . . sniffed.

Was that . . . smoke?

She sniffed again.

Yes. The odor was faint, but definitely smoke.

Through the dim light, she peered up toward the ceiling. Were those vapory tendrils seeping in where she'd removed the piece of tile from the drop ceiling?

Yes.

"Laura . . . ?"

The tendrils grew more robust.

The smell got stronger.

"Laura . . . is that smoke?"

"Yes." She limped to the door and pressed a palm against the flat surface. Jerked it back.

It was way too hot.

Her heart began to hammer.

Was Hamilton's house on fire?

Whatever was happening, her plan suddenly took on a new urgency. They had to get out of here *now!*

"I don't know where the smoke's coming from, but get ready. I'm going to start banging."

Repositioning herself under the duct, she began to hit the metal with the support rod.

One minute passed.

Two.

Three.

The smoke was black now. And thicker.

Lord help them, the house *was* on fire!

And Hamilton was either ignoring their banging or had already vacated the premises.

But someone outside would see or smell the smoke, wouldn't they? Except . . . who would be outside at this hour of the night?

Dev!

He was out there, watching. He'd eventually notice the smoke and call 911. The fire department would respond, and if she kept banging, they'd hear her, wouldn't they? *Please, God, let them hear me!*

Her eyes began to sting, and she started coughing.

Not good.

Smoke inhalation could kill faster than fire. She had to stave it off, buy herself some time.

Letting the metal rod drop to the floor, she limped to the bathroom, filled the sink with water, and soaked as many washcloths and towels as she could find.

"It's getting hotter in here, Laura." There was panic in Darcy's voice.

"I know, sweetie." After wringing out the towels, she joined her sister near the door. Fortunately, Hamilton's soundproofing had sealed the room tight. No smoke was seeping around the door or under the walls. Most of it was coming in from the ceiling. But the temperature was several degrees warmer closer to the door. "I'm going to move you to the other side. Just lie still."

She slipped her hands under Darcy's arms and pulled her as gently as possible across the carpet—but not gently enough. Every one of Darcy's moans was like another thrust of Hamilton's knife.

Fighting back tears, she settled her sister near the far wall and placed a wet towel over her nose and mouth. "Keep this here, okay? It will help protect you from the smoke."

No response.

Had Darcy passed out?

Her throat tightened, and she swallowed past her fear. In light of their dire situation, maybe that was for the best.

Laura wrapped a wet towel around the lower part of her own face, cringing as the weight rested on the bridge of her tender nose, then picked up the metal rod. Crouching as low as she could to avoid the smoke gathering near the ceiling, she resumed pounding.

If the house was on fire, emergency vehicles would arrive soon. The firefighters were trained to search for victims, so they'd be listening for evidence of life. The odds were strong they'd hear the banging and know someone was trapped below.

But could she escape the fire—and the effects of smoke inhalation—long enough for her message to be heard?

And even if she did . . . would they be able to reach her and Darcy through the fire that must be raging just outside the door?

28

Giving the front of Hamilton's house his full attention, Dev punched in Connor's number on speed dial. After covering the broken window with what looked like a blanket, Hamilton had turned on every light in the place. They'd been burning for twenty minutes now.

Weird.

"You rang?" As usual, a U2 song was playing in the background in Connor's car.

"Anything going on from where you sit?"

"Nope. Quiet, as usual. Did you check in with Cal?"

"Yeah." An odd glimmer of light darted around the edge of the blinds on an upstairs window, and he picked up the night vision binoculars. "Considering he's got day shift here tomorrow, he's probably regretting his offer to come down tonight. Maybe I'll . . ." His voice trailed off as an amorphous shadow appeared on the blanket in the first-floor window. It wasn't a person. It was wavering too much, shooting up and down. Like . . .

A surge of adrenaline kicked in and his heart skipped a beat.

"Get out your night visions. I think I'm seeing the shadows of flames behind the blanket over the broken window on the first floor." Even as he spoke, he was scanning the rest of the house. Door, windows, rooflines . . . there! Was that smoke seeping out from under the eaves?

"I see smoke." Connor's confirmation was clipped and curt. "I'll call 911 and let Cal know."

"You take the back door. I'll cover the front. Bring your ax."

Before Connor could respond, Dev was out the door of the Explorer and charging to the back. The flame-retardant jumpsuit he'd lugged around since his ATF days—much to the amusement of his partners—might not be part of the standard equipment in Phoenix vehicles, but it was going to come in handy tonight.

In fifteen seconds, he'd shoved his legs and arms in, zipped it up, and grabbed the ax, a bottle of water, and the fire extinguisher from the supply box.

As he raced toward the house, Cal was sprinting from the other direction carrying similar equipment. The closer Dev got, the more the air smelled of smoke—and the more it became obvious there were dancing shadows behind *all* the windows.

The whole house was ablaze.

Even with a leg up, the broken window in front was too high above the ground to reach, so he homed in on the door. Dumping everything but the ax on the ground, he began hacking at the wood near the knob.

The door was solid—but it was no match for an ax and a strong set of determined arms. When the wood began to splinter, he backed off, angled sideways, and smashed his right heel below the lock. The door slammed back . . . and a bellow of heat surged out.

Lifting his arms to protect his face, he stared into Hamilton's house.

It was a raging inferno—a man-made one, based on the distinctive smell of gasoline permeating the air.

An accelerant had been used.

Bad news.

He looked at Cal and read his partner's thoughts.

No one could survive this.

But he wouldn't accept that.

Couldn't accept it.

If Laura and Darcy were inside, they might somehow be sheltered from the brunt of the fire. It was possible. Anything was possible.

He had to believe that.

Had to believe they could get to them in time.

Except there was no way in through the wall of flames blocking the doorway.

"Let's try the back." He grabbed the items he'd dropped and tore toward the rear of the house, Cal on his heels.

They arrived just as Connor delivered a kick to the back door. Like its counterpart in front, it crashed open.

There was better news back here. No fire and less smoke. He could get through this in his protective gear.

Dev ripped off his neck warmer, twisted the cap off the bottle of water, and soaked the material. "I'm going to take a—"

"Wait." Connor cocked his ear. "Listen."

A banging sound, faint but distinct, echoed in the silence.

Dev's pulse surged. "It's coming from the basement."

"Someone's down there." Connor grabbed the bottle of water from him, doused the balaclava he yanked from his pocket, and tossed it to Cal. He used the remainder of the water on his own headgear. Then he picked up the fire extinguisher he'd set on the back stoop and gripped his ax. "Let's do this. We can't wait for the fire department."

Cal pulled on the balaclava. "Fast. The smoke's gonna do a number on us even if we stay low, and assuming the furnace is gas, it could blow any minute."

"Listen . . . I can handle this." Dev yanked the neck warmer over his head, covering his nose and mouth. His partners weren't dressed for this—and Cal had a new bride. The risk was too high. "You guys don't have to—"

"You're wasting time." Connor dived in.

"Move it." Cal shoved him from behind.

Man, he loved these guys.

Ducking low to stay as close to the floor as possible, Connor advanced toward the open door on the left that was belching smoke, fire extinguisher in hand. Dev followed, his own ax and extinguisher at the ready. Cal took up the rear.

At the door, Dev eyed the steps, staying as much out of the path of the rising smoke as possible.

It looked like the descent into hell.

"Laura!"

His shout produced no response—but the banging continued. More muted with the basement door open, oddly enough. Was it coming from somewhere else?

"How come the sound isn't . . . louder?" Cal began to cough, even though they were all crouched low, well under the cloud of smoke that hung in the top half of the room.

"I don't know." Connor wiped the back of his gloved hand across his watering eyes. "But it's from ductwork. I think it's coming from down there."

The faint, keening wail of a siren penetrated the chaos.

Dev looked at his partners. Waiting for the pros to get here would be safer—for them.

But if Laura was caught in those flames, every second counted.

"I'm going down."

Without giving them a chance to reply, he pointed his fire extinguisher at the flames on the steps and sucked in a lungful of air. At least he had two things going for him—the higher-end equipment capable of handling burning liquids that Phoenix had sprung for, and the ability he'd perfected to hold his breath for longer-than-usual periods, thanks to his summer job as a lifeguard in high school.

The smoke continued to roll upward as he took the steps as fast as he dared, one hand on the railing, eyes burning, tears streaming. At the bottom, the banging became more audible. It was coming from his left—from behind the door on the far wall.

Dodging the pockets of fire, continuing to hold his breath, he gauged how much time he had before the smoke got to him.

Not much.

And he couldn't hold his breath forever.

In front of the smoldering door, he dropped as close to the floor as he could get. The air was clearer here, and he took a small breath.

"Laura!"

At his call, the banging stopped. A few seconds later he heard coughing—and a voice calling his name.

It was her.

Thank you, God!

"Back away from the door!"

Parsing out the air in his lungs, he rose to his knees and attacked the door with the ax, near the handle. It gave much more easily than he expected.

As he yanked it open and did a sweep of the room, one thing became immediately clear. While there was smoke inside, there wasn't a lot of it. And there was no fire.

That was the only reason Laura was alive.

But she was a mess. One eye was black, her nose was swollen, and there was blood all over her clothes.

"Get Darcy . . . out." She gestured to the figure huddled on the floor, under a blanket, her voice hoarse. "She has . . . an abdominal . . . stab wound."

"I've got her." Connor spoke behind him and shoved his way past.

As he reached for Laura's hand, Dev hoped Cal had stayed topside. His third partner had neither the lifeguard nor scuba training that gave him and Connor a breathing edge in this situation. "Can you walk?"

Coughing, she nodded. But as she started forward, she swayed.

He caught her as she folded.

"Can you handle her?" Connor tipped his head as he passed, Darcy in his arms.

"Yeah."

"Take a deep breath. The air's better in here."

Bending low, he took in some air, then crossed

to the scorched stairs as fast as he could. Cal was waiting at the top, off to one side, crouched low. He sprayed the steps with the fire extinguisher as they ascended.

The last step cracked when Dev put his weight on it, and Cal grabbed his arm, hauling him up as the wood broke apart and fell into a pile of smoldering kindling.

Too close to even think about.

Doing his best to shelter Laura as much as possible, he sprinted through the kitchen and burst through the back door on Connor's heels.

As he stumbled down the alley, sucking in lungfuls of the cold night air, firefighters streamed past him toward the burning structure, already activating the flame-suppressing foam in their hoses. The cops were out in force too, evacuating neighboring buildings and cordoning off the area.

Larson appeared out of the dark and took his arm, guiding him farther away from the house, toward the waiting paramedics. "I don't think there'll be any charges pressed for that rock-throwing incident."

"Yeah." He coughed again. "As far as I know, Hamilton's still inside."

"I'll let the fire department know."

The officer disappeared into the night as the paramedics converged on them. Two of the technicians lifted Laura from his arms. Another tried to lead him a different direction.

He shrugged the guy off. "No. I'm staying with her."

"At least put this on." The paramedic tugged an oxygen mask over his face.

Still hacking, he tried to shove it away. "I'm fine."

"Humor me, okay?" The guy positioned it firmly in place. "You have any other damage besides too much smoke?"

"No."

"You did better than your buddy, then." He gestured over his shoulder to Connor, a few yards away. His partner had an oxygen mask on too, and a paramedic was cutting the bottom off one leg of his jeans. "Probably thanks to your jump-suit."

"What's wrong with him?"

"Second-degree burns, from the fast look I got on my way to you. He wasn't dressed to go traipsing through a fire."

Yet he'd gone down to the basement, anyway.

Dev owed him for that. Big-time. He'd never have managed to get both Darcy and Laura out by himself before the steps collapsed or he succumbed to smoke inhalation.

"Dev?"

At Laura's hoarse summons, he dropped to one knee beside the technician who was putting a pressure bandage on her leg. "I'm right here."

Her oxygen mask obscured her vision, and she

tried to push it aside. The paramedic on her right restrained her.

"We need you to keep that on, ma'am."

She groped for his hand, and he folded her cold fingers in his. "How's Darcy?"

The guy who'd pressed the oxygen mask on him rose. "I'll find out." He joined his colleagues a few feet away, where a hushed exchange took place.

That gave Dev a chance to focus on the woman whose hand was gripping his. Despite her battered and bloodied appearance, despite terms like airway edema and bronchodilator and CO toxicity the paramedics were bantering around, the strength in her fingers gave him hope. "You're going to be okay." She had to be. There was no other option.

"I'm more worried about Darcy. She's been . . . through hell."

They both had, as far as he could tell.

The paramedic rejoined them. "Her BP is low and she's in shock. Pulse is steady but weak. They'll have to assess the stab wound at the hospital. Once the IV is in, they're going to transport. The cold out here isn't the best environment for treatment, and she's stable enough to be moved."

"I want to stay with her." Laura tightened her hold on his hand, panic threading through her voice.

"We're taking you both to the same trauma center." The paramedic working on Laura taped her IV in place and looked at his partner, who was listening to her chest with a stethoscope. "Any problems?"

The other man shook his head.

"Then let's get out of this cold." He transferred his attention to the technician hovering beside Dev. "Does he need to be transported?"

"No." Dev answered for him and took off the oxygen mask. "But I'm going to follow you there." He leaned closer to Laura. "I'll be right behind you. And I'll stick close at the hospital, okay?"

"Okay."

The paramedics shouldered him aside and whisked her toward the waiting ambulance.

"You want some company?"

At Cal's question, Dev dragged his gaze away from the stretcher carrying Laura. Connor stood beside Cal. Both were covered in soot.

"Do I look as bad as you guys?"

"Worse."

"That's what I was afraid of. You getting that burn treated?" He gestured to Connor's leg.

"Nah. It's only a small area. I know how to deal with it. I'm just mad they ruined an almost-new pair of jeans."

Dev thought about arguing. Decided against it. Connor was tough, but he didn't take chances. He was also a whiz at first aid, thanks to his

Secret Service training. If he needed medical attention, he'd get it.

"You guys go home. I could be awhile—and I'll have company." He gestured toward the stretcher being loaded into the waiting ambulance.

Cal regarded him through narrowed eyes for several beats, then nodded. "Okay. We'll deal with the police. You need anything, call."

"I will." As the two of them started to turn away, Dev grabbed their arms. Both stopped and glanced back. "Listen—thanks for . . ." His voice choked as he searched for words to express his gratitude.

One corner of Connor's mouth twitched. "Dev speechless. That's a first. Wait till I tell Nikki."

Cal grinned at him. "Don't worry. I'll run interference for you." Then his demeanor grew more serious as he clasped his shoulder. "No sweat, okay? This is what partners do."

"Yeah," Connor seconded. "Now go keep the pretty lady company."

The two men moved away. And as Dev jogged toward his Explorer to follow the ambulances, he gave thanks.

For faithful friends and answered prayers.

Voices were talking. Deep, male voices.

One of them was Dev's.

Laura tried to pry her eyelids open.

They refused to budge.

506

How could she possibly have let herself fall asleep before she had word on Darcy's condition? They must have given her some drugs. Morphine, maybe, because she wasn't hurting very much anymore.

No. Wait. They'd said something about repairing a vein in her leg. They must have put her out to do that.

But she didn't intend to stay out. Not until she had some answers about Darcy.

She tried again to lift her eyelids. This time they raised halfway.

A strong, warm hand enfolded hers. Dev's.

Bliss.

"Laura?"

Exerting a supreme effort, she managed to open her eyes.

Her favorite PI was inches away. His face was cleaner than the last time she'd seen it, but a stray streak of soot bisected the fine lines of fatigue at the corner of one eye.

"You stayed."

"I said I would."

Yeah, he had. And as she'd learned over the past tumultuous days, James Devlin was a man you could count on.

"Can you find out about Darcy for me?"

"Your timing's perfect." He eased aside to reveal the white-coated man behind him. "The doctor just came in."

The physician circled around to the other side of the gurney. "Do you want me to start with your condition, or your sister's?"

"My sister's."

He folded his arms. "Aside from multiple contusions, dehydration, and signs of malnourishment—including an electrolyte imbalance—her biggest issue is an abdominal wound. The knife did penetrate the peritoneal cavity, so we'll be watching for peritonitis and treating with antibiotics as a precautionary measure. She also has a small laceration in her liver, which produced internal bleeding."

Laura drew an unsteady breath. "I was afraid of that. I knew she was going into shock."

"The rest of the news is better, though. On a scale of one to six, with six being the most severe, her liver injury is a two. Also, by the time we did a CT scan, the bleeding had stopped, so no surgery should be required. We'll be monitoring her with regular blood tests to confirm that, and we'll keep her on bed rest for a couple of days, but she should be fine. The liver has amazing regenerative properties."

The knot in Laura's stomach began to loosen. "Thank God!"

"Not a bad idea. You were both very lucky. Which brings me to your condition. Your nose isn't broken, but you have quite a shiner—as well as a concussion. The stab wounds on your arms are straightforward. No nerves, blood vessels, or tendons were injured, so we just cleaned and bandaged them. You were also fortunate with the wound on your shoulder. It was far enough to the outside that there was no damage to the rotator tendons or brachial plexus, which control the arm. We were able to repair it with a few stitches. And neither you nor your sister suffered any serious effects from the fire. No burns, no major smoke inhalation."

"What about her leg?"

At Dev's impatient query, the doctor raised an eyebrow. "I'm getting to that." He turned back to her. "Any questions so far?"

She shook her head and squeezed Dev's hand. The doctor might not like his demanding tone, but his proprietary concern warmed her heart.

"You weren't as lucky with the leg. A major vein was nicked, and we had to have one of our vascular surgeons go in and do some fine suturing. On the plus side, you should make a full recovery, and we didn't need to transfuse you or your sister."

"When can I see her?"

"We're about to admit you both, and you'll be sharing a room. Someone will be in to take you up in a few minutes. If you need anything in the meantime, press the call button."

As the doctor exited, Laura let out a long, slow breath and looked at the man who had saved her life. "I don't even know how to begin to say thank you."

One side of his mouth hitched up as he stroked his thumb over the back of her hand, but his attempt at a smile didn't alleviate the lines of strain and fatigue around his mouth and eyes. "Have dinner with me when you're on your feet."

"That hardly seems an adequate thank-you."

"Consider it the first installment. Because if you're willing, I'd like to see a whole lot more of you now that you're no longer my client."

She wove her fingers through his, those promise-filled words better than any painkiller the hospital could have given her. "Ready, willing, and almost able."

"It's a date, then. We've got a gig in Costa Rica for a few days, but once I get back, clear your social calendar. We're going to . . ." A yawn caught him unawares, and he lifted a hand to stifle it. "Sorry about that."

"What time is it?"

He twisted his wrist. "Six-thirty."

The man had to be dead on his feet. "Go home. Get some rest."

A nurse pushed through the door, followed by an aide. "You're set to go upstairs. You'll meet up with your sister in the elevator."

As they prepared to roll her out, Dev maintained his grip on her hand. The temptation to let him stay was strong—but selfish. He needed to crash.

She tried to tug her hand free, but he didn't release it. "Please, Dev. I'll feel better if I know you're getting some sleep. You can come back and see me later."

The aide began wheeling her out. Dev followed along, still holding her hand. "I'll just go with you as far as the elevator."

She didn't argue.

As they trundled down the hall, another gurney came into sight, and she caught a glimpse of Darcy. Their gazes met when the aide maneuvered her next to her sister inside the elevator, and tears welled in Laura's eyes. Darcy's hand snaked out between the safety rails, and Laura grabbed it, holding fast.

"You're going to be fine." Laura's voice wavered, then strengthened. "We're both going to be fine."

A tear trailed down Darcy's cheek, but she smiled back. "Yes, we are." Angling her head, she looked at the tall man who was holding Laura's other hand, her expression curious.

"Are you going up with us?" The aide directed the query to Dev, her finger hovering over a button on the control panel.

"No." Laura didn't give him a chance to answer. "But he's coming back later."

Dev slowly released her fingers. "Count on it."

Instead of exiting at once, however, he bent, brushed her hair back from her face with a whisper-soft touch, and pressed his lips to her forehead.

Her eyes drifted closed.

Mmm.

That was one way to boost a girl's blood pressure.

He lifted his head a few inches, and his next, whispered words were only for her. "Get used to that."

Then, with a wink and a grin, he straightened up and exited, watching her from the hall until the door closed.

"Who is that, Laura?"

She turned her head toward Darcy. "James Devlin. He's the PI I hired to find you—and one of the guys who saved our lives."

"Do you two know each other . . . well?"

"Not well enough. But he'd like to change that."

"I say go for it. He's pretty hot, even if he is kind of old."

One of the aides closer to Laura's age snickered, and her own lips twitched as she squeezed her sister's fingers. "You're my top priority for now, but once we're both back on our feet, I think that's very sound advice."

The door opened, and as the aide wheeled her past the window in the elevator lobby, she

512

caught a glimpse of the rising sun as it gilded the edges of the clouds and tinted the sky a lustrous pink.

A smile touched her lips. How apt.

For the night was over, and this was a new day—shining bright and filled with promise.

Epilogue

Five Months Later

Dev stepped onto Laura's front porch and reached for the bell—only to have Darcy fling open the door before his finger made contact with the button.

"Hi, Dev."

He retracted his hand and smiled at the teen. In the five months since her traumatic runaway experience, she'd blossomed. The fear lurking in the depths of her eyes receded with each passing day, she'd made a slew of friends at school, and her hair was blonde again . . . except for a brand-new neon purple streak on one side.

"Hi, yourself."

"Hey, Dev." Nikki's brother followed her out.

He had to give the kid credit. Despite Laura's resistance to the notion of Darcy going on single dates, Danny had hung in there for the past five months. Today was the reward, even if their first date was Phoenix's annual Fourth of July BBQ at Cal's house—a crowd scene, where they'd have zero privacy. But they were going and coming together, and Darcy seemed content with that.

In fact, she seemed content in general these days, thanks in large part to the love Laura had lavished on her . . . which was returned in full measure, as far as he could tell.

"Hi, Danny. See you guys at Cal's, right?"

"Right." Danny claimed his date's hand. "But we're going to swing by the Webster carnival first. Laura and Nikki both know."

"Sounds like a plan."

He waited until they reached the end of the walk, then stuck his head in the open door. "Laura?"

"In the kitchen. Come on back."

He strolled through the living room that had become his second home over the past few months. He'd lost count of the number of nights he and Laura—and sometimes Darcy—had watched movies here or played Scrabble or worked on plans for the teen outreach church project the two of them had agreed to chair at their pastor's request. It was getting harder and harder to return to his cold, sterile apartment.

But if all went well, maybe he wouldn't have to for much longer.

Fingering the small box in the pocket of his

jeans, he tried to rein in the sudden uptick in his pulse as he approached the kitchen.

"Hi." Laura glanced over her shoulder at him and smiled as she finished covering a large plate of brownies with plastic wrap. "You must have run into Darcy and Danny at the front door. Either that or you picked the lock."

"No lock picking on my agenda today." He moved beside her and propped a hip against the counter, taking a leisurely sweep of the red toenails peeking through her sandals, her white Capri slacks, and a red knit top that showed off her curves to perfection. Nice. "What's with the purple streak in Darcy's hair?"

Laura rinsed her hands in the sink, pulled a towel off the rack, and scrunched up her face. "I don't like it, but one thing I've learned over the past few months is to be more flexible and pick my battles."

"Your strategy appears to be working. Darcy seems happier every time I see her."

"I give the counseling sessions most of the credit for that. And getting involved with the youth group at church has made a huge difference in her outlook too. Of course, a boyfriend doesn't hurt, either. Danny's a good kid."

He took her hand and tugged her close, looping his arms around her waist. "Yeah, he is. And speaking of boyfriends—is that part of the reason you seem so happy too?"

A faint flush rose on her cheeks, and an endearing dimple appeared in her cheek. "Doesn't hurt."

A rush of gratitude tightened his throat as he looked down at her. He'd been there when she'd given the police her statement, and he'd read Darcy's. Despite Laura's heroic plan to save them, both had come close to dying.

Too close.

But that was over. She was safe in his arms. And if this day turned out the way he hoped, she'd be close at hand for the rest of his life.

He brushed back a stray strand of hair that had escaped her French braid, letting his fingers linger on her cheek. "You look especially beautiful today."

If she noticed the sudden huskiness in his voice, she didn't comment. Instead, she fingered the collar of his golf shirt. "You're not too bad yourself. Though I have to say I prefer the green version that matches your eyes. But blue is in keeping with the holiday."

"I could go home and change."

"That would make us later than we already are. We need to get moving."

She started to tug free, but when he held fast, she sent him a quizzical look.

"I don't think they'll mind if we're a few minutes late. Connor can take the first shift guarding the grill so Cal doesn't char the burgers. I want to get a head start on the fire-works."

Chuckling, she slipped her arms back around his neck, tipped her chin up, and closed her eyes. "No objections."

The temptation to give her the kiss she expected was strong—but first things first.

"I had something else in mind."

She opened her eyes, her expression puzzled. "Such as?"

Keeping one arm around her, he reached into the pocket of his jeans and withdrew the small velvet box.

Her eyes widened and her mouth formed an *O*. "Is that . . . what I think it is?"

"Since our thinking is usually in sync, I'd venture to say it is." He flipped open the lid to reveal a solitaire flanked by smaller stones on a gold band. As he angled it in the sunlight, the facets glittered and twinkled and sparkled. "See? Fireworks. The kind I hope will last a lot longer than the ones we'll see tonight."

She lifted her gaze, and the love shining in her eyes chased away the flutter of nerves in the pit of his stomach. "Yes." She held up her left hand.

He gave her a slow blink. "I didn't ask you yet."

"Sorry. I guess I got carried away." She exhaled. "Go ahead."

He let a beat of silence pass. "It seems kind of anticlimactic now."

517

She withdrew her hand. "Do you want me to retract my answer?"

"No!" He tugged the ring from the box and grabbed her hand. "But I'm going to give you part of my speech, anyway. Although I guess it's safe to skip the if-this-is-too-soon-I'll-try-again-later part."

"Definitely a safe deletion." She traced a finger along the line of his jaw.

He grabbed her hand. "Stop that or I'll never get through this."

"Okay." Eyes twinkling, she gave him a demure look. "I'll be good."

A grin tugged at his lips. "I have no doubt of that."

Giggling, she played with a button on his shirt. "Now who's straying off subject?"

He tucked her straying hand in his. "You know . . . this isn't quite how I imagined this moment."

"Do you want to get down on one knee?"

"Do you want me to?"

"I kind of like the present arrangement." She snuggled closer.

"Can we be serious for a minute?"

"I'll try, but my heart's already singing the Hallelujah Chorus."

"Then I'll keep this short." Shifting gears, he launched into the condensed version of his prepared speech. "You know my history. You know I wasn't in a hurry to rush into romance, and you know why. It seemed safer—and wiser—to walk a wide circle around commitments . . . until I met you."

He took a deep breath and linked his fingers with hers. "The truth is, as I fell in love with you, I began to realize God had given me a priceless gift the day you came into my life. Because you helped me see that loving is worth every risk. And now I can't imagine anything closer to heaven on earth than falling asleep in your arms every night and waking up beside you every day for the rest of my life."

There was a sheen in her eyes as he finished, and when she spoke, a tremor ran through her words. "That was beautiful, Dev." Then a radiant smile lit up her face. "Now?"

"Now."

"Yes!"

He slipped the ring on her finger without further ceremony and moved on to a different kind of fireworks.

When they at last drew apart, Laura sighed and rested her forehead against his chin. "I guess we have to go to the BBQ."

"Yeah. I've got the sodas and you've got the brownies. Besides, we have some exciting news to share."

"I don't know that I'd call it news."

He frowned and pulled back a few inches. "What do you mean?"

"I think Nikki suspects."

"Why?"

"You know that day I stopped in your office last week on my lunch hour? When I asked her where you were, she said you were on a personal errand—and she had this smug expression I've never seen before."

He grimaced. "I see it almost every day. I think she has some kind of funky ESP."

"Maybe . . . but Darcy's on to us too. She's been humming the wedding march lately."

Dev huffed out a breath. "Is anyone going to be surprised?"

"Not Moira. Last time I saw her, she asked if I was shopping for a dress yet. I'm sure she's shared her suspicions with Cal."

"That only leaves Connor."

"Don't count on it. We haven't exactly been hiding our interest in each other."

"What about you?" Dev played with her braid. "Were you surprised?"

"By the timing. I was beginning to think you were going to wait until Christmas." She tugged his head down toward hers, until their noses were inches apart and the blue of her eyes filled his field of vision like a bright summer sky. When she spoke again, her voice was soft—and serious. "But I'll tell you this, James Devlin. I'd have waited for you until this Christmas, or next Christmas, or the Christmas after that. However long it took. Because you're a man worth waiting for. And I love you with all my heart."

The joyous strains of the Hallelujah Chorus began to resound in his own heart—the full symphony version. "Not more than I love you."

She smiled up at him. "Prove it."

And so he did.

Acknowledgments

With each suspense novel I write, I'm amazed at how much I still have to learn. Every book takes me into new territory, and the research challenge is immense. I am deeply grateful to the following people who lent me their expertise during the writing of this novel.

Tim Flora, president of Mid-West Protective Service, Inc., whose twenty-eight years of experience in federal and local law enforcement, private investigation, and security made him the perfect PI source for this book—and the entire Private Justice series.

Lieutenant Tom Larkin, commander of the St. Louis County Police Department's Bureau of Crimes Against Persons, who once again answered my police-procedure questions with promptness and patience.

Marc Ulses, assistant chief/fire marshal of the Frontenac Fire Department, who steered me through the key scene leading up to the climax.

Patricia Davids, fellow author and nurse, who critiqued the medical sections.

Captain Ed Nestor from the Chesterfield, Missouri, Police Department, who continues to be my go-to person for amazing sources.

My deepest thanks, also, to the amazing team at Revell—you rock!

And love—always—to my wonderful husband Tom and my fabulous parents James and Dorothy Hannon, whose love, support, and encouragement I treasure.

About the Author

Irene Hannon is a bestselling, award-winning author who took the publishing world by storm at the tender age of ten with a sparkling piece of fiction that received national attention.

Okay . . . maybe that's a slight exaggeration. But she *was* one of the honorees in a complete-the-story contest conducted by a national children's magazine. And she likes to think of that as her "official" fiction-writing debut!

Since then, she has written more than forty contemporary romance and romantic suspense novels. Irene has twice won the RITA award—the "Oscar" of romantic fiction—from Romance Writers of America, and her books have also been honored with a National Readers' Choice award, a HOLT medallion, a Daphne du Maurier award, a Retailers Choice award, and two Reviewers' Choice awards from *RT Book Reviews* magazine. In 2011, *Booklist* included one of her novels in its Top 10 Inspirational Fiction list for the year.

Irene, who holds a BA in psychology and an MA in journalism, juggled two careers for many years until she gave up her executive corporate communications position with a Fortune 500 company to write full-time. She is happy to say she has no regrets! As she points out, leaving behind the rush-hour commute, corporate politics, and a relentless BlackBerry that never slept was no sacrifice.

A trained vocalist, Irene has sung the leading role in numerous community theater productions and is also a soloist at her church.

When not otherwise occupied, she and her husband enjoy traveling, Saturday mornings at their favorite coffee shop, and spending time with family. They make their home in Missouri.

To learn more about Irene and her books, visit www.irenehannon.com.

Center Point Large Print
600 Brooks Road / PO Box 1
Thorndike ME 04986-0001 USA

(207) 568-3717

US & Canada:
1 800 929-9108
www.centerpointlargeprint.com